AN UNHOLY TERROR
STALKS THE GODLESS EMPIRE . . .

The Soviet premier hesitated, wondering what effect
the next item would have.

"Our Party leader wishes to appoint Colonel
Valarian to the post of Minister of the Interior," he
said.

"NO!" Somoroff screamed. "No! That man is a
murderer. He destroyed my son. He has been responsible for murder in one hundred cities and towns.
And you will make him a Minister? He will burn in
Hell before that!"

RED DEVIL

Books by David Saperstein
from The Berkley Publishing Group

COCOON
METAMORPHOSIS
RED DEVIL

RED DEVIL

DAVID SAPERSTEIN

BERKLEY BOOKS, NEW YORK

RED DEVIL

A Berkley Book/published by arrangement with
the author

PRINTING HISTORY
Berkley edition/February 1989

ISBN: 0-425-11408-2

A BERKLEY BOOK® TM 757,375
Berkley Books are published by The Berkley Publishing Group,
200 Madison Avenue, New York, NY 10016
The name ''BERKLEY'' and the ''B'' logo
are trademarks belonging to Berkley Publishing Corporation.

PRINTED IN THE UNITED STATES OF AMERICA

10 9 8 7 6 5 4 3 2 1

The author gratefully acknowledges the help and inspiration provided by the following people:

Rabbi David A. Mersky, Director of Campaign and Development, Combined Jewish Philanthropies of Boston, Boston, Massachusetts

Rabbi James Perman of the Free Synagogue of Westchester, Mount Vernon, New York

Rabbi Noah Hefetz of the Institute for the Heritage of Zefat in Halacha and Kabbalah, Zefat, Israel

Nira and Arie Posner of Tel Aviv, Israel

Mr. David M. Szonyi for his wonderful research efforts

Mr. Anatoly Shcharansky for his extraordinary spirit, will, and inspiration

The late James "Yasha" Smith, my true Russian uncle

Father Colm Murphy of The Columbian Order, Brussels, Belgium

Qin Shi Huangdi, the first emperor of China who created the terra cotta soldiers of Xian (Sian), and the Government of The People's Republic of China, which has taken great care to preserve them for us all

Natalee Rosenstein, my editor who caught the "spirit" . . .

Susan Schulman, my agent who inspires

To
Cherie and Lou Bernard
and
Iris—the Fabulous Siri
for always sharing the dream
and
Aunt Lil Eisen—my teacher
Aunt Henri Luchan—my other mother
Uncle Harry Luchan—my pal
May God bless

⚊ PROLOGUE ⚊

The chill January dawn was the first morning of total silence. Hardly an inch of earth was not covered with the blood of Soviet heroes on Mamai Kurgan Hill. Below, the Volga River flowed slowly past the awesome scene of death and destruction that was Stalingrad in early 1943.

But the German invader was gone—stopped and forced to retreat. Beaten. The price was clear on the bloody hill that morning as a sea of bodies, Soviet and German, lay twisted and contorted in silent testimony to the madness of war.

A Soviet staff car worked its way slowly up the hill. Once in a while a waft of smoke, carried on the frosty wind, crossed the hillside. The man driving the car was oblivious to the carnage around him. He slowly approached his goal, a concrete bunker near the crest of the hill.

The man had a regal bearing, even as he sat behind the wheel of the battered Mercedes, a gift from Adolf Hitler to his one-time friend and ally, Joseph Stalin. How ironic the car's history was on the hill that day. But to the driver, it meant nothing. His deep black eyes were cold, lifeless bloodstones set in a gaunt, pale, scarred face.

Waffen SS Colonel Wilhelm Hendricks's staff car eased to a halt in front of the abandoned Soviet bunker. He was dressed in the uniform of a Russian major. The cold, dead body of a Soviet captain, Vladimir Barnowski, lay near the entrance. The colonel stepped over the corpse and went down the concrete steps into the bunker's main room. He was alone.

Although the day was bright outside, the interior of the

1

bunker was dark. But from a shaft of light angling from the firing slit onto the wall to his right, he could make out the form of another body draped over a machine gun.

Colonel Hendricks was unmoved by the sight of death as he pushed the dead soldier to the side and peered through the opening. The landscape in front was barren and scarred from the battle. Bodies, in whole or part, were scattered in front of him like toy soldiers left behind by a child. It had been a fierce battle. Some would say later that this was the exact point where the Soviet Army stopped the Germans and turned the tide of the war on the Eastern Front.

The Nazi Colonel went back outside and dragged the Soviet captain's body several yards from where he found it. He went through the man's pockets and removed his identity cards. He tore off the battalion insignia and rank marking from the uniform. He then took a small bottle of acid from his pocket and poured it onto the fingertips of the dead man. He did the same to the dead man's hair. A twisted smile appeared on the evil, burn-scarred face of the German officer. He compared his hands, also badly scarred, to the Soviet's. They were almost the same size.

After looking around to see that he was alone, the SS Colonel went to the car and took a spare gasoline can from the back seat. He poured the gasoline over the dead Soviet officer. Then he removed a jade and silver ring from his finger and put it on the middle finger of the corpse's right hand. He struck a match and the body burst into flames. Satisfied, he turned and walked back into the bunker. Within a few seconds it exploded violently. A cloud of black smoke rose high in the sky.

— 1 —

Outside the Kremlin, Moscow was in the grip of winter. The sky was grey. Snow had fallen all week. It was Friday. The bureaucrats and government officials of the modern communist era were taking leave for the weekend. The premier's office still showed a light.

Premier Ivan Ivanovich Alexeyevich, Premier of all the Russias, President of the Presidium of the Union of Soviet Socialist Republics, was sitting in his favorite chair by a small fireplace. He sat alone, staring into the flames and sipping his tea. His face appeared troubled and deep in thought. The jacket to his blue serge suit hung in the closet. He still wore the vest.

There was a knock on his door. He looked up and smiled. He stood and crossed the room to greet his visitor—a man who had been a good friend long ago, in another place.

Peter Ilyavich Somoroff was tall and close in age to the premier, but he did not show his fifty-five years, as the premier did. His step was firm on the soft Persian rugs.

The two men met in the middle of the room and clasped hands. The premier then reached for his friend's shoulders, brought him toward his face, and kissed him on the cheeks. "Peter . . . Peter, my dear old friend. You look well."

"Premier Ivan Ivanovich. Thank you. You look tired."

The premier laughed. "Yes . . . tired. You think it is easy to be the premier of all the Russias? Come and have some tea."

"Yes, tea would be good. It's a Moscow winter out there."

The two men's eyes met and locked. The premier was the

first to look away as he put his teacup down near the samovar. "Peter, I asked you to come because I have a problem—a personal problem. I asked you to come here . . . to this place . . . at this time . . . because I am deeply disturbed with things that I do not understand."

Somoroff immediately became interested. "Well, old friend, I cannot imagine a problem that you, I mean a man who sits in this room, cannot solve one way or another."

Ivan Ivanovich shook his head. "Ah, Ilyavich, you would be surprised at what can't be solved in this room. Let me show you something."

The premier slowly crossed the room to his large desk. Peter followed. It was a neat desk with papers piled along one side and a telecommunications console on the other. An ornate fountain pen and inkwell set made of onyx stood proudly on the desk. The inscription read: *Ivan Ivanovich Alexeyevich—a citizen of Odessa—a friend of the people—true son of Russia.* It was signed by the City Council of Odessa and dated on the day he was elected premier.

Ivan Ivanovich stood at the right side of the desk and bent to pull out a file. It was sealed with a leather binding and strap that doubled around the file and joined with a locked clasp. The premier reached into his vest pocket and took out a small key.

"Here it is. Come, sit over here. This will be a long night. Let's be comfortable by the fire."

They walked to their chairs near the glowing fireplace. Peter was staring at the file and wondering why the premier had to keep files locked in his own office. His mind drifted for a moment to his own office and the rows and rows of locked files that were there. But that was normal business for the KGB. Files and locks, locks and files . . . the things that dreams are made of—mostly bad dreams for the names in those files.

Settled again the premier spoke. "What I am about to show you, and tell you, could be the end of me in this office, but I believe, deeply believe, that what happens to me is now of little importance. There is a danger. A long sharp bloody knife is aimed at the heart of our great country. I believe that. It is like a kukri, you know, the curved, double-edged knife the Gurkha use. And it is in the hands of a man who knows how to use it."

Somoroff stared at the premier. He could hardly believe the words he had just heard. There was fear in this voice. They had been through much together—wars . . . women . . . death . . . depravity . . . even murder, but this was a different thing he heard. This was a man who was sincerely frightened, and because it was the premier of the Soviet Union speaking, Peter felt a chill pass through him.

The premier sighed and continued. "Well now. This file was started two years ago by Boris Menoff. He did it on his own and gave it to me just one week ago. We met the next day after I had read it, and we talked for several hours. I must admit that I did not believe him, but you know, he was a dear friend like you, and he was a man I trusted."

Peter stopped him. "Was?"

"He is dead."

"When . . . how . . . ?" Peter was shocked. "I heard nothing."

"You will hear nothing. Perhaps in a few weeks a heart attack or something, and a private funeral."

The premier reached for a bottle of brandy next to the samovar and poured a glass. He gestured questioningly to Peter and then poured another glass. Both men quickly downed the warming liquid. The premier poured another.

"Boris died in my arms here, in this office, on Wednesday afternoon at six thirty-three PM. He died in a way I cannot begin to describe. Words are inadequate. He was . . . he was . . . destroyed from inside."

The premier's eyes moistened. Peter came to his side.

"Ivan Ivanovich . . . what happened?"

The premier reached for his key and opened the file. He handed it to Peter and gestured for him to sit down and read it. Then he leaned back in the chair and stared at the fire.

Peter Ilyavich Somoroff was a Georgian. He had been in the Cossack guard and had served as a tank commander in World War II. He moved to counterintelligence during the occupation of East Germany. He rose fast in the NKVD, and transferred to the KGB when it became an independent agency, but had the sense to move into the background when Stalin was on a rampage. It was in those years that he had met Ivan Alexeyevich in Odessa. Peter made it his business to be near a seaport when Stalin was in one of his moods. One never knew when a knock on the door would come. It was easy to shoot down a plane or stop a car, but it was hard to find a ship at sea. Ports were the best hiding places. Besides, a fast speedboat could make it across the Black Sea to Turkey in less than a day—perhaps a bit more if you had to dodge patrols.

Ivan Alexeyevich had such a boat, and it was in this way that the two men had met.

Peter noticed the boat in the harbor one Sunday as he lunched at a restaurant near the shore. It was low, sleek, and very official looking. He watched it move slowly out of the harbor and then, just beyond the seawall, the sound of the engines changed pitch and the boat seemed to rise out of the water, moving toward the point on Karkinitskiy Bay called Ak-Mechet. It moved faster than any boat he had ever seen. It was an early hydrofoil, and Ivan Alexeyevich was its designer and builder. Peter vowed to find the owner and to become his friend. With such a boat his security was guaranteed.

Boris Menoff was a Jew. He was also one of the few people who could communicate with the German scientists whom Ivan Alexeyevich had brought to the Soviet Union after the war. Boris, it was said, had a way of convincing the Germans that their lives depended on how he wrote the reports that Commissar Alexeyevich required before the scientists were allowed to work. He used to liken his role to that Dr. Mengele had played before the long lines of Jews in Auschwitz. This one to the right . . . this one to the left. He also let them know that he was born a Jew.

At one meeting late in 1945 he had gathered thirty-eight German scientists in the meeting room at the compound in Smolensk. He had been having some difficulty with this group because they had banded together and refused to work. There originally had been thirty-nine of them. But at this meeting one was missing. Menoff never mentioned where he was, but he wore the missing man's ring on his finger. No one missed this fact. At the end of the meeting he brought a box into the room and displayed the severed head of the missing scientist. He then promised a head a day if work did not immediately proceed. It did.

Actually, the unfortunate scientist had died in the night of a heart attack. Boris only took advantage of his body, which was of no use to the Soviet Union anymore. When Stalin heard about the incident he personally telephoned Boris and congratulated him.

Ivan and Boris met at a Party function in Leningrad in 1953. Boris had lived there all of his life, even in the days when it was called Petrograd. He had survived the pogroms and finally renounced his religion for the Party. He did this out of conviction, not fear. He was a communist through and through. He was also rising in the Party and had the reputation of being a very thorough and precise man. Ivan and Boris immediately became friends, for what Boris lacked in poise and political finesse, Ivan had. Alexeyevich on the other hand could feel the power and strength of this diminutive man. From the day they met, they became a team and a power to be reckoned with in the Party.

On the day Peter spotted the hydrofoil, they were cruising to Yalta. The boat was handling well, and Ivan ordered top speed as soon as they were out of sight of land. They ran at seventy knots for ten minutes, and then Ivan ordered the boat back to cruising speed for the rest of the journey. He put his arm around Boris and, laughing, they went to their quarters. The rest of the journey was spent with vodka, two beautiful Mongol girls from Chita, and sleep.

Peter Somoroff met Ivan Alexeyevich one week after he learned that it was he who controlled the hydrofoil. Boris Menoff introduced them. It took little time before the three men became close friends, a friendship they kept to themselves.

Ivan was the politician.

Boris was the activist.

Peter was the organizer.

Together they formed a synergistic troika. They often joked about the strength of threes, long a symbol of Russian might.

2

An hour passed before Peter looked up at the premier. He had gone through the file three times. Boris Menoff had been his usual efficient self. The material was well organized, but some conclusions seemed to be missing from the file. What was inferred had never been quite spelled out. It had been difficult even to surmise the purpose after the first reading. During the second reading Peter entertained a thought so bizarre that he dismissed it. After the third reading there was little doubt in his mind as to the conclusion Boris was heading toward before he died. But to believe that was pure fantasy. And Somoroff was a pragmatic policeman.

The file was filled with facts, events, names . . . and toward the end, a great deal of innuendo.

It began in 1952, one year before the death of Premier Stalin. A long list of young officers and party members assigned to keep tabs on the Jewish population of the Soviet Union was the first document. A name was circled—Major Nickolai Valarian. Nothing more.

The next entry was a series of articles from a Leningrad newspaper. The first reported the suicide of a man after he had murdered his wife and three children. As in all Russian papers, the details of the murder were withheld, but the suicide could not be hidden. The man, a rabbi, had immolated himself in front of the Opera House.

The second article dealt with a minor protest by the congregation of the dead rabbi. They maintained that the rabbi had not committed the crime and, in fact, had been murdered himself. The name of Nickolai Valarian was neatly underlined. He had been the investigating officer at the protest that took place at police headquarters in Leningrad. Valarian was not a member of the Leningrad police but was attached to Internal State Security. His headquarters were nearby in the city of Pushkin. The article also mentioned that Major Valarian and his men had taken several of the protesters into custody.

The final article in the series was dated two months after the occurrence of the presumed suicide. It was not from the Leningrad newspaper but was rather a small clipping from an Estonian weekly. It stated that the third synagogue fire in as many weeks had taken place in Leningrad and that a Major Valarian from Internal State Security had completed an investigation showing that the fires were being set by the congregants themselves in an attempt to disrupt the "People's Government" by claiming anti-Semitic actions. Once again Boris had underlined Valarian's name.

There followed in the file several more articles and newspaper clippings, official internal documents, clippings from German, American, Israeli, and Canadian papers, and a letter from a Mrs. Katarina Barnowski from Gorki requesting that her husband, Captain Vladimir Barnowski, missing in action in 1943 near Stalingrad, now called Volgograd, be removed from the rolls of deserters and given the proper honors of a hero of the USSR. Thus far the clippings had all pertained to the treatment of Jews in the USSR from 1952 to 1977. As a collection they were a damning statement of anti-Semitism. That was not a surprise to Peter Somoroff, nor was the fact that a former Jew, Boris Menoff, had gathered this data. What was surprising was the letter from Mrs. Barnowski. It didn't fit. Then Peter noticed that the request had been answered officially and denied. The answer was dated July 15, 1957, and was signed by Colonel Nickolai Valarian. The major had become a colonel and was now assigned to the Security and Records Division of the Army.

The next entry in the file was a blown-up black and white photograph taken from an Army identity card. The face was badly scarred from burns. The expression was alert. The eyes were piercing even through the softness of the blowup. There was no hair on his head, only scar tissue. It was a photo of Colonel Nickolai Valarian.

The two men sipped their tea and brandy.

"Was Boris ill when he wrote this last entry?" Somoroff asked.

"He was changed. Something was dying inside . . . here." The premier touched his hand to his heart.

"I don't understand. Boris gave up his religion long ago, yet this file is filled with . . . I don't know what to call it."

"I call it God. Boris Menoff was reaching for his God."

"How did he die?"

"Horribly. In agony . . . in my arms. Even in death, his face was not at peace."

Peter leaned toward his old friend. "Ivan Ivanovich, this is the twentieth century . . . almost the twenty-first. These fantasies that Boris infers . . . they are unbelievable. Don't you think so?"

"Yes," the premier answered softly. "But Boris was a rational man, and a friend. And I have seen things happening . . ." His voice drifted off wistfully. The premier stopped talking for a moment. Then he caught himself and focused back on Somoroff. "Peter Ilyavich, I want you to pursue this affair." His voice was now businesslike.

"Of course."

The premier stood, signaling that the meeting had ended. Peter stood too. Both men studied one another again.

"Boris was afraid of this Colonel Valarian. Are you?" Peter asked.

"I can deal with him, but his ideas, his methods—those can hurt us. This is the USSR on the move," the premier said proudly as he swept his hand toward the relief map of the Soviet Union that dominated one wall of his office. "We cannot tolerate negative world opinion for policies that do not emanate from this office. We are old friends, and I tell you I am frightened for this country that we love. Boris was a good man. He was always a Jew at heart. Superstitious. But sometimes things can get out of control . . . people can gather power in this bureaucracy we've built and destroy everything Russia might become. Do you understand?"

"Yes," Somoroff answered. He suspected the premier knew more than he was telling. "Let me get to work."

"Good." Ivan Ivanovich Alexeyevich slapped his old friend on the back. "It's good to see you. You look well. How is your family?"

"They are all well. My son is an officer now. Armored."

They walked to the door of the premier's office and embraced as they had done when they first met earlier that evening.

"Let me know if you need anything, Peter Ilyavich."

"I will." He started to leave, then turned back to the premier. "And Ivan Ivanovich, please rest easy. We'll get to the bottom of this business and clean it up."

The premier looked kindly at his old friend. "Yes. Make me an airtight case against this Valarian, and we can both put dear Boris's bones to rest."

The Kremlin was quiet when Peter Somoroff left with Boris Menoff's file tucked neatly in his soft leather attaché case. The premier remained in his apartment behind the forbidding Kremlin walls, a man alone at the head of a great nation. A proud man.

"It's yours now," the premier had said, gesturing to Menoff's file. "Be careful. I have lost one dear friend. I don't want to lose another."

"You won't. Let me attack it my way, plodding as that may be. I promise you and the ghost of our old friend Boris that I will get to the bottom of this thing." The men had embraced once again and Peter had clamped his hand on the premier's shoulder. "He was my friend too, Ivan Ivanovich. Good night."

— 3 —

Detective, in a word, described Peter Somoroff and his approach to his work. Facts. The case must always be built on facts. And he knew that sometimes facts were not exactly what they initially seemed to be. He had the distinction of being above politics in his role in the KGB, due mostly to his superior abilities as a detective. After all, espionage aside, a good policeman was always an asset to a security organization.

The next morning Peter Somoroff ate breakfast with his wife, Nadja, and her mother, Maria. The old woman, nearly eighty now, lived with them in their three-bedroom flat on the south side of Lenin Square. His position in the government allowed for the spacious apartment. The Somoroffs had two children. The girl, Anya, was a student at the Polytechnical Institute in Omsk. They only saw her once a year since the central Soviet city was more than 1500 miles from Moscow. Their son, also named Peter, was serving with the Army in Chita, near the Mongolian-Manchurian border, as a tank commander.

Peter had awakened early and made three calls. The first was to his assistant, Leonid Chomsky, telling the young lieutenant to meet him at the office later that morning. The second was to Katarina Barnowski in the city of Gorki. The late captain's wife was at home and surprised to hear from an official regarding her request that her husband be taken off the rolls of deserters. Peter told her that he would like to speak to her and would arrange to be in Gorki the next day.

The last call was to the widow of his good friend Boris

12

Menoff. Celia Menoff sounded cold and distant on the phone but agreed to accept his visit that afternoon.

Peter finished his breakfast, kissed both women, and left. His car was parked in front of the apartment house. It was a late model Skoda, another symbol of his status. After three tries, the small engine caught and he drove across Lenin Square toward his office.

Peter had made a decision. He would involve as few people as he could in the initial investigation. They, in turn, would know as little as possible about the overall operation. He would be the central control and the only one who knew all of the facts.

When he arrived, Chomsky was waiting in the office anteroom.

"Good morning, Leonid. Sorry about this. I hate to disturb your weekend, but it is important."

The young lieutenant dismissed the apology. He was totally loyal to his boss. He also knew that Somoroff was a personal friend of the premier. Contacts like that never hurt a career. Both men entered Somoroff's office. Peter chose his words carefully.

"Leonid, last night I had a call from the premier. We met in his office. He asked me to do him a favor. But it is very delicate. It can go no further than this office, and until I tell you otherwise, no one—I repeat no one—is to know what you are doing. Is that clear?"

"Absolutely, sir."

The young man was excited. He sensed something important was happening.

"Good," Peter answered. "Now, first I want you to go over to our records department and get everything you can on a Colonel Nickolai Valarian. Be careful. Speak to no one. Get the file yourself. Don't sign it out."

"Don't sign it out?" questioned Chomsky. "You mean steal it?"

"I mean get the damn file over here before two this afternoon. How you do it is none of my business."

Peter's voice was stern. It surprised Leonid because his boss was normally a very mild-mannered man.

Chomsky answered quietly, "Yes, sir." He got up. "Will there be anything else?"

"Yes. Understand this is serious business. I want you to

turn over anything else you are doing to Captain Servioff. Tell him it is my order. If he has any questions, have him see me.''

''Very well.'' The lieutenant started to leave. Peter spoke again.

''Leonid? How well do you know Pushkin?''

''I was born there.''

''Yes. Next week you will have a holiday. I'm sending you home on leave . . . officially. Unofficially you will have some work up there.''

''Very well, sir.'' He closed the door and pondered the change in his boss's manner. Although Leonid was only twenty-eight years old, he had gathered wisdom far beyond his years. His teacher, Peter Somoroff, was the best. Yes, something big was up. Okay, he thought, if it is this Valarian you want, then it will be Valarian you will get, Peter Ilyavich Somoroff. And anything else you ask me to do. Loyalty was one of Chomsky's great strengths.

After Chomsky departed, Peter engaged the scrambler on his phone and called the premier. In a moment the familiar voice came on the line.

''Good morning, Ivan Ivanovich,'' said Peter.

''Good morning, old friend. How are you?''

''Just fine. I wanted to tell you I am at work, and we are already making progress. I will need someone to act as a liaison to you. I thought we might consider Boris's wife, but I called her this morning and she sounded strange. I am going to see her this afternoon. Any thoughts?''

There was a pause on the phone.

''No, Peter. I haven't seen her since well before the . . . ah Boris's . . . accident. It went through official channels. She may even blame me. Let me know what you think.''

''Very well,'' Peter answered. ''If not her, then perhaps we can arrange a leave for my son.''

''Where is he now?''

''Chita. With the 294th Armored Brigade.''

''Like father, like son, eh, Peter?''

''For his sake, I hope not. But he's trustworthy. That I can guarantee.''

''Fine. If Celia is no good, we can arrange for your young Peter to have some leave. Call me later.''

"Good. Later then, Alexeyevich."

"Goodbye."

The next few hours went quickly for Peter Somoroff, so quickly that he was surprised to see Leonid Chomsky standing before him. Somoroff had reread Boris Menoff's file on Valarian several times.

"That was quick, Leonid. Any problems?"

"No, sir. Well, a small one . . . not really a problem."

"What happened?"

"The file was not in the general access area, and it was not on the computer. That can happen, but it is rare."

"Where did you find it?"

"In the secure section. I used your entry code to the computer."

"My code? You have my code?"

"You said how I got the file was my business."

"Correct. Good," he said, smiling.

"There is something else that is sort of funny."

"Yes?"

"The file is incomplete. On both ends."

"Explain."

"It begins in 1943. It ends in 1977. Look."

The young man put the printout sheet on Peter's desk. The first page heading read:

VALARIAN, NICKOLAI. Colonel, USSR Army, 1957, Bachelor Officers Quarters, Building 347. USSR Army, Security and Records Division. Member Communist Party, 1952, status—current.

Then an asterisked notation interrupted what appeared to be a normal file.

***All records on VALARIAN, NICKOLAI prior to 1943 destroyed in Leningrad by fire. Subject suffered acute amnesia and third-degree burns on 68% of his body in battle, Stalingrad, 1943.

Hospitalized at Grozny Burn Institute, 1943–1950. Recuperation in Baku, 1950–1951. Military pension refused by subject. Readmitted to active duty, Internal Affairs, 1952.

The file then continued normally, outlining Valarian's career. Much of it was in Menoff's file. In 1977 the file ended abruptly. Peter Somoroff noted the last entry. He knew it had been made by Boris Menoff himself.

Subject: VALARIAN, NICKOLAI. Colonel, USSR Army, Security and Records Division, Department of Internal Jewish Affairs. Budget request for extraordinary increase by Colonel Valarian denied by Commissar B. Menoff acting as Deputy Minister, Bureau of Budget, Internal Affairs.

Finally, the computer printed a curt closing on the file.

File transferred July 14, 1977. Secure code entry terminated. See Division Chief, Security and Records Division, USSR Army.

In effect, if you wanted to know more about Colonel Valarian, the computer was telling you to see Colonel Valarian personally.

"Clever," commented Peter.

"I don't recall ever seeing anything quite like it," said the young lieutenant.

"There are ways, Chomsky. But in a government like ours it is difficult to hide everything. We will see."

Somoroff stood behind his desk. He folded the printout and put it into his briefcase.

"Now, Leonid . . ." The KGB colonel moved around to the front of the desk and put his hand on Chomsky's shoulder. Both men walked toward the office door. "I want you off on holiday to Pushkin. Cut the orders yourself and sign them for me. Send me a copy. Our friend Valarian was in Internal State Security headquartered in Pushkin in 1952. See what you can find out, especially about some business with the Jews in Leningrad."

Peter had made copies of the articles from Menoff's file regarding the dead rabbi and the protests. He gave them to Chomsky.

"These will help. Just get whatever you can and be back here next Saturday morning. We will talk. Have a good trip."

Chomsky started to leave through the anteroom. Peter called after him.

"Leonid."

The young man stopped. "Yes, sir?"

"Be careful. Keep things to yourself. It's important."

"Yes, sir. I understand."

The lieutenant left Peter standing at the office door. No, thought Somoroff, you don't understand. But you will soon enough.

— 4 —

There were 478 cinder blocks surrounding Isadore Vogel, former rabbi of Congregation B'nai Jesherin of the city of Minsk in the western Soviet Union. He could not remember when he had first counted the blocks, but now he could look at any wall in the compound and immediately tell you how many blocks it contained.

Outside, the Siberian winter made a Moscow winter seem like spring. His room, his home, was exactly twelve feet by twelve feet by six feet. There was a door, a bed, a table and chair, a small dresser, and no window. A small, oval woven mat covered the center of the floor. It always reminded Rabbi Vogel of a yarmulke.

He had been in Tostuya, in the science compound, for seven and a half years. Before that there had been three other camps. He had not seen his family in all that time. Once in a while there were letters, but he could not answer them. For all he knew they might have been told he was dead. There hadn't been a letter for over two years. He tried not to think about them. Sometimes a week would pass and then he would remember. But he didn't cry anymore.

Today he had been washing the bathroom floor near the reception center processing section. He saw a group of very well-dressed men being processed. He knew one of them. The man was a well-known scientist, a mathematician, named Yasha Mendel. Yasha was from Minsk but had moved away twelve years ago. He hadn't been a religious Jew. When the rabbi saw Mendel he thought, Mendel . . . Yasha Mendel . . . what have you done to bring you to this place? You were

18

always the Russian first and the Jew second. What has happened? Rabbi Vogel knew he might have to wait a long time for the answer. But one thing that he had developed as a prisoner was patience. Without patience you either went mad or killed yourself. So the rabbi cleaned the floor and asked God what Mendel had done. It made his day quite interesting as he speculated on the possibilities.

5

Celia Menoff's appearance shocked Peter. He was so riveted by her emaciated condition that he didn't notice the physical change in the Menoff apartment until after they had sat down in the living room. She looked terrible. What has happened to you, Celia dear? thought Peter. The once vivacious and beautiful woman had aged overnight. Her long dark hair was matted and streaked with grey. Her dark eyes looked glassy and hollow. She had always taken pride in her figure, which for a woman in her late forties was remarkably young. Now Peter observed a thin, shuffling ghost of the woman he had known.

"Tea?" she asked.

"That would be nice, Celia. How are you?"

She pointed to a chair near the window. "You sit down, Peter Ilyavich. I'll be a moment." She went to the kitchen for the tea.

Now he noticed the apartment. It sent a chill through his body.

The room was dark. The only light came from the window near him and, from far off in the corner, a menorah, the Jewish candelabrum, which was burning with seven candles.

As his eyes adjusted to the light he saw that the furniture in the room was covered with black cloth. Only his chair and a small wooden bench nearby were uncovered. The large wall mirror was covered with black paint. But something was written, or drawn, on the mirror. He walked toward it for a closer look. There was a square painted on the mirror, and the square was divided into forty-nine boxes. In each box was a letter. He walked closer to read the letters as Celia came into the room.

"No, Peter. Get away from that!" There was panic in her voice.

"What is it, Celia?"

"Something . . . nothing . . . Sit. Please sit near the window."

She put the tea tray on the floor near the wooden bench. "One sugar, right?"

"Right," he answered, watching her squat to prepare his tea.

She handed him the glass, took her own, and sat on the bench. "I knew he would call you," she began, "and I knew you would get involved. Boris knew too."

"Boris was my friend. I loved him and so did Ivan Ivanovich. Of course I am involved."

"Of course." She seemed to stare into empty space, as though he were not there.

"Are you all right?" he asked.

"Yes."

A noise entered the room. A moan. It came from the corner near the menorah. Peter looked up and saw two of the candles go out. Celia dropped her glass onto the floor. It didn't break, but the tea spilled. As he looked back at her she was on her feet and moving quickly to the mirror. She stood in front of the box of letters and muttered words he didn't understand. Then she lit the two candles with the center candle. The noise stopped. Peter shivered again.

"You should not be here," she said as she returned to the bench.

"Tell me about it, Celia."

Life and anger suddenly came to her face.

"*No!*" she screamed. "I can't."

He leaned to her and grabbed her shoulders. He felt her bones through the grey sweater.

"Celia. Listen to me." His voice was firm. "I want to know what happened. I want to know everything Boris told you, everything you saw, everything you know he did. It is very important."

She looked up at him. The anger and fear were gone. The blank expression returned.

"Everything?" she said. "You won't believe me. You'll

think I am insane." She laughed a hollow laugh. "Perhaps I am insane. Boris thought he was, you know . . . at least for a while. Then it became real, and he knew he wasn't insane. Then he was just frightened."

She looked at Peter, and some life came into her eyes. She reached out and touched his face.

"It was the first time in his life that he was frightened. You knew him well. He was your friend . . . I know you did many things together. He didn't speak of them, but I knew . . . I know. He loved you, Peter Ilyavich. He loved me, too."

He watched her relax a bit. Peter released her from his grip and leaned back in the chair. "Tell me, Celia. I have to know."

She braced herself and her eyes cleared. She took a deep breath and let the air out slowly. Then she spoke.

"Boris was a Jew. You know he gave it up long ago . . . for the Party . . . for new things that he learned to love and believe in. I am not a Jew. You see the way this place is? Boris did that before he died. He brought an old man here. A rabbi, I think. The man showed Boris what to do. It took them a whole day. The man said it was the only chance Boris had. He said it would protect me."

Peter was confused. "Protect you . . . from what?"

Her face became frightened again.

"From that man—that evil man." She began to shake, then she screamed. "Oh, God, how I hate him. I hate him. I hate him."

Somoroff was on his feet, pulling her up into his arms. Her strength was surprising. He held her tightly and tried to calm her.

"Easy, Celia . . . easy. It's all right. Try to be calm. I'm here . . . you are not alone. Easy . . . relax."

He felt her tightness ease.

"Let's go into the kitchen," he suggested.

"No! I have to stay here. It is safe in this room. Please." She pushed herself away from him.

"I'm all right now. Sit."

They both sat again, he in the chair, she on the bench. But she didn't speak.

"Whom do you hate, Celia?"

She remained silent. He decided to push her.

"Is it Valarian?"

Slowly she raised her eyes until they met his. Her face was contorted, and pure hatred filled the room around her.

"Yes." Her answer was a hiss.

And then she would speak no more. It was as though she were in a trance, or a catatonic state. He shook her, yelled, hugged her, lifting her off the ground. Nothing worked.

He went to the phone and dialed the duty officer at KGB headquarters.

"This is Colonel Somoroff. I need an ambulance and medical attention at Commissar Menoff's apartment." He gave the address and told the officer he would be waiting there.

Peter then sat Celia in the chair and went into the bedroom to get her coat. The bedroom was unkempt, and the bed had not been slept in. In the center of the bedspread were several bits of cloth, placed in an arrangement that resembled a five-pointed star. Peter took out his notebook and drew the arrangement on a blank sheet of paper. He found her coat and a warm Persian lamb hat. When he came back into the room she was not in the chair. For a moment fear gripped him. Then he saw her in the corner near the menorah. She was kneeling and muttering what sounded like a prayer.

"Celia?" he called to her as he rushed to her side and knelt.

"Peter," she spoke softly, "you must love God." Then she went into a trance again and he knew he could not reach her.

In the distance he heard the sound of the ambulance siren. Quickly he pulled her to her feet and dressed her in her coat and hat. Then he sat her in the chair.

He didn't know why, but he began to pull the sheets from the furniture. He threw them in the bedroom. Then he took his notebook and copied the letters from the mirror, being careful to get the configuration exact. He took a sheet and wiped the mirror clean.

There was a knock at the door. He let the attendants and a doctor into the apartment, telling them that Mrs. Menoff had had some kind of a breakdown while he was visiting. He instructed the doctor, a young woman, to put Celia in a private room under observation.

"No one is to talk with her until Dr. Brodsky arrives. I will call him. This is official business."

His firmness was not missed by the young doctor.

"Yes, Colonel. Is there anything else?"

"Yes, Doctor . . . ?"

"Karkov," she answered.

"Karkov." He wrote her name down in his book. "Please sedate her now."

"As you say, Colonel." She took her medical bag to the windowsill and removed a syringe. While she gave Celia Menoff an injection Peter called the duty officer again and instructed him to contact Dr. Brodsky and to have the doctor call him at home after he had seen Mrs. Menoff.

Before they left the apartment, Peter took the keys from Celia's handbag and double-locked the door.

He watched the ambulance pull away. As he walked toward his car he took out the notebook and studied the letters. They appeared to be an anagram but made no sense to him. This is what he had written.

```
T H I R A M A
H I G A N A M
I G O G A N A
R A G I G A R
A N A G O G I
M A N A G I H
A M A R I H T
```

Now he would have to involve a cryptographer in the investigation. The team was growing.

~6~

Pushkin is a city that lies southwest of Leningrad, near the Baltic. As a young man growing up there, Leonid Chomsky had been able to enjoy the cultural activities that nearby Leningrad offered. He was a well-rounded Army officer with a passion for the ballet and, in particular, for a beautiful young ballerina with the Leningrad Company.

As soon as he arrived in Pushkin, he called Marina Grochenko and made a date to see her on Monday. It turned out to be her one day off. He was pleased with the timing.

It was now Sunday, and although he knew the Internal State Security office would be open, he didn't want to appear there on the weekend. Instead, he called his parents from the hotel and arranged to have dinner with them that night.

Five hundred miles to the southeast, in the late afternoon, Peter Somoroff waited inside the Gorki train station. The Moscow express was due in half an hour, so he had some time to contemplate his meeting with Katarina Barnowski.

The woman had been cordial. She lived alone in a small house in a suburb of the industrial city. She was grateful for the attention that Somoroff was giving her request, but very surprised that he was interested in an event that had happened so long ago.

They had exchanged greetings and sat in a small sunroom. She served cake and coffee.

"I found the letter denying my request, Colonel Somoroff," she began. "I kept it because my husband was a very special man . . . to me."

"I understand. May I see the letter?" asked Peter.

25

She passed the letter to him. He quickly glanced at the signature.

"Did you try to contact this Colonel Valarian?"

"Yes. I remember the conversation to this day. It was three days after I had received the letter. I really didn't think he would take the call personally, but he did. He was . . . adamant about the denial. I told him that my husband was a career officer. That he would never desert, especially in a battle. He hated the Nazis. He was from Riga, you know. Both his brothers had been killed by the swine. When I told Colonel Valarian that, he laughed."

"Laughed?"

"Well, not a laugh exactly, but his tone of voice had some pleasure in it. I remember his exact words. 'My dear Mrs. Barnowski, in a war millions of people die. I am not impressed.' "

Somoroff listened intently.

"Then," she continued, "he told me that my husband was a goddamned deserter and would forever remain so in the records of the Soviet Army."

She was visibly upset. Tears came to her eyes.

"Forgive me, Colonel, but it's been a long time and the memories are flooding back . . ."

"I understand," Peter said in a soothing voice. "May I ask you a few questions—if you don't mind, that is?"

"Certainly you may. I am grateful for your attention."

"I find it interesting that Valarian used the word *goddamned*. You are sure he said exactly that?"

"I am certain. It was a strange word for an official to use, so I remember it clearly."

"Do you have any photographs of your husband? Especially any taken around the time he disappeared?"

"Yes," she answered. "He was on leave during Christmas of 1942. We spent some time at a friend's cottage near the Caspian Sea." Mrs. Barnowski got up to get the picture, but Somoroff stopped her. "Excuse me. Just a moment. I want to show you something." He reached into his pocket and took out the black and white photo that Menoff had put in the file. He handed it to her. "Do you know this man?"

She gasped. Then she put on her glasses and studied the picture carefully.

"For a moment . . . just a moment, I thought it was my

husband. But, no. The face . . . the shape of the head is similar. Poor man. Those are terrible burns. Who is it?'' she asked as she handed back the photo.

"Colonel Valarian."

Mrs. Barnowski was a kind woman.

"Poor man," she said softly. "No wonder he is so difficult."

She left the room and returned with a yellowing photograph of Captain Barnowski and herself, taken in front of a small cottage by the sea. A moment of happiness captured on film before the horror of Stalingrad the following month.

Somoroff heard his train approaching. She was a sweet woman, and he believed her when she said her husband was not a deserter. He studied the photos side by side. There *was* a similarity. But why Boris Menoff had singled out Mrs. Barnowski's letter was a mystery. Peter made a note in his book to get Barnowski's records from the military record center in Riga. He then bought a bag of peanuts from the station vendor and walked onto the platform as the train entered the station. He looked forward to the ride home and a long nap on the train.

As his train made its way toward Moscow, night had come to Siberia, thousands of miles to the east. You could tell night there only by the clock, for at this time of year the frigid wasteland stayed in almost total darkness. The camp slept by the clock.

This night Rabbi Vogel was assigned a special detail. He and several other prisoners were taken to a building that had been recently reopened. They were put to work cleaning the floors, windows, and toilets. As the rabbi scrubbed the floor near the shower room he noticed Yasha Mendel working in there. Vogel pushed his bucket toward the shower room, then rose to his feet and went into the room to refill the bucket. The guard paid no attention. He came up behind Mendel, who was wiping the shower stall walls.

"Don't turn around, Mendel. It's Rabbi Vogel from Minsk."

The mathematician stiffened and whispered. "Rabbi Vogel? You aren't dead?"

"Almost like dead, but we Jews are tough. What happened to you that they sent you to this hell?"

"It's a long story." Mendel moved around to face the

rabbi. The shock of seeing such a change in his old rabbi registered on his face. "My God, Rabbi. What have the years done to you? You look one hundred years old."

Vogel smiled. "If I look one hundred that's good. I feel one hundred and fifty. Give it time, my friend . . . you'll catch up. Forget that. We haven't too much time. They don't like me to talk to anyone. Tell me what has happened. Tell me if you have seen my family. Tell me the news."

Mendel spoke rapidly. "I haven't been in Minsk for more than five years, so I know nothing of your family. But Minsk is relatively good for the Jews. I was in Kiev, at the Physics Institute. A few months ago they came in one day and took us, all the Jews, out to trucks. Just like the Nazis. They said it was a secret project, that our families would be notified. We went to the military airport, and they brought us here in a plane. All Jews. Jews in the Soviet Union are going to have very bad times."

The news hit the rabbi hard.

"So it continues." He sighed. "It always continues . . . always a final solution."

Then he put his hand on Mendel's arm. "Yasha," he said in a soft voice, "in this place you must be strong. You must believe that it will be over some day, and you must live for that day. I am still a rabbi . . . your rabbi, and I am here. Now I must go back to work. We will talk again."

"Thank you, Rabbi," said Mendel. "Please say a blessing for me tonight. I never really left our faith."

Vogel was touched. "Of course, Yasha. That is because our faith never left you. Stay strong."

The men parted. Vogel filled his pail and returned to scrubbing floors. He scrubbed toward the southwest corner of the building—in the direction of Jerusalem—and prayed for Yasha Mendel and all the Jews of Russia.

7

The cold air outside the Moscow train station drew the warmth from Peter's face. If the world were a simple place, I would be on a sunny beach now, he thought. But it is not, definitely not.

He found his car and drove toward the hospital. Twice he reached to use the radio phone in the car but thought better of it and decided to control his curiosity until he reached the hospital.

The guard at the entrance to the secure wing of the hospital snapped to attention when Peter showed his ID. At the information window inside he found the room number of Celia Menoff and checked to see if Dr. Brodsky was in the hospital. The inside guard checked his records and affirmed that the doctor was still in the building. Peter asked that the guard have Dr. Brodsky paged and tell him to meet him in Mrs. Menoff's room.

As he approached the room Peter was aware of the smell of the hospital. It was not pleasant to him. That antiseptic odor was forever linked in his mind to the mental institute where he had spent so much time interrogating prisoners of the state. The idea of putting them into a mental hospital had been Boris Menoff's brainchild. Now he was dead, and his wife lay in a hospital bed suffering from some form of mental disease. A strange twist, thought Peter to himself.

The room was dimly lit by a small bedlamp. Celia lay sleeping, her face still not relaxed. From time to time it contorted as though in pain. Sadness filled Peter's heart, and

29

he reached and touched the frail woman's hand. It was cold. As he drew away Dr. Brodsky entered the room.

"She is resting," said Brodsky behind Peter's back. Somoroff turned to face the doctor. Brodsky was a large man, over six foot six, weighing about 250 pounds. Yet for his size he was a most gentle man and an excellent diagnostician. Peter reached out his hand in greeting.

"How are you, Dr. Brodsky?"

"Well, Comrade Colonel. And yourself?"

Peter liked the big man and responded to his genuine warmth. "I am fine. But how about Mrs. Menoff? What is it?"

The doctor moved over to the bed and gazed down at the sleeping woman. He shrugged.

"I don't know. A severe trauma, perhaps. Physically she is healthy enough. We did a blood test. It was good, a little anemic perhaps, but within the parameters for a woman her age. She has been sedated, you know, but it looks like shock to me—just a guess. Tomorrow we will know more." The doctor motioned for them to leave the room. Out in the hallway he continued.

"Let her rest tonight. I will be here first thing in the morning, and as soon as I examine her I'll give you a call."

Peter was grateful for Dr. Brodsky's attention. Celia was in good hands.

The two men walked to the elevator. Brodsky draped his arm over Somoroff's shoulders. "Don't worry, Colonel. You look after affairs of . . . whatever you look after, and I will tend to the healing."

Peter smiled and then shook hands with the large man. "I won't worry. And thank you."

The elevator arrived, and Peter entered and waved good night.

After the elevator door closed, Dr. Karkov, the young female physician who had originally tended to Celia Menoff, approached Dr. Brodsky.

"Did he speak to her?" asked the young doctor in a firm, almost commanding voice.

"No. She is still sleeping. How much did you give her anyway?"

"Enough to keep her quiet. What did he ask you?" Her voice again held a tone of command.

"Just the normal questions. Nothing unusual. I told him I would examine her in the morning." His tone was questioning. Dr. Karkov thought for a moment. Brodsky waited for her to speak. Finally she looked up into his warm brown eyes and answered in a cold, distant voice.

"I will meet you here in the morning. It is possible that the patient may not last the night. Good night, Dr. Brodsky."

The woman turned and left the tall, heavyset chief of diagnostic medicine standing as though he were a brand-new intern admonished for some vague medical error.

Damn you, thought Brodsky. But he knew he was impotent to act against her will. Valarian had made sure of that.

Before retiring for the night, Peter Somoroff had to make one final visit to his office, which was not far from the hospital. He placed the slowly growing file into his private safe after first making a copy of the anagram taken from Celia Menoff's mirror. He then placed a call to the premier on the secure phone.

"Good evening, Ivan Ivanovich."

"How are you, Peter? How was your journey?"

"Interesting, but not conclusive. It will take some time, but the wheels are in motion."

"Good. How is Celia?"

"I am afraid she will be of no use to us now. Dr. Brodsky is letting her rest tonight. I saw her a little while ago. She is ill, Ivan . . . very ill, I am afraid."

"Then we will have to send for your son. I will arrange things, and he will be en route by the morning."

Peter weighed involving his son for a moment. The premier understood his silence and spoke again.

"Don't worry, Peter. He will be with me. We will not arouse any suspicion. I have checked into the matter already. General Kubyshev is commanding in that region. I'll tell him we are going to honor you, and as a surprise we are gathering your family for the festivities."

Crafty of you, thought Peter, but he felt relieved.

"That sounds good, Ivan. But I won't need him for a few days, so have him travel by train. A plane might show favoritism and arouse suspicion."

The premier listened and knew there was more to Peter Somoroff's suggestion than just avoiding favoritism.

"What is it, Peter Ilyavich?"

Somoroff chose his words carefully. Secure phone or not, one never really knew.

"It is a puzzling business we have, Ivan Ivanovich. Puzzling and rather complex. But by all means let's have our young man from Chita come to us. I think we will have need of trusted allies in the days ahead."

"Good. I understand. Let us talk again tomorrow. Good night, Peter."

"Good night, Premier Alexeyevich. Sleep well."

Before leaving the KGB building he had one more stop to make. First, Peter Somoroff checked the duty roster to see who was covering the cryptography section that night. The officer in charge was Major Rosteveli, a brilliant Georgian who, because of an inability to tolerate incompetence, had been passed over for promotion three times. However, his natural curiosity drove him to be one of the best cryptographers in the country. Peter found good luck in the fact that Rosteveli was on duty.

He found the major in his office in the basement. Rosteveli was an old friend and greeted Peter with a hug.

"An honor, Colonel Somoroff. A great honor for you to visit us in the bowels of this behemoth of an edifice."

Peter was smiling, almost forgetting the reason for his visit. "May I sit?"

"Please, Comrade. Forgive my bad manners."

"I have a little job for you, Major." The Georgian immediately became interested. When Peter Somoroff had a "little job," it usually turned out to be a challenge, and Rosteveli loved challenges.

Before Peter continued, he took the copy of the anagram from his pocket. The major leaned over his desk with interest. "Before I show this to you, I want it understood that this is . . . well . . . personal. I want you to keep it to yourself. Show no one. Clear?"

"As a bell, Comrade, as a bell. Now what is it?" He was curious to the straining point.

Peter passed the paper to the aging major, who glanced at it, then looked up at Somoroff and back to the paper. He spoke as he looked at the document.

"Ah. A crossword puzzle. Well, if this is for a contest, I want a commission for the answer." He looked up smiling, but Peter Somoroff was not smiling back at him. The major immediately became serious.

"A bad joke. Forgive me."

"This is serious, Major Rosteveli, and very private as I said. I want you to give it your full attention . . . no matter how long it takes."

The major spread the paper on the desk in front of him and stared at the anagram. He was at work already.

Peter rose from his chair. "Thank you, Serg. Call me on my direct line when you have something."

Rosteveli looked up and nodded. "It may take a while, Colonel, but I will have an answer. Of that you can be sure. Good night."

Peter left the building and walked slowly to his car. The night air was cold. The events of the day raced through his mind. Things were in motion. The first steps had been taken. Exactly where they were leading, however, was still a mystery.

As he drove toward home a thought gnawed at him. Boris Menoff, an old and dear friend, now dead, might have been slightly insane to reach for the conclusion hinted at in the file. There was still no proof, and Celia's condition didn't make things any easier. Perhaps Boris and Celia had gone off the deep end together. Perhaps. But he would press on and gather the facts in his own plodding way. With facts you got answers. With answers you got solutions. And with solutions you solved problems.

— 8 —

Dawn came to Pushkin while most of Russia still slept. It was a brisk winter morning outside as Leonid Chomsky, KGB officer, slept in his warm hotel bed. It was an uneasy sleep in spite of the wonderful dinner he had had last night with his parents. The dreams were a constant nocturnal visitor to the young lieutenant. Always the faceless questioner. The cold room. The light. And a raspy persistent voice pounding at him from inside his brain.

He was grateful for the knock on his door that woke him. The room was chilly. He wrapped the blanket around him and went to the door.

"Yes? Who is it?"

A woman's voice answered. "Chambermaid."

"Chambermaid? What time is it?"

"Time for you to open the door. I have only one day off!" It was Marina.

Leonid quickly opened the door, and she slipped inside the room. He opened his arms to her and the blanket fell to the floor, leaving him naked, but he was so excited at seeing her that he didn't realize he was not wearing pajamas.

"Can't you wait a moment to say hello?" she joked.

"What? Oh, forgive me . . . I didn't . . ." He scrambled to put the blanket around him, but somehow it didn't cover him completely. Marina Grochenko began to laugh at his clumsy attempt. The more he struggled, the funnier he looked. Finally she came to him and put her arms around his neck. They kissed long and softly and spoke no words. He took her toward the bed. She slipped off her coat and let it fall to the

34

floor. He began to unbutton her blouse and was clumsy at that, too. One button came off. He knelt, pulled off her boots, and kissed her feet. She stood and slipped her skirt down over his head, but he kept on kissing and moving his way up her body. She fell back on the bed as he worked up to her face. Their lips met again, but the skirt was around his shoulders now and his hands were trapped under it. She rolled over on top of him and pinned him to the bed.

"Now I have you. You are my prisoner."

"Please show me mercy," he begged. "I have no arms."

"It is not your arms I need. It is this."

She reached down to his erection and held him.

"Oh, that," he said casually. "Well you can have that, but leave it attached to me. It works better that way."

"Show me."

They made love, and although Marina was a ballet dancer who lived in a world of grace and fluid motion, their passion for each other and the long absence grew into a wild, almost frenzied, joining. They were deeply in love, each trying to convey this to the other with the strength of youth.

Later at breakfast, which they ate in the small restaurant in the hotel, they held hands and spoke softly.

"Can you stay with me tonight?" Leonid asked.

"Yes, but I have a class early tomorrow. How long will you be here?"

"Just for a few days. I have to go out today for a while."

"Why?" She was disappointed.

"Some business for the boss. It will only take an hour or so. You can use the room and sleep."

"I don't want to sleep. I want to love you."

"Only an hour. Sleep now because you won't get any sleep tonight."

"Is that a promise?"

"A commitment!"

She reached across the table and touched his face with the back of her hand. Her fingers were long and slender, like her dancer's body. He had fallen in love with her before they ever met as he watched her dance in Leningrad a year ago. He would sit in the balcony and see her face as though she were right next to him. Her eyes, those Tatar eyes captured him. They held passion and fire—black fire and a faint suggestion of a heritage and pride dating back to the glorious days of

Genghis Khan. No one would ever dominate those eyes, nor the soul behind them.

As the lovers finished their breakfast, a young Peter Somoroff was awakened by his orderly in the barracks near Chita, thousands of miles to the east.

"Lieutenant. Sorry to wake you. These orders came directly from Commanding General Kubyshev."

The sleepy tank commander focused sharply when the General's name was mentioned.

"Let me see."

The orderly handed him the teletype page.

"Moscow? Immediately. Yet by train?"

He knew that somehow his father was behind this sudden interruption in his life. He also knew about his father's work. A telephone call was out of the question. If he was wanted in Moscow then he would go to Moscow.

Two hours later he waited in the Chita train station, contemplating what the mysterious journey might mean and why he was to report to the premier directly. He knew this must involve his father. In the distance a train whistle blew. It would take two days to get to Moscow. The time couldn't pass quickly enough for the young Somoroff.

The senior Somoroff was up early that Monday morning as his son began his journey. It was too early to call the hospital. Peter made himself a cup of tea and sat at the small kitchen table. He took a pad and pencil and began to chart out the investigation. So far he had made a solid beginning. The next step would depend, in part, on what Lieutenant Chomsky was able to uncover. Peter also wanted to have a look at Valarian himself. He toyed with the idea of just walking in on the man and presenting himself as an adversary. The phone interrupted his train of thought.

"Hello."

"Colonel Somoroff, this is Major Rosteveli."

"Yes, Major. You have something?"

"Yes, sir."

"Where are you now?"

"In the office. It didn't take too long."

"Not over the phone, Major. Meet me in the park on the south side of the monument to the cosmonauts. You know the place?"

"Yes, sir."

"In an hour, Major. And keep it to yourself."

"You told me that last night. When a Georgian makes a promise to another Georgian, he keeps it."

"Sergei!"

"Yes, sir."

"Someday that mouth of yours will get you fired."

"Yes, sir. One hour."

Peter hung up. He was excited. Information was beginning to filter in. Rosteveli would have some; Chomsky would have some; Brodsky would have some; Celia would tell him more . . . and slowly Comrade Valarian would become known.

The duty officer at Internal State Security in Pushkin was a captain of Artillery, ill-suited for a desk job. He was a man of action, not a pencil pusher. Now this young lieutenant flashed his KGB identification, and he was supposed to jump. Pushy cop, thought Captain Bonyon, as Chomsky rattled off a list of files he wanted to examine.

"Well, Lieutenant, those files are very old. It will take some time to get them up from the basement."

"I have time, Captain. Let me call you tomorrow morning."

"They may not be here by then."

Chomsky sensed a problem and responded firmly. "Captain . . . sir . . . this is a top-priority KGB matter. I know you understand the importance of such a request. Surely you can have someone work on it today. I need those files."

The captain stood up behind his desk as if to dismiss Chomsky. Leonid sat in the chair, immovable. If the captain wanted an argument he would get it, and he would lose. That was apparent to both men.

"I am sure that we can have those files for you by tomorrow morning."

"Good." Chomsky now got up and prepared to leave. He turned at the door and addressed Captain Bonyon again.

"One more thing, Captain, if you have a moment."

The captain waited. Now what? he thought.

"There was a synagogue near the central square. Is it still there?"

"They had a fire there last year. But it is still there, although there are not too many Jews left."

Bonyon smiled a knowing smile at Chomsky. The young man didn't smile back.

"Thank you, Captain. Until tomorrow morning."

Chomsky saluted and left the room.

Bonyon returned to his desk and telephoned the corporal in the records section downstairs. He gave him the list of files that Chomsky had requested and a clear order to have them in his office early that afternoon. Before you have those files, thought, Bonyon, I want to see what is so interesting to the KGB.

The Moscow train moved swiftly west. By nightfall it would be in the super-secure Omsk region, a nerve center for the Soviet missile system. The windows would be covered and anyone found peering out would be subject to immediate arrest. Even the young tank commander did not have the authority to view this area, but Peter would be sleeping as they passed through.

The monument to the cosmonauts soared above the small park, rising angular and smooth into the winter sky. Major Rosteveli sat waiting for his boss. The news he had for Somoroff was certainly unique. The code had been easy. The translation had been a little harder to come by.

Peter approached the major only after he had carefully checked the rest of the park. No one was there, as well no one should be on this cold morning. He sat next to the major and felt the icy bench through his wool pants.

"Good morning, Rosteveli. What have you got?"

"Good morning, Comrade Colonel. I have a great deal, and I need to know more, but for that I will need an expert and I didn't want to involve anyone without consulting you first."

Somoroff was grateful for the major's caution.

"That is one of the few times I have heard you admit you don't know everything, Rosteveli my friend. Perhaps you are mellowing in your old age?"

The major chuckled. "No, Colonel Somoroff. This kind of knowledge is extremely specialized. I don't know if we have anyone in the Soviet Union who can supply all of the answers."

Now Peter was intrigued. "Go on. Tell me everything you know."

Rosteveli took his notes from a small briefcase. There were several pages. He began to speak. Peter did not interrupt, although he was bursting with questions.

"It is not an anagram. It is called an acrostic; actually this one is a double acrostic. A complete specimen. The words are Hebrew and some older language, too. I think perhaps Chaldean. Very old, and very complex in meaning. It would help to know where you found this, but since you did not tell me I assume that I have no need to know, for now."

Peter nodded.

The major passed a copy of the acrostic to Peter Somoroff so that he could follow the explanation and translation. This copy was boxed.

"I have a rough translation of some of the words, but only rough, because they are a mixture of languages. It really is quite interesting and very ancient. You see that the words are the same across and down. The first, *Thirama*, is from a language I do not know. *Higanam* is derived from Hebrew. It means something like *defending* or *defend*. The next word, *Igogana*, was tough, but I think it is also Hebrew or derived from a Hebrew word meaning *roof* or *covering*. Of that I am not sure. The next, *Ragigar*, I can't ascertain at all. It has the feel of the oriental about it. *Anagogi* is simple. It is derived from Greek—*anagoge*; it means *raise* or *elevate*. *Managih* is also Hebrew and has several meanings. I put down those that seemed to be in keeping with the others. So we have *managih*, from the Hebrew *mno*, to restrain, stop, put up a barrier, or even contain with a barrier. The final word, *Amariht*, is also Hebrew, from *armth*, which means *word* or *speech*.

"So this acrostic is talking about either containing or protecting something or someone, or perhaps penetrating something, or someone. But it is very old, and I do not know how it was used."

Peter corrected him. "Is used, my friend. It is used."

"Do you know how?"

"No."

"Can you tell me where you found it? How it was placed?"

"Why do you say 'placed'?" The major's findings had captured Somoroff's confidence.

"Because these acrostics had a definite use to ancient peoples. They could conjure up spirits and protect against evil. Things like that."

"How do you know this, Rosteveli?"

"Well, Comrade Ilyavich"—the major used the familiar name—"I am not exactly a student of Hebrew, so I had to use some research books. I must admit that I found the key to it quite by accident while flipping through a dictionary. My eye caught one of these acrostics, and there it was, in black and white." He smiled and shrugged. "Accidents can happen in my business, too. All is not science."

Somoroff liked the man's honesty. He decided to share his confidence and told him the story about finding Celia Menoff, but told him nothing of the file or Valarian. He never mentioned the premier.

After Somoroff had finished, the major let out a slow whistle. "We have something very special here, Comrade Somoroff. What do you want me to do now?"

"We have to find an expert who can translate the rest of this for us and tell us about its meaning. Any ideas?"

Rosteveli thought for a moment. "Must it be someone in KGB?"

"No. But it must be someone we can either trust or control."

Again the major thought for a moment. He spoke now in a softer voice, even though the two men were alone in the park. There was conspiracy in the air.

"I have a friend . . . an acquaintance. She is a Jew. Sort of religious, but we've known each other a long time. She has a friend whom I have met a few times. He is old and immersed in his God. I know he doesn't know where I work, but when I am around he always talks about retribution to me. He says that we, meaning the atheists, will pay a price for our godlessness. Things like that. I know he deals in mysticism, and the Jews treat him with great respect . . . and fear.''

"Can you find him?''

"Yes. He worships every day in the big synagogue.''

"Fine." Peter paused for a moment, then gave Rosteveli Celia Menoff's address. "Find him and bring him to this address at three this afternoon. I will meet you there. But don't tell him what it is about.''

Both men rose from the bench, shook hands, and went off in opposite directions. Rosteveli made his way toward the synagogue, while Peter drove toward the hospital, wondering what surprises the day would bring. He hoped that Celia was better, because he had many more questions without answers . . . yet.

9

"She died in her sleep. There was no suffering, Colonel Somoroff." The large doctor sat with Peter in the anteroom at the end of the hall, away from the main flow of the hospital traffic. Peter's sadness filled the room.

"How did it happen, Brodsky?" An anger was swelling inside him, and Peter wanted the doctor to know he was angry.

"An embolism in her sleep. It went right to her heart. I am sorry."

"Who was on duty when it happened?"

Dr. Brodsky was taken aback by the question. He thought of lying but knew Somoroff's reputation for details. When the KGB section chief asked a question, he always checked out the answer.

"Dr. Karkov was on duty."

"The young woman who came for Celia?"

"Yes. She is a very good doctor. There was nothing to be done, believe me, Colonel."

Peter wondered why Brodsky was pushing so hard.

"Is she here now? I'd like to speak to her for a moment."

Brodsky got up and went to the house phone. He had Dr. Karkov paged.

"How about some coffee, Peter?"

"Not now, thank you. I would like to see Celia. Is she still in the room?"

"I believe she is," answered Brodsky. He was nervous. They walked down the busy hallway to her room. As they entered, Peter stopped, turned, and caught sight of Dr. Karkov ducking into a doorway. She had been watching them. Brodsky missed it, but Peter Somoroff suddenly realized that he had engaged the enemy. From this point on, no one was to be trusted.

Celia lay under a sheet that was pulled up over her face. Peter drew the curtains apart and filled the room with sunlight. Then he carefully pulled back the sheet to reveal the corpse. The look of death was on her face, and something more. In death she should have been calm. However, her face was a mask of fright, the skin pulled tight over sunken cheeks, the eyes closed; yet beneath the lids fear still dwelt. She was rigid, her bony hands clenched in fists.

"Please leave me alone in here with her." It was an order to Brodsky. The large man let himself out of the room quietly.

Peter moved quickly to the body. His hands explored the arms, legs, and neck. He was looking for something, and he found it behind her left knee—a small needle mark. As he touched it, the door opened and Dr. Karkov entered. Peter knew she was there, but he kept on examining the tiny wound.

"Dr. Brodsky said you wanted to see me, Colonel Somoroff."

"Yes. Please just wait a moment." He took his time so that there would be no doubt in Dr. Karkov's mind that he had found the injection mark. He replaced the sheet over Celia and turned to his adversary.

"You were on duty last night, Doctor?"

"Yes, sir. I found the patient, Mrs. Menoff, dead this morning at about four o'clock."

"Did you try to revive her?"

"Yes, sir."

"How?"

"I gave her adrenaline and then used the defibrillator. It was no use."

Peter removed the sheet and opened Celia's nightgown. There were slight burn marks, signs that a defibrillator had been used. He closed the gown and looked at her arms.

"I see no injection marks here."

"I couldn't find a vein there, so I used the large vein in her leg, behind the knee, Colonel."

"I see," answered Peter. Now I have you, he thought. He

went to the room phone and called his office. Captain Servioff, his adjutant, was on the phone in a moment.

"Captain, send my driver and two of the Special Branch people to Central Hospital, room six-six-seven. I will meet them." Peter hung up and escorted Dr. Karkov to the door. "Thank you for trying to save her, Doctor. She was an old friend. I will take care of the body. You may put that in your report."

Once outside the room, Peter closed the door tightly and called down the hall to a guard. He instructed the man to allow no one to enter the room without his permission. He repeated, "No one."

The guard snapped to attention. "Yes, sir."

Dr. Brodsky stood across the hall watching the proceedings. He was frightened by Peter's official attitude and threw a glance at Dr. Karkov. Peter saw the exchange.

"Doctors, can we have a little talk in the anteroom? I have to be here until my men arrive." He didn't wait for an answer but walked down the hall. The two doctors followed.

At the same time, Major Rosteveli parked his car across from the synagogue and waited. He knew the rabbi would emerge eventually, and he was sure the old man had not seen him following along to the synagogue earlier. As he waited he thought about Fannie Beshevsky, his lover, a Jewess and his friend for many years. Would this be considered a betrayal if Somoroff arrested the rabbi? Surely Fannie would know it was Rosteveli's doing . . . or would she? So many Jews were being picked up these days. Perhaps it would be just another arrest to her. He would be kind and understanding and offer to find out what had happened to the old man. Yes. That would appease Fannie. It would be all right. His thoughts were interrupted as an Army vehicle pulled up in front of the synagogue and six soldiers, led by a tough-looking major, entered the building. Fear gripped Rosteveli. He must act quickly.

At another synagogue in Pushkin, Lieutenant Chomsky, dressed in casual civilian clothes, sat with another rabbi. The man was very old and poorly dressed. His clothes were ragged but neat. The collar on his black coat was frayed with age. The rabbi spoke slowly.

"The fires were set by hoodlums, even if they were soldiers. I don't care what they tell you. They were soldiers. Under orders."

Leonid didn't argue. He was sure the old man was correct. "I am sorry about the fires, Rabbi, but that is not my area of responsibility."

The rabbi nodded. "No one is ever responsible. But God knows, and I know. That is enough."

Chomsky tried to move the conversation to what interested him. "I was asking about the other rabbi. The one who killed his family and immolated himself in front of the Leningrad Opera House. Did you know him?"

"Rabbi Levinson? Yes I knew him. But it wasn't that way. Everyone knew it wasn't that way."

"What happened?"

"They killed his family. They burned him. They blamed it on him. It was all lies."

"What really happened? Who did it?"

Now the rabbi stared deep into Leonid's eyes. It was a piercing look, wise and angry. Chomsky stared back, unable to break away from the other man's gaze. Then the rabbi shuddered and broke off contact.

"No. There is nothing to tell. A family was killed . . . a rabbi was killed . . . a synagogue was burned. It happens all the time, here, Europe, America. It's been that way for thousands of years. I don't know who did it. I only know why."

Chomsky knew he had lost the man's confidence. One last try. "Then why did they do it, Rabbi?"

Now the old man smiled. "Before I tell you perhaps I should pray that after you arrest me, you'll let me die quickly."

"I am not going to arrest you, Rabbi." Leonid was sincere, yet he understood the old man's fear. The KGB has a reputation that always precedes it. But now the rabbi was silent again. Leonid played his last card.

"Do you know a man named Valarian?"

Immediately the rabbi uttered a prayer, put on his prayer shawl, and pulled it over his head. He stood, bowing toward the torah ark of the small synagogue and rocked back and forth, chanting rapidly in Hebrew. Leonid was startled. The rabbi spoke to him no more. After a few minutes Leonid left the synagogue. The rabbi was still praying with a fervor, and although the words were strange to Chomsky, he knew the sound of fear in any language.

It would be several hours before he was able to forget the fear and make love to Marina.

～ 10 ～

Things had gone well at the hospital. Peter Somoroff was pleased as he waited in his office. Doctors Brodsky and Karkov were being processed downstairs. Each would have a private cell in which to spend a few hours thinking about why they were there and what was going to happen to them. Let them stew for a while, thought Somoroff, then we will get some answers. Meanwhile he had removed Celia's body to the pathology section of another hospital under another name and ordered an autopsy. He had particularly instructed that the needle hole in the back of the knee be checked for adrenaline. The report would be to him by the end of the day. Now it was time to get over to the Menoff apartment and keep his appointment with Major Rosteveli and the old Jew.

The day had grown grey, and a light snow was beginning to fall. Rosteveli kept the motor running, and the heater on high. Even so, the old man still shook in the seat next to him. He had good reason to be afraid.

When Rosteveli had seen the soldiers enter the synagogue he had acted quickly, leaving the car and following them into the building. They had gone to the office that was down a long hallway to the left. Rosteveli had gone directly into the sanctuary and found the old man praying in the last row. He slid into the pew next to the old man and touched his shoulder. At first the Jew didn't recognize him and was confused. The major reminded him that he was Fannie's friend. The man remembered and returned to his praying.

"We must leave here, Rabbi."

47

"I am not a rabbi, atheist."

"Fine. But there is danger here for you. There are soldiers searching the synagogue. You have to come with me."

"I am not afraid of soldiers."

"Nevertheless, old man, you are going to come with me. We have business to discuss."

"I have no business to discuss with atheists."

"It is for Fannie. She sent me," Rosteveli lied. "She needs you now."

"Is she sick?"

"Yes." He was willing to say anything to get the old man out of the temple. "You have to come right now. I have a car outside."

The old man hesitated. "Are you a policeman?"

"Yes. KGB. But I am Fannie's friend."

"I know. We talk about you sometimes. She says you are a good man."

"Fine. But we have to go quickly." He heard the soldiers coming back down the hallway. In a moment they would be in the sanctuary. Rosteveli had to think fast.

"What is your name, old man?"

"Isadore Kantrowitz."

"Fine, Isadore. Listen to me carefully. The soldiers are coming. You get down and hide near the aisle. I will stop and distract them. You understand?"

The old man nodded, his eyes bright and alert.

"When I speak to them, you slip out the door and go across the street to a dark green car. Get into the back seat and lie down. Hide yourself. Do you understand?"

Again the old man nodded. He got to his knees and crawled to the aisle. The major stood up and walked to the opposite aisle as the soldiers, led by the other major, entered the sanctuary. Rosteveli took out his KGB identification and called to the major.

"You. Major. What are you doing here?"

The Army major was startled to see a Russian in the synagogue. He was distracted by the loud voice and the tone of command.

"Who are you?" asked the soldier.

"Major Rosteveli, KGB. Come here. All of you." Once again a command.

As the group of soldiers came toward him, Rosteveli retreated back a few rows so that when he confronted them, their backs would be to the door. As they passed the row where the old man was hidden they didn't notice him. Their eyes were glued on the KGB officer.

Rosteveli presented his ID to the Army major. They saluted each other.

"I am Major Anton Metsky, adjutant to Colonel Nickolai Valarian, Security and Records Division."

"Nice to meet you, Major. May I ask why you are here?"

"We are looking for someone, a man. An old man. Have you seen anyone?"

"Just those people in the front." Rosteveli gestured toward the front of the sanctuary where three men were praying.

"Ah," said Metsky. "Thank you." He signaled for his men to surround the worshippers.

"One moment, Major," commanded Rosteveli. He noticed that the old man had just left the room, and he wanted to give him time to get out of the lobby and into the car.

The soldiers hesitated, looking toward their major, not knowing who was the senior in the room.

"Yes, Major?" answered an annoyed Metsky.

"May I ask the name of the man you are seeking?"

"Why?"

"Because I am asking. That is enough." The Georgian could be tough when he asserted himself.

Metsky thought for a moment. The men in the front of the sanctuary were looking back at them now, and he could see that they were all young men. His prey was not among them. "His name is Isadore Kantrowitz. May I do my work now?"

"Certainly. Don't let me stop you from your duty."

Rosteveli couldn't hold back a smile, but he had misread the major. Instead of sending his troops toward the front of the room, he ordered them back into the street. Rosteveli looked up and saw the outside door just closing. Kantrowitz was an old man and couldn't move fast. As the soldiers moved toward the door the KGB major stopped them again.

"Wait. Major Metsky, just another moment. I think I can help."

The Army men stopped again and faced him.

"How, Major?" said Metsky. "All you seem to be doing is delaying us from our duty."

Ignoring the dig, Rosteveli spoke. "This man . . . Kantrowitz. Is he a small man with a beard? Does he wear that black Jew clothing?"

"Yes," answered Metsky. He was interested. "Do you know him?"

"No. But there was a man here about ten minutes ago. He had a terrible cough. I thought he was dying. The others sent him home." Rosteveli gestured to the men in the front, who had resumed their praying. He hoped that they had heard what he told the soldiers and that they would confirm his story. He had spoken loudly enough, but to be sure he continued, even louder now.

"Yes. I am sure they called him Isadore. He went home. You just missed him."

Metsky was sure that the men in the front had also heard the KGB officer. It would do no good to check with them now. Somehow he felt he had been fooled, but he didn't know why.

Rosteveli was now sure that Kantrowitz was safe in his car. He snapped a salute to Metsky. "Well, Major. I must be going myself. Glad to be of service."

"May I ask what business you had here this morning, Major . . . ah . . . Rosteveli?"

Arrogant bastard, thought Rosteveli. You want a game? I'll give you a game.

"You may ask, but I cannot answer. Unfortunately regulations do not permit me to share KGB work with you. But I can say it was a routine matter. Good day, gentlemen."

As the green KGB car pulled away, Major Anton Metsky watched carefully. He was sure he saw a head pop up in the back seat as the car turned the corner. Colonel Valarian would find this matter interesting.

When he was sure that they weren't followed, Rosteveli spoke to the old man. He used a soft voice to allay the man's fear. "Why did the Army want you, Mr. Kantrowitz?"

"Do they have to have a reason? I am a Jew, that is enough."

"I don't think that is the reason, Rabbi."

"I am not a rabbi, I told you that. And we are not heading to Fannie Beshevsky's house either. You are arresting me."

"No, Mr. Kantrowitz. Not an arrest. But we do have some

questions for you. You may not believe me, but I don't know what the questions are. We will meet someone else in a while. He has the questions."

"Then *he* will get the answers." The old man folded his arms in defiance and was silent.

~11~

The shades on the Moscow train were drawn and locked by the Military Police, who had boarded as the train entered the Omsk region. Young Somoroff slept.

In Pushkin, Leonid Chomsky returned to the hotel. Marina had slept and was now in the bath. He was still upset by the rabbi's reaction to Valarian's name. He called hello to Marina, who was luxuriating in a tub full of suds.

"Are you here for good now?" she yelled back.

"All yours, love. Take your time. I have to make just one call."

The lieutenant placed a call to Peter Somoroff in Moscow. He caught him just as he was about to leave for the Menoff apartment. Since the call was not on a secure line, Chomsky had to be discreet in what he said.

"I am just checking in, Colonel Somoroff."

"How is your holiday going?" The section chief immediately understood that Chomsky wanted to speak in code words. Somoroff listened carefully, making notes on a pad.

"It's going very well, but the weather is a bit cloudy. Tomorrow I hope it will be clear."

"Is the forecast good?"

"I think so. I saw my parents last night. They are well. I visited an old uncle, and he is sick. It is puzzling as to what is wrong with him."

"What do the doctors say?"

"He only saw one doctor. The same one whom we discussed."

52

Somoroff knew that he was talking about Nickolai Valarian. "Did the doctor prescribe anything for your uncle?"

"Yes, but he had a very bad reaction. Sort of lockjaw, but not as bad a reaction as your friend had. I'll visit him again soon and see if he is any better."

"Fine. Things here are interesting, but they will wait until you are back from holiday. When do you plan to come home?"

"A few days. I'll know better tomorrow. Why don't you call me in the evening tomorrow?" He gave Somoroff the number so that the call could be scrambled.

"Fine, Leonid. I'll check with you tomorrow night at about eight PM."

"Good. Until then, Colonel."

"Yes. Until then. Have a good time."

Somoroff broke off the call. Three blocks away Sergeant Mikolov, aide to Captain Servioff, was pleased with his first information from the phone tap. He called Captain Servioff with the pertinent information.

"Captain, I got the tap in just in time. Chomsky called. He is in Pushkin at this number: six-eight, four-four, oh-two. Room twenty-two."

The captain was pleased—and he knew Major Metsky would also be pleased with his efficiency. It had taken only one hour to get the tap operative. He called Metsky and told him the news.

Major Anton Metsky was totally committed to his superior officer, Colonel Nickolai Valarian. He was mesmerized by the power and self-assurance that emanated from the badly scarred officer. He entered Valarian's office quietly after calling him to say that there was information to be discussed. No matter how many times Metsky went into that office he still found it an awesome experience.

Valarian sat behind a huge mahogany desk. A communications console was the only item on it. The top was kept dust-free and shiny. The rich deep red of the wood reflected the one light in the room, a large chandelier made of ornate wrought iron, kept barely lit by a dimmer switch. The chandelier was in the shape of a pentangle, a five-pointed starlike figure enclosed by a circle. Tiny lights ran along the outline of the star and circle. Valarian's bald, scarred head and face were not reflected onto the desk though the chandelier was.

The bare walls were also paneled in mahogany. There was no window in the room. A special thermostat allowed the colonel to keep the room temperature exactly the way he liked it, which was very cold.

This was the second time that day that Metsky had visited the office. When Rosteveli had duped him, and he was sure that the major had done just that, he quickly returned to headquarters and went immediately to Valarian. It took a few minutes at the console for Valarian to find out who Rosteveli worked for and what he did. Valarian had just a few questions.

"Why would a cryptographer be out in the field? What does his boss Somoroff want with the Jews? Who else is close to Somoroff?"

The first two questions were unanswerable at the time. The third could be responded to—Leonid Chomsky, Captain Viktor Servioff, Premier Alexeyevich, and the Somoroff family. Also, a most interesting fact, Somoroff had been close to Boris Menoff. This made Valarian uneasy. He instructed Metsky to get a phone tap on Somoroff and have their agent in the Kremlin check out the premier's visitors' log for the past few weeks to see if Somoroff had been there.

A few hours later, Metsky returned to the office with the information from the phone tap. Servioff had been on Valarian's payroll as an informer. He was an ambitious man with an eye for Somoroff's job, and, as Valarian's files revealed, a not infrequent taste for young boys, which Valarian had been happy to arrange to supply.

"Colonel Somoroff's aide, Lieutenant Chomsky, is in Pushkin. We are checking the number, but we are sure it is a hotel. They spoke in code. Somoroff will call him on the scrambler tomorrow night. That will not be enough time for us to install the equipment necessary to overide the scrambler."

Valarian listened intently, then responded. "Let me know when you have confirmation on the hotel. Alert our people in Pushkin. Anything else?"

"We were not able to put a tail on Somoroff. He left too quickly."

"What about Karkov?"

"She is in Lubyanka in the Internal Security section. So is Dr. Brodsky."

"Then they moved them from headquarters? When?"

"A few moments ago . . . just before I came down to see you."

"Can we reach them?"

"No, Colonel. We have not been able to penetrate that part of the prison."

"What about the Kremlin log?"

"Nothing yet. It is too soon."

Valarian was annoyed. His body tensed. A battle was joined. He knew Somoroff's reputation and understood that he was not dealing with an amateur. Valarian enjoyed the challenge.

"Very well, Major. Keep on top of things and feed me information as it comes in, no matter what time it is. Do you understand?"

Metsky knew that tone of voice. He stood and snapped to attention.

"Yes, sir!" He turned and walked toward the door. He knew Valarian was displeased with the day's events. But it hadn't been Metsky's fault. Still, that didn't matter. It never mattered. Valarian was his master. It was a pact they had joined long ago. Success earned him great reward, but failure meant pain. That was the bargain.

Metsky's body tensed. Then it came—the hot, searing flash in his spine. A fast deep pain, right to the nerve endings. A reminder to obey orders. Metsky screamed and fell to his knees. He pleaded with Valarian to stop. The colonel glared at the fallen major. He spoke in a low, disdainful voice. "Get up, you weakling. Get to work."

As the cringing major left the room, Valarian turned to his communications console and entered his private code. The computer responded quickly, as if it too knew the caller could inflict pain. Valarian requested the complete record and service file of Colonel Peter Ilyavich Somoroff, Internal Security, KGB, Moscow.

Within a few moments the long printout of Somoroff's history began to appear on Valarian's terminal printer.

At that same moment, Peter Somoroff opened the locked door to Boris and Celia Menoff's apartment and pulled a reluctant old man inside. Major Rosteveli followed after them.

Isadore Kantrowitz was frightened. The apartment was just

as Peter had left it. He walked to the center of the living room, but the old man would not follow. "Please come in, Mr. Kantrowitz. There are things in here that I want to ask you about."

Isadore Kantrowitz backed away toward the door. He bumped into Major Rosteveli, who held his shoulders.

"*No . . . No!*" screamed the old man. "Not in there."

Rosteveli was surprised at the man's strength but held him firmly. Peter Somoroff found the man's actions most interesting. Then he recalled Celia's words about an old man who came to the house with Boris before he died. A man who did things to the walls, mirrors, and furniture. Could Isadore Kantrowitz possibly be that old man? Peter took a chance.

"Mr. Kantrowitz, we know you were here before. We know you did things in this apartment. Boris Menoff is dead. Celia Menoff is dead. This place is safe now."

The shock of hearing about Boris Menoff caused Major Rosteveli to release the old man.

"Did you say Boris Menoff is dead, Colonel? I did not hear anything about that."

Peter realized his mistake, but it was too late to recall his words. Now he had to draw Rosteveli in deeper.

"Commissar Menoff died over a week ago. It is a secret. His wife died this morning. That too is a secret. Do you understand?"

"Yes, sir."

"I will fill you in on the details later. Now we have to get this old man to talk to us."

Peter walked toward Kantrowitz and put his hand on the old man's shoulder. He spoke gently and guided the man into the disheveled room.

"Please, Mr. Kantrowitz, please sit down. We will not harm you. The Menoffs are dead. Whatever was in this room will not harm you, either."

Trembling, the old man responded to Somoroff's plea and slowly entered the room. But he was afraid. What did this policeman know about harm of this nature?

"Do you have a match, Colonel?" asked the old man. Peter dug into his pocket and handed a box of wooden matches to the Jew. The old man then lit all the candles on the menorah, muttered a prayer, and sat on the small wooden bench near the window.

"What do you want from me?" he asked.

"First let me ask you if we may turn on the lights in here."

"Yes."

Peter motioned for Rosteveli to turn on the living room lights.

"Now, Mr. Kantrowitz, please be at ease. We are not going to arrest you. We are not going to harm you. We can protect you if you wish."

Isadore Kantrowitz did not respond. He just stared at the colonel. Rosteveli sat down in one of the armchairs, intent on what was happening.

Peter continued. "I was here yesterday with Mrs. Menoff. She became ill, and we took her to the hospital. She died early this morning. I don't yet know why she died, but we are doing an autopsy. Before she fell ill we spoke . . . we spoke about many things. You did this to the room, didn't you?"

Kantrowitz nodded affirmation.

"How did you come to Boris Menoff?"

"He was my nephew." The old man now spoke in a monotone.

Rosteveli hadn't known that Menoff was a Jew. The news came as a shock to him, but he remained silent and absorbed.

Peter went on. The pieces were coming together. "What did you do here? Why was the room this way?"

Slowly the old man raised his face until he was staring directly into Peter Somoroff's eyes. He spoke slowly and carefully.

"I will answer you. What I say is the truth, but you will not believe it. Even I know little about it. What I did here I did from memory, from things long ago, before the War and the Nazis . . . before the revolution . . . when there were no Reds . . . when there were no Whites . . . only the czar and oppression. They are things I saw as a boy in my home village of Melitopol, in the south. Boris was born there, too. He was a good boy. He was a Bar Mitzvah. He was a Jew. In the end, he came to know that being a Jew was the only possible road to safety for him and his wife. But as you can see it was too late."

The old man paused. Peter remained patient until the old man spoke again.

"I told Boris that I didn't know enough. These things . . ." He gestured around the room toward the menorah and the mirror. He noticed that the acrostic was gone, erased by Peter Somoroff before Dr. Karkov arrived. "Oh," exclaimed the old man, "it is gone . . . well, no matter. The evil one is also gone from this place."

Peter spoke. "What evil one?"

"The one who killed Boris and Celia. The one who is once again trying to destroy my people. The one who will destroy Russia. I think you know him." The old man smiled.

"You mean Valarian?" asked Peter.

"That is what he calls himself now. We know him by many names."

"What do you mean, many names?" Peter felt a cold sensation in his spine.

"He is the ungodly. He is the fallen angel. The evil one."

Peter drew a deep breath and asked the question that Boris Menoff's file had inferred. "You mean the devil?"

The old man raised his hands and spread them in a plea to heaven above. He spoke a prayer in Hebrew, then looked back at Somoroff. "That is a fairly new name for him. The ancient ones, blessed be they, called him Shaytān. That is Aramaic. Others call him Lucifer . . . Leviathan . . . Belial . . . Satan . . . Antichrist—there are many names."

Rosteveli was on his feet. "My god, what are you talking about? The devil? Colonel, surely—"

Peter cut him off. "Major, sit down and remain silent. Mr. Kantrowitz is speaking. There will be no interruptions."

"Yes, sir." Rosteveli sat again, staring at his superior officer in disbelief.

"But," said Peter, "you were able to do things in this house to stop him. How?"

"Boris and Celia are dead. It was a feeble attempt. It was not done properly. I told you I only know from long ago—my knowledge is incomplete."

"Celia was safe until I took her out of here," said Peter.

"He didn't want Celia anyway. It was Boris he was after."

"Why?" Peter asked.

"Because Boris was after him. I warned Boris, but he didn't believe, until it was too late . . . may he rest in peace."

"In peace," Peter responded. "Can you tell us about the things you did in this room? What do they mean? How do they work?"

The old man realized that this KGB colonel believed his story. It was fantastic. Perhaps this was a chance for his people. He knew there were good, kind Russians. He knew they had a fierce pride in their nation, in their Mother Russia. It was, after all, his country too. He spoke hesitantly.

"I can tell you some things, show you some things, but it will be incomplete."

"Is there anyone else who knows more?"

Now Kantrowitz perked up. Yes, perhaps this was the way . . . a beginning.

"Yes, Colonel," he answered, "if they are still alive. Some rabbis, one in particular—from Minsk."

"What is his name?" Peter asked.

"Isadore Vogel . . . Rabbi Isadore Vogel of Minsk. But I don't know what happened to him. He was arrested many years ago, and we have not heard about him for a long time."

Peter was on his feet. Rosteveli stood also.

"Major, I want you to take Mr. Kantrowitz to the office and make him comfortable. Show him what you have done so far with the acrostic and see if he can help you. I want a guard on him twenty-four hours a day. If he needs anything—anything—get it for him."

"Yes, sir." Rosteveli gestured for Kantrowitz to come with him. As they headed for the door Peter stopped them.

"One more thing, Mr. Kantrowitz. Could you come into the bedroom for a moment?"

The three men went into the bedroom. Peter took out his notebook and showed the old man the drawing of the pentangle he had made from the cloth arrangement he had found on the bedcover.

"This was on the bed yesterday. Do you know what it is?"

The old man smiled. "Yes. The Christians believe it is Satan's sign. But it has no power for us. Celia did it when I was here."

The three men left the apartment together. As Major Rosteveli and Isadore Kantrowitz drove off toward headquarters, Peter Somoroff drove in the opposite direction toward the Kremlin.

—12—

Premier Alexeyevich met with Peter in his private conference room.

"Your son is on his way by train. He will arrive the day after tomorrow, in the morning. He is to report directly to me."

The premier seemed distant and distracted. Affairs of state, thought Peter. I wouldn't have his job for anything. It is too much responsibility for one man.

The premier continued. "Before you tell me your news, I think you should know that Valarian knows I am investigating him."

"What happened?" asked Peter.

"He is trying to locate a copy of my visitors' log. I have loyal people around me, but now I suspect he too has people on my staff."

This fact unsettled Peter Somoroff.

"Then he knows you have Boris Menoff's file?"

"He must. That puts you in danger. I'm sorry."

Peter was touched by his friend's concern. "That comes with the job, Ivan Ivanovich. I can protect myself."

Premier Alexeyevich had more news.

"I have spent the morning with the Presidium. This business with our Jews grows worse. There are pressures from America. The dissidents get publicity. I will have to act soon."

"Can't you ease off a bit . . . let some time pass?"

The Soviet leader was on his feet. His voice raised in protest. "Don't you get the picture yet? I'm not ordering these things to be done. Valarian is behind it. His people are scattered throughout this damned bureaucracy of ours. If I stop one, then another arrests Jews somewhere else, or burns a synagogue, or rounds up a few and sends them off to Siberia. It's a big country, comrade, and filled with anti-Semites."

"You are sure Valarian is behind it?" asked Peter.

"Most of it—of what gets out to the world press anyway. He has powerful allies and an organization of fanatic followers. We must be very careful with this man. He has been able to gather many to his side. Caution, Peter . . . caution."

Peter paused before speaking again. The things he had to tell the premier were of a different order than how the premier viewed Valarian. Peter was not really sure he grasped these things himself.

The premier sat down again. "So what has the KGB to report?"

"Several things . . ."

It took an hour for Peter to relay all of the information to his friend. He was careful not to conclude anything regarding the motive behind Valarian's deeds. His final statement was cautious.

"The man holds some power, but I don't know enough about him yet to define his goals. There is a sense of . . . strangeness . . . something mystical, religious about this thing. I hope to have more for you in a few days, but for now conjecture will serve no purpose."

The premier had a question. "This old Jew you have with Rosteveli. Do you trust him?"

"Yes. He is genuinely frightened. In his way, no matter what you and I think, he did try to help Boris and Celia. That is more than we were able to do."

Premier Alexeyevich stood to announce that the meeting was ended. As the two men walked to the door of the conference room, Peter asked, "Do you have one more moment?"

The premier stopped and nodded.

"I need someone else to help in the investigation. I can't take any more of my staff or others will become suspicious. My son will be able to relieve me of contacting you in this way, and I will be able to get out into the field. Then I can dig into Colonel Valarian's past in detail. But for now I must have someone you trust implicitly."

"What do you want this person for, comrade?"

"I have to send someone to Siberia or one of the camps to find a certain man for me."

"The rabbi the old man spoke about?"

"Yes," answered Peter, a little embarrassed that he was following the suggestion of an old Jew. But the premier understood. No stone should be left unturned.

"One of our special embassy agents is here for a debriefing. She has been in America for two years. She is one of our best. I trust her with my life, Peter Somoroff. Her name is Sasha Andreyev. I will send her to you tomorrow."

"Thank you, Premier Alexeyevich." Peter left the room reflecting that perhaps he should have asked for a man. He knew the rabbi about whom Isadore Kantrowitz spoke would surely be in Siberia, and that was a brutal place at this time of year, especially for a woman.

When Peter reached his Skoda the snow was falling hard. It took a few minutes to brush off the windows and warm the car. He maneuvered around a soldier plowing the parking lot, passed through the Kremlin's northeast gate, and drove through the still streets toward Lubyanka Prison. It was time to have his talk with Doctors Brodsky and Karkov. As he drove slowly through a Moscow turning white, Peter Somoroff's thoughts remained with the premier. His mind drifted back to those early days on the hydrofoil as the three, Ivan Alexeyevich, Boris Menoff, and Peter, cruised the Crimea from Odessa to Sevastopol. Those were the days of Stalin and purges. But to these three rising stars in the Soviet political system, they were days of warm sunshine, a fast boat, and beautiful women.

After Peter had seen the hydrofoil leave Odessa harbor he had stayed all day, hoping for it to return so that he could meet the owner. By nightfall he knew it was futile to wait any longer. Each day after that he waited at the docks. On the third day he was rewarded beyond his expectations when, as the boat docked, he saw the familiar figure of Boris Menoff on the fantail. He also knew the man with Boris by sight. It was Ivan Ivanovich Alexeyevich, Commissar of Odessa. Peter waited patiently on the dock as the two men approached. Boris, always aware of the physical world around him, noticed Peter Somoroff.

"Peter Ilyavich," the little man called out, "how glorious

to see you." They hugged, and that brought a smile to the waiting Ivan Alexeyevich, because Peter was a good foot taller than Menoff and had lifted him from the ground.

"Now, if you will put me down," declared Menoff, "I will introduce you to the man who runs this city."

"It will be an honor to meet the man who, as you say, runs this city, but it will be a delight to meet the man who runs that marvelous boat," Peter answered, and in so saying made a friend for life of Ivan Ivanovich Alexeyevich, now premier of Russia.

As he drew closer to Lubyanka, another memory passed through Peter's mind, of the day that he had revealed to Alexeyevich why he had wanted to meet the owner of the hydrofoil.

They had been swimming and drinking on a beach near Yalta. The boat was moored offshore. Boris was on board with the women sleeping off a horrible hangover.

Ivan lay back on the warm, golden sand with a satisfied sigh. "This is the good life, my new friend. It would be wonderful to always be this serene . . . this safe."

Peter picked up the cue. He knew that the commissar was close to Stalin, but Boris had hinted that these days Alexeyevich kept away from Moscow. Premier Stalin was on the warpath. He took a chance and spoke his mind to Ivan Alexeyevich.

"The good life, that's true. But I don't know about safe. One never knows about that . . . these days."

Alexeyevich knew that Somoroff was NKVD. For a moment he thought that his time had come, that Comrade Stalin had sent Somoroff to collect him. He sat up and stared at Peter. "What do you mean, Peter?"

Peter saw the fear in the man's eyes and knew that he had played his cards right. Alexeyevich was also afraid of the madman in Moscow.

"I mean that we have a leader who is . . . shall I say . . . a bit erratic when it comes to the security of those around him?"

Ivan felt it was a test. He was wary. "Well," he said, "perhaps, but these are difficult times for the country. There is too much devastation from the war. Too much unrest in the world. Atomic weapons. Revolutions. The job he has is a big one—I would never want that responsibility."

Prophetic words.

Peter decided to go all the way with his new friend.

"There is no excuse for the purges. I have friends who have felt his wrath . . . unjustified. I think he is a madman."

There. He had said it. Suddenly there was relief on Ivan's face, and he fell back onto the sand laughing.

"You hate that lunatic bastard, too?"

"That's why I wanted to meet the owner of the hydrofoil. I thought it was the perfect escape vehicle—if I ever needed one, that is."

Tears of laughter were in Ivan Alexeyevich's eyes.

"Yes, yes. That's why I keep it down here, especially this summer. And you are welcome to it, my friend . . . always."

He kept laughing and laughing. Peter knew it was emotional relief Ivan was letting out, the relief that any of them might experience after feeling he had escaped from a one-way ticket to the Gulag or, perhaps, the grave.

As he entered the stone walls of Lubyanka, reality came back. It was Moscow . . . it was winter . . . it was snowing, and he, Peter Ilyavich Somoroff, held prisoners in this place. He also had business in Siberia. Time changes only the cast of players, the game remains the same.

Leonid and Marina finished making love for the third time that afternoon and napped peacefully in each other's arms. Downstairs, two men, a police sergeant and a plainclothes detective from the Pushkin central police station requested the register from the hotel manager. They would report Chomsky's whereabouts to Major Metsky immediately.

Young Peter Somoroff's train passed through Omsk. As he ate in the dining car, news of his orders reached Nickolai Valarian through the computer. Valarian had programmed the computer to supply background on all of those close to Peter Somoroff. He kept the information foremost in his mind as he studied his adversary's file. It might be useful to know exactly where his son was going to be for the next few days.

Sasha Andreyev found a message from Ivan Alexeyevich's secretary to call him. She had been out shopping for dinner. Her roommate, a cousin from Kiev, had taken the message down carefully.

"I couldn't believe it, Sasha. She actually said she was

calling from Premier Alexeyevich's office." The young woman knew that Sasha worked for the embassy in America. Since apartments were so hard to get in Moscow, she had been happy to take care of the place while Sasha was away. But she never realized how high in the government Sasha's job went. The young diplomat never talked about her work.

Sasha called the Kremlin number, but the premier was out. However he had left a message. She was to see Colonel Peter Somoroff at KGB headquarters in Moscow the next morning. She was to call him first. He was expecting her call. The premier also said that she was assigned to Somoroff until further notice. KGB in America or KGB in Moscow—to Sasha it was all the same thing. She was one of the best, and she knew it.

The dull Siberian winter sky never changed. However, within the Tostuya compound many things were changing. There was an influx of new inmates, all Jews. More buildings had to be opened, cleaned, and quickly filled with the new arrivals. Rabbi Vogel was kept busy day and night on detail after detail. At least it gave him a chance to talk to Yasha Mendel once in a while. The conversation was always the same—why so many Jews? Was it happening all over again? Why? They were allowed little contact with the new arrivals, who were themselves bewildered and lost in the snowbound surroundings. Vogel had to know what was happening. He had to chance talking to some of them. He shared this idea with Mendel, who by now had grown accustomed to the camp rules and regulations.

"Rabbi," Mendel whispered as they moved musty mattresses from a truck into the barracks, "if you have to do this thing, be careful. There are new people here in the administration, too. And some new guards arrived yesterday, Cossacks."

"I will be careful, Yasha. Something has happened. I feel it."

"Me, too," said the mathematician. Rabbi Vogel noticed as they entered the lit barracks that Yasha Mendel had aged considerably in the few short weeks since he had arrived.

~13~

Dr. Brodsky's room in Lubyanka was comfortable, if small. He stood nervously at the barred window, averting his gaze from Peter Somoroff's. With or without eye contact, the interrogation continued. Brodsky was beginning to crack.

"Once again, Doctor," said Peter, "I must have an answer from you today. Who is this Dr. Karkov that she has a hold over the Chief of Psychiatric Medicine?"

"She has no hold over me, Comrade Colonel." The doctor answered formally.

Peter had found the autopsy report waiting for him at the prison. It confirmed that Celia Menoff had died of a heart attack, an embolism. It also stated that adrenaline had not been used, especially behind the knee. So he knew that Karkov had lied, and Brodsky knew she had lied. Now there was no time for games. Peter felt an urgency to know more about their plans.

"The woman was murdered. You are accused as an accomplice. It won't go well with you, Doctor, I promise. On the other hand, if you cooperate with me, and because of our long friendship . . ." He let his voice trail off.

Brodsky spun around on the word *murder*. His face was white, the blood drained.

"Murder? Me murder? You are insane."

"Very well. If you wish to spend the rest of your life in prison, that is your business." Peter stood and turned to leave.

"*Wait*," yelled the doctor, "please wait." He sat on the bed, dejected and beaten. After a deep sigh, he told Peter Somoroff the truth.

A half hour later, Peter left Brodsky's room feeling good. Now he had some ammunition. Before questioning Dr. Karkov he called Major Rosteveli.

"How is Mr. Kantrowitz?"

"Settled in, Colonel. We are working on the acrostic. He is unable to fill in some of the translations; still we are trying. There is something else, Colonel."

Peter didn't like the tone of his voice. "Yes?"

"I received a call from that Army major I met at the synagogue today. He tracked me down to my office. His name is Anton Metsky."

"Where does he work?"

"I checked it out. He works for the man you mentioned to the old Jew today. Colonel Valarian."

So they're tracking us here, too, thought Peter. Fine. Still he hadn't made a link between Karkov and Valarian. Brodsky's story made no mention of Valarian or Metsky. It would be troublesome if there was a link. However, Brodsky had given a plausible reason for why Dr. Karkov would want Celia Menoff dead. Peter knew he needed more facts before confronting Karkov.

He told Rosteveli, "Major, I want you to leave Mr. Kantrowitz under guard. No one is to see him. *No one.* Go to the terminal in my office and use this entry code: K-RR-sevenXB plus. Do you have that?"

The major answered in the affirmative.

"Get a printout on Dr. Tania Karkov, now attached to the Psychiatric Unit at Central Hospital. Bring it to me at our section in Lubyanka."

"Yes, Comrade Colonel. It may take a while."

"I'll wait for you, Rosteveli . . . and, Major, be careful. When you get here I will explain much of this to you."

Within minutes Rosteveli had a guard on the door to his office and was on his way upstairs to Colonel Somoroff's office.

Peter called home to Nadja and explained that he would be working late. She was disappointed, so to cheer her up he told her that their son was coming to Moscow on leave. Nadja quickly forgot her annoyance with her husband.

While Peter waited for the file, across the city in the headquarters building of the GRU—the Intelligence Directorate of the General Staff of the Soviet Army—Colonel Nickolai

Valarian, Security and Records Division Chief, sat and listened to Major Metsky's third report of the day.

"Chomsky is in Pushkin at the Grazeed Hotel, room twenty-two. He is with a lady friend"—he looked down at his notes—"a Miss Marina Grochenko. She is a dancer with the Leningrad Ballet."

"Do we know why he is in Pushkin?" the colonel asked.

"Not yet, sir. But we will have a tail on him when he leaves the hotel."

"Good. Any news from Lubyanka?"

"Both doctors are still there. Somoroff is in the prison. Also, Captain Servioff reported that the major whom I met at the synagogue today—"

Valarian interrupted, "Rosteveli?"

"Yes, sir. Rosteveli is in Somoroff's office using the computer."

"Do we know why?"

"No, sir. I tried to locate the request, but it came in on a secure entry code. Somoroff has such a code similar to yours, Comrade Colonel."

"What about the old Jew?"

"He is in Rosteveli's office under guard."

Valarian put both of his scarred hands on the shiny mahogany desk. He glared at Metsky.

"Kill him!"

Anton Metsky had received orders like this against Jews from Valarian in the past. But never a job to be done in such a dangerous place. "In KGB headquarters, sir? That will be a problem."

"You don't have to attack the place, idiot. But the Jew will have to eat."

Metsky understood. Servioff could take care of that.

"Is there anything else, Colonel?" The major wanted to get out of the cold room quickly. Whenever there was killing in the air Valarian's cold, calculating demeanor changed. He would become excited, issuing orders until he reached a frenzy. But this time Valarian remained calm.

"Yes, Major Metsky. One more thing. I want to know the schedule of the stops that the train from Chita to Moscow will be making for the next few days. Also a list of people we have at those locations."

Metsky knew better than to question the reason for the

request. "Yes, sir. I will have that delivered to you within the hour."

The major stood, saluted, and left the office quickly. He had no desire to return again that day. Three visits were enough.

Rosteveli arrived at the prison on Dzerzhinsky Square after nightfall. He sat patiently as the colonel read the file on Dr. Karkov. When Somoroff had finished he spent the next hour telling Major Rosteveli the whole story, and since he had been in Menoff's apartment, he also told the major some of the conclusions that Boris Menoff had suggested in his investigative file. But the KGB cryptographer refused to believe those conclusions.

"You are right, Major, but we have to follow the case—wherever it leads us."

Both men stood. Peter walked with Rosteveli to the elevator. "You go back to the office and tuck our guest in for the night. I will see you in the morning. Thank you, Major."

As the major left the prison, he didn't notice he was being followed by someone in another car. There was too much on his mind. The snow was falling more heavily now. He had to drive with caution.

Isadore Kantrowitz hadn't ordered anything to eat, but he was hungry. The guard outside the door told the mess orderly that Major Rosteveli did not mention food would be coming up to the office. However, it was the dinner hour, so he accepted the tray. He unlocked the office door and gave the food to the old man. Isadore Kantrowitz nibbled on the chicken and boiled potato while he pored through the Hebrew-Greek translating dictionary in search of another meaning for *anagogi* or *anagoge*. He was dead within twenty seconds. The guard outside heard nothing as the old man slumped forward onto the dictionary.

—14—

"I demand to know why you are holding me here, Colonel Somoroff!" There was arrogance in Dr. Karkov's voice. Peter also detected a slight tremor of fright underneath. Good, he thought. She is not sure.

"In good time, Tania Karkov. It will all be clear to you in time. Now I have a few questions for you, if you don't mind."

Keep it polite and low-key, thought Peter. He was sure she would not be thrown off her guard by his manner, but there was no need for extreme interrogation techniques yet.

The pretty, blond Bielorussian doctor stood defiantly. "Ask your questions, policeman."

"Good," said Peter. He deliberately sat down and opened his briefcase methodically. String her out. Raise her anxiety. He had, in his life, questioned hundreds of prisoners. He knew all of the techniques. Soon, this murderer would understand whom she was defying.

"Now, Comrade Doctor. The reason you are here is murder. You are accused of being an accomplice in the murder of Celia Menoff, wife of a member of the Supreme Soviet. We have charged Dr. Brodsky, and he has implicated you. I have just a few loose ends to tie up before you are formally charged."

Tania was stunned. Murder? How did they know? Brodsky wasn't there when she did it. She knew Somoroff was lying and felt contempt for his clumsy approach.

"That, of course, is a lie, Comrade Colonel. I am an accomplice to no such act, and you know it."

70

"Perhaps. But he did implicate you. He seems to hold a great animosity toward you. Frankly, Tania, he hates you."

She shrugged and folded her arms across her bosom. Peter noticed that she had an attractive body underneath her white lab coat. What a strange species we are, Peter mused. I am attracted to this female while at the same time I have such contempt for her actions. He changed tactics.

"Have you had your dinner, Doctor?" he asked.

"Yes. Swill for pigs."

"Well," he said, standing, "you had better get used to it. You will be here for a long time." He began to fold his papers.

"Is that all you have to say to me?" she questioned.

"No, there is more. Brodsky is not the murderer—you are. We have the autopsy report. There was no adrenaline administered. You injected air into Celia Menoff's vein behind her knee, causing a heart attack. It was clumsy, and you, my dear doctor, were stupid to think you could get away with it."

"I had no reason to kill the woman. I had no motive."

"Ah, but you did. Dr. Brodsky told us about your hatred of Boris Menoff. About how he imprisoned your brother for anti-Soviet activities. You had an excellent motive."

Actually Brodsky had only casually mentioned it. Peter Somoroff had confirmed that tidbit in Karkov's file. He also found that her brother, Misha Karkov, had been released from prison a few months ago at the direction of none other than Nickolai Valarian. The circle grew tighter.

"But my brother is free. And Boris Menoff is dead—" She stopped herself but too late. He had tricked her.

"Yes, Comrade Doctor. Boris Menoff is dead. But how do you know that?"

"The woman told me," she countered quickly. "She . . . ah . . . she woke during the night. She was delirious . . . muttering about her husband. I was shocked to hear the news—"

"Garbage. You told me she was sedated, that she didn't waken at all. That she had the attack in her sleep. Get your story straight."

Tania Karkov knew that her words were being recorded through a bug hidden somewhere in the small detention room. She fondled a ruby ring on her finger. Peter noticed the action. He bore in for the kill.

"I know that you are only an instrument in this matter, Tania. It will go easier for you if you tell me about the man who gave you the order to kill Mrs. Menoff."

Tania Karkov felt the cold shock of entrapment surge through her body.

"What man? What are you talking about?"

Peter changed tactics again. He shouted at the attractive doctor.

"I am talking about Valarian. Colonel Nickolai Valarian, the man who instructed you to murder Mrs. Menoff. You have just a moment to speak, Doctor, so do it quickly. Otherwise the next time you talk it will be before a magistrate of the court."

Tania Karkov lunged at Somoroff, trying to slash him with the ruby ring. As though captured in a frozen moment, Peter saw the small needle point projecting from the center of the bright red stone. *Poison.*

He backed away toward the door, shouting for a guard. She lunged again, barely missing him as he stepped aside. As she passed him he kicked her in the stomach. She fell forward, clutching her groin, as the guard opened the door with his pistol drawn. Tania looked up and knew she was trapped. Peter ordered the guard to shoot if the prisoner made any attempt to attack.

"Now," Peter spoke in a shaky voice, "give me the ring."

"You will have to take it, Colonel." There was cold defiance in her voice.

"Then we will take it," Peter answered coldly.

A look of hatred came across Dr. Karkov's face. She knew the man meant to have his way. She knew she was finished. For her, failure was death, from either the men in this room or that strange and powerful man to whom she owed her total allegiance. She spoke to Peter Somoroff, and her words cut the air like knives.

"You will never have me, Somoroff. You will know soon enough who we are, and what we can and will do. You are weak, impotent, ignorant. He will break you like a dry twig in winter. I curse you . . . I spit upon you . . ."

Her face twitched; her eyes grew glassy; spittle ran from her mouth. Peter saw that she had plunged the needle ring into her wrist.

As he knelt over the dead woman, a guard arrived to tell him that Major Rosteveli was on the phone with an urgent message. Peter told both guards to remove the woman to the prison morgue. He rushed to the phone only to hear of another death. Rosteveli was furious.

"He was poisoned. Someone sent food to him. The guard is not at fault, I didn't instruct him properly, Colonel—it is my fault."

"Calm down, Major," Peter instructed with a commanding voice. "Calm down. Have the body removed to the morgue here at Lubyanka, then go home. Take all of the acrostic papers with you. I will call you in the morning at home. Stay there until I call."

"Is it safe for me, Colonel?" Rosteveli was worried.

Peter thought for a moment.

"I have a better idea. Go to your lady friend's house. The one who knew the old man. Call me in the morning. And be sure you are not followed."

The major understood. The colonel was talking about Fannie Beshevsky.

"Don't worry, Comrade Somoroff. I won't make any more mistakes."

He hung up the phone. No, Peter thought, and neither will I.

~ 15 ~

Moscow was white with the new-fallen snow and as hushed as a soundproof room. Peter Somoroff sipped his morning tea and watched Moscow waking up out of the kitchen window. His mother-in-law was up and about, puttering and cleaning so that things would be perfect for her grandson's arrival tomorrow. Both women had been excited when he came home last night. It was always difficult to leave the happenings of the day behind when he came home. Usually it took two shots of vodka before he could relax. Last night it took four, and Nadja had noticed his alcohol consumption. She was gentle with him. Supper was hot and delicious. Talk was kept to a minimum, although both women were bursting with questions about young Peter's leave. He told them it was a special leave given to soldiers who had performed exceptionally well in Afghanistan. Another lie in a life of lies. But it satisfied them.

Peter reviewed his plans for the day. Major Rosteveli would call soon. Peter glanced at the kitchen clock. Seven fifteen; yes, he would be calling at any moment. Assuming the major had not been followed, they would meet away from the office. Peter knew that Lubyanka was a secure place. The KGB diplomatic agent whom Premier Alexeyevich had recommended would also be calling, but at the office. Other than Chomsky and Rosteveli, Peter knew he could trust no one. Somehow he would have to divert her call. Then there was Chomsky in Pushkin. He would have some news tonight. Peter considered calling him now to warn him of the danger, but he knew the young lieutenant would be out working. The

74

thought made Peter anxious. First things first. He went to the phone and called the premier.

"Good morning, Premier Alexeyevich. Can you put this call on scramble?"

Peter heard a high-pitched squeal. Then the premier was on the line again. "Good morning, Peter."

"I would appreciate your calling your friend Sasha and asking her to meet me at Lubyanka, in my section. Tell her to be there by nine AM."

"Is anything wrong?"

"A few problems. I will come by later with a full report."

"Fine. Make it before five. I have a state dinner tonight with the Hungarians. Goodbye."

Satisfied, Peter waited for Rosteveli's call, which came immediately after he hung up with the premier.

"Good morning, Colonel."

"Good morning, Major. Meet me at Lubyanka at eight-thirty. Goodbye."

Nadja came into the kitchen and wrapped her arms around her seated husband. She felt warm and soft. He loved her and bent his head backward into her breasts and the warm robe. She kissed his neck.

"Good morning, Peter Ilyavich," she murmured into his Adam's apple.

His response was even more muffled.

"Good morning, love."

Nadja's mother watched from the kitchen door. Her son-in-law was a good man. It pleased her to see their love. She smiled and shuffled off to clean the house as only a grandmother can for her only grandson.

The Moscow train traveled into dawn near Chelyabinsk. Ahead lay the Ural Mountains. Now the train would slow down as it wound its way through the mountain passes and tunnels across the majestic range. Peter had been trained in this region in nuclear and biological warfare at the highly secret Kamyshlov Range and Proving Grounds. The weapons they studied surprised the young man. He thought about whether he would really use them against an enemy one day. Thoughts about the Afghanistan action flooded his mind. He was glad to be out of that business. You fought an invisible enemy who seemed to be part of the rocky, barren terrain.

They appeared and disappeared at will, hitting with rocket and mortar fire sporadically as they moved through the forbidden hills. He had come to admire the tribesmen who defended their mother country with the same intensity and abandon described by his father when he talked about the Soviet Army defending Stalingrad against the Nazis. Young Somoroff had kept a diary of his adventures in Afghanistan. Now, as the memories came to him he took paper and pen and began to write. Someday, he thought, I will tell the story of this chapter in Russian history.

Peter brought Rosteveli up to date on last night's events. The major was still angry with himself and was pacing back and forth in the cell that Peter had set up as a temporary office.

"Please, Major. No one blames you. Please sit down and listen to me."

The Georgian slumped into a chair opposite the Colonel.

"We have to begin to anticipate these people effectively. I am convinced they have tapped my office phone, and probably my home phone. We will assume that your line is also tapped. This wing of the prison is mine. I know every man and woman here, but I want you to spend the day checking their files for any contact with Valarian—or anyone at GRU in Moscow. Be thorough. From now on our lives depend on it."

Peter could see that Rosteveli was completely involved. It felt good to have the crusty fellow Georgian on his side.

"Did you tell the woman about Kantrowitz?"

"No, sir. But I felt like a shit, that I can tell you."

The intercom buzzed.

"Colonel Somoroff, you have a visitor in reception." Peter glanced at his watch. It was 9:00 AM exactly. A good sign. He instructed Rosteveli to leave the room and use the office at the end of the hall. The files were there.

Sasha Andreyev, although born in the Ukraine, grew up in Tallinn, in Estonia. Her clothes reflected a life style oriented to the west. She wore a lynx coat and matching hat, sealskin boots, and black suede gloves. The boots and gloves set off the dark, silky black hair. As she removed her coat, Peter saw she wore an American sweater and jeans underneath. The jeans were skin-tight, revealing a full figure. He noticed her gun neatly tucked into the right boot on the inside. The flare of the jeans hid it well. She spoke first.

"I have heard a great deal about you, Comrade Colonel. It is an honor to work with you."

"You have me at a disadvantage, madam. I know nothing about you, but if Ivan Alexeyevich recommends you, then that is good enough for me."

They shook hands. Hers were warm and smooth. He lingered with them for a moment thinking how long they would last if exposed to a Siberian winter storm.

"Is there something wrong?" she asked.

He let her hand go. "No . . . nothing. Now come and sit down. I have a job for you that needs to be done immediately."

She took a notebook from her shoulder bag. Before she could get her pen out, Somoroff stopped her.

"Nothing on paper, Miss Andreyev. The matters we will discuss are for my ears and the premier's only."

"Yes, Colonel. And my name is Sasha, please."

"Good. Now, Sasha, first you will locate a man. His name is Rabbi Isadore Vogel."

She looked at the KGB chief. "Excuse me, Colonel—"

"Yes. I said *rabbi*," he answered before she could ask, "and my name is Peter." He continued, "I believe Vogel is from Minsk. He is in a camp. I assume in the Siberian area but possibly somewhere else. When you locate his whereabouts, report back to me."

"Can you tell me why you want this man . . . what the case is about?"

Sasha was curious but respectful of her superior officer.

"Not now. I will tell you what you need to know as you need to know it. I'm sorry, but it will all make sense to you in time. Just one more thing. Do not connect my name or that of the premier or my section with this research. And if you can help it, keep it away from the GRU. We have enemies there. As a matter of fact, try to involve as few people as possible and leave no trail from here. Be sure you are not followed when you return."

Sasha knew how she would like to get the information—firsthand, at the source. She had to ask.

"Comrade . . . ah, Peter, do we have a budget for expenses on this case?"

"What do you need?" he asked. It hadn't occurred to him yet to set up a budget. This woman asked good questions.

"It is an hour by plane to Minsk. I can make the flight if I get to the airport by noon. I can be back by tomorrow afternoon. That way I can go to the court records without using the computer or the GRU, as you instructed."

"Do you have a government travel card?" he asked.

"Yes," she answered, "but for the diplomatic section only."

"Fine. Use it for your trip. By tomorrow I will have the premier transfer us to his special discretionary budget."

"Very well. I will see you here by three tomorrow afternoon." She thought for a moment, then asked, "Do you want me to call you from Minsk?"

"No. The phones are not secure. And when you leave here, go through our section to the main prison and out the front gate. Good hunting, Sasha, and be careful."

As Sasha Andreyev drove toward the airport she made several quick turns to be sure she wasn't being followed. It was strange to be on assignment inside her own country, taking the same precautions she had so often taken in the United States. There was something very sad about Soviets spying on Soviets. But the premier had been specific . . . "You are to be totally committed to this man Somoroff as though he were me." Now that she had met the famous Peter Ilyavich Somoroff, she liked him. Her only complaint at this point was her ignorance of the case. In a few days, she would wish that her ignorance had remained.

In Pushkin, the files gathered for Chomsky told Captain Yuri Bonyon that the KGB was interested in Nickolai Valarian. The captain put two and two together quickly. Inside, the KGB agent was reading files of Jewish arrests and incidents going back several years—all involving Valarian. Outside, two of the most anti-Semitic policemen in Pushkin sat waiting and watching. Well, thought Bonyon, this is none of my affair. Let the hyenas eat their own. He went down the block to the neighborhood coffeehouse.

Police Sergeant Zalitski nudged the detective next to him. "That was the duty officer who just left. Chomsky must have had to see him."

Lieutenant of Detectives Vladimir Zorbin was a patriotic Russian. He followed orders explicitly, but his actions were always tempered by his love of his country. Police work was satisfying but local in scope, so when he was approached by Sergeant Zalitski to get involved with a special project for GRU chief Valarian, he was thrilled. It had been explained that both men could be of great service to their country, and to the GRU in particular, if as they went about their daily work they took special assignments from Valarian's office. Most of those assignments had involved actions against Jews. Now, for the first time, they involved a KGB agent, and this made Lieutenant Zorbin uneasy.

"Yes, he probably did," answered Zorbin. "Put it in the report."

"Shouldn't one of us keep an eye on him?" asked the zealous sergeant.

"He probably only went to the coffee shop."

The sergeant moved to get out of the car. "I'm going to have a look anyway. I'll be back in a few minutes."

Zorbin didn't argue. He was glad to be alone for a while.

As he sipped his coffee, Captain Bonyon was amused by the clumsy sergeant's attempt to spy on him. It also made him uneasy. This KGB agent in his office might be involving him in a matter he didn't want any part of. He decided to speak to Chomsky and hurried to finish his coffee.

Chomsky sat absorbed in the files. Separately, they were just records of arrests and imprisonments of some citizens of Pushkin. Collectively, they were an indictment of anti-Semitism in that fair Russian city. Each file was signed by Major Nickolai Valarian, then head of internal affairs for his section. Leonid wondered if it would be worth while to stay another day to compare the arrests of Jews after Valarian had been promoted out of that job. As he tried to make that decision, the door to the office opened, and Captain Bonyon stood staring at him with a funny look on his face.

"I'm not finished yet, Captain. I'll be about a half hour more."

"What is it exactly that you are looking for, Lieutenant?"

"That is my business . . . KGB business. I'm afraid it doesn't involve you."

"Ah, but it does," said Bonyon as he sat down in the unfamiliar chair opposite his own seat, "it most certainly does."

"And how is that, Comrade Captain?" Chomsky asked sarcastically.

"I have just had a cup of coffee at the corner, and I believe because of your presence here, I had to drink it under the surveillance of our local police."

Chomsky grew alert. He felt a tingle in the pit of his stomach.

"Police? Are you certain?"

"Oh," said Bonyon, enjoying the KGB agent's interest, "I am quite certain. I know those rats. But they don't know me . . . at least I think they don't."

Chomsky relaxed. "Just a coincidence. I know they have no business with me."

The captain sat back in the chair and smiled. "Ah, but I think they are here because of you. I think they followed you."

"What makes you think that?" Leonid was worried again.

"You have to know this neighborhood, its businesses. The police just don't come around here too often."

Chomsky believed the man. He had to know more about the police outside, and that meant involving Captain Bonyon. But in order to do that he first had to speak to Colonel Somoroff.

Peter Somoroff's secretary took Chomsky's call. He was told that the colonel could be reached at Lubyanka. Somoroff took the call as he was on his way to see Dr. Brodsky.

"Yes, Leonid. What is it?" Peter was annoyed that Chomsky had called, even though he knew these lines were still secure.

"I apologize for calling, but something has come up. May I speak freely?" The KGB lieutenant had asked Captain Bonyon to leave the room while he placed this call.

"Go ahead," answered Somoroff.

"The files are full of interesting information about our friend. But for some reason I seem to have two local policemen on my tail."

"How do you know that?"

"The captain of this section spotted them. I believe him."

"Who are they?"

"I don't know exactly, just that they are from the local police. A sergeant and a lieutenant."

"Get me their names. I'll hold on."

Chomsky put down the phone and called the captain into the office. "Do you know the policemen's names?"

"Yes."

"Good," said Leonid. "Please write them down for me. I'll be just a moment, then you can have your office back."

He was especially nice to the captain, sensing that he would need him. After Bonyon left the room, Leonid read the names to Somoroff. Peter copied them down.

"Good, Leonid. Now, get those files photocopied, and get out of there. I want you back here by tomorrow morning."

Chomsky was startled by his boss's insistence.

"Is everything all right, Colonel?"

"No. It is not all right, and this business of those policemen worries me. Be very careful, Leonid."

Chomsky thought for a moment, then risked Somoroff's wrath with a question. "Colonel Somoroff, I may have to involve the captain of this section a bit. He gave me the names of the policemen, he knows which files I have viewed, and . . . and I am worried about Marina Grochenko. She was with me last night."

Peter hesitated. It was dangerous to involve any stranger, but he trusted Chomsky's judgment.

"If you must, then tell him only what he needs to know—but, Leonid, be sure of him, please. This business is getting nasty. And give me his name."

He gave Somoroff Captain Bonyon's name.

"Yes, sir. I will. See you tomorrow morning?"

"Yes, Leonid. But meet me at Lubyanka. We are using this wing for our office in this matter. See you tomorrow."

Somoroff hung up. He stopped by the office where Rosteveli was working.

"Major, hold off on those security checks for a while. I want you to pull the files on these people. Bring them to me as soon as you have them."

Rosteveli took the three names, noting that two were with the Pushkin police and one was an Army captain. "May I use your secure entry code to pull them?" he asked.

"From now on use only that code for the computer. Everything we do is to be as secure as we can keep it . . . until we want them to know our business."

Rosteveli felt the anger in Somoroff's voice. It was a controlled anger, tempered with the patience of a first-class detective and a man of intellect. He also sensed that the chase was on. In typical Somoroff fashion, it first involved information—as much as they could gather against their enemies—then, when they knew everything there was to know about these people, Colonel Somoroff would move in for the kill. And it would be a kill without pity, based on solid evidence.

Somoroff moved down the hall to Dr. Brodsky's room. He was not finished with the traitor yet. Before the day was out, the Chief of Psychiatric Medicine might need a psychiatrist himself.

A copy of Premier Alexeyevich's visitors' log lay on Nickolai Valarian's polished desk. The notations of Peter Somoroff's meetings with the premier were neatly underlined. Valarian now knew he was confronting a clever enemy. The KGB chief's file was thick with success. His reputation was awesome. How swiftly he had moved to collect Brodsky and Karkov. But how did he find the old man so fast, and what was Lieutenant Chomsky up to in Pushkin? He needed answers, but first he would move to slow Somoroff down, to punish him enough so that there would be no doubt about Valarian's power. He stretched his mouth and squeezed his eyes shut as though he were a lion yawning. Valarian felt the tightness of his burned body. Aging scar tissue became less flexible with time.

Anton Metsky watched the GRU colonel contort before him. He recoiled inside at the sight of those long, yellowing teeth and the bunching flaps of twisted flesh that covered his boss's face. The colonel spoke as if from deep inside a musty well.

"Have you heard anything more about Brodsky or Karkov?"

The major hesitated, knowing he must give his chief bad news. "Yes, Colonel Valarian. I am afraid it is not good." He waited for a reaction, but the colonel only looked.

"Dr. Karkov is dead. She is in the Lubyanka morgue. There is no news of Brodsky."

"How did she die?"

"Poison. She took her own life."

Once again the yellow teeth parted scarred lips. A smile?

"She was loyal. I want her body brought here."

"That may not be possible . . . not just yet. Somoroff has it under guard."

"Bring it when you can. How did they react to the old man's death?"

"Captain Servioff said the body was also taken to Lubyanka's morgue. It is being guarded."

Valarian stood and leaned over the desk. The hollow voice pierced the cold room. "You will be busy today, Metsky. We will have to teach this Somoroff a lesson. A lesson he will never forget!"

Metsky concentrated on the orders as they were issued rapidly. Was there, he thought, anyone more evil or more powerful in the world than this man before him? The pleasure of serving Valarian's wishes excited the major. He loved the action. And the power.

~16~

As night fell in Moscow, Peter Somoroff left the Kremlin. The lights in the great hall were burning, and the strains of music from the Soviet Army Orchestra announced the beginning of a state dinner. Peter's meeting with the premier had been short and to the point. Starting tomorrow his son would be the liaison to the Kremlin chief of state. That thought made Peter Somoroff feel proud. He still had not told the premier what his gut feelings were regarding Menoff's file and the conclusion one might draw from the events of the investigation. He found his Skoda and prepared to head home.

The words of Alexeyevich still echoed in his brain. "When you sit in my chair, Peter Ilyavich, you feel the undercurrents of the powermongers. They will use anything to control the destiny of the Soviet Union. This Valarian has organized many people to his cause. Make no mistake, I know his cause. It is my position he seeks. Others have tried. If we misjudge him, then we will be punished. He knows he has me by the throat with this Jewish business. He is clever. And he has powerful friends in the Presidium. Be careful."

Peter drove toward home, welcoming the thought of a warm apartment, a good meal, and a loving wife. Tomorrow he would see his son. He felt no compassion for Dr. Brodsky. The man had been stubborn, pleading ignorance. Now he would spend a few days in Somoroff's psychiatric ward with a different breed of doctors. Peter knew Brodsky was his. The man would crack in a short time. Peter put Brodsky out of his mind until the KGB doctors were ready to give him back in a more cooperative mood.

• • •

Leonid Chomsky was looking forward to his return to Moscow. Captain Bonyon offered to drive him to the Leningrad airport. The soldier was extremely buoyant and talkative. He was alive with excitement. Now he had more than a desk job. He had been enlisted by the KGB in a field operation, working for the fabled colonel Peter Somoroff. The young lieutenant next to him was a good man. It had been fun watching him handle the Pushkin policemen this afternoon.

After copying the files, Chomsky and Bonyon had left the building. The two policemen still sat in their Zim watching the front door. Chomsky walked directly to the car and motioned for the driver, the sadistic sergeant, to roll down the window.

"May I see your identification?" Chomsky asked directly.

"Who the hell are you?" the belligerent sergeant answered as he opened the car door to get out.

Chomsky slammed the door on the man's legs. He screamed in pain. The lieutenant started to draw his gun and then thought better of it when he saw Captain Bonyon pointing a large service revolver at him through the window. Chomsky dragged the sergeant to his feet and told him to spread-eagle against the car. He searched the man and took his revolver.

"Now turn around slowly and show me your identification. Take it out slowly."

Sergeant Zalitski took out his ID. "You are making a mistake, you arrogant KGB bastard." The sergeant was still in pain.

Leonid took a perfunctory glance at the ID and returned it to the man. Then he spoke to Bonyon. "It's all right, Captain, these men seem to be with the police."

Detective Zorbin was out of the car in a flash. "Seem to be? You two are under arrest!"

Chomsky smiled. These policemen were dumb. Even the detective hadn't picked up the sergeant's mistake. Leonid pressed his point home. "You had better have solid grounds for this arrest, because you knew I was a KGB officer. Your friend here just insulted my rank."

"And you knew we were police," the detective answered.

"That, sir, you will have to prove, and I suggest that unless you can, you will quickly feel the wrath of my office in Moscow on your fat necks."

Zorbin knew he had lost the argument. He motioned for Zalitski to get into the car. They sped off as Bonyon and Chomsky had a good laugh.

Before heading for the Leningrad airport, Chomsky made one stop at the Pushkin synagogue, but the temple was deserted and locked, and the old rabbi was nowhere to be seen. As Chomsky bade farewell to Captain Bonyon at the Leningrad airport, he could not have known that, at that moment, just fifteen miles away in the artists' section of the fabled city, Sergeant Zalitski was carrying out the first of Nickolai Valarian's orders for the day. His partner, Lieutenant Zorbin, sat on the young dancer's chest and pinned her arms, while Zalitski smashed a sledgehammer down on her right kneecap. She fainted from the pain. The crunching sound made Zorbin sick, and he vomited on the bed.

Zalitski laughed. "You should have done that on her face, Comrade Lieutenant. Now get off."

He then took a bag containing a dead cat from his overnight satchel and slit the cat's throat. Major Metsky had been specific about this part of the action. He held the bleeding cat over the young dancer and let the blood pour onto her body, especially the legs.

"Must you do that?" Zorbin asked, aghast at the gory sight.

"We must do whatever Comrade Metsky tells us to do. Now mark her!"

The shaken detective smoothed out the blood on the dancer's belly and drew the six-pointed Jewish star onto her skin with his pocket knife. Zalitski then smeared the cat's blood so that it mingled with Marina Grochenko's blood, and the deed was done. The final act was to call the Leningrad Ballet and leave a message that Marina Grochenko had been in an accident and was at home. They would discover her by morning, but by that time Zorbin and Zalitski would be safely back in Pushkin. Sergeant Zalitski wished he could see the KGB lieutenant's face when he heard about his little dancer.

The second of Valarian's orders was carried out in Lubyanka Prison. It was done by Misha Karkov after Valarian told him that his sister was dead. The young criminal wanted revenge. It was easy for the colonel to guide his vengeance toward the KGB enemy.

Using GRU identification papers, young Misha Karkov, recently paroled by Valarian, entered the Lubyanka main prison with orders to pick up GRU autopsy reports for that month. This allowed him access to the morgue. He asked the desk sergeant, who was on Metsky's payroll, for the reports, taking notice of the KGB guards standing near the storage drawers in the cold room. One drawer would contain his sister, the other the old Jew. He signaled to the desk sergeant who rose and called to the guards.

"Hey! This guy wants to talk to you two."

Misha drew his pistol and hid it under his coat as the guards came to the cold room door. When they were both through the door he put the pistol to the sergeant's head and instructed the KGB soldiers.

"Put your machine pistols against the wall behind the desk. Quick!"

The guards followed his orders. He pushed the sergeant in front of him and ordered them all into the cold room. He then made all three men get into the storage drawers and slid them shut. He crossed the room and took the machine pistols and used them as wedges to keep the drawers shut, all but the sergeant's. The small but powerfully built Karkov then checked the hallway outside. No one was around. He pulled a surgical scalpel from his leather greatcoat and went to the first drawer. In it was his sister, cold and white in death. Tears came to his eyes and anger welled up in him. He bent and kissed her cold lips, then slowly closed the drawer, turning his attention to the other where the body of Isadore Kantrowitz was stored. With the scalpel he mutilated the old man's body, cutting large slashes, pulling out the intestines, and finally cutting off the old man's penis and testicles and stuffing them into the cadaver's mouth.

Tomorrow morning the Jewish community of Moscow would be informed that the KGB had murdered one of their members. Since Valarian knew that the Jews rushed to bury their dead, they would demand the body. Let Somoroff explain the mutilation to them.

Anton Metsky felt removed from the third order, but he knew it was the most dangerous. It had to be carried out no matter how much he questioned the wisdom of such an act.

Valarian had studied the Chita-to-Moscow train schedule along with the list of loyal people along the train's route.

He pinpointed the city of Kazan, just two hundred miles east of Gorki. The city lay near the Volga River. Their agent there was a civil engineer named Valya Pernick. She specialized in hydroelectric dam construction and was a totally committed disciple of Valarian's. They had met when he was recuperating at the Burn Institute in Grozny. Her mother had been Valarian's nurse, and until her unfortunate death in 1970 in an airplane crash, both women did his bidding. Metsky placed the call to Valya Pernick himself. She never questioned orders from Colonel Valarian.

In the early morning hours, as the Chita-to-Moscow train left the Ural Mountains behind, speeding toward Kazan and eventually Moscow, Valya Pernick bought her ticket at the Kazan station and waited. The ticket read Kazan to Gorki, one-way. She wore the black dress, black coat, and veil of mourning. The station agent might remember her, but he never saw her face through the heavy veil.

A few hours later, young Peter Somoroff awakened to the conductor announcing Kazan as the next stop. By the end of the day he would be in Moscow and would see his family. It was exciting. He dressed and went to the dining car for breakfast. There were many travelers boarding at Kazan, and he was glad that he had eaten breakfast before the morning rush began in the dining car. He casually noticed the woman in mourning when she entered the car.

Two hours later there was a knock on Lieutenant Somoroff's door. He was surprised to see the veiled woman before him.

"May I help you, madam?" he asked politely.

The woman was crying. "I saw you in the dining car. Aren't you the son of Colonel Peter Ilyavich Somoroff?"

"Yes . . . yes I am. How do you know me?"

"I know your father. May we talk?"

Peter invited her into his sleeper compartment. He turned to ask if she would like some coffee just as the woman drove a long stiletto upward from below his rib cage into his heart. In a few seconds he was dead, killed by an expert. Valya propped him up on the sofa and covered him with a blanket as though he were sleeping. She then returned to her seat, took a book from her handbag, and read for the rest of the trip to Gorki.

• • •

Peter Somoroff parked in Lubyanka and walked toward his sector. It was going to be a full day, he thought. Leonid and Sasha will both be back. As he walked in the cold morning air, he had no idea that it would be a day he would remember for the rest of his life.

~ 17 ~

Somoroff, Chomsky, and Rosteveli sat in the office-cell and discussed their next moves. The major and the colonel had read the Pushkin files thoroughly. There was no doubt that Valarian had been ruthless and brutal in his treatment of the Jews in that part of Russia.

Rosteveli reported on his check of the KGB Lubyanka people in this section. None of them had any link to Valarian or the GRU. The three men then discussed the previous night's happenings in the morgue. The news was all over the prison. Somoroff ordered Tania Karkov's body to be moved. There was little he could do about the mutilation of Isadore Kantrowitz's body. Peter questioned Rosteveli.

"You say that the KGB men were locked in the drawers, but the desk sergeant was not?"

"Yes, Comrade Colonel."

"Strange. Was this sergeant included in the people you checked out yesterday?"

"No, sir. He is not in our section; however, the guards were and they checked out fine."

Another mistake, thought Somoroff, betting to himself that the sergeant would have a GRU or Valarian connection in his file.

"I want you to pull that sergeant's file and check it, Major. Do it now."

Chomsky had sat quietly through the last exchange, amused by the thought of the three men locked in cold storage drawers. Somoroff turned to the young lieutenant as Rosteveli left the room.

"You were not able to find the rabbi again?"

"No, Colonel. The synagogue was deserted. I think the man was a little crazy anyway. He withdrew when I mentioned Colonel Valarian."

Peter sensed that Chomsky was taking this too lightly. He had not yet told him all of the facts. It was time to sober up the young man.

"If you think that rabbi was crazy, Lieutenant, then you are a poor judge of character, or your little romantic interlude has softened your brain."

Leonid Chomsky sat upright in his chair, alert to the colonel's tone of voice. Peter told him the facts, especially stressing the fanatical way in which Tania Karkov took her life. He ended the lecture with a question. "How do you think those Pushkin police got on to you?"

"A phone tap? I apologize, Colonel."

Then he realized that if the police checked his hotel yesterday, they also knew that he had spent the night with Marina. A knot tightened in his stomach.

"What is it, Leonid?" Peter asked.

"Marina. They must have seen Marina. Perhaps there were more of them . . . perhaps they followed her back to Leningrad. . . . She may be in danger."

He was on his feet, searching for a phone. He located it and picked up the receiver.

"May I call her, Colonel?"

"Go ahead. These phones are still safe."

There was no answer at her apartment.

"Perhaps she had an early rehearsal," suggested Somoroff.

Leonid was close to panic. "It's too early. They don't start until noon. She had a performance last night . . . so they rest in the morning."

"Are you sure?" Peter felt a chill. He took the phone from Leonid and flashed the operator. "Give me KGB Central in Leningrad." While he waited he told Leonid to write down Marina's address. Leningrad answered. "Give me Major Bazak."

Somoroff instructed his man in Leningrad to take a few men and to go around to Marina Grochenko's apartment. If she was not there, they were to check the Leningrad Ballet Theater. And they were to move immediately. Peter instructed them to call him back at the Lubyanka number as soon as they located the girl. He hung up.

"Thank you, Colonel."

"You're welcome. Now if we can dispense with your love life and get onto our problems . . ." Secretly Somoroff feared for the young dancer.

Leonid Chomsky smiled nervously. He could not really concentrate until he knew Marina was safe.

The head rabbi of the Great Synagogue in Moscow received the news about Isadore Kantrowitz by telephone. The caller was anonymous. He checked with the regulars who confirmed that Kantrowitz had, in fact, crept out of the synagogue with the help of a KGB major. He had not been seen since that happened yesterday morning. But a lone Jew in Moscow is not a person with position. There was no free press to inform. There was no politician to call. There was nowhere to complain except through the international links established by the dissidents. In the end, the rabbi knew that he would have to go to Lubyanka and ask questions. He would have to gather what facts he could, and he would perhaps have to beg for the body of Isadore Kantrowitz, so that it might be buried according to Jewish custom and law.

Rabbi Posner was himself an old man weighed down by a life of oppression and prejudice. From the Pale to the pogroms. The miraculous escape from the Nazis. The dark days of Stalin. The faint hope of immigration to Israel . . . And now, the steadily growing pressure, squeezing his dwindling congregation once again. How much must a people take? He knew the answer. As much as God wills. He grunted as he struggled with his heavy overcoat. By now, he thought as he left the synagogue, my feet know the way to Lubyanka all by themselves.

Peter was about to have Major Rosteveli bring in the sergeant from the morgue when the phone rang. Leonid jumped to answer, but Peter told him to sit.

"I will get it."

"Speaking." He listened intently as the major from Leningrad related the scene he had found when his detail entered Marina Grochenko's flat. Peter fluctuated between anger at the deed and compassion for his young assistant, who sat with his eyes glued on Somoroff.

"Thank you, Major. Call me when you have a doctor's

report." Leonid jumped to his feet. "And, Major," Peter continued, "I want a guard on the woman at all times."

"What is it?" asked an anxious Chomsky. "Is she hurt?"

"Sit down, Leonid." Somoroff was firm, yet gentle at the same time. He told the young lieutenant what the major had found. He left out the part about the blood and the Jewish star.

"I have to go to her . . . please, Colonel," Chomsky pleaded.

"Not today, Leonid. She will be sedated, and the surgeons will have to do a full workup before we have answers. There is nothing you can do for her now. I promise that you will be there when she wakes up."

Somoroff put his hand on Chomsky's shoulder. He wanted to say more to the young man, but a fear was gripping him. Like some giant chess game, they were all players, trapped in a battle with life and death as its outcome. He knew more than the others . . . Chomsky, Rosteveli, Sasha . . . even the premier. He knew they were losing at every turn.

"Leonid, listen to me." Peter spoke softly. "I will make you another promise. When we find who did this, you can have him for a while . . . alone. All right?"

"If you give him to me, you will never get him back, Colonel!"

"I know." The answer seemed to calm the young man.

Premier Alexeyevich took General Kubyshev's call in his office. The morning had been spent busily preparing for a Presidium meeting that afternoon. Kubyshev was insisting that he speak to the premier directly.

"Yes, General, what is it?" Ivan Alexeyevich didn't like interruptions.

"I am sorry to disturb you, Ivan Ivanovich." The premier noted that the general, an old friend, used the familiar form of address. He narrowed his attention to the far-away voice in Chita.

"What is it, Comrade General?"

"I have very sad news for you. A few moments ago I received a message that young Peter Somoroff was murdered. They contacted me because he was carrying orders from my command." A sledgehammer seemed to hit Ivan Alexeyevich. He thought of the boy's father.

"What happened?" His voice was filled with anger.

"We don't know. He was stabbed sometime this morning after the train left Kazan. They found his body in Gorki. A conductor found it. The train is being held and searched, but I am afraid many passengers got off in Gorki before the discovery."

There was a long pause as the premier thought, trying to gather his senses.

"Is there anything I can do at this end?" asked General Kubyshev.

"No. Just keep this as quiet as you can. I will take care of the matter from Moscow. Thank you, General . . . thank you for calling me directly."

He hung up the phone and leaned back in his large leather chair. Death. Death was in this office, he thought, picturing Boris Menoff twisting in agony on the floor of this very room, cursing the name of Nickolai Valarian as he clutched Ivan Alexeyevich's arm. Blood had oozed from Menoff's eyes, nose, and mouth as if some awful hemorrhage had exploded in his brain. Still he cursed Valarian. Then as death came to him he had muttered in Hebrew, "Shema Yisraeil: Adonai Eloheinu, Adonai Echad. Hear O Israel: The Lord Our God, The Lord is One." That moment of death brought to an end Boris Menoff's torment. Ivan Ivanovich wondered what young Peter Somoroff had thought as he died.

The premier called his deputy with instructions to delay the Presidium meeting for two hours. He then telephoned Lubyanka.

Peter was on his way to the front desk to meet Rabbi Posner when Rosteveli caught up to him in the hallway.

"There is a call for you from the premier."

Peter stopped and instructed the major to bring the rabbi up to their office.

Chomsky sat in the office-cell, about to begin his interrogation of the morgue sergeant, when Peter entered the office. "Excuse me, Leonid. Take this man to an empty room and question him there. I need the phone here."

Leonid gestured to the nervous sergeant, and they left the room. The premier told Peter to come to his office immediately. From the tone of Alexeyevich's voice, Peter knew not to question the order. He waited until Rosteveli brought the rabbi into the room.

"Major, make this man comfortable and have him remain

here until I return." He then addressed the rabbi. Peter knew what the man wanted because the duty officer at the front gate had insisted that the rabbi state his business. Rabbi Posner had specified the KGB and mentioned Isadore Kantrowitz's name. Peter was not surprised. The game grew more intricate by the minute.

"Rabbi, I have some urgent business that will take me an hour or so. I know why you are here. Please be patient."

He thought about having Rosteveli show the man the acrostic but thought better of the idea. There was no point in involving another person.

The rabbi sat in a chair and folded his hands in his lap. Never had a KGB officer spoken so politely to him. He felt that the man's concern for his comfort was genuine.

"Major, Lieutenant Chomsky has our friend in a room down the hall. See that the prisoner does not leave this floor or communicate with anyone. Also, call over to the section where Dr. Brodsky is located and tell them that I want him ready to speak to me this afternoon. I will call you if I am delayed."

He crossed the room and reached to shake the rabbi's hand. "Thank you for your patience, Rabbi. We will answer all your questions shortly."

As Peter left Lubyanka and drove through Dzerzhinsky Square, Marina Grochenko was being wheeled into the x-ray facility at Leningrad Hospital. A scab in the shape of a Star of David had formed on her abdomen, causing raised eyebrows from the technicians.

Downstairs in Lubyanka Prison a KGB captain racked up the videotape of yesterday's visitors as the two KGB guards sat in front of a monitor and waited to identify the man who had locked them in the morgue drawers.

In Tostuya it was mealtime. Rabbi Isadore Vogel listened with great interest as a new arrival from Kiev told of Jewish roundups and the desecration of the synagogue in that great Ukrainian city.

Meanwhile, a few hundred miles northwest of Kiev, in the city of Minsk, Sasha Andreyev committed as much of Isadore Vogel's file as she could to memory. Somehow she knew that she would be meeting this learned man within a few days. The thought of being in one of those fabled camps excited the pretty agent. The thought of winter in Siberia did not. She looked at her watch and realized that she would have to hurry to make her flight back to Moscow.

One paragraph in the file was fascinating. This rabbi had been accused of sorcery and witchcraft. Certain pieces of evidence had been presented at the trial by the State Prosecutor. When questioned, the rabbi had stated that they were used to exorcise devils, dybbuks, from fellow Jews. The judge had asked the rabbi to repeat the answer and then requested a complete psychiatric workup on the man. Sentence had been passed.

She noted that the arrest and charges had been made by Major Nickolai Valarian.

In the request log on the face of the folder, she saw that the file had been recently examined by a very high official of the government. The name was familiar. It was definitely the signature of Commissar Boris Menoff, Deputy to Premier Alexeyevich, member of the Supreme Soviet, and Minister of the Interior.

~ 18 ~

When a son must bury a father there is solace in the fact that a long life had been completed, that continuity was established. But when a father must bury a son, there is devastation and despair.

Ivan Alexeyevich watched his friend Peter Somoroff carefully. Several moments had passed in silence since the premier had told Peter of his son's murder. There was no easy way to give his friend the sad news. He tried to comfort Somoroff, telling him it had been quick, that the boy did not suffer, that the police were rounding up suspects in Gorki.

His words fell on deaf ears. Peter Somoroff's mind was light-years away, tripping through the birth, growth, and death of his one and only son. He pictured the fair hair and bright blue eyes of an eight-year-old on their first trip to the resort on the Black Sea. Young Peter had taken to the water like a fish. The image of the boy swimming faded to a young Nadja, gently holding the baby in her arms and nursing him. Peter could hear the sounds of delight coming from his son as he nursed. How he loved them both at that moment. Then he was at the Military Academy, and the brand-new Lieutenant Somoroff hugged his father, and his father wept with pride in his son. And that was gone. That bright, handsome, loving child turned to man was gone. Peter Somoroff's heart was breaking inside, alone as though he had fallen into a chasm of endless depth with only the echo of his despair around him.

"Peter Ilyavich, speak to me." The premier was standing next to his friend, unable to comfort but trying to establish

human contact. Peter looked into the premier's eyes and
slowly came back to reality.

"May I have a brandy, Ivan Ivanovich?"

The premier brought Peter a stiff drink, which he drank in
one gulp. Peter shuddered, unaccustomed to alcohol midday.
"Why?" he asked. "Why would anyone want to kill him?"

Both men kept their thoughts to themselves. Could it possibly be connected with the Valarian investigation? For what
purpose?

"Was it robbery?" That crime was so rare in the Soviet
Union that Peter knew the answer before the premier spoke.

"Nothing seems to be missing. I spoke with the Chief of
Police in Gorki. He is personally handling the investigation."

Peter began to drift away again.

"Why don't you go home . . . take a few days off . . .
however long you need. I'll take care of the arrangements."

Home. It hit Peter like a shot. Nadja . . . Grandmother
Maria . . . Anya . . . He had to tell them. It would be
unbearable. He knew he needed time to gather the strength
required.

"Can we keep this quiet, Comrade Alexeyevich . . . for a
few hours? I don't want to go home just now . . . I need
some time . . ." His voice trailed off, and the premier
understood.

"Of course. The police would like to do an autopsy in
Gorki. They will send the body on tomorrow. There can be a
funeral with full military honors. He was a hero of the
Afghanistan action."

Yes, thought Peter, a military funeral would be right.
Nadja's mother will go to the old church and do things her
way, but he knew the old woman wouldn't insist on a religious service.

He prepared to leave. Then Peter remembered the events in
the Lubyanka morgue and the attack on Marina Grochenko in
Leningrad. He related these to Premier Alexeyevich.

"You are convinced Valarian is behind this business?"
questioned the premier.

"I am certain. I want to arrest him!"

"You had better sit down again, Peter. I too have some
news for you on matters pertaining to this case."

The KGB chief didn't like the sound of Alexeyevich's

voice. It was going to be more bad news. He sat quietly. The premier sat behind his imposing desk.

"This afternoon I will attend a meeting of the Presidium. I delayed the meeting because of this terrible business with your son, but I must tell you that you cannot arrest Comrade Valarian."

Peter was stunned at the use of the word *Comrade* attached to the name of the man whom the premier suspected of murdering Boris Menoff. He waited for the Soviet leader to continue.

"The general secretary of the Party, with whom you know I share leadership, called me a few moments before you arrived to ask why I had delayed the meeting. When I told him, he was understanding but insisted that we convene this afternoon. He has put a new item on our agenda."

The premier hesitated, wondering how his news would affect Peter Somoroff.

"The new item is that our Party Leader, General Secretary Marshall Serge Malenkov, wishes to appoint Colonel Nickolai Valarian to the post of Minister of the Interior—Boris Menoff's old job."

It was too much. The world had gone crazy. Peter felt dizzy, nauseous. His heart, broken moments ago, was about to explode. Anger welled up inside.

"No!" he screamed. On his feet, leaning across the large desk, the blood vessels in his neck and face bulging, he screamed again, *"No!* Are you mad? That man is a murderer. He destroyed my son as though he had driven the knife in himself—I know it, and you know it. He has been responsible for murder in Pushkin, in Gorki, in Kiev, Minsk, Tostuya—in one hundred cities and towns. And you will make him a minister? He will burn in *hell* before that!"

The dam had burst and spilled its angry contents onto Premier Alexeyevich. He knew he must respond, but there was too much at stake to allow anger, even murder at this point, to interfere with the delicate balance of power that he held precariously in his hands.

"Sit down, Peter," he commanded, "and listen! Marshall Malenkov and Valarian have kept their friendship secret. They have planned this carefully, orchestrated every move. This is not all they want. I'm not too sure where they are heading, but I do know that to fight them on this thing will bring down our government and perhaps turn the whole world into chaos. You are a policeman. I am the premier. It will be done *my* way.''

Somoroff knew the premier was right, but the anger didn't subside.

''I will kill him, Ivan Ivanovich!''

''Good,'' answered the premier. ''But when I tell you . . . and not a moment before. Is that clear?''

''I know he murdered my son.''

''Perhaps. It is possible. That thought also entered my mind. But you are a policeman. You wrote the KGB handbook. Use it. Make your case. Build it like a castle, stone upon stone. Then we will take that scum and his friends, including Malenkov, and grind them to dust. But let us do it right!''

~ 19 ~

The trip back to Lubyanka was dreamlike for Peter Somoroff. His thoughts wandered and the pain would not subside. It was a knot . . . a knife . . . a huge sadness piercing his heart. Anger dissolved into agony, then into a profound hurt. He felt as if a part of him had been torn out.

As he parked the Skoda and turned the ignition off, he experienced an uncontrollable emotion rising from within. His hands shook, then his legs, and from deep inside this calm and sensitive man released a primordial cry that vibrated through the car. It made the steel doors and thick glass windows reverberate harmonically. Then the tears came. He bent his head forward onto the steering wheel and sobbed for his lost child, for that sweet, proud part of his world he would never again know.

Rosteveli, Chomsky, and Sasha Andreyev looked up to see a very different Peter Somoroff standing in the doorway of the office-cell. They knew something was very wrong. Sasha wanted to go to her new boss. She sensed he needed help. But it was Major Rosteveli who crossed the small room and touched the colonel.

"Peter Ilyavich . . . what has happened?"

The others rose in anticipation. Rabbi Posner stood also. He, perhaps more than the others in the room, knew the look of great loss that was upon Peter Somoroff's face.

Peter gently removed the major's hand and entered the room. He closed the door behind him and asked them please to sit down. It didn't occur to him to ask the rabbi to leave. In fact, it was a comfort for Peter to see the understanding in the old man's face.

"My son is dead," he announced in a quiet voice. "He was murdered on the train this morning."

Now Sasha did cross the room to embrace Somoroff. "I am so very sorry, Comrade," she whispered.

Leonid came to Peter's side and said nothing. He just stood staring at the floor.

Rabbi Posner closed his eyes and silently said Kaddish, the Hebrew prayer for the dead.

Rosteveli knew what had happened. His old Georgian bones told him that Valarian was behind this brutal deed. He was furious but kept it inside. Peter's eyes met his, and they both understood.

Somoroff gestured for them to sit down. He spoke first to the rabbi. "I am sorry to detain you, Rabbi. Thank you for your patience. Mr. Kantrowitz was working with us on a case. He was poisoned. I am sorry to say that it happened right in KGB headquarters. That is the truth. On this day, of all days, I hope you will believe me."

The rabbi knew the pain of the man who spoke, and he did believe what he was told. "I understand. I only wish to be able to take the body for a proper burial."

"Of course. Do you know who called you about this, Rabbi?"

"The man did not give me his name. He just said that Isadore—Mr. Kantrowitz had been murdered by the KGB and that his body was here in Lubyanka."

Peter studied the rabbi's face carefully. It was a kind face. He decided to trust the man.

"I want to ask you a few questions, Rabbi. I am taking a chance in speaking to you, and everything I say must remain secret. No one may ever know what I am about to tell you."

The rabbi looked around the room at the other three KGB agents. They were all looking at him. He felt uneasy but turned to Peter Somoroff and spoke. "Colonel, may I speak for a moment . . . before you share confidences?"

Somoroff nodded.

"I am a Jew. I am a Russian." His lower lip quivered. "So on two counts I am a proud man. Believe it or not, I love my country . . . but . . . it is not normal for the KGB to request . . . to enlist . . . the help of Jews. I know that it is a sad and bitter day for you, and you have my deepest sympathy. They told me that a KGB major took Isadore yesterday.

They also told me that this major helped Isadore escape from some soldiers—"

Peter interrupted. "It was Major Rosteveli here who took Mr. Kantrowitz. Your description of what happened is accurate."

The rabbi nodded and paused in thought. Peter also paused. The two men stared at each other for a moment, suspended across years of persecution and suffering. Each wondered if trust was possible. Peter decided it was, and that it was also necessary.

"Rabbi, if I tell you what Mr. Kantrowitz was doing for us—and by doing so I must tell you a very strange story—then it is possible that your life might be in danger. I have lost my son today . . ."

The words choked in Peter's throat. A tear came to Leonid's eye.

". . . and others have died or been hurt with this business. I don't want to put your life in danger, Rabbi, but if they called you and told you about Mr. Kantrowitz's death, then you may already be involved."

The rabbi smiled. "To be a rabbi is to be involved, Colonel Somoroff. I am many things, but I am not afraid. Let me help you if I can."

"Thank you." Peter reached and touched the rabbi's shoulder. "We are working on a case that involves the death of a high official of the government. This man and his wife were helped by Mr. Kantrowitz."

Peter then spoke to Major Rosteveli. "Serge, do you have a copy of the acrostic?"

The major opened his attaché case and took out a copy of the acrostic.

"Please let Rabbi Posner see it."

The rabbi studied the paper carefully. Leonid and Sasha strained to see it. Noticing their curiosity, Peter spoke. "I will fill you in on all the details later. We all have a need to know everything now."

The rabbi looked up from the paper and directed his words to Peter. "Do you know what this is, Colonel?"

"Not entirely, Rabbi. I hoped you might help us. It was what Mr. Kantrowitz was doing when he was killed."

"Yes," said the rabbi, "Isadore would know about these

things." His tone was one of disdain. "But I do not." He passed the paper back to Rosteveli.

"But you are a rabbi?" Peter questioned.

"Yes, but not that kind of rabbi," he said, gesturing with his hand toward the paper. "That is magic and superstition . . . not my work."

"Do you know Rabbi Vogel from Minsk?" Peter asked.

Rabbi Posner let out a deep sigh as Sasha Andreyev leaned forward in her chair. "Yes, Colonel, I know . . . knew him. I believe he is dead."

"No," corrected Peter, "we think he is alive, in . . ." He turned to Sasha questioningly.

"In Tostuya, Comrade Colonel. Camp Eleven."

The rabbi did not change expression. "Well, it is good he is alive, but I really knew him only by reputation. We met once after the war, briefly." Then it dawned on the rabbi why they were asking about Rabbi Vogel and the acrostic. Still he wanted to be careful. This was the KGB.

Peter pressed the point. "Do you think that Rabbi Vogel will know about the acrostic . . . about the things that Mr. Kantrowitz tried to do?"

"What things?" the rabbi asked.

Peter sensed his caution. He asked the others to leave the room. When they had gone Peter told Rabbi Posner the whole story. When he finished the old man just shook his head in amazement.

"I can tell you that if you wish to do those things—that superstition about evil that Kantrowitz did, about devils and archangels—then Rabbi Vogel is your man. If anyone knows these things, he knows, believe me. But, God help you. This is the world of mystics and darkness, not the twentieth century. Can you be so desperate, Colonel?"

"It is not a matter of desperation, Rabbi. We just want to examine every possibility in this case."

"Then Vogel is your man."

"Thank you. Please remember that what I have told you must remain secret. Your life depends on it."

The rabbi agreed and stood. "It is already forgotten. Now if I may make arrangements to take Mr. Kantrowitz's body . . ."

Peter hesitated. "There is one more thing, Rabbi. It concerns the body."

Peter explained the mutilation. When he finished, the rabbi sighed again. "I am not surprised, and I believe you had nothing to do with it. Isadore has no family left. Only a few friends will mourn him. I will keep the coffin closed."

"You must make a complaint, Rabbi."

Posner understood. "I will do it through official channels, the police. I suppose there will be an investigation . . . they will question me . . . you?"

"Yes. I will deny it," answered Peter, "and if I guess right, then Colonel Valarian will try to make trouble for me. Please be careful with him, Rabbi. Be outraged at the desecration, at me."

"I will, Colonel. He is a man, not a devil."

Peter wrote out a release for Kantrowitz's body and handed it to the rabbi.

"This will allow you to take the body. Thank you for your patience, and for your help. We will talk again, I hope . . . after all of this is put to rest."

"That would be nice," said the rabbi. He walked to the door, then turned back to Peter Somoroff.

"Colonel. If you find Rabbi Vogel tell him that . . ." He hesitated, then spoke clearly. "That Kemiot still exists. He will know what I mean."

Peter wrote the word down and checked the spelling with Rabbi Posner. "'K-E-M-I-O-T?"

"Yes. And, Colonel, my sympathies to your family. I will say a prayer for your son tonight . . . If you don't mind."

"I would be honored," Peter answered, "and thank you."

The rabbi left to collect the remains of Isadore Kantrowitz as Peter Somoroff called his team back into the room. The four then spent the next two hours filling each other in on the mysteries and terrors of Colonel Nickolai Valarian and his followers. However, Peter did not tell them about Marshall Malenkov's friendship with Valarian and the plan to have him sit on the Supreme Soviet as Minister of the Interior.

When they finished, each went in separate directions. They would meet in three days, and by then their little band would have grown by three members.

Leonid Chomsky was to contact Captain Bonyon in Pushkin and cut orders assigning him to KGB, then the two men were to question Marina Grochenko about her attackers.

Sasha Andreyev was to go to Tostuya, Camp Eleven, after

first setting up a financial account through Premier Alexeyevich's office. If she found Rabbi Vogel she was to bring him to Moscow and keep him in the secure wing of Lubyanka Prison.

Major Serge Rosteveli was to complete the interrogation of the morgue sergeant, clear the files on all KGB people working the prison wing, and organize a squad of men to be available twenty-four hours a day. He was also to move all the files on the case from Somoroff's office over to the prison. He was to trace the phone tap and see who was involved at headquarters.

Finally, he was to open an investigation into the death of Isadore Kantrowitz. Peter suggested that Captain Servioff handle the matter.

Rosteveli remained in the room after Leonid and Sasha left. The old Georgian wanted a moment with his friend.

"Have a drink, Peter Ilyavich?" The major poured two glasses of vodka from his flask.

Somoroff took the glass and stared at the clear liquid. He then looked up at Rosteveli. The major's eyes were tearful. "Colonel, I wish to drink a toast to your son . . . if you don't mind . . . and to say that I will not rest until that animal Valarian is dead by my own hand!"

Peter was moved by the fury of his friend.

"Thank you, Sergi. Let's just drink to the boy . . . to Peter, and keep our minds clear. I now know this business is far from over. The journey is just beginning."

The major felt the weight of Peter Somoroff's words. He lifted his glass.

"To Lieutenant Peter Somoroff," he toasted.

"To Peter . . ."

Both men emptied their glasses and tearfully embraced one another.

~ 20 ~

The front page of *Pravda* carried the story of the deaths of Boris and Celia Menoff in an automobile crash while vacationing near the Black Sea. An official state funeral was to be held the following week.

Inside the paper, on page four, a brief account of the death of Lieutenant Peter Somoroff, son of Colonel Peter Somoroff, was printed. The young man's death was listed as the work of imperialist agents because the boy was a hero of the Afghanistan action. It further stated that he was posthumously promoted to captain and would be buried that day in a military cemetery with full honors.

Letters of sympathy lay unopened on the foyer table in the Somoroff apartment. The funeral had been painful for Nadja and Peter. Their daughter Anya had been strong despite her long trip from the Polytechnical Institute in Omsk. Peter, Nadja, and Anya sat in the small kitchen on the morning after the funeral.

"Grandma is in church," said Anya.

Nadja sipped her tea, nodded, and spoke softly. "She will go every day now, to light candles for Peter and to pray for his soul."

"But Peter wasn't religious," answered Anya. She was twenty-two and quite beautiful. Her dream was to be a cosmonaut, and she was taking the equivalent of a masters degree in aeronautical engineering at the institute in Omsk.

"No," said Peter, "but your grandmother is, and if that is her way, then let her do what she thinks is right. It can't hurt. She's old . . . let her be."

His voice didn't scold, but it was firm.

"Okay," said Anya. "Now can you tell me what happened to my brother?"

Nadja and Peter looked up from their food at her.

"What are you talking about?" said Nadja.

"I'm talking about how my brother died. I don't believe that stuff about foreign agents. Peter wasn't that important . . . was he?" She looked directly at her father for an answer. Peter knew that he must keep up the charade. His daughter was more like him than young Peter had been. She was tenacious when it came to getting answers to questions, and her trained mind had a cold logic about it that wouldn't let go until a problem was solved.

"Your brother was killed. The police believe that it was a foreign assassin. I have not seen any reason to doubt them."

"Why was he on a train? Why was he coming to Moscow?"

"He was on leave . . . to attend a ceremony for me. The premier was going to give me a medal . . ." His voice trailed off.

"And I wasn't invited?" Anya questioned.

Peter tried to be firm. *"No."*

Anya caught him glancing over at her mother. Nadja was crying.

"I'm sorry, Mom, Dad. It's just so frustrating. I'm sorry." She reached across the table and took her mother's hand. Both women began to cry.

The phone rang, and Peter rose to answer it. Anya stopped him. "I'll get it, Dad. You stay with Mother."

Moments later she came back into the kitchen. "It's Premier Alexeyevich's office. He would like to speak to you."

Peter went to the phone. "Premier Alexeyevich?"

Peter heard the squeal of the scrambler and adjusted his own, which had been installed two days ago after Rosteveli informed him that his home phone was tapped.

"Good morning, Peter Ilyavich. How is it today?"

"It will take time, Comrade Ivan Ivanovich, but it will heal. Thank you for asking."

"I have been able to delay Valarian's appointment for a few weeks, but Malenkov will press me after that. The Americans haven't been making that much noise about the Jews lately, and unless they do, I will have nothing to delay with. Do you understand?"

Peter thought for a moment. An idea passed through his mind to use the desecrated body of Isadore Kantrowitz to arouse the American Jews. He would have to put Rabbi Posner in touch with the dissident underground.

"Perhaps I can arrange some press for us, Premier. Give me a few days. I'm going back to work today."

"I hate to bring it up, Peter, but we still need someone to be liaison between us in this business."

"I'll give it some thought."

"Fine. I will be in Poland for a few days. Call me when I return."

"Have a good trip, Ivan Ivanovich."

"Good hunting, Peter Ilyavich. Take care."

Rabbi Isadore Vogel sat in his cell and sipped tea. It was different from his cell in Tostuya. This place was warm, and the tea was fresh. The door was not locked either, and the walls were smooth and plastered. No cinder block here. It seemed a palace compared to his last residence. Yet he knew it was Lubyanka, and he didn't know why he had been brought so far by the pretty KGB officer. Still, his treatment had been kindly, and he didn't feel threatened. It's a mystery, he thought, but it's better than Tostuya . . . at least for now. He only regretted that he had been unable to tell Yasha Mendel where he was being taken. They will think I am dead, thought Vogel. Maybe I am. Maybe this is just a dream. He reached across the table and touched the prayer book that the KGB major had brought him. Next to it lay a yarmulke and a tallith, also supplied by the wondrous Major Rosteveli. And he was so polite, Vogel thought, so . . . concerned for my comfort. But with the patience of a man who had kept his sanity while denied freedom for almost twelve years, Isadore Vogel relaxed and enjoyed the relative freedom of the moment. Later he knew it would change. It always did.

Leonid met Captain Bonyon at the Leningrad Hospital. He asked the soldier to remain outside Marina's guarded room for a moment while he spoke to her. The captain understood.

Marina lay with her leg in a cast suspended on wires attached to a frame above her. She was asleep. Leonid noticed the flowers he had sent, plus a large bouquet from Colonel Somoroff. He would have to be back in Moscow tomorrow. Although he made no noise Marina sensed his presence and opened her eyes. Leonid stood above her. He held her hand.

"Hi," she said dreamily.

"I love you," he answered, and bent to kiss her. She touched the back of his head and caressed his hair, squeezing his hand in her other hand with all of her strength.

He stood and breathed deeply. "I love you," he said again.

"Why did they do this to me?" she asked. "Why?" Now she was crying, and she turned her face away into the crisp pillow.

"I don't know," he lied. "Do you feel like talking about it?"

"No." The answer was long in coming.

"I want to find them, darling. We have to know what you saw . . . who . . ."

"If I tell you what I know"—she hesitated—"will you promise me something?"

"Yes."

"Promise me that I will never have to see them."

"I promise. Before you tell me I want to bring another man into the room. He is working on the case. Okay?"

She nodded, and he called Bonyon into the room.

It took just a few moments before both men knew who had attacked Marina Grochenko. An hour later they were on their way to Pushkin with a KGB squad, and shortly thereafter, using a small ball peen hammer, Leonid Chomsky smashed both of police sergeant Zalitski's kneecaps with relish. Marina might never dance, but this man would never walk again. Captain Bonyon held Marina's other attacker and made him watch. Lieutenant Vladimir Zorbin then talked for over an hour, but he never took his eyes off the hammer that Chomsky held in his hand.

After the interrogation, both prisoners were sedated and brought to Leningrad KGB headquarters. Ironically, Zalitski was placed in the room next to Marina Grochenko's. He was chained to the bed and given only minimal medical attention. Orders were issued to keep him sedated and under guard. Bonyon and Chomsky took Lieutenant Zorbin back to Lubyanka with them for further questioning.

The team now gathered for their first meeting in three eventful days. Somoroff listened as Sasha related that it had been relatively easy to find and secure the release of Rabbi Vogel. The camps were quite crowded, and his cell could be used for at least three new prisoners. She had not been followed, and Peter was fairly certain that Valarian could not connect her to this investigation.

Leonid Chomsky reported on his actions after introducing Captain Bonyon to the group. Peter thought it might be useful to have the crippled Sergeant Zalitski brought to Lubyanka. Leonid agreed, and steps were taken to notify the KGB in Leningrad. The detective, Lieutenant Zorbin, was being held in a cell in their wing. They talked about Marina for a few minutes and agreed that she should have a guard at all times.

Major Rosteveli had the longest report. He had been very busy organizing the unit, clearing all the people in the wing, establishing a secure squad, equipment, and a budget and completing the questioning of the morgue guard who had confirmed the identity of the man who desecrated Isadore Kantrowitz's body. But he was unable to make a link with the guard and Valarian.

At the end of his report he spoke directly to Peter Somoroff. "I have established and traced the tap on your office and home phone, Comrade Colonel. Either they are clumsy or very arrogant, because it was simple. Our own KGB Sergeant Mikolov, Captain Servioff's aide, operated the tap. To me that means they are a small group, with perhaps fewer staff than we possess. On the matter of who poisoned the old man, there is not much to report. The kitchen received a call using my authority to order the dinner. My guess is that Mikolov did the deed, but no one in the kitchen actually saw him. Perhaps we should ask Sergeant Mikolov to come over here for a few days?" A smile crossed Rosteveli's face.

"Not yet," said Peter. "As long as we know whom we have to watch, we can be careful. Let them feel secure. We must build our case."

Sasha spoke up. "In all the activity, I almost forgot to tell you, Comrade Somoroff, that Minister Menoff had recently inquired into the court records of Rabbi Vogel. His name was on the log sheet."

That was bad news. If Boris Menoff knew about Vogel,

then it was possible that Valarian would also have interest in the rabbi.

"I think we must consolidate all of the information we have," ordered Peter, "and begin to set up a method of operation. I want to interrogate all of the people we now hold. I will do it in the main interrogation room. Put it all on videotape. I want all of you to observe the questioning through the one-way mirror."

The group rose as one, but Peter held them for a moment.

"First I want to meet with Rabbi Vogel alone. Then let's see the morgue sergeant, then Lieutenant Zorbin, and finally Dr. Brodsky."

The group dispersed under Major Rosteveli's leadership. Peter walked down the grey hallway toward Rabbi Vogel's cell. Instinctively he knew he was about to enter a strange, forbidden land. In his bones he sensed that Rabbi Vogel held the key to combating Valarian. Whether the rabbi would, or could, share it willingly was another question. Years of imprisonment did strange things to people. Perhaps the rabbi felt he had nothing to lose. Perhaps he might even welcome death itself, rather than aid his captors. Somoroff had to know. He opened the door to the cell. Rabbi Vogel stood opposite the door with his back to Peter. The tallith, a large black and white prayer shawl, was pulled over his head, and the man swayed from side to side in prayer, muttering Hebrew words from the prayer book he held open in his hands.

The rabbi turned to the intruder.

"Please finish," said Peter. "I will wait."

The rabbi nodded and returned to his prayers. Although he said the words, thoughts raced through his mind. This is the man who wanted me, I know it. . . . I feel his eyes behind me . . . Yet he allows me to pray. . . . Gather yourself together, Vogel—this will be a day to remember.

Anya grabbed the phone in the middle of the first ring. Her mother napped in the bedroom, and she didn't want her disturbed. Her grandmother prepared lunch in the kitchen. The woman, aged as she was, had returned from church strengthened by her worship. Anya was jealous of the old woman's strength. She seemed to accept young Peter's death with a fatalistic attitude. Youth is not necessarily strong, Anya was thinking, but wisdom is. Then the phone rang.

If it is possible to feel hatred over a telephone line, then Anya did. She said, "Hello," but there was no immediate reply. Someone was at the other end. She could hear the sound of breathing, like that of an asthmatic.

"Hello," she said again.

"Tell your father I will crush him. I will destroy all of you."

Death on a telephone line. The voice had an icy breath like the wind in Tostuya. Anya tasted fear in her mouth.

"Who is this?"

"Tell your father I curse him to damnation!"

Anya grew strong.

"Coward," she said. "Whispering threats on the phone is the coward's way."

"Do not offend me, little girl. The blade that tore into your brother's heart still lives. . . . It can find yours, too."

"Fuck you, pig." Her own words shocked her.

The voice chuckled with an evil hiss into her ear. She slammed down the receiver in anger, but she was shaking from that last sound. It still hissed in her brain. Looking up she saw her grandmother coming across the room. The old woman looked at Anya and came to her.

"What? What is it, darling?" she asked.

Anya embraced her. The warmth of age comforted the frightened girl.

Valarian continued to chuckle to himself after the girl had hung up. He called to his secretary and told her to send Misha Karkov into the office. A moment later the young criminal stood before his mentor.

"Did you see the young Somoroff girl at the funeral, Misha?"

"Yes, Colonel. She is very pretty." He smiled.

Karkov was a small man with closely cropped hair and dark eyes. His hands were large for his body, and his high cheekbones spoke of Mongol heritage.

"Would you like to have her?" Valarian asked.

"Yes. I would like that, Colonel."

"Then have her. She is at home now with two other women. They will not bother you. Go!"

Misha reached across the desk and kissed Valarian's scarred hand near the jade and silver ring. He felt heat from the ring. It gave him strength. Valarian allowed him to linger in its warmth for a moment.

"Do it well, Misha, and I will reward you."

— 21 —

Vogel was stunned. There was no playing around with Peter Somoroff. The KGB colonel was direct and obviously in a hurry for answers. After he introduced himself, Peter got right down to cases.

"You are here because we believe we need your services and your knowledge. But before I begin, I must tell you that there is great danger in what we are doing. Perhaps you best of all will know that danger."

The rabbi listened. The man across the small cell table was obviously an intellectual and a leader. The name Somoroff was familiar, but vague . . . something from long ago.

"I am here at your request, Colonel."

"Do you know Rabbi Posner?" Peter asked.

"Yes. I knew him long ago. Is he still in Moscow?"

"Yes. Do you know Isadore Kantrowitz?"

The rabbi thought hard for a moment. "No. That name is not familiar to me."

Peter was annoyed. He knew the man was lying, yet he didn't want to bully him.

"Rabbi . . . what is a dybbuk?"

Shock. The KGB wanted to know about dybbuks. Had the world gone mad? Vogel composed himself and stared at his interrogator. Who was this man?

"You know, Colonel Somoroff, that was the last question a judge in Minsk asked me before I . . . ah . . . went away. Surely you didn't bring me here, all this distance, to ask the same question?"

"I am not a judge, Rabbi Vogel. I am a man who seeks

115

some answers. And that is one of the questions I want answered.''

"Very well," Vogel answered. "A dybbuk is a spirit, a bad spirit, that enters a body and possesses it. Makes it crazy, or sick, or inhuman. That's a dybbuk."

"Do you know Isadore Kantrowitz?"

"Yes. It was a long time ago. He asked me to come to Moscow to help him with a dybbuk."

"Did you come?"

"Yes."

"Did you help him?"

"Yes."

"How?"

"We drove it out."

"How?"

The rabbi stood and walked over to the cot. He felt oppressed, as if the smooth grey walls were closing in on him, crushing him. He sat on the squeaky bed and ran his hand over the rough grey blanket.

"I don't remember that one in particular. . . . There were so many in those days . . ."

"Is each one different? I mean, each time you do it, do you have to drive it out differently?"

"Yes, Colonel. Well, basically it is the same, but there are different techniques. It depends on how strong the dybbuk is . . . or what it is doing to the person."

"Must the person be a Jew?"

Rabbi Vogel was startled by the question. He thought hard about his answer.

"No. It is not necessary, but I never did it to a non-Jew. I was never asked."

"What do you do, Rabbi? Is it like the Catholics do exorcism?"

"It is and it isn't. I really can't explain."

"Try. It's important to me."

"Well, our way is older. We were around before the Catholics, so much of what we do, what we believe, is in their ceremonies. But they attack these spirits in the name of Christ . . . through Christ."

"And you? The Jews!"

"We just attack the dybbuk directly. It is driven away, but it is never destroyed. You can't destroy them."

Peter took the copy of the acrostic from his pocket and handed it to Vogel. The rabbi studied it. His lips moved as he gazed at the paper.

"Do you know what that is, Rabbi?"

"Yes. But it's just a protection . . . a precaution. It is not very powerful." He handed it back to Somoroff.

"Mr. Kantrowitz made that for someone. You are right. It didn't work."

The rabbi nodded, then there was silence in the room. Vogel began to hum under his breath.

"Rabbi," Somoroff began again, "do you remember the man who brought the charges against you in Minsk?"

Now Vogel's attitude changed. His face became pale, and he stroked his beard nervously and withdrew to himself. Peter noted the reaction and knew he was at the moment of truth. But the rabbi didn't answer. He just looked off into space and hummed louder, as if to block out the next question.

"Do you remember Nickolai Valarian?"

The rabbi grasped his own shoulders and drew himself up tightly. His humming became high-pitched, a wailing bordering on crying.

"Isadore Kantrowitz is dead, Rabbi Vogel. He died trying to help us."

"Rest in peace," said the rabbi. "He was a fool to try and fight that . . . that . . . thing."

"What thing?"

The rabbi suddenly composed himself, stood, and walked back to the small table. He sat and looked directly into Peter Somoroff's eyes. Now Vogel knew what the KGB wanted. He felt curiously strong, and for the first time in many lonely years, he felt a purpose in his existence. A new voice came from his lips. Peter noted it with alarm. He did not expect such strength.

"Colonel, I believe you know what I mean—Valarian is not a man. He is a thing. He has hurt you, hasn't he? Yes. I can see that in your eyes. But understand something. It is very important. This is not a dybbuk. Forget dybbuks. This beast is stronger, more important than a mere dybbuk. He is evil! He is an abomination doing the devil's work."

Peter Somoroff listened. And at that moment his life was forever changed. Vogel was the ally that he, the premier, all of Russia needed.

"I want you to help me kill him." Peter's voice was insistent.

"You cannot kill him. You can never kill him!"

The room filled with silence once again. Peter refused to accept defeat.

"What can we do?"

"I don't know. Really. He is very powerful, and you must be careful. Now I know—" The rabbi stopped in midsentence.

"You know what?"

"The camps . . . all the camps are filling up with Jews again. Like with the Nazis. It is his work. Now I know."

"Then we must stop him."

"For Jews you want to stop him?"

"For Russia."

Vogel touched his hand to the prayer book and looked up at Somoroff.

Peter knew he needed this man. Somehow he had to reach and use the real power that the rabbi possessed.

"Rabbi Posner asked me to tell you something. He said to tell you that Kemiot still exists."

"Posner said that? Kemiot?"

"Yes. What does it mean?"

"I can't say." Vogel's voice was calm, but Peter could see the man's mind racing.

"Is it important?"

"Can I see him?"

Peter stood. "Within the hour."

He left the rabbi pulling the prayer shawl over his head, and as he closed the door the prayers began again.

Rosteveli had the morgue sergeant brought to the interrogation room. Now he sat with Bonyon, Sasha, and Leonid waiting for Colonel Somoroff. They watched the sergeant through a one-way mirror. The man was frightened. Peter entered the room, glanced through the mirror, and then instructed Rosteveli to take a few men and bring Rabbi Posner to Lubyanka. The major left immediately.

Peter went into the interrogation room and sat down opposite the sergeant.

"I will make this brief, Sergeant. The man who came to the morgue was Misha Karkov. He has been identified. We know whom he works for. All I want to know is whom do you work for?''

''I work for the prison, Colonel. In the morgue.''

''Sergeant, don't be a fool. There are two guards that you made look stupid, and all they would like to do is get their hands on you for a few minutes. Do you understand?''

''But, Colonel, I was attacked too.''

Peter stood. ''I have no time for this bullshit. I'll send them in, and you will tell them what I want to know.''

He moved toward the door.

''No! Please, Colonel, I'll tell you.''

It was just a matter of money. The sergeant was not a follower of Valarian. Major Metsky paid him from time to time for services. He reported about prisoners in Lubyanka. He copied some records. Small stuff. That night the major had called him and told him to do whatever Misha Karkov requested. He was promised protection, and he felt betrayed. He was also afraid of Metsky.

Peter turned the sergeant over to Leonid Chomsky for a complete statement that would serve as an indictment against Major Metsky when the time came to prosecute.

Anya sat alone in the apartment. Her grandmother had gone to church again, and her mother still slept deeply in the bedroom. It had been two hours since the call, and she was still debating whether or not to call her father. The late afternoon light faded, yet she made no move to turn on a lamp. Darkness crept into the apartment, turning all colors to grey and black. The Siamese cat sat in her lap sleeping. She did not hear the door latch being violated. Suddenly the cat perked up. Then Anya heard the scratching sound. It's Grandma trying her key, thought Anya. She went to the door to open it just as Misha Karkov popped the lock. She surprised him, and for a moment he was startled. Then he pushed by her, closing the door and grabbing her around the neck. The two fell to the floor onto a small area rug that slid with the weight of their bodies. Anya gasped as the intruder tightened his grip around her neck. She could not cry out. His other hand was on her breasts, rubbing and pulling her blouse open.

The little man was strong. Anya realized she was being raped. The man was excited, and she felt his hardness against her buttocks. She relaxed her body and gently began to move against his.

"Ah," he whispered. "You want it . . . good."

She continued to rub and slowly slid her hand toward his crotch. He grabbed it, leaving her breasts for a moment.

"No tricks, little girl. I'll tell you what to do."

He rolled her over onto her stomach, keeping his arm around her neck in a tight grip. With his other hand he pulled her dress up and slid his hand into her underwear and between her legs. It was cold. She remained calm and slowly parted her legs to allow him to touch her vaginal lips. His finger pushed inside her with difficulty because she was dry with fright. Then he pulled his hand out and opened his belt. She heard his fly unzip and then felt his hard penis on her buttocks. Time was running out, but she didn't panic. As long as she felt his penis she knew she was still safe. He was getting excited and began to mutter obscenities in her ear. She tried to react positively, as though she enjoyed what he was doing and saying. She spread her legs for him.

"Good," he said. "You want it."

He put his hand on her again, but she was still dry. Then he spit on his hand and rubbed the spittle on his penis.

"I'll get it in . . . I'll ram it up your ass if I have to, bitch."

She felt him raise up, and in doing so he loosened his grip on her throat. She pictured his penis and testicles in her mind and felt sure of their position above her. He was a short man, and she knew they were within her reach. Her right hand opened slowly once, then balled into a fist. Anya struck quickly back with her fist and at the same time rolled in the opposite direction.

Misha emitted a sickening scream and released her. The pain was intense. Nausea rose in his throat. Anya was on her feet and delivered a powerful kick to his groin . . . then another . . . and another. The last landed directly on his testicles again, and he fainted.

Nadja stood in the door of the bedroom.

"What is it, Anya?" She saw the man on the floor and screamed.

Anya's eyes searched the room for a weapon. She didn't know how long the attacker would be out.

"Mama, call Dad. Tell him to get here immediately. Do it

quickly." She then pulled a lamp cord out of the wall and tore it from the lamp. In a flash she was tying his legs. She repeated her action with another lamp and secured his hands just as the man began to awake.

The rabbis spoke in yiddish while Peter sat in the room, ignorant of their conversation. There seemed to be an argument, with Vogel admonishing Posner. The word *Kemiot* came up several times. In the end Posner prevailed. He spoke first.

"My friend here is unaware of many things. We have been discussing a little history, mostly about Israel and the Jews of Russia. I told him that I trusted you, but you must understand that he has been in prison for a long time. He is out of touch with our life today."

Peter nodded his understanding.

Rabbi Vogel then spoke. "You want me to help you with this Valarian? I believe he is possessed by an evil spirit. We cannot kill him, but it may be that we can drive him away. Rabbi Posner does not agree or believe in such things. We have the same God, it's just that from time to time we approach him differently."

"Then you will help us?" asked Peter.

"That depends on how far you are willing to go. It is not a simple matter, and I can't do it alone."

"Whatever you need, we will get." Peter felt relieved.

"Then we will have to go to Israel."

And by the tone of his voice, Peter Somoroff knew that Rabbi Vogel was serious. Somoroff was about to discuss the ramifications of Vogel's request when Leonid Chomsky broke into the room to tell Peter he was needed at home immediately.

~ 22 ~

The marshall paced back and forth in Premier Alexeyevich's office. The two men had run the Soviet Union as a team for ten years, with Premier Alexeyevich handling external affairs, thus controlling the KGB, and Marshall Malenkov handling internal affairs, with control over the Army and the GRU.

"Ivan Ivanovich, it is absolutely unforgivable that this thing should have been done by the KGB. The American press is full of the story. They even have a picture of the Jew's body."

"But what makes you think the KGB had anything to do with it?"

"What am I, a fool? The man died in KGB headquarters. He was in the morgue at Lubyanka. That idiot Somoroff gave the body to the Jews. What did he think was going to happen?"

The premier knew that this was the price he would have to pay for allowing Somoroff to release the story to the western press. If he could contain the marshall to abuse in this office, then they had bought the time they needed to deal with Valarian. He pressed harder on the general secretary.

"Somoroff thinks that this was done by the GRU in order to make the KGB look bad in our eyes. I don't know why yet, but I am investigating. Give me a few weeks and I will have the matter cleared."

"I warn you, Comrade Alexeyevich, the politburo won't stand for this publicity. What we do in our country is of no concern to anyone else outside."

The premier was on his feet. He smashed his fist onto the desktop.

"But, my fellow comrade, what we eat in this country is our concern, and since you have been unable to produce enough food for our people, we have to rely on the west for grain. And when they have us by the balls they like to squeeze a little from time to time."

The marshall calmed down. This round goes to you, Alexeyevich, he thought, but soon, very soon, Colonel Valarian and I will crush you and your precious KGB bootlickers.

"How long will it take for them to calm down in America?"

"Too long for us to wait. We have to respond. I want this business with the Jews to stop for now, and I want you to allow them to begin to emigrate again."

"How many?"

"That is your business, but it had better be substantial. And none of the stupid payment business. Let them leave with their belongings, just no money."

The marshall poured himself a brandy. Premier Alexeyevich toyed with the idea of warning Malenkov about Valarian and telling him about Boris Menoff's file, but thought better of the idea. Let him play with fire . . . Let him get burned.

"Will you be at Menoff's funeral?" the premier asked.

"No. I have to be in Murmansk. The new submarine is being tested."

Alexeyevich watched his partner with sadness. Once they had been close, sharing dreams for their great country. But the marshall had changed. His whole life centered on power, on winning, even at the expense of the nation. It was madness.

"Boris was a friend. He loved the Soviet Union."

"Menoff was a Jew!" The word sounded like a curse.

"What has happened to you, Comrade Secretary? Why this obsession with the Jews? There are so few of them."

"They are a cancer to be cut out and destroyed."

"Even if it means destroying our country?"

"That will not happen."

"You sound like the Nazi madman. He tried it too and almost took us with him. It cost us twenty million lives. Do you forget?"

Marshall Malenkov spun around and pointed a shaking finger at the premier. "Forget? My wife and child died in Kursk. I have a piece of German steel in my neck." He slapped his neck. "Forget? I will never forget. But in the beginning it was the Jews, not the Nazis, who brought the war.''

"Bullshit. You are a stupid old man if you still believe that. You forget our dear Comrade Stalin and his love affair with that Nazi. The world was ours until he drove the knife into our backs. It was Hitler not the Jews who burned Soviets.''

Malenkov suddenly grew tired. He dismissed the argument with a wave of his large hand, put down his brandy glass, and moved to leave the room.

"I will take care of the emigration matter, Ivan Ivanovich. You take care of the Americans. Two weeks. Not one day more, and I will have that bastard Somoroff's head!''

He slammed the door behind him. Ivan Ivanovich Alexeyevich gestured an obscenity to his departed partner, then turned on his scrambler and telephoned Peter Somoroff with the good news.

The squad of six enlisted men and one officer dispersed around the Somoroff apartment. Two men in the apartment, two in the hallway, one at the back entrance to the building, and the officer and one man in the van out front. All had walkie-talkies. All were armed with submachine guns. There would be no easy access to the Somoroff apartment now.

Back at Lubyanka, the interrogation of Karkov began.

"This man is not possessed.'' Rabbi Vogel was firm in his statement. Misha Karkov sat in the straight-backed chair with his hands and feet bound tightly. Peter stood next to the rabbi. Leonid remained near the door of the interrogation room. Down the hall, Sasha Andreyev talked quietly with Anya Somoroff.

"I could have killed him,'' Anya said.

"I'm glad you didn't.''

"Did he kill my brother?''

"No, I don't think so. It seems he was in Moscow when that happened.''

"Who killed him?''

"We don't know.''

Sasha could see that Anya didn't believe her, but it was the truth. It was not her place to convince the pretty daughter of her boss otherwise.

"Do you know why he died?''

"It is not for me to say, honestly. Perhaps your father will talk with you now . . . after this business."

Anya liked Sasha's honesty. She decided not to press the matter further. In time her father would tell her.

Leonid felt the hair begin to tear from Misha Karkov's head. He relaxed his grip.

"You can't scare me," Misha said defiantly to the KGB colonel seated in front of him.

"Would you like to die?" Peter asked.

"I don't care. It is not in your hands."

Rabbi Vogel stepped closer to the prisoner. Suddenly something about the man struck him. Something that he had not seen before. As he approached, Misha's eyes locked on the rabbi. Fear began to creep into his face, and he tried to pull back from the old man. Vogel reached slowly toward Misha's neck and pulled away his shirt. There was a mark on Karkov's shoulder. It was red and shaped like an arrowhead, wide at the shoulder and coming to a point at the neck. Inside the mark was a yellow backward C, and under it three yellow dots.

$$\overset{\textstyle\supset}{\cdots}$$

"This man is marked." Vogel directed his words to Peter. "He will be able to tell us much, but first I must get some things. Leave him for now but guard him carefully. Don't let him sleep or even close his eyes."

He then gave Leonid Chomsky a list of things that they could get from Rabbi Posner at the Great Synagogue of Moscow. Captain Bonyon was assigned to stand guard over the prisoner. Vogel went with Major Rosteveli to have a look at the morgue sergeant, Dr. Brodsky, and the Pushkin lieutenant Zorbin. Perhaps they too were marked.

"Are you feeling better?" Peter was extremely gentle with his daughter.

"I'll be all right, Dad. But please tell me what is going on. I know this has to do with Peter's death, and I want to know."

The case had cost him one son, and he certainly didn't want to put his only remaining child in danger. But Valarian had a reach throughout the Soviet Union, with many disciples whose identities were still unknown. It would be better, Peter decided, if Anya was kept in Moscow and within the tight circle of the investigation. He told her the whole fantastic story. It was too much for her to believe.

"You are mad, Father. Spirits . . . Devils . . . Possessed people? Do you really believe all of this?"

"Yes," he answered, "and it would be better for you to at least keep an open mind. In any case, I want you near me for a while. You will act as liaison between our group and the premier. It was the job that your brother came to Moscow to do."

She grasped the significance of what her father had decided and felt very close to him.

"I won't let you down . . . and I will keep an open mind."

"Don't leave here without a guard. Don't go anywhere—no matter what happens—unless we know where you are, and, Anya . . . never alone. Is that clear?"

"Absolutely."

They hugged.

"For now," he told her as they left the room, "stay close to Sasha."

~ 23 ~

At the first taste of wine, Valarian spit. Metsky, startled by Valarian's action, drew back from his mahogany desk. The colonel spit again.

"Arghh . . . damned Jew."

"What is it, Colonel?"

"Leave the room," commanded Valarian. The discomfort was growing, and he knew he had to be alone.

As soon as Metsky left, Valarian lay down on top of his desk and stared into the pentangle of lights above him. His eyes milked over, pure white. One of the points of the pentangle turned red, and the color expanded down the length of the point to the middle of the star, which now took the shape of the mark on Misha's shoulder. The small lights formed the same backward *C*, and three lights became dots under the letter. Valarian's body stiffened.

At the same time, back in Lubyanka, Misha Karkov's body also stiffened. Rabbi Vogel watched carefully as he stopped pouring wine into Misha's mouth. The prisoner's eyes rolled back, and the sound of Valarian's voice roared out of his mouth.

"Damned Jew!"

Vogel was pleased. He spoke in ancient Aramaic. *"There is but one God—Yahweh."*

He then diminished the name of God. *"Yahwe . . . Yahw . . . Yah . . ."*

The rabbi moved quickly and, with a pointed instrument, using the remaining wine, drew an acrostic on Misha's forehead.

The KGB investigation entered a new and quite unexpected

127

phase as it elevated before the Soviets' eyes from the natural to the supernatural.

Peter, Leonid, and Bonyon watched in fascination. It was a square divided evenly into nine boxes. In each box Vogel wrote a number. As he did it he explained.

"The names of God are many. This is one of the most ancient. It can be diminished to three letters, *Y-A-H*, and their numerical value is fifteen—and a very powerful number when written this way."

Each box had a number and no matter what direction you added, the total was fifteen.

4	9	2
3	5	7
8	1	6

As he entered the last number, a six in the lower right-hand box, another sound came from Misha's mouth, but its origin was deep within his body.

"Awww . . . Awww . . . meechawww . . ."

Vogel then placed a highly polished mirror in front of Misha's face. The others in the room looked into the mirror and saw Valarian's face. Chomsky gasped.

"Who is that?"

"Valarian," said Peter Somoroff.

"Yes," said the rabbi, "the evil one himself. But I can't hold him too long."

Peter tried to be businesslike. "What is happening?"

"We have been able to reach him and let him know that he has been discovered. Misha is a disciple. This one always has five attached to him . . . in a sense he owns their souls, but it is a temporary thing. Soon he will release this one, because we have used his body and because we control it. Then Misha will be of no use to us . . . to anyone."

Suddenly words tumbled rapidly from Misha's throat.

"I will kill you, Jew. Foul stench of the earth. Your children will burn, your people will vanish. I swear this."

Vogel reacted immediately with a firm voice. *"Silence.* I do not speak to the fallen. I speak only to Yahweh. To *Him* you may swear. Do it, Belial . . . Leviathan . . . Lucifer . . . Shaytān . . . I know you."

The mirror began to glow in Vogel's hands.

"He is leaving Misha. Stand back."

The others moved away as the mirror glowed brighter. Vogel released it, yet it remained hovering over Karkov's face. Then it burst with a flash. It was gone.

Misha screamed and contorted in the chair. Spittle ran from his mouth, mucus from his nose. The acrostic on his forehead shriveled and disappeared. Then he passed out.

There was silence in the room.

"He is gone," said Vogel. He pulled Misha's shirt back, and the arrow was gone, too.

"This man is no longer bound to his service. A small victory, but of little consequence."

"What do we do now?" asked Peter. He was sitting, exhausted by the events.

Rabbi Vogel folded his prayer shawl, placed the pointed silver instrument in a blue velvet case, and cleaned the wine cup carefully.

"Do you want to meet Valarian, Colonel?"

"Will there be a danger?"

"Yes, but I think you should face your enemy and know him for what he really is. We can do it next week, on Tuesday."

"Why Tuesday?" asked Rosteveli.

"It is Yom Kippur, our Day of Atonement. On that day he may not harm us. But we can do some harm to him . . . perhaps delay him for a while . . . make him reexamine his plans."

Peter Somoroff stared at the rabbi, wondering how a man, so long in prison, so long out of touch with the world, could be so positive and so quickly involved.

"What will happen, Rabbi Vogel?"

The rabbi took an old twisted ram's horn from another velvet case. He held it up for all to see.

"This is the shofar—the ram's horn. On Yom Kippur, evil is powerless over those who are truly penitent."

He passed the shofar to Peter. "I will teach you to blow the horn by Tuesday, and I will teach you the words. Oh, how I wish I could be there, but only one may approach him. He will not expect this from you, Colonel Somoroff."

Peter put the horn to his lips and tried to blow. No sound came out. The others in the room laughed at his huffing and puffing. It broke the tense atmosphere.

The rabbi took back the shofar, placed the mouthpiece between the second and third finger of his right hand, and held the end of the horn high in his left hand.

"This is the way it is held. Blow steady and use the tongue." He put the mouthpiece to his lips and blew. A loud, mournful sound came from the horn—*tekeeeawwww*. . . .

At GRU headquarters, Valarian, sitting alone in his office deep in thought, shuddered as the sound of the shofar dimly reverberated in the room. Outside in the anteroom, Major Anton Metsky also shuddered but didn't know why. He clapped his hands over his ears to block out the strange sound.

∞ 24 ∞

GRU headquarters stood facing the People's Park in a northern suburb of Moscow. It was one of the few military installations in the city, and unless one knew there was a military presence inside the structure, it would appear to be another government building. A high wall surrounded the white marble structure. The main gate was guarded by two military policemen in uniform, with the bright blue and red GRU patch and crest on their uniforms.

Peter Somoroff eased his Skoda to a stop at the guard booth. He flashed his KGB identity card, and the guard snapped to attention, bringing his machine gun up vertically to salute the colonel.

"Good afternoon, sir. Please state your business."

"I have an appointment with Colonel Valarian."

"Just one moment, sir."

The guard entered the booth and checked his list of visitors. Then he telephoned to confirm the appointment. A moment later he waved Peter through the gate. "Please park in the visitors' spaces on the right, Colonel. Colonel Valarian is on the fifth floor." He saluted again.

Peter parked and entered the building's main entrance. Once again a guard, seated at a desk in the lobby, questioned him, and once again a phone call confirmed the appointment.

Peter noticed the metal detector as he passed through the lobby to the elevator. He felt the ram's horn in the pocket of his greatcoat, thinking about the problem there would be if it were metal and how he would explain the instrument. He passed through another metal detector outside Valarian's office.

131

The secretary was a middle-aged woman, plump and red-faced. Her steel-grey hair was pulled back severely into a bun. She wore a high-collared blouse and black wool skirt.

"An honor, Colonel Somoroff. Welcome. Colonel Valarian will be with you in a moment. May I bring you tea?"

Peter looked carefully at the woman. Rabbi Vogel had spent the past few days instructing him in the various ways to recognize disciples, among other things. The mark on the shoulder was the obvious sign, but there were more subtle ways, now that they knew Valarian had taken disciples to him. But the woman moved too fast, and Peter was unable to look at her hands or directly into her eyes. She stood with her back to him and made tea. Behind him he heard a click, and the door to Valarian's office opened slightly. Without looking she spoke.

"You may go in now, Colonel. I will bring the tea in a moment."

Peter felt a cold rush of air coming from the office through the small crack of the door, now ajar. Then he smelled an odor somehow musty yet acrid. It reminded him of a mixture of wet wool and burnt hair.

Nickolai Valarian, murderer of his son, smasher of dancers' legs, killer and epitome of evil, sat behind the shiny mahogany desk in an arrogant pose, both hands folded on the desktop. The reflection of the pentangle chandelier above him gave the aura of a crown of lights around Valarian's hands.

"I have anxiously awaited this moment, Comrade Somoroff," Valarian said caustically. "You are a courageous man."

Peter was about to respond when the secretary entered the office. She passed by him and placed the tea service, an antique silver one with one white porcelain cup, on a small table along the wall.

"Will there be anything else?" She directed the question to Valarian.

"No, thank you. We do not wish to be disturbed."

"Yes, sir." She left the room quickly, with a grace that belied her portliness. The door closed softly behind Peter. He turned to face Valarian.

"May I sit down?" Peter fought his fury and remained calm on the outside.

Valarian gestured to a chair near the tea service. Peter sat, picked up the teacup, and poured himself some tea. He noticed that Valarian's image was not reflected in the shiny silver teapot. This was as Vogel had said it would be. He then glanced up at the light above the desk and noticed that one of the star points was dark. Vogel would be glad to hear this news. It meant that a new disciple had not yet been ordained since Misha Karkov had been freed.

"Now, Colonel Somoroff," Valarian began as he leaned back in the black leather chair, "what can I do for you?" His tone was sarcastic.

Peter sipped the tea. "There is no point in being coy, Colonel Valarian. I know who and what you are. I came here to tell you that you have no place in this country. We do not want you here!"

The evil man's face became hard. A grunt of contempt growled in his throat.

"*We?* Who is *we,* Colonel Somoroff? You little man. Bureaucrat. You don't tell me where I belong. I am of this world, free to be where I want to be, when I want to be!"

His voice was strong. There was no doubt about Valarian's will. Peter started to answer when he felt a burning sensation begin to creep down from his shoulder to the hand that held the teacup. The cup began to shake, slowly at first, then violently. It shook out of his hand and crashed to the floor. The heat stopped. The shaking stopped.

Valarian was smiling.

"I could destroy you now—just as I destroyed your Jew friend Menoff."

He leapt to his feet and pointed at Peter. The KGB colonel was thrown from his chair onto the floor, then rolled over and over toward the opposite wall, finally crashing into it. His body vibrated against the rich mahogany paneling. His head banged violently against the wall and floor. Valarian laughed and relaxed, and the shaking stopped.

"Little man. Do you really know who I am? Do you know what I can do if I wish it?"

"I know who you are . . . what you are."

Peter sat up on the floor. He slid his hand into his coat pocket and gripped the shofar firmly.

"No, Colonel Somoroff, I don't think you know." Valarian laughed. "Now you have seen me. You have felt my power. But you are tiring me, and I must get on with the business of this nation. Ahhh, such a business it will be when I am

ready.'' He laughed again and settled back in his chair. He
didn't see Peter ease the shofar out of his pocket.

Peter lifted himself slowly to his feet, keeping the shofar
hidden from his adversary. He began to move toward the
door, bent in defeat. Valarian kept laughing at his back.

Suddenly Peter brought the shofar to his lips and in one
movement sounded the ram's horn while turning to face
Valarian. The sound filled the room. *Teekeelaww* . . . Quickly,
another blast—*shvoooawww* . . .

Valarian froze in midlaugh. Then, as though hit by a
sledgehammer, he was thrown back into his chair with a force
that caused the chair to topple him over onto the floor.

''*Damn you,*'' he screamed.

Peter moved to the front of the desk and looked down at
Valarian.

''*Silence,* godless one. You are fallen forever from His
grace!''

Then Peter began to speak in Hebrew as Rabbi Vogel had
taught him.

''*Praise be the Lord our God, who has given us his
commandments!*''

He blew the horn again.

Valarian was slammed into the rear wall of the office. He
sat there, unable to move, and it was obvious to Peter that he
was inflicting great pain upon the man. Peter continued with
the commandments.

''*I* am *the Lord, thy god!*''

Valarian shook.

''*Thou shalt have no other gods before me!*''

Valarian's legs split. Peter heard a bone crack.

''*Thou shalt not take the name of the Lord thy God in
vain!*''

Valarian's eyes rolled back into his head, leaving only the
whites showing.

''*Remember the sabbath day, to keep it holy!*''

Valarian's arms slammed against the wall, as though he
were being crucified.

''*Honor thy father and thy mother!*''

Valarian bled from his nose and mouth.

''*Thou shalt not kill!*''

Valarian was lifted off the floor, slowly, up toward the
ceiling.

"Thou shalt not commit adultery!"

Valarian was jammed into a corner of the ceiling. He moaned.

"Thou shalt not steal!"

Valarian, now spread-eagle in a corner of the ceiling, was slammed down onto the floor. His hands and feet were burning.

"Thou shalt not bear false witness against thy neighbor!"

Valarian was spun in a circle on the floor. Blood and fire flew from him.

"Thou shalt not covet thy neighbor's house, nor his wife, nor his servants, nor his cattle, nor anything that is thy neighbor's!"

Valarian stopped spinning abruptly. He fell in a heap on the floor at Peter Somoroff's feet.

"Praise be the Lord our God, who has given us his commandments!"

Peter lifted the shofar to his lips again and sounded a blast that drowned out Valarian's scream.

He looked down at the twisted, bloody, burning man at his feet.

"Little man, you say? I will show you who is little. I am *Russia,* and I *damn* you!"

He left. There was much yet to be done.

~ 25 ~

It was midmorning before Andy Taft could catch the shuttle back to New York. He had to encourage the D.C. cab driver to speed a bit on the parkway, but they made the plane.

The plane was half-full, and Andy had time to sit by himself and ponder the events of the preceding night. Sasha Andreyev was a known KGB agent attached to the Soviet Embassy in Washington. They had met on a few occasions, each knowing that the other knew his or her work. Andy was with DIA—Defense Intelligence Agency—a secret and little publicized intelligence arm of the U.S. government.

The meeting had been requested by a direct phone call to Andy at his New York apartment. The phone was unlisted and secure, yet Sasha had had no problem getting through. She was resourceful, and quite attractive, too.

They had dined at a small French restaurant in Georgetown, just off Wisconsin Avenue. The food had been superb and the wine had served to loosen the conversation. After dinner they had gone to his Georgetown apartment. Sasha had suggested this, and because Andy knew it was secure, he agreed. He was a little surprised the next morning when he played back the tape he had made of their conversation. It was completely jammed with a high-frequency disturbance. She must have hidden a device in her pocketbook lining. He had checked the pocketbook when she went to the bathroom after they had made love and found nothing, but he hadn't checked the lining.

Now he leaned back in his seat and pondered the conversation. It had all been small talk through dinner. When they arrived at his apartment he took her coat and went to the bar

136

to make stingers. She sat on the barstool across from him and immediately presented him with her request.

"Andy, we need to use your contacts in Israel. We want you to set up a meeting with one of my superiors and the chief of the Israeli service."

Andy was shocked. "It would be easier to set something up for you with the Chinese. Are you mad?"

"No, not mad, just in need of a favor. We are willing to pay you for your troubles."

He shook his head in disbelief. "Well, beautiful, assuming I know who the chief of their service actually is, and assuming they could be convinced that the meeting was in their interest, it will take more than money to pull this thing off. You people haven't been . . . shall I say . . . close with them?"

He offered her a stinger mist, and as she took it he leaned over the bar and kissed her.

"It comes with the drink. . . . You're beautiful."

She licked her lips and answered. "You too . . . but later. Do you think it could be done?"

"Anything can be done, sweetheart. Just give me a good reason to do it, and then give me about ten good reasons for the Israelis to do it, and we have a deal."

Sasha became very businesslike.

"Okay. What I am going to tell you, you will just have to believe. I can't prove anything now. We will prove it for the Israelis later. Also, this meeting comes from the premier, directly. He called me last night."

Andy was impressed. "No shit. Alexeyevich himself?"

"Yes . . . no shit. It knocked me right out of bed, but there is no doubt. It was him. Each of us has a code for such direct contact. He knew mine. There are only two people in the world who know that code, and I'm one of them. It was his idea, but I think this was the first time it was ever used. In any case it was Ivan Ivanovich . . . I am sure."

Andy leaned over the bar toward her. "I know you are going to tell me a story now, and I'm going to listen with great interest, but no matter what you tell me, I am going to have to have confirmation. From what you have told me so far, I'm going to have to eyeball the man himself. There is no other way."

She answered quickly. "Granted. It will be done."

Andy was tingling inside at the prospect of meeting the premier. He cleared his senses and lowered the stereo. He

gestured to Sasha to sit on the couch, then seated himself at
the other end.

"Comfortable?" he asked. She nodded and began again.

"The premier has a situation that is beyond his control. It
is an internal situation. The code name is *Flame*. It deals with
things that we would call supernatural. Understand that for a
country without religion this comes very hard, but there is no
other explanation. We are dealing with a—I will use his
word—a dybbuk. That is what the premier said to me."

"That's not Russian. It's Yiddish. An evil spirit?"

"The premier is convinced that such a person, spirit, force
. . . whatever you want to call it . . . that it exists, and that it
lives now in the Soviet Union."

Andy leaned toward her with a small smile on his lips.
"Excuse me, dear, but has it occurred to you that Ivan
Ivanovich Alexeyevich has gone bananas?"

She remained serious.

"Andy, this morning I was visited by a man you know. A
man who is not supposed to be in this country. Nevertheless
we met at the Mayflower this morning, and he showed me a
file. The premier is not bananas. The premier is deeply
concerned. Not only for the Soviet Union, but for the peace
we now enjoy."

"Who is the man you saw today?"

"Peter Somoroff."

Andy whistled. "You tell me this—and he's still here?"

"Yes. He will see you tomorrow . . . if—if—I can convince you, and he will also make arrangements for you to see
the premier."

This was the real thing, and it was big.

"Okay. Please go on. I'm hooked."

Their conversation lasted three hours. Sasha did most of
the talking, with Andy interrupting only to clarify certain
points. When Sasha finished Andy was as excited as he had
ever been in his life. Her final plea had brought tears. She
loved her country, and she was frightened. The premier was
right—things were out of control and beyond understanding
within the framework of a rational world. She recalled the
rabbi's words to the premier: "You are dealing with things
that you refuse to recognize. When you evicted God from
your midst you opened your door to evil. Why are you
surprised that it came in?"

~26~

America, being an open society, gives those who practice espionage a fairly simple task. Peter Somoroff had to move quickly after his final meeting with the premier. Time was against them.

He now sat in room 1174 of the Mayflower Hotel in Washington, D.C., just a few blocks from the White House. If Sasha did not convince the American DIA agent, they might soon be celebrating Somoroff's capture in that White House. But so far things were going well. Sasha had checked in each time with the correct message. The first call had come from the restaurant in Georgetown. All she said was "blue." The next call was four hours later from the American's apartment. The message was "bright light." The final call this morning at precisely 7:43 was "Flame." They would be here at 9:15, and they would have thirty minutes to talk. Then Peter had to leave. He looked at his watch. It was 9:10.

Four minutes later he left room 1174 and walked to room 1166. He opened the door, and Sasha took her gun away from the American's temple. Andy Taft was sitting in a chair staring at Peter Somoroff. When Andy spoke, Peter sensed the excitement in his voice. "My God, it's actually you," said Andy. "Sasha, now I believe you have a problem. Maybe we all do."

Peter Somoroff spoke quickly. "I am relieved to hear you believe us. Sasha says you are one of the best. I will tell you that we also have a file on you, and you are categorized as . . . ah, what is the word . . . an independent thinker. Most of the time that is dangerous for us, but this time we gambled that your independence could keep our secret . . . for a while, anyway.

139

Andy kept his eyes on the KGB chief. "If you think you've bought me, you're way off base. You know I have to report all of this."

"Yes. Shall we get down to business?"

"Not yet. I want something from you first."

Peter smiled. "Yes . . . the negotiations begin."

Andy got up from the chair and walked over to Peter Somoroff. He reached out and shook hands with the security chief. He then asked Peter Somoroff to open his mouth to further confirm his identity. Andy looked in to see the small piece missing from the tip of Somoroff's tongue as the DIA file had so stated. He was satisfied.

"Thanks. Now part two. How the hell did you get into the country?"

Somoroff relaxed. "Good. If I tell you then can we get down to cases?"

Peter spoke as he moved toward the window. "We have a number of sleepers in America. That I am sure you know. They are just plain American citizens, and most of them will die having never been used. In cases of extreme emergency— and this case is an emergency—we just have one of them take a trip somewhere, and then we bring him in, to an embassy, whatever. So it is simple for me to get his passport and ticket, and I am through customs and immigration. *Poof* . . . I am here, and a loyal sleeper comes home."

"And how do you leave?"

"Ah, I thought you said we could get down to cases if I answered your question. I did."

Andy realized that his excitement had made him phrase his question improperly and that he had lost this round. He also knew that there were at least five DIA agents in the hotel at that moment. Peter Ilyavich Somoroff would be spending the night courtesy of the DIA, so he played along.

"Okay, you're right. Now what?"

Peter moved toward the bed and sat. "I wanted you to see me so that there would be no doubt in your mind that the premier is serious. We need your help. We know that you will have to report the happenings of last night and today to your superiors. We expect that, and we expect that you will be able to convince them that you should help us . . . help the premier."

Andy nodded. "Go on."

"You are to arrange a meeting between you, the chief of Israeli intelligence, and me. The stakes are simple. You will convey the message that the lives of five million Jews depend on his making that meeting."

"Those people don't respond well to threats. You know that."

Somoroff held up his hand. "Please let me finish. We have only a few moments, and then I must leave. You will tell him that fact. Second, you will tell him that the Soviet KGB wishes to enter into a joint operation with the Israelis—for the benefit of both nations. You have heard the story from Sasha. It is true. Third, you must not tell the reason for the meeting to the Israelis."

Andy stood up. "Hold it. You can't possibly mean that. They just won't accept. That man—their Mossad chief—his identity is super-secret. I'm sure that's a no-buts situation."

Somoroff continued as though he did not hear Andy. "Finally, you will give him this letter. The contents of the letter are unknown to me. They are to have their laboratory people open it and check to certify that it has not been opened previously. You are to tell him that the security of the letter is their code *Kemiot*. I believe it means amulet, or something like that . . . a charm. He will know. He will understand."

Andy took the letter and held it in his hand. It felt dangerous. The envelope was the official stationery of the USSR. The entire envelope was encased in a fine, almost silky, transparent film.

Peter Somoroff rose from the bed and walked toward the door. "I must tell you one more thing. I am leaving, and you will have to stay here for twenty minutes. Your colleagues are already outside of my room, but we know that I am no longer there. I will be out of the country by tomorrow morning. Sasha will remain. She will go to your office with you if you wish."

Sasha protested. "Is that necessary, Comrade Somoroff?"

He answered directly. "Absolutely. You will now be the contact. When the Israelis agree—and they will—we will talk again."

Peter walked over to Sasha and kissed her lightly. He shook hands with Taft, then turned and left the room. Andy stood holding the envelope. A million thoughts raced through his head. He noticed Sasha's gun drawn again. He told her to put it away; he wasn't going anywhere. She didn't.

~ 27 ~

The wheels were set in motion. First the call from the office stating that an American DIA agent had brought a letter for General Arie ben Kagan with specific instructions that code Kemiot was to be used. That code was known only to the inner circle of Israeli intelligence. The utmost care and security had to be followed. It was required by the code that ben Kagan be informed of its use. He immediately had the American checked out through channels and then authorized the lab to examine the letter. It would take ten hours for the examination to be completed. By then he would have the information about the American. He left instructions to be called when the letter was ready to be opened.

Kemiot is a Hebrew word frequently mentioned in Talmudic literature. Its meaning was tied to the verb meaning *to bind,* but the general use of the word had to do with amulets and sacred ornamentation worn by the ancient and forbidden gods. The use of the code by Israeli intelligence had come from one place. The Soviet Union.

Arie ben Kagan cleared the lab after his people assured him that the sealed envelope had not been compromised. They also confirmed the watermark on the stationery as Official Soviet—Diplomatic.

His hands were steady as he opened the letter with a sharp knife, but his heart fluttered when he saw the signature at the bottom of the letter. Ivan Ivanovich Alexeyevich. The letter was written in longhand. The message was precise.

To the People of Israel:
It is not with humility but with pride that I write this letter and ask you, in the name of God Almighty, to

heed its contents. Our nations could be no further apart, even if we were at war. I cannot apologize for this condition. It is sorrowful, and it is my sincere hope that the coming days will see an end to animosity, and a new beginning.

We knew nothing of Kemiot. Rabbi Posner, of the great synagogue of Moscow, gave us the information. He will arrive in Tel Aviv whenever you request his presence.

We have discovered that an evil spirit, a demon, is in our midst. He plans to destroy our nation and, with it, much of the world.

I have learned too much to express in a letter; I feel too much to do less. I beg your trust in this matter.

The American DIA agent, Andrew Taft, is authorized to contact us. We wish you to meet, in Israel, with our Chief of the KGB Investigative Section, Peter Ilyavich Somoroff, three members of his staff, and Rabbi Isadore Vogel, formerly of Minsk. They will have more details. Rabbi Vogel has informed us that part of the solution to this dreadful circumstance lies in Israel. He requests that Rabbi Sholem Asher also attend the meeting.

We are but men and filled with centuries of mistrust and suspicion. I put all of that aside. We are human. We are threatened. I pray you will act with conscience and deliberate speed.

In friendship extended,
Ivan Ivanovich Alexeyevich
Premier, USSR

It was signed in the premier's hand. Arie ben Kagan couldn't breathe. He read the letter twice, then called Michael Gross, his closest aide, into the lab.

"My god," said Michael after reading the letter, "can it be true?"

Ben Kagan blinked and cleared his mind of a million pulsing thoughts. "Get Rabbi Asher down here by morning. And get me that DIA agent." Gross handed Arie the letter and turned to leave. "Michael, one more thing. Pull the complete file on Rabbi Posner—everything . . . dental records, birth certificate, the works—and the file on Colonel

Somoroff, too. Drop them at my office. I'll be working all night.''

Gross responded to the orders with a nod. "Shalom, General. I'll go up for Asher myself. He's at the dig under the mosque.''

"The Siloam tunnel?''

"I think so, General. I'll check the museum first.''

Rabbi Asher's voice echoed in the cavern as Gross made his way along the tunnel. Bare light bulbs illuminated the smooth walls and dusty soil beneath his boots. He listened to the great archaeologist as he approached the cavern.

". . . captured by King David about one thousand BC. So Solomon's Temple extended the city and elongated its shape along the eastern ridge above us. In a way we are lucky that Antiochus destroyed the temple, because in doing so, he sealed this tunnel and the treasures it holds—''

Michael entered the chamber, disturbing the small group of students who sat listening to Rabbi Asher. The rabbi turned his attention to the intruder.

"May I help you, young man?''

"Rabbi Asher? I need you for a moment . . . alone.''

"Who are you, may I ask?''

A few of the students stood and faced Gross.

"I am Captain Gross, aide to General Kagan in Tel Aviv. The museum told me I would find you here.''

The rabbi told his students to remain in the chamber. He then led Gross back through the tunnel to the entrance below the Old City Wall. The guards at the mouth of the tunnel checked them and let them through the tunnel entrance, which was in the rear of a coffeehouse.

"We can speak here, Captain Gross.''

Michael checked behind him in the tunnel. The guards were out of sight. He then opened the door leading to the shop's storeroom. Empty too.

"I am sorry to disturb you, Rabbi, but you will have to come to Tel Aviv with me—now.''

"Just like that? Perhaps you have a reason for this journey?''

"I am to tell you very little.''

To be sure of the proper words, Gross took out his notebook and read the instructions. "General Arie ben Kagan said that I was to tell you that Kemiot requests your presence in Tel Aviv!''

"That's impossible!"

"Well, Rabbi, I have lived in Israel all my life. Nothing is impossible. Shall we go?"

"Let me tell my students I am leaving. Just give me five minutes."

"Fine. But, please, don't say where you are going."

The helicopter ride from Jerusalem to Tel Aviv was less than sixty kilometers, and within the hour Rabbi Asher began the strangest journey of his life. Although it was a journey for which he had prepared, he had never really believed it would come to pass.

The preparation began, for Rabbi Asher, over seven centuries before, when the great Jewish physician and philosopher Maimonides, known also as Moses ben Maimon, wrote his famous text denying the use of magic, demonology, and conjuring. He stated that these ancient practices were no more than base idolatry and forbidden in the Torah. From that time on, the battle raged as to whether these practices are allowed or prohibited under Jewish law and God's Law.

Rabbi Asher was born in Poland. He was ordained as a rabbi in Bialystok in the Hasidic sect, whose people claim direct descent from the Chaldean tribe of Abraham. Their history and worship is filled with mysticism based on ancient and Biblical texts. It was in the early days of his rabbinate that Sholem Asher met Rabbi Isadore Vogel, also a Hasid. They gathered with several other rabbis in Bialystok to choose one rabbi who would go to Zefat, in Palestine, to study under the followers of the famous Rabbi David ben Zimrah, a sixteenth-century scholar, who refuted Maimonides' writings and who, it is rumored, brought back the old ways and the ancient rites of demonology, magic, and conjuring. Rabbi Asher, then a young and zealous man, was chosen. He returned to Poland a few times before the holocaust of World War II and shared some of his knowledge with Rabbi Vogel. They spoke of the unthinkable and of rituals that, when practiced by the holy believers, could work miracles.

It was all very secretive. An underground was born at that time, with the code name of Kemiot. Its purpose was to transmit this forbidden information into Eastern Europe if and when it was needed. During World War II it became a channel by which military information was passed. Later, after the war, it was used to resettle Jews in the newly formed State of Israel. In the modern era, Kemiot had been buried and sealed in the minds of those few who remained under the communist regimes and of one sect in Israel.

Now Rabbi Asher knew Kemiot had been resurrected and that his knowledge and services were needed somewhere in Eastern Europe. The day had come. He was ready.

"Do you know the contents of the letter?" General Kagan sat at his apparently disorganized desk, puffing on an old corncob pipe and staring into the eyes of the young DIA agent.

Andy Taft was not sure that ben Kagan was the head of Israeli intelligence, but he suspected this was the man.

"No, sir. They only asked me to deliver it."

Arie nodded. He passed a copy of the letter across the desk to the American.

"This is a copy. The original has gone to the prime minister."

After he read the letter, Andy placed it carefully on the desk. "Wow! Do you believe it?"

"I will withhold judgment until we have checked further. One thing is clear. They wish to have this meeting. Whether we do is not my decision. You will find that your embassy has temporarily attached you to this section as a liaison officer. We wish to see Rabbi Posner in Israel as soon as possible."

The buzzer on the general's desk console flashed.

"Excuse me," he said and picked up the receiver. The voice at the other end told him that Captain Gross had arrived with Rabbi Asher. "Fine. Have them wait in the conference room, and bring those files in to me for a moment."

Ben Kagan stood. Andy Taft followed suit.

"Mr. Taft, do you know how Rabbi Posner will arrive?"

"No, sir. I am just to contact the KGB in Washington. They did say he would be here within twenty-four hours. They will notify the American Embassy of the details."

Kagan walked to the door as his secretary brought in two files, one blue and one red.

"Thank you, Shoshanna. Hold all my calls, except for the prime minister's."

He then turned to Andy and extended his hand.

"Welcome to Israeli intelligence, Mr. Taft. Please take steps to have Rabbi Posner come to us. We will expect him tomorrow."

"Excellent. What about the others?"

"Mr. Taft, this is a risky part of the world. We are a small nation, and therefore cautious. Let's have a talk with Rabbi Posner first. I am sure the KGB expects that of us. When you can confirm the details of his arrival, contact Captain Gross. He will meet the rabbi and bring him here."

Ben Kagan gestured Andy toward the door. As Andy was about to leave the room, the general stopped him.

"You have no doubts about seeing Somoroff in Washington? You are sure it was him?"

"Absolutely, General. And I believed him, too."

The general shook his head. "Fantastic. Absolutely fantastic."

～ 28 ～

Lod Airport was relatively quiet. Intermingled with travelers were armed soldiers moving in groups of twos and threes, their Uzi machine guns always present, always ready. Michael Gross flashed his ID and escorted Andy to the Swissair gate. The red and white 747 stood off to the left, and a long stream of passengers moved slowly toward the gate. Both men scanned the column. Both strained to find the priest. Andy saw him first but then became confused when three other priests emerged from the forward door of the huge jet.

"I hope there isn't a convention of priests," he mused.

"There he is," said Michael. He pointed to a small, old priest who, as arranged, walked slowly with a limp and was aided by a heavy shillelagh-like cane. By design, they would not approach him in the open. Israel is one of the few countries in the world whose citizens are constantly on guard within their own borders. Gross told Andy to keep an eye on the old man while he slipped away for a few minutes. It would take at least twenty minutes for the passengers to clear customs and immigration. Gross had work to do. If the rabbi had been followed or if his presence was known to the various enemies of Israel, Michael wanted to know before contact was made.

Rabbi Posner was in another world mentally. Here he stood on the actual soil of Eretz Israel, the homeland, dressed as a Catholic priest. He had always imagined he would drop to his knees and kiss the ground if he were ever so fortunate as to see Israel. But he concentrated on his limp and handled his cane as though it had been an appendage for many years. Still, tears filled his eyes and his heart beat joyfully.

Colonel Somoroff had shown him the picture of the young American DIA agent. The image was burned into his mind, but the man was nowhere to be seen.

He approached the stern customs officer, noting the Star of David on his uniform, and suppressed a strong desire to reach across the desk and kiss the man. Do they realize, he thought, what it means for me to see a Jewish soldier? The officer took his Swiss passport and looked up.

"How long will you be in the country, Father?" The man spoke perfect German.

"Three weeks," answered Posner, wondering if this man knew who he really was and if his rusty German had fooled the soldier.

"Have a nice visit. Shalom." He stamped the passport. "Your luggage will be coming out over there." He gestured toward a blue door. "Just go through."

On the other side of the door Andy Taft extended his hand to the rabbi. It was a small room, bare and sterile white. For a moment Rabbi Posner was disoriented and didn't recognize the stranger.

"Rabbi Posner? Are you all right?" Andy spoke in English.

"Mr. Taft? Yes, Mr. Taft." Posner was relieved. He took Andy's hand and shook it several times.

The rear door to the room opened, and Michael Gross entered.

"Shalom aleichem, Rabbi. Welcome to Israel." He spoke in Yiddish. The rabbi could no longer contain himself—he burst into tears and hugged all six feet two inches of Captain Gross. It was a scene that the intelligence officer had seen many times. And each time it happened his eyes were never dry.

The two rabbis sat across from each other later that afternoon. Arie ben Kagan was satisfied that Rabbi Posner was who he said he was. The dental records checked; the fingerprints and the scars from Nazi beatings were correct. Kemiot had come home. The link was made.

But all was not harmony. The rabbis were from different schools of thought regarding the mystical aspects of Judaism. Asher knew, by oaths taken long ago, that he could not convince this fellow rabbi and that it was dangerous even to argue the point. Perhaps it had been a mistake to share the Kemiot pipeline with the non-Hasidim. Arie ben Kagan settled the argument quickly, without offending either man.

"We are not here to discuss the merits of rabbinical thought and teaching, gentlemen. We have a rather momentous decision to make regarding our contact with the KGB and the Soviet government. Rabbi Posner is Rabbi Posner, and from what he has told me of Colonel Somoroff and of Rabbi Vogel, I am just about convinced that this meeting should take place. Do either of you have any objections?"

Rabbi Asher answered first. He spoke rapidly and with firm conviction.

"I cannot make that judgment." He hesitated now, gathering his thoughts so that his words would be effective. "And, in the end, if I am convinced that there is truth in the story, then we will have to convince my associates in Zefat. That will not be an easy task."

It was an old story for ben Kagan. The religious against the state. How many times had he fought with them? His concern was always the survival of the state; their concern was always on what they called a "higher plane" or, as one had said before the Yom Kippur War, "from a higher authority." It was at once their strength and their weakness. Was it better that the Jews of Europe walked into the concentration camps without a struggle? Should each have taken a Nazi with him? Still, these rabbis like Asher felt they held the final answer to the question. Perhaps they had some special link to the Almighty. Arie ben Kagan still trusted his links to his agents in Moscow, Washington, Cairo, Damascus, Tehran, and the rest of the crazy world. They might not hold the final answer, but until the world was ready to live and let live, he knew the "final solution" to the "Jewish question" was alive and well and living in many of these nations.

Rabbi Posner spoke slowly in Yiddish. "You ask me if I believe this problem is real? I must say no, because I reject the premise. But if you ask me whether Colonel Somoroff and Rabbi Vogel believe it is real, then I must answer yes. This Soviet is different. Perhaps he is mad, and perhaps Vogel has been brainwashed by all those years in Siberia . . . I don't know. But the business with Isadore Kantrowitz was real, and the Menoffs are dead. It was enough for me to expose Kemiot. I say they are sincere—but I am not a politician.''

Ben Kagan studied the two men. He knew that Andy Taft was waiting in the outer room for the signal to bring the Soviets to Israel. The prime minister had met all night with the cabinet. The arguments were heated. Twice ben Kagan had been called into the Spartan room to be questioned by shirtsleeved ministers. The last holdout was Ruth Goldstein, Minister of Internal Affairs, and on paper ben Kagan's boss. She was dead set against the meeting.

''Let those Soviet bastards stew in their own juices. I don't believe this mystical crap for one minute. It's a trick to discredit us. Besides, what can we do to help them anyway?''

The general could answer the question, but only in part. ''Madame Minister, in my interview with Rabbi Asher, he told me there was—is—some possibility of helping the Soviet premier.''

''Can he assure that?''

''No. He must meet this Rabbi Vogel, and then he must convince the others in Zefat to help.''

''How?'' she asked. ''How could they help?''

''He won't say, Mrs. Goldstein. They are a very secret group up there.''

She knew ben Kagan was telling the truth and that she would eventually be overruled by the rest of the cabinet. But before she gave in, she fired one more shot.

''It has always seemed strange to me that we can know what is happening in all the secret conclaves of all the capitals of the world, yet we cannot know what a few old rabbis in Zefat are up to.''

She leaned back in her chair and lit a cigarette.

The prime minister, a quiet, soft-spoken man, who had risen to the highest office in Israel through the tumultuous politics of a nation under constant attack, leaned to his left and tapped Ruth Goldstein on her hand, as a father might do to a child.

''Ruth, therein lies our strength. If we ever come to the day when we must spy on God and those who do His work, we shall surely break the covenant of our people.''

The woman could not hold back her smile. She crushed her cigarette in the ashtray and then covered the prime minister's hand with hers.

"Well, Myron, there have been times in my life when I wondered if that might not be a good idea. This business of being chosen gets to be quite a burden from time to time."

A vote was promptly called, and Arie ben Kagan was given the mandate to proceed within the guidelines he thought best for the security of Israel. The operation was now in his hands.

He made the decision with the same assuredness as he gave the order to destroy the Egyptian airfields in the Six-Day War. Within hours Sasha Andreyev boarded the El Al flight at John F. Kennedy Airport in New York, and the special Illutian aircraft assigned to the KGB filed a flight plan from Moscow to Stockholm.

Project Flame was on the move from Moscow to Tel Aviv.

— 29 —

The small dacha was set back a kilometer from the dirt road. It was another four kilometers to the blacktop and several more until one reached the main road to Moscow. The frame house gave the appearance of a gingerbread and vanilla cake decoration as it sat surrounded by the new-fallen snow. A wisp of smoke rose straight up from the chimney, indicating an absence of wind. The two black official cars stood silent at the front door, their drivers huddled in the small gatehouse beyond the driveway.

As a disciple, Major Metsky was far more comfortable in this place than in the GRU office to the south in Moscow. Valarian was calmer here, more deliberate, and definitely more powerful. This was sanctuary.

Anton sat in the large central room admiring Valya Pernick as they waited for Valarian to dress. She was a handsome woman, not beautiful but strong and feminine. She was dressed entirely in black, as she had been when she killed young Peter Somoroff, a silk blouse over a turtleneck sweater, long wool pants, and sealskin boots. She wore no makeup. Her dark round eyes leaped out of a pale, angular face. He fantasized, imagining her long legs wrapped around his small body, pumping furiously on the large black velvet bedspread in Valarian's bedroom. He knew that Valarian had had sex with her many times, as he had with her mother. Metsky suspected that he had even slept with both women at once. She never spoke of it. He considered whether a disciple could be sexually equal to the master.

Valarian broke through his thoughts as he entered the room. He was all business.

"Tell me what they did, Valya. Everything." He sat in the large chair near the window farthest from the fireplace.

"Three of them went to Stockholm. Somoroff was still in East Germany. They took a small jet. Our GRU people in Sweden tracked them to Göteborg. From there they took a ferry to Copenhagen, where Somoroff met them. They flew SAS to Amsterdam and then KLM to Tel Aviv. At Schipol they presented Israeli passports, and the Jews passed them right through. It had obviously been arranged."

Valarian stared out the window at the winter landscape. Since the ordeal with Somoroff he had rested at the dacha. His body had recuperated from the battering, but valuable time had been lost. Two weeks had passed.

"Who went from Moscow?"

"Somoroff's daughter, the KGB lieutenant Chomsky, and the old Jew."

Valya looked at Major Metsky, indicating that he should add his information to her story. He spoke calmly.

"I have traced the Jew. He was taken from Camp Eleven in Tostuya three weeks ago. The authority was KGB, but the signature was that of Sasha Andreyev, an agent assigned to America. It must have been a forgery."

"It was no forgery," snapped Valarian. "I know that bitch. She is a personal pet of the pig Alexeyevich." There was venom in his voice.

"But, Colonel Valarian, she is still in Washington."

"She was here, I tell you!" he shouted. "She is part of their gang now. Check with Washington again tonight. See if she is still there. Please continue, Valya." His voice grew softer. "They were met at Lod by an Israeli agent and whisked away by helicopter transport. I believe Major Metsky can tell you where they went."

Anton was proud of himself. He had alerted the Soviet fleet radar ships in the Mediterranean and requested a complete log of all Israeli air traffic from the time the KLM flight landed. He now referred to the computer printout that he had removed from his briefcase.

"Assuming that the time of takeoff of the helicopter from Lod is accurate, we have seven helicopters in that area at the given hour. Two went to Jerusalem, one returned to Lod, three went south to Ashdod, Gaza, and Beersheba, and one went north to Tiberias."

Valarian watched a hawk circle above the bare trees. Suddenly it swooped down out of sight but quickly rose again with a small animal in its talons.

"They went to Tiberias," he said. "Now tell me about the Jew."

"He is a rabbi named Vogel, Isadore Vogel, from Minsk. You charged him, Colonel, and signed the complaint. His wife and two children emigrated to Israel in 1977. They were told he was dead."

"I should have destroyed him. He is a dangerous Jew."

It was clear to Valarian now. Vogel had instructed Somoroff and taught him to inflict the punishment.

"When this is over I want that Jew alive," Valarian hissed. "What steps have you taken at Lubyanka?"

"The wing is still under their security. Major . . . ah"— Metsky checked his files—"Rosteveli is in charge of the section. He spends time with a Jewess . . ."—once again he checked his notes—"named Fannie Beshevsky. She was a friend of Kantrowitz. We can move on them at your command."

"Good." Valarian was pleased. "Just keep them under surveillance for now. What have you prepared in Israel?"

Major Metsky was proud of his foresight. He shuffled through some papers and continued. "I have a strike team ready to move immediately in Bint Jubayl, across the border in Lebanon."

"PLO?"

"Yes. Al Fatah. Tiger Cubs, all devoted."

"Good." Valarian stood. "Wait here. I will be back in a short time."

He walked from the room into his bedroom and closed the door. This windowless room was much smaller than the main room, and without heat. He removed the covering from a small, round table near the left of the bed. Inlaid on the tabletop in black and ivory was a small pentangle, shaped exactly like the chandelier that hung in his office. He removed five black candles from a drawer in the table and placed each on a point of the star. He touched one with his jade and silver ring, and it burst into flame. He then gripped the candle with both hands and stared into the flame. The flame grew more intense, and hot wax poured onto his hands. When his hands were completely covered with wax he withdrew them, scraped the wax, and rolled it between his palms. His fingers worked quickly, manipulating the wax as a sculptor would clay. His hands parted, and there, in his palm, was the head and detailed face of a man. Valarian brought the figure to his lips and blew softly into its mouth.

In the coffeehouse Three Figs, in the Arab section of Acre, Achmed Sharit sat sipping his morning coffee and watching the ship traffic across the Bay of Haifa in the direction of Haifa. It was a warm, sunny morning. The old man felt his shoulder tingle and immediately knew he had been summoned. Within seconds he was on his feet and moving quickly, despite his age, to his small flat in the basement of a rug shop. The owner, his landlord, greeted him, but Achmed pushed past the man without recognition.

"Salaam alecheem, Achmed," the shopowner shouted after him.

It fell on deaf ears. A moment later, Achmed fumbled with the door lock and entered his tiny basement apartment. It was dark and musty. He reached under his sleeping cot and unrolled a threadbare rug. It was marked with a red triangle, within which was a backward C over three yellow dots. He lay down on the carpet so that his body covered the arrowlike triangle completely. Then he pulled his clothing down off his shoulder, revealing the same mark as the carpet bore. His head turned toward the marked shoulder, and his tongue slid from his mouth to touch the backward C there.

His eyes glazed over, and he heard his master speak.

"Those who would destroy you are near Tiberias. Three or four Soviets and an old rabbi. They are with Israeli agents. Find them and tell me where they are. Do it by tonight."

Achmed felt the pain and delight that only a true disciple of Satan may experience. The tip of his tongue burst into flame, and he swallowed the flame as though it were the finest meal he had ever eaten. Then he left for Tiberias after carefully packing his rug in a weatherbeaten satchel.

Valarian returned to the room. "By tonight I hope to know where they are in Israel. I want an immediate attack launched."

"Just tell me where they are," said Metsky, "and we will get them."

Valarian noticed the large black limousine coming up the driveway.

"You will have to go now," he said to Anton and Valya. "Has the Moscow rabbi returned yet?"

"Yes," answered Metsky.

"Pick him up and hold him at GRU headquarters. It is time we took a few hostages."

As Major Metsky and Valya Pernick left in their own cars, each saw the heavy figure of Marshall Serge Malenkov enter Valarian's dacha.

~30~

It was for more than security reasons that General Arie ben Kagan chose Kibbutz Ginnosar as the meeting place. The small settlement nestled on the shore of the Sea of Galilee, which provided a shield from the east. The commando base at Migdal, to the south, gave additional protection and crack troops to add to the kibbutz defenses. Security was good.

The other reason was the Michael had informed him that Rabbi Vogel's wife and children were members of this kibbutz.

The three Soviet visitors had been secluded in a special army trailer, away from the main settlement on the shore of the Sea. Gross had handled the arrangements. Now Michael was on his way back from Tel Aviv with the final member of the Soviet group who had arrived that evening.

But first, Arie had a mitzvah, a good deed, to perform. He walked along the rock-lined path toward the cottage that contained Rabbi Asher and Rabbi Vogel. It was a white stucco house with a tile roof that served as a guest house for the kibbutz. A faint smell of fried fish reached ben Kagan's nostrils, and as he passed the guards after showing his ID, he could see the rabbis sitting at a table on the porch eating dinner. The light within the long shadows gave the setting a conspiratorial feeling.

Rabbi Isadore Vogel had changed his drab Soviet clothes for the khaki slacks and white shirt of a kibbutznik. He had even obtained a blue and white yarmulke with a Star of David knitted on the top. The two men were deep in discussion and only noticed his approach as he ascended the three steps onto the porch.

"Shalom, Rabbi Vogel. I am Arie ben Kagan. Welcome to Israel!"

"Shalom aleichem, General. It is an honor to meet you."

Ben Kagan sat and took a pear from the fruit bowl on the table. He took a deep bite and the juice ran down his chin.

"Only in Israel can we grow such fruit," he said as he wiped his chin with a cloth napkin. Rabbi Asher laughed.

"The general is a farmer. He will tell you that it is because we grow it with love that it is so sweet."

"And because we grow it on our own land," added ben Kagan.

Vogel stared at Arie ben Kagan. Both Israelis could feel the man's words before he said them, but both also knew that they had to be said. Arie prolonged the moment by biting the pear again. Then he spoke.

"Nu Sholem. . . . So how is your old friend?"

"He has told me a great deal, but we have to hear more from the Soviets. It sounds to me like they have uncovered a nest of deadly vipers, maybe more.

Ben Kagan didn't want to get into the matter yet. He knew that Vogel had been cleared by Asher, and he knew that the two men had spent the afternoon discussing events in the Soviet Union.

"May I speak?" asked Rabbi Vogel.

"It's a free country, Rabbi," joked Arie.

"Less than a month ago I lived in a small, cold room. There were 478 cinder blocks surrounding me. Today I sit by the shore of Galilee . . ."

He fought back his emotion. "Excuse me." He reached into his pocket, brought out a handkerchief, and blew his nose. "It has been quite a trip. Overwhelming. When they brought me to Moscow I asked about my family. It took several days, but Colonel Somoroff finally was able to ascertain that they had emigrated to Austria and possibly on to Israel. We were waiting for word from the Relief Agency when this trip came to pass."

Asher looked to ben Kagan, but the general remained impassive.

"To be in Eretz Israel is beyond words for me, and to ask a favor is perhaps . . . perhaps rude . . . but if it is possible, is there some way to see if they are somewhere in Israel?"

"Would you like to see them now?" ben Kagan asked.

"What did you say?" The rabbi thought that he hadn't heard the officer correctly.

"Why don't we take a walk, Rabbi Vogel? It's a beautiful kibbutz."

He got to his feet and leaned across the table to take Vogel's arm. The rabbi was trembling. Arie steadied him as they walked down the steps toward the main settlement. Two guards with Uzis fell in behind them. A female sergeant with her pistol case unsnapped walked off to their right.

"Did you say I could see my family now?" the stunned rabbi asked.

"Well, in a few minutes. We have to walk down to that third building on the left." He pointed to a row of Quonset-type structures below them.

Selma Vogel washed the last dish and turned off the tap. "David," she called. "It's your turn to dry."

A thirteen-year-old boy, tanned and handsome with blond hair, stuck his head into the small kitchen.

"It's not my turn. Talia does it tonight."

"Talia has to study for her exams. You do it tonight, and she will do it twice in a row."

"But, Mom—"

"No arguments, young man." Selma was firm. The years in Israel had been good for her and for the children. She thought often of her husband and how he would have so enjoyed living here on the Galilee. The adjustment had been hard at first. The fact that she spoke Hebrew helped.

When they had told her that Isadore was dead, she had no reason to stay in the Soviet Union. Many times since then she had thanked God for her courage to leave all behind and bring her children to Israel. When they were bar and bas mitzvahed, she had cried for her lost husband and the joy he would have had in seeing his children grow up so well.

David Vogel came into the kitchen reluctantly and reached for a towel to begin drying the dishes. Selma also turned to dry her hands and for a moment caught sight of two men walking down the hill in the purple light of dusk. Strange, she thought, when she saw the armed soldiers behind them. And then for a moment—an elusive, wispy, ephemeral moment—she thought . . . and then turned away from what could not be.

Talia settled on the sofa with her geometry book on her lap and her worksheets scattered on the floor. The yellow lamp illuminated one side of her young face. She was deeply immersed in her work but looked up when her mother entered the room. The women smiled at each other. Talia's was a beautiful smile. Her father's smile, thought Selma. Symphonic music played softly on the radio. And then the image of the old man on the hill came rushing back to her . . .

As she turned there was a knock on the door.

"*Yes!*" she screamed. "*Yes . . . yes . . . yes . . . yes . . .* She was running to the door. Talia was on her feet, the textbook crashing to the floor. David came from the kitchen, plate and towel in hand.

"Yitzak!" she screamed and threw open the door.

She was in his arms. "Oh . . . oh, God . . . Yitzak . . ."

The children surrounded them. They engulfed each other and fell to their knees in one embrace. A plate broke on the wooden porch.

Arie ben Kagan signaled for the sergeant to place her men near the house, and he walked, back up the hill to Rabbi Asher.

And the fruit is also sweet from our tears, he thought as his own fell on the sandy soil of the path.

~31~

The young Arab boy sat facing Achmed Sharit. He was the third to return to the apartment in Tiberias. Two more were still out scouting the surrounding settlements. As soon as the boy finished his report, Achmed paid him and left the city in his old Chevrolet. It was nearly 9:00 PM, and he knew he had to contact Valarian quickly. The wrath of his master was to be avoided at any cost. He had the information Valarian wanted.

He drove southwest toward Mount Tabor. There was very little traffic on the road. After five minutes without seeing another vehicle, he pulled off the road among a stand of trees. He took his satchel and walked up a hill, away from the road. It was a clear, starry night. The air was crisp and cool.

He lay with his head to the north, once again covering the red arrowhead on the blanket with his body. As soon as his tongue touched the backward C on his shoulder he was in contact with Valarian.

"I have found them, Master. They are in a kibbutz called Ginnosar on the Sea of Galilee. It is a quiet place, but today and tonight there have been helicopters landing and leaving. Many soldiers from Migdal have also come to the kibbutz. A great deal of activity."

He then waited for his reward, and as his tongue glowed and flamed he sighed with joy.

"Rabbi Vogel will join us in the morning," announced Arie ben Kagan to the three Soviets seated in front of him. He then introduced Rabbi Asher to Peter Somoroff, Anya Somoroff,

162

and Leonid Chomsky. As they shook hands, the sound of the military helicopter could be heard landing on the beach. Arie continued after the introductions were completed. "The others are here. They will be with us in a moment. If this meeting goes well, then tomorrow I will take Colonel Somoroff to the chief of our intelligence service. But first I must be convinced. I trust you will understand our caution."

Peter Somoroff nodded his agreement. He expected to be questioned before the most secret man in Israel was revealed to him. General ben Kagan was known to him, to the KGB. Though they spoke of him many times as an adversary, Peter held the deepest professional admiration for General ben Kagan's accomplishments.

The sound of a jeep coming to a halt outside the trailer announced the arrival of Captain Gross and Sasha Andreyev. Now they could begin.

It was more of a negotiation than a conference. Arie asked Peter Somoroff to relate the entire story, and it was recorded on tape. He then asked each of the Soviets to tell their own version of the story from the time they became involved to the present moment. That too was taped. Then Rabbi Asher began to question Somoroff.

"You say that you were able to inflict pain on Colonel Valarian? Can you repeat the words that Rabbi Vogel taught you and indicate when you blew the shofar?"

Somoroff did as Asher requested. He could never forget those words.

"Now, if you can, will you do it once more, but this time tell me how Colonel Valarian reacted after each commandment. Please take your time . . . it is very important."

"Rabbi Asher, that is a day I will never forget. It is burned into my memory, action by action."

Peter again related the events of Yom Kippur in Valarian's office. No one other than Rabbi Vogel had heard the story before this night. Peter had only told them that it had been an amazing experience and that in time he would relate it to them. When he finished ben Kagan had a new respect for the KGB colonel. Rabbi Asher was the only one in the room who took it in stride. He wanted more details.

"He did not bleed until you said, 'Honor thy father and thy mother'?"

"That is correct."

"Tell me how he bled again."

"From the nose and mouth."

"Not the eyes?"

Peter closed his eyes and conjured up the image of Valarian at the moment he pronounced the fifth commandment. "Not the eyes, Rabbi. I am sure."

"And what was his position on the floor after the last commandment?"

Peter answered again. "He was lying on the floor in a pile . . . with his legs drawn up and his arms crossed over his face."

"Would you say that it was a fetal position? Think carefully."

"Yes . . . no! Not fetal. His arms covered his face, not his chest."

The rabbi smiled.

"Good . . . very good. One last question. When you left his office, what did the secretary do?"

"Why do you ask?" Peter was curious.

Asher glanced over at Arie, but the general was speaking already.

"Let us ask the questions, Colonel."

"Very well," Peter responded. "She said goodbye to me as though nothing had happened. I thought surely she must have heard the shofar and Valarian's screams, but she just sat there typing, looked up as I came out of the office, and said goodbye."

"Excellent," said Rabbi Asher. "She is not a disciple, then. If it were so she would have been devastated by the shofar."

"Is this important?" asked Michael Gross. He was caught up in the story and forgot that ben Kagan had told him to keep a low profile this first meeting. But Rabbi Asher was too excited and answered quickly.

"Very important. If what they say is true about that Karkov fellow, then there are only two disciples left in Russia. This man does not take disciples quickly."

Now Arie's curiosity was also peaked.

"Why only two? You said he could have five."

"Yes." Rabbi Asher was standing and moving about the room. "But he will always keep at least two disciples far from him. They are his long-range eyes and ears, and through them he can escape if necessary . . ." His voice trailed off as he realized he had said too much. Ben Kagan spoke to the Soviets.

"Is there anything else to tell . . . anything you think is important?"

Peter spoke up. "Yes, General. I have just spent several days in East and West Germany and France. There is more to the story, but . . . no one in this room knows these new facts except me. I will wait to see your superior to repeat that information."

Gross showed his annoyance at the arrogant Soviet colonel.

"Touché, Colonel," said ben Kagan. "I will make my report, and we shall see what tomorrow brings. Now, I think we have all had a long day and face perhaps a longer one tomorrow. Let's all rest." He stood and formally shook hands with the Soviet visitors.

"General?" Somoroff asked as ben Kagan was at the door. "Is Rabbi Vogel all right?"

Arie liked this Soviet. He was a compassionate man, as Rabbi Posner had said.

"Yes, Colonel. He is fine. You may be pleased to know that he is with his family tonight for the first time in over twelve years."

A big smile came to Somoroff's face.

"Good, General. Excellent. I will sleep well tonight."

The movement of the Al Fatah unit in the hills above the kibbutz and the deliberate underwater swimming of the PLO frogmen as they approached from the Galilee would give lie to that statement.

~ 32 ~

Lubyanka had been quiet since the departure of the people to Israel. Major Rosteveli had spent his time consolidating forces, finishing security checks on all KGB people in the wing, and interrogating the prisoners.

The morgue sergeant had told all he knew and was now safely under lock and key in the cell section. Captain Vladimir Zorbin, the Pushkin detective, had also been questioned in great detail. He too was on Metsky's payroll and had had no contact with Valarian. On the other hand, Dr. Brodsky, the tall ex-Chief of Psychiatric Medicine, had been able to identify at least one other enemy.

After Tania Karkov took her life, Brodsky had been under the control of the KGB psychiatric unit. He had cracked quickly, simply because he too had administered such interrogations, and he knew that no matter how strong the will, eventually everyone broke under the strain. Many became catatonic, useless vegetables for the rest of their lives. That was a fate he didn't want, so he decided to cooperate as soon as he saw that Somoroff had ordered the full treatment for him.

Rosteveli was not surprised when Brodsky told him that Dr. Karkov had mentioned a KGB captain whom Valarian and Metsky supplied with young boys. From her description Rosteveli knew it was Captain Viktor Servioff, an aide to Peter Somoroff. Several things now made sense to the major, including the death of Isadore Kantrowitz inside headquarters and the facility with which Somoroff's phones had been tapped.

He did not bring Servioff into Lubyanka immediately. Colonel Somoroff had instructed him to clear all overt actions with him unless it was critical. Servioff could wait, but Rosteveli swore to deal with the captain himself when the time came. He took Kantrowitz's death personally. Somehow he would make up for the heartache it had caused his lover, Fannie Beshevsky.

With everything secure in Lubyanka, he sent Captain Bonyon to Leningrad in a military medivac aircraft to bring the sedated Pushkin police sergeant Zalitski and his victim, Marina Grochenko, back to Moscow so that they too could be kept under secure conditions.

All that remained was to have Rabbi Posner met at the Moscow airport and kept under surveillance. He had arrived from Israel that afternoon via Beruit on a Şyrian airliner. The old man who had entered Israel as an Irish priest on a pilgrimage returned to the Soviet Union as a Moslem. He had played his role well, and there was no incident at the airport. Although Rabbi Posner could have remained in Israel, it was his own choice to return to Moscow. He had a congregation, small as it was, to serve. He felt that this was his place until all Jews in the Soviet Union were safe. But that was a day he feared he would never see.

When he arrived at the Great Synagogue of Moscow, Rosteveli was waiting with Fannie Beshevsky. The major dispersed several KGB men around and in the building, posting two of them outside the door of the small apartment that Rabbi Posner occupied. Fannie watched with amazement as Rosteveli greeted the old man warmly.

"I didn't think you would want to come back, Rabbi," he said.

Posner smiled and shrugged. "To tell the truth, I didn't. But what would my congregation do without me?"

"You should have stayed there, Rabbi. It was safe," said Fannie.

"And wonderful, Fannie—you should see it! Jewish soldiers . . . cities . . . farms—wonderful. Just wonderful."

"Did you see the others?" asked Rosteveli.

"No. I left before they came. I knew that the longer I stayed, the harder it would be to leave. But one wonderful thing I learned was that Rabbi Vogel's family is there. He should be with them by now."

Rosteveli was obviously pleased, and Fannie saw it in his face. She took his arm and squeezed it. He was a little embarrassed in front of the rabbi.

"You must be tired. I have my men all around here. No one will be allowed to see you unless you clear it with them."

The rabbi protested, but Rosteveli reminded him of poor Isadore Kantrowitz and the unscrupulous men they were battling.

"Do what the major asks," said Fannie, "please . . . for the congregation you came back to serve."

Rabbi Posner nodded his consent. "Fine. Perhaps I'll convert a few of them before this is over."

They all laughed. Rabbi Posner yawned.

"You get some rest, Rabbi," commanded Rosteveli. "We'll be in touch with you when we hear from Israel."

Fannie kissed Posner gently on the cheek with deep affection. "You have done a wonderful and courageous thing for us, Rabbi. No one will ever forget."

Rabbi Posner laughed. "No one will ever know," he said as he looked at Major Rosteveli. "Perhaps, Rabbi, perhaps. Who knows what the days ahead will bring?"

"Good night, Major. Good night, Fannie." The man was tired and showed his age.

The couple left the synagogue and drove toward Fannie's apartment. As they left, a GRU corporal, slumped down in the seat of his car, radioed his report to Major Metsky.

"The KGB major left with a woman. The rabbi is home, but there are at least seven KGB men guarding him."

Metsky thought for a moment. "Keep up your surveillance and report if anything changes."

He then called KGB headquarters and asked to be connected to Captain Servioff.

"Viktor?"

"Major Metsky. I haven't heard from you in over a week. It's quiet around here . . . boring, if you get my meaning?"

Metsky understood. "Yes. We will have to do something about that. But first I have a little mission for you."

Several kilometers to the north, Colonel Nickolai Valarian began the process of initiating a new disciple into his fold. The large, meaty body of Marshall Serge Malenkov, General

Secretary of the Party, lay naked on the black velvet cover of the bed. He was totally hypnotized and rigid. His breathing was slow and labored, and deep sighs emanated from his slightly parted lips. Five black candles were placed on the small table in the room. Four of them were lit. The fifth was without form, just a blob of wax.

Valarian studied the marshall. He circled the bed, reaching toward the huge body, touching it from time to time as though he were caressing a woman. He bent over the bed, and his long tongue slid out of his mouth and licked the marshall's shoulder. The big man shuddered and sighed. A small mark, a backward C, remained on his shoulder, half-way to the neck.

Valarian then went to the table and took the shapeless wax in his hands. It immediately became soft, and he flattened it into a circular sheet, taking care that it remained smooth. He laid the flattened wax over the center of the table covering the ivory pentangle. His eyes glowed deep red.

"I bring another to me."

The pentangle showed through the black wax as though it were transparent.

"He, like all, comes with a free will."

The center of the wax rose in a bubble that took the shape of the marshall's face. Valarian then touched the other four candles with his finger and they burst into flame.

"Know him as your brother, protector of our way."

The bubble face, a duplicate of the sleeping Malenkov's, slowly turned to face each of the candles. As it faced each, that candle burned a little brighter than the rest.

When the face had been presented to all the candles, Valarian carefully lifted the bubble and the remaining wax and brought it over to the bed. He beckoned with his free hand, and Malenkov sat upright. Then Valarian stretched the base of the bubble and fit it over Marshall Malenkov's head, like a mask. Inside, Malenkov's eyes popped open. He could not breathe, and his eyes grew larger as he sucked for breath that could not come through the tough wax. But he did not struggle. His chest swelled as he silently gasped and sucked at the pliable wax.

Valarian removed the black robe he wore and stood naked before the large man with the black wax head. The colonel's body, like his face, was badly scarred from burns. He moved to the bed and placed himself behind the seated marshall, gently kneeling so that his head was above Malenkov's. Their bodies touched. Malenkov stopped gasping and nestled back into Valarian, who took the marshall's head in his hands and bent it backward so that he looked down on it, upside down.

"I am your nourishment. I am your life. Come to me and you are with me forever."

Valarian slid his tongue through the wax into Malenkov's mouth, breaking the seal. A rainbow of colored fluid dripped down his tongue into the new disciple's mouth and through his body, which began to glow with the same rainbow of light.

The large marshall arched his back, as though in orgasm, thrusting his pelvis toward the ceiling. Still Valarian kept his tongue in the man's mouth, still the fluid flowed until it seemed to fill Malenkov's body and began to spill out of his mouth onto his black waxed face.

Valarian withdrew his tongue. He was in ecstasy. He placed his jade and silver oriental ring, which had the image of a dragon carved on it, on Malenkov's eyes, one at a time. The ring melted the wax over the eyes. Valarian then took the wax in his hands and lifted it from Malenkov's head. The large man fell back on the bed, still in a coma-like state.

Valarian removed the ring from the middle finger of his right hand and placed it on his left thumb with the face pointed downward. He pressed the ring into Malenkov's left shoulder between the mark he had previously made and the neck. Then he covered the ring with his other hand and pressed hard. The marshall screamed. Valarian quickly slid the ring, with both hands still pressing on it, down the marshall's heavy body to his penis. A red scar was left in the wake of the ring, stretching from the man's shoulder to his genitalia. As soon as the ring touched his penis, the screaming stopped and a sigh of pleasure came from him.

Valarian withdrew from the bed. Malenkov was in a deep sleep. He went back to the small table and fashioned the wax into a candle, carefully placing it at the fifth point of the pentangle, recently vacated by Misha Karkov.

"And now you are mine forever, Marshall Serge Malenkov. Forever."

He touched his hand to the wax, and it burst into flame like the others. On the bed, the general secretary stirred as though waking from a deep and restful sleep.

~ 33 ~

No one could approach Kibbutz Ginnosar undetected. It was strategically located close to Syria. The approaches across the Galilee were constantly monitored. Several sophisticated listening devices had been carefully placed to assure early warning of an attack on the kibbutz.

The pretty commando sergeant joined Arie ben Kagan, Rabbi Asher, and Michael Gross as they crossed the center compound after leaving the trailer.

"We have trouble, General," she reported.

"How much?" Arie asked as they continued to walk.

"Two Al Fatah squads on the hill above the dock. One more crossing the road to the south."

"Heavy weapons?"

"Yes, sir. Rockets and mortars. Snipers with night scopes. Automatic weapons."

"Very well. They will wait until we are settled in for the night."

He ordered Gross back to the trailer, instructing him to take the Soviets to the bomb shelter under the main dining hall.

"Walk slowly, Michael. When you move them be sure it looks casual. Don't group together. Keep close to the buildings."

Gross stopped, bent to tie his shoe, then walked back toward the trailer.

Ben Kagan continued walking with the sergeant.

"Tell Major Horowitz to disperse as planned. I want prisoners. Tell our snipers with the infrared scopes to stay in place."

A beeper sounded on the sergeant's belt. She took a small radio from her pocket.

"Steiner here."

A voice cracked back at her. "They are coming from the sea, too. We have at least three frogmen heading toward the trailer."

Ben Kagan smiled. Few people knew the extent of the Israeli defense system. Every inch of border, every inch of shoreline was monitored twenty-four hours a day, above and below the surface.

"Tell them to put our own people in the water. I definitely want one of those frogmen alive."

The sergeant relayed the order, then left the general as he and Rabbi Asher continued toward their quarters in the guest house.

Gross knocked on the trailer door, then opened it.

"Everyone get up quietly. No lights. We must leave immediately."

None of the Soviets had gone to bed yet. Peter Somoroff jumped to his feet as Gross turned out the lights.

"What's going on, Captain?" he demanded.

"Please, Colonel, we don't have much time. Our friends, the PLO, are about to pay us a visit. We must leave now!"

As he spoke he heard the muffled sound of a mortar firing. He sprang into action.

"Down on the floor. Fast!"

The round was long, exploding on the beach past the trailer.

"Now, out of here—quickly. The next round will be on us."

They were out the door, following the Israeli captain as he ran a zigzag course along the buildings toward the dining hall.

When the mortar round exploded, Arie ben Kagan was surprised. It was too early. He felt stupid. The longer they remained at war with their neighbors, the less predictable and more proficient the enemy became. The second round was a direct hit on the trailer. He prayed that Gross had been efficient.

Major Chaim Horowitz reacted fast. He was the commander of a crack commando battalion. He crouched in a bunker near the docks and barked orders into his walkie-talkie.

"Get that mortar. I want all the snipers to concentrate on it. And watch below the road. They have a rocket launcher down there."

All of the lights were out in the kibbutz. Suddenly a flare burst above the dock area, illuminating a group of Israeli frogmen as they crouched adjusting their equipment. One by one they fell to accurate rifle fire.

"Damn," Horowitz muttered to himself. Then he spoke into the radio again.

"Avram . . . Avram? Where the hell are you?"

"We're behind them now, Chaim. They have begun early. We're ready now."

"Then for God's sake hit them—hard—push them down to us."

Avram Leiter immediately ordered his commandos into action. They had taken positions behind the attackers, but they were below them, firing up toward the top of the hill. The enemy was prepared, and a whole squad opened fire down on the commandos, pinning them in place.

Captain Leiter sized up the situation quickly. He was on the radio again, crouching behind a large rock, cursing the enemy.

"Honey Bear . . . Honey Bear . . . this is Stick. . . . Get those gunships up here fast—and I mean fast . . ."

Honey Bear was back to the captain immediately. He was Lieutenant Jonas Balek, helicopter pilot and commander of the two gunships that hovered three miles to the west of the hill.

"Okay, Avram . . . I copy. Here we come."

Even as Balek spoke, Avram could hear the whine of the chopper motors, or at least he imagined he heard them. He twisted over and watched for their approach. In less than twenty seconds he spotted them rising over the hilltop behind him.

Back on the dock the Israeli frogmen were all dead or wounded. Major Horowitz watched the trailer take two direct hits and disintegrate. Then rocket fire came from below the road leading to the main gate of the kibbutz. Another flare burst above the dock.

Anya Somoroff ran alongside Michael Gross. Peter Somoroff and Sasha were close behind. Chomsky, who had never been in combat before, took up the rear. He was frightened. The smell of cordite and gunpowder filled the smoky air. The light from the flares threw eerie shadows across the compound. As the group passed a building that housed the fish processing plant a rocket scored a direct hit. The concussion threw Leonid to the ground, and he was splattered with chunks of fish. At first he thought he was wounded, but when he reached to touch his supposed wounds and felt and smelled the source of his fear, it brought a smile to his lips.

Ahead of him, Michael Gross had thrown Anya Somoroff to the ground and covered her with his body. Peter did the same for Sasha. Thank you, thought Peter to himself when he saw the courageous deed that Gross had performed

Arie ben Kagan and Rabbi Asher had never reached the guest house. When the first mortar hit, Arie had grabbed the rabbi and directed him toward the dining hall. As they ran down the hill past the living quarters, General Kagan was pleased to see that Selma Vogel was leading Rabbi Vogel and their children toward safety, too. Both kids had their weapons at port arms. The oldest, Talia, was firing her carbine up toward the Arab positions as she ran. Before they reached the dining hall, both children left their parents and moved to their assigned positions inside the compound.

Now, with most of the young children and older people safe in the shelter below the dining hall, General ben Kagan took a position behind the water pump at the rear of the building and watched Michael Gross and the Soviets approach. He was again pleased when they got up after the hit on the fish factory. They were only fifty yards away when the second rocket swooped into the compound and totally destroyed the Vogel home.

From cover near the base of the hill, Avram Leiter blew his whistle and his commandos withdrew away from the devastating Arab automatic weapons fire. Two of his soldiers were hit. He screamed for the medics and directed them to the wounded soldiers.

Lieutenant Jonas Balek banked his Cobra gunship to the left and released a rocket package. Five seconds later the top of the hill was an inferno. The machine gunners on both ships raked the hilltop with thirty-caliber gunfire. The second gunship, piloted by Lieutenant Miriam Felder—the famous "Angel of El 'Arîsh," who had been responsible for the evacuation under fire of fifteen wounded tankers in the Yom Kippur

War—banked off to the right and turned to face the hill from below. She fired a cluster of phosphorus rockets directly at the Arab positions, but as she fired, a ground-to-air missile was launched by the Al Fatah at her Cobra. Her rockets and the missile exploded simultaneously. Jonas muttered a prayer as he watched her gunship disintegrate and fall to the ground.

Then his radio crackled again, and Captain Leiter spoke. Since he was on the opposite side of the hill he had not seen Miriam's chopper go down.

"That did it, Jonas. Miriam nailed them. . . . We can take it from here."

Jonas Balek had little time to answer the captain. Major Horowitz was on the radio immediately.

"Jonas, get down toward the road. To the left. They have a rocket launcher down there, and Steiner can't get to it. Copy?"

"Yes, sir," answered a stunned Jonas Balek. "Did you see Miriam?"

Major Horowitz answered slowly and sadly. "Yes, I saw her. . . . She's gone. She got them . . . God bless her."

Jonas swung his Cobra toward the road with a vengeance as Captain Leiter signaled for his commandos to move up the hill and clean out the remaining attackers.

The explosion on top of the hill and the destruction of the gunship startled Peter Somoroff. He knew in his bones that this attack was for his benefit . . . that it was meant to destroy his mission. Michael Gross was on his feet pulling Anya by the hand behind him and yelling back to the others.

"Let's move—that way . . . to the dining hall. . . . Hurry . . ."

Peter grabbed Sasha by the hand and followed. Leonid Chomsky came from behind and took Sasha's other hand when he noticed that she was bleeding from the leg. Even though she was supported by both men, she fell as her right leg buckled. Peter looked down and saw the blood. He motioned for Leonid to help him pick her up. Both men carried her toward the dining hall.

When Major Horowitz saw Balek's gunship swoop down below the main gate toward the road he felt better. Jonas unleashed his second cluster of rockets and followed in with napalm. That will take care of that, thought Horowitz, turning his attention to the seashore. He knew the Arab frogmen were still in the water and still a threat.

"Shmul," he called on the radio. "Shmul . . . what's your position?"

Shmul Kantor—formerly Sam Kantor of Stamford, Connecticut—drifted with his engines off about three hundred yards off the kibbutz dock. He was out of range of the mortars, and the rocket squad that was below the kibbutz was unable to see him. His powerful patrol boat had been placed to intercept a possible escape route across the Galilee.

"I'm here, Major . . . due east about three hundred yards."

"Good. They have three or four frogmen in the water. Their last position was about seventy yards offshore directly in front of the trailer."

"The trailer is gone," answered Shmul, "but I have the position."

"Okay. Keep your engines off and watch the beach if you can. I want those bastards to think we don't know about them. I will move some troops to the beach as soon as that rocket squad is silenced. How many frogmen do you have aboard?"

"Two," answered Kantor.

"Good," replied the major. "Stand by, and be ready to turn on your underwater lights."

Down near the road, three of Sergeant Steiner's squad were wounded, two dead. The gunship had done the trick and silenced the rocket launcher, but the enemy had taken defensive positions. Several of them were still alive and hidden in the rocks below the road. The young sergeant had a piece of shrapnel in her left arm. As she bound the wound with a khaki bandage, she motioned for her B team leader to join her. He moved quickly among the rocks and was at her side in a moment.

"You're hit?" asked the corporal.

"A nick, not serious . . . Listen. I want you to take your squad and cover the road and below. Cut them off. Major Horowitz wants some prisoners, so we will wait them out. As long as the rocket is out of business, we can sit here. Okay?"

"I have only seven men left," answered the corporal, a young sabra. He was enjoying the fight. "How many prisoners does he want?"

"A few—an officer is possible."

"You have it!" The corporal smiled and moved off to his

men. In five minutes they were in position, and the young corporal was making his plans to capture an Arab officer.

The kibbutz was suddenly as quiet as it had been before the firefight began. The Soviets led by Michael Gross never made it to the dining hall. The attack stopped when they were a few yards short of their goal. General ben Kagan ran out to greet them.

"Is she wounded?" he asked, motioning toward Sasha Andreyev.

Peter answered. "Yes, in the leg. It missed the bone."

Arie knelt and examined the wound as Sasha sat on the ground holding her left calf. Leonid knelt next to her, allowing Sasha to squeeze him around the neck as the pain of the wound grew more intense. Ben Kagan shouted for a medic.

"You'll be all right, Miss Andreyev," he said in a comforting voice. "It did miss the bone."

"Have they gone?" asked Anya, still shaken from the action and holding on to Michael Gross.

"No . . . but they are subdued," answered ben Kagan.

The smoke was clearing from the compound. A few cracks of gunfire came from the hill above. Peter Somoroff looked up in that direction.

"Those are our weapons," assured ben Kagan. "Mopping up."

People began to move about the kibbutz, clearing debris and moving to new defensive positions outside the perimeter of the compound. Peter was impressed with the efficiency of the Israelis.

"You knew they were coming?" he asked ben Kagan.

"No . . . but we knew when they arrived. How does it feel to be fired upon with your own weapons, Colonel?"

"I recognized them—not pleasant." His voice drifted; he didn't know exactly what to say.

"Let's have a cup of coffee and unwind, if we can," said Arie. A medical crew had arrived and was removing Sasha, now on a stretcher, toward the kibbutz infirmary. Leonid started to go with her, but Michael stopped him.

"She will be okay, Lieutenant. It's better if you stay with us." As he started to object a burst of gunfire was heard from the road below.

"Isn't it over?" asked Chomsky.

"It's never over," answered Gross.

The group moved quickly toward the dining hall.

Major Horowitz was now on the beach directing a squad of men to positions along the shoreline.

"Stay down and watch for breaks in the surface. Keep flat. Look for bubbles . . . any disturbance."

Offshore, the three frogmen were confused. The firing had stopped too soon, before they were able to reach the beach. They lay on the sandy bottom communicating with hand signals and by touch. The leader, a stocky man, fumbled along his weighted belt and removed a small flashlight. He cupped the lens in his hand and lit it. He checked his watch. It was too soon for the fight to be over. Either the early attack had taken the Jews by surprise, or . . . or they had been ready. In either case he had to know. After turning out the light he motioned for one of his men to move toward the beach. The frogman swam slowly ahead. The two others followed. They had trained as a unit and could anticipate each other with certainty. Their cautious movements were rehearsed.

Below the road, Corporal Ahron ben Levi finished placing his squad in position. The road was blocked and the ground below the Arab position sealed off. A squad of Captain Leiter's men had joined his own. Seventeen Israeli commandos had the enemy trapped, with the only route of escape toward the sea. Lying flat, Corporal ben Levi slipped his cartridge belt off and loosened the sling on his Uzi machine gun. His face was blackened and glistened from sweat and grease. He tucked his blond hair under the wool stocking cap and removed his boots. Then he checked himself for any loose or shiny objects. Satisfied, he crawled over to a commando nearby.

"David," he whispered.

A commando peeked out of a foxhole. "Ahron? That you?"

"Yes. Look, I'm going in there to have a look at them. You take the squad. Just hold your position, and if any of them run, try to grab one—but don't let any get away . . . okay?"

"You sure you should go in there? We have them trapped . . . why don't we just wait?"

"Just do as I say. I have my reasons."

David Blumberg knew his squad leader well. Ahron ben Levi's brother had been a hero of the Six-Day War, and the younger ben Levi's ego drove him to top his brother. The other soldiers in the unit liked the young, blond corporal, but they thought he was slightly crazy when it came to heroics. He took too many chances, but always with his own life; he never endangered his men.

"Be careful," chided Blumberg. "Those are PLO Tiger Cubs out there—they love to castrate Jews."

Ahron smiled and took a halfhearted swing at David. "You just watch the perimeter and keep them in there. I'll be back."

He crawled off toward the Arab positions as David Blumberg moved in an opposite direction to warn the others that Ahron was going in.

The lead frogman carefully broke the surface and looked toward the beach. He was in four feet of water and his flippers rested gently on the sandy bottom. He slid off his mask and peered into the darkness. Beyond the beach he watched the activity inside the kibbutz compound. The Israeli's had beaten off the attack, he knew that immediately. He slipped on his mask and dropped under the surface to join his companions.

Shmul's voice on the radio gave Horowitz the message. "I spotted one of them about thirty yards offshore, just in front of the trailer area, Major."

Major Horowitz trained his infrared binoculars toward the designated area and saw the water ripple as the frogman dipped under the surface.

"Okay, Shmul . . . we have them . . . about thirty yards off the trailer. Do you copy?"

"Yes, Major. I have them in my scope."

"Good. Okay, let's go. Try to get me a prisoner."

Shmul Kantor turned the ignition and the twin diesels roared into action. He hit a switch on the control panel and the underwater lights flashed on, illuminating the water in front of the patrol boat for twenty yards. He threw the clutch, and the sleek speedboat leaped ahead. Within seconds it was up to forty knots, heading straight for the beach in front of the destroyed trailer. At the same moment, large spotlights were turned on above the beach and aimed at the exact spot where the frogman was spotted. A loud siren sounded to add to the confusion.

Below the water, the frogmen were confused. Their leader knew they had been spotted—they had to get out of the lights and into deeper water fast. Then he heard and felt the sound of the patrol boat. He spun around to see the underwater lights coming straight for him and his men. He tried to get their attention, but they panicked and were swimming frantically away from the oncoming speedboat. He flicked his flippers and dove to the bottom, where he dug rapidly into the sand and, lying on his back, began to cover himself with sand and rocks.

Above, Shmul Kantor saw the two frogmen swimming away from him. He slowed the engines and, keeping them in his light, signaled for the two Israeli frogmen to get ready to drop over the side. Before he could position the boat, however, the Arabs turned and, realizing they were trapped, surfaced and began firing at the boat. Shmul cursed them and ducked. In a few seconds both frogmen were dead from sniper fire from the shore. He eased the boat near the bodies and ordered the Israeli frogmen to pick them up. When the bodies were aboard he turned off the underwater lights and radioed to Major Horowitz.

"We have two of them—dead. Your guys are trigger-happy over there."

"They had orders, Shmul. You okay?"

"We're all right. I'm going to leave our men out here for a while, just in case there are some more. Turn out those spotlights."

"Good idea . . . but do it quietly. They may be watching."

Shmul spoke to the two Israeli frogmen for a moment and turned the patrol boat parallel to the shore. They were in darkness again. He lined the boat up with the destroyed trailer and then dropped the frogmen over the side away from the shoreline. The two men slipped into the water quietly and sank to the bottom. One of them held a small sonar device, pointing it toward the shoreline.

Arie ben Kagan sat with the Soviets in the dining hall and sipped his coffee. He had a radio nearby and listened to Major Horowitz and the patrol boat. Somoroff was fascinated at the sophistication and coordination of the Israelis. Chomsky

glanced around the large hall and watched groups of commandos as they sat and relaxed after the firefight. He felt a new
respect for a people he had always been told were cowards.
He now knew that was a lie, and he wondered how Soviet
soldiers would fare against these tough commandos.

At a table nearby, Michael Gross brought Anya Somoroff a
cup of tea and continued to calm her. She was quite pretty.
Gross was attracted to her. He spoke to her in Russian for the
first time. Before this he had only spoken English.

"Feeling better?" he asked.

She answered, "Yes, thanks," and then realized he had
spoken her language. "You speak Russian?" she immediately said.

"Yes, Miss Somoroff. My grandfather was from Kiev."

"Does this kind of thing happen often here?" she asked.
Her voice was still subdued and her legs shook slightly.

"Not often, but the potential is always there."

"How do you live with it?"

"We live. Someday there will be peace."

"It's awful." She was sincere. He felt her compassion and
liked her even more.

Corporal Ahron ben Levi passed his second Arab. He
wanted an officer, and both men had obviously been too
careless to hold a rank. He lay under an outcropping of
porous rock and listened carefully. The noise from the beach
had stopped, and he knew he had to be extra-quiet now. Off
to his left he heard a body shift position. Then, from the same
direction a soft whisper in Arabic, which he understood.

"Ali . . . pass the word. Three minutes and we will break
toward the road. On my command."

Got you, you bastard, thought ben Levi. He slid a blackjack from his sock and twisted the leather strap around his
right hand. Then he began to count seconds off to himself.
Around him he heard the Tiger Cubs preparing to make a run
for it. He marked their positions and prayed that his squad
was ready for their rush. His only interest was in the man off
to his left. The Israeli corporal judged that the man would be
first up and would run right, toward the road. That meant he
would pass just above the outcropping where ben Levi would
be a one-man reception committee.

• • •

On the sea floor, the frogman leader carefully brushed the sand and rocks from his rubber suit. Several minutes had passed, and the silence reassured him that the Israelis had left. The darkness was friendly. He oriented himself away from the shoreline and began to swim slowly out to sea. When the Israeli frogmen grabbed him he thought for a moment that he had hit a rock or a fish. Then he felt their hands and knew he had been trapped. Both Israelis gripped the frogman firmly and rushed him toward the surface. As they broke through into the night air they felt their prisoner go limp in their hands. He had swallowed his poison capsule and died instantly. One of them shouted toward the shore, and the spotlights picked up the sight of the frogmen as they pulled the dead man toward the beach.

Avram Leiter completed the mop-up on the hill. There were no prisoners. Most of the invaders were burned beyond recognition from the phosphorus rockets Miriam had fired from her gunship, before she was hit by the missile. He radioed the news to Major Horowitz, then set up a perimeter of defense and walked down toward the kibbutz.

As ben Levi's counting reached two minutes and fifty seconds, he heard the Arab officer rise and issue a command. The remaining Al Fatah were on their feet all around him opening fire toward the road and running in that direction. He immediately heard David Blumberg's squad fire back. Good, he thought. That will keep them busy. He crouched, sensing the approach of the Arab officer. At the moment of truth he leaped up and knocked the man down. Then he swung the blackjack wildly in the direction of the man's head. Before the stunned Arab could regain his footing, ben Levi heard the crunch of his weapon as it made contact. He then draped himself over the unconscious man and waited for the firing to stop. Ten minutes later he yelled toward the road for David Blumberg to bring a stretcher. He had Major Horowitz's prisoner.

Down on the beach, in the harsh spotlights, Major Horowitz pulled the mask from the dead frogman. His first surprise was that the man was older than one might expect. The second was that he had blond hair and blue eyes. Not very typical for an Arab.

"And who are you, my little dead water baby?" Horowitz spoke aloud. "Did they send a Soviet to kill Soviets?"

He ordered two men to take the dead man to the infirmary, then he turned to his second-in-command.

"Secure the beach and take care of those men on the dock. Tell Shmul to patrol for another hour and then have him report to me in the armory. I'll be in the dining hall for a while if you need me." Then he activated the radio. "Sergeant Steiner? How is it?"

"Under control, Major. They tried to break out, but we stopped them."

"Any prisoners?"

"Yes, sir. Three. Two Cubs, wounded, and an officer with a headache."

"Good. Bring them to the armory. I'll be along in a few minutes."

He walked briskly toward the dining hall to report to General ben Kagan.

~34~

DIA headquarters in Washington had been appraised of the raid on Kibbutz Ginnosar. Andy Taft waited in the American Embassy in Tel Aviv for their reply. He wanted to get up to Galilee fast once he heard that Sasha Andreyev had been wounded. He was growing fond of her.

The message came via satellite just before noon. Andy waited with the cryptographer and read the transmission as it was decoded.

RE GINNOSAR ATTACK. STRONG DIPLOMATIC OBJECTIONS WILL BE RAISED THIS PM AT UNITED NATIONS. PRESS INFORMED OF DETAILS. EXPECT HEAVY COVERAGE. TWENTY-EIGHT SENATORS SENDING STRONG MESSAGE TO SOVIET TRADE MISSION. ADVISE PROGRESS OF PROJECT FLAME AS IT DEVELOPS. SIGNED— BURGESS/COUNTERSIGNED—SUPERBOWL

The countersignature meant that the chief of DIA was personally involved in Flame. Andy put the message in his safe and called Israeli intelligence to request a helicopter to take him up to Galilee. An hour later he was dropped off on the beach near the dock at Kibbutz Ginnosar.

Earlier that morning, while Major Horowitz was questioning the Arab officer, General ben Kagan ate breakfast with Peter Somoroff. Afterward they stopped by the infirmary to see how Sasha was feeling. She was still asleep, but the

doctor told them she would be able to move around by
evening.

Ben Kagan then took Colonel Somoroff to view the body
of the dead frogman.

"We don't think he's an Arab, Colonel."

"Who do you think he is?"

"A Soviet, to be honest." Ben Kagan studied the KGB
officer.

"General, anything is possible in this world. Perhaps I can
help you to identify him?"

Ben Kagan was delighted. He had hoped the colonel would
offer his help, but he knew it was a long shot.

"Perhaps you can," Arie answered quickly. "We will get
you a set of his fingerprints and a complete set of dental
x-rays. Then when you return to the Soviet Union you can
trace him . . . if he is one of your people."

"I doubt that he is KGB," said Peter. "We don't use
frogmen in our line of work—not on staff, anyway." He
smiled at ben Kagan and continued. "Might I make a
suggestion?"

"Please."

"Why not have Mr. Taft send the data to Washington?
They can pass it on to Miss Andreyev's contact at the Soviet
Embassy. He will be able to order a computer search of our
military—I suspect the Navy will be most fruitful—and get an
answer for us tomorrow."

Arie put his hand on Somoroff's shoulder. "I had hoped
you would suggest something like that. Thank you."

"There are no thanks necessary. I want to know if he is a
Soviet as much as you do."

"I think it's time for you to meet the head of the Mossad,"
ben Kagan said to Somoroff. He motioned him toward the
door. Both men left the infirmary and walked up the hill
toward a small building beyond the guest house.

Once inside the one-room house, ben Kagan closed the
door and turned to face Peter Somoroff.

"This is the meeting you wanted," he said, staring directly
into the Soviet's eyes.

"It's you?" Peter was surprised.

"Yes. A few months ago there would have been another
man in this room. Now he lies in a small cemetery near
Beersheba. An old clockmaker who died in his sleep. Perhaps

his countrymen will never know how much he did for Israel.''

"We are in a sad business, General."

"Yes, well . . . So it is my decision. I believe you. I believe your story. We will try to help the premier."

"Thank you."

"All I can do is hope to arrange for us to have a hearing in Zefat. Rabbi Asher's people are there. It's all very secret—even to us—but they are the ones to help you . . . if they will. I can't promise anything. I can't order them to help."

"May I ask why?" Somoroff felt slightly defeated.

"They live in another world. Sometimes I think that the religious fanatics are as much trouble as you atheists. There is no middle ground. They live a life of mystical seclusion. This group in Zefat is the most secretive. We can only try."

"When can I see them?"

"Tomorrow. We will travel up there today, but I know that Miss Andreyev will have to remain. Also your daughter. They will not allow women. They will not allow Lieutenant Chomsky either. It will be you and me. Vogel and Asher will go ahead of us."

"Fine."

"I want them to go down to Tel Aviv as soon as Miss Andreyev can travel. Captain Gross will take care of it."

"He is a brave man," said Somoroff. "He took good care of Anya last night. I appreciate that."

"Yes. He is good. I also think he is getting a little sweet on your daughter . . . if I may say so?"

Somoroff laughed. The general certainly spoke his mind.

"I noticed that myself, General. Imagine a colonel in the KGB with a Jewish son-in-law in Israeli intelligence? What is the world coming to?"

"Perhaps a better place, Colonel. . . . It's a thought."

Peter looked at the man who had revealed one of the most closely guarded secrets in the State of Israel to him moments ago. He genuinely liked him and had the deepest respect for him, too.

"Perhaps it is becoming a better world, General," he responded, "and maybe we are going to help it along in that direction."

"Maybe . . ." ben Kagan remarked softly. "Maybe . . ."

They left the small house and walked down toward the guest house where Rabbi Sholem Asher waited with Rabbi Vogel.

On the opposite side of the small house a section of siding slid open, and a small man, bald except for a rim of white hair, wearing a grey shirt and black work pants, slipped out of the hidden opening. Although the house appeared to have only one room, there was actually a small narrow enclosure that ran its length. Anyone inside that enclosure could hear the conversation in the house.

The old man walked slowly away in the opposite direction from ben Kagan and Somoroff. He was pleased with his subordinate's performance. No, he mused, I am not a clockmaker any more . . . and I am certainly not dead yet . . . but it is true that when the time comes, I will be buried near Beersheba. Until that day he would remain the most secret man in Israel and, as the head of the legendary Mossad, one of the most powerful.

Michael Gross walked along the beach with Anya Somoroff. The sun was warm, the water calm and smooth. The boats had long since left the dock and were out fishing on the Galilee. Only Shmul Kantor's patrol boat remained moored at the end of the dock. Two crewmen were on duty, operating the boat's radar and sonar.

"Do you know about this place?" asked Michael, sweeping his hand out toward the sea.

"You mean the Galilee? Yes, I know about it. It was where Jesus lived and performed his miracles." Anya would never forget the stories her grandmother had told about Jesus and the Holy Land. She would tell the old lady about her visit someday, and she knew the woman would delight in knowing her grandchild had actually seen the blessed place.

"Are you a religious person?" Gross was curious.

"No," answered Anya, "not at all. But my grandmother is. She goes to church every day. She prays for my brother."

Anya stopped. It was the first time she had thought of young Peter Somoroff in several days. She felt suddenly very sad.

Michael didn't understand. "Is something wrong? Did I say something?"

"I was just thinking about my brother . . . about his

dying . . .'' She began to walk again. "It's so calm and beautiful here this morning, so peaceful . . . I forgot about last night for a moment. I forgot about a lot of things." She looked at Michael.

"Was he a good man, your brother?"

Anya thought it was a strange question. "What do you mean? He was my brother. I loved him."

"I just wondered if you knew him. Your father said that he was stationed far to the east and that you were in school . . . so I just wondered if you had time to know him."

"It's a strange question."

"Yes. I—" Gross hesitated. He wasn't sure how the pretty Soviet would take what he wanted to say. He wasn't sure if he should say it at all because it went against everything he had learned and felt about the Soviets. He stopped and sat down on the warm sand.

"Come," he said as he reached out his hand to Anya. "Sit down for a moment. We have time."

Anya sat beside him. Michael kept her hand in his. She didn't pull away. It felt good to her.

"Your father and General ben Kagan will share many secrets in the next few days. Many things that even I don't know about."

"Me, too," said Anya. "I'm not in the KGB, you know."

"I know. Let me talk for a minute. It's that I have spent time traveling to many places . . . I have been a busy man. A man with a purpose, with a country to defend. I think you understand that now."

Anya nodded and looked down the beach at the destroyed trailer.

"I understand a lot more than I did yesterday."

"Good. I asked you about your brother because I—we— forget that our enemies are people sometimes . . . that they have families . . . that they hurt like we do. They are our enemies, so who cares?"

He sifted the bright sand through his large hand and gently squeezed her with his other hand.

"You care," she said.

He looked at her and frowned. "No. Not really. I don't care about those bodies we brought in after the attack. They are the enemy, and they wish to destroy us. If their wives and mothers weep today, I don't care. We lost twelve people last night. There are wives and mothers weeping here, too."

"So what are you trying to say, Michael? I am an enemy too."

"That's the problem. Are you? Your country is, I'm sure of that, but . . . are you? Here we sit by Galilee, and you tell me that your grandmother told you about God and Jesus—it doesn't make any sense to me."

"What doesn't make sense, Michael? Say what you mean!"

"I can't. I don't know what I mean."

"Maybe you don't want to know."

Anya released his hand from hers. She stood and looked down at him.

"I like you, Michael, and it is confusing to me, too. But I can say it."

He stood quickly and grabbed her by the shoulders.

"You can say it because you don't have to kill people tomorrow. I may have to, and maybe it will be a Soviet. It might even have been your brother, if he were alive. Don't you see that?"

She looked up at the tall Israeli and saw that his eyes were filled with tears. There was anguish on his face. She slid her body toward him and he embraced her.

"Yes, I see that," she whispered, "but you didn't kill him. A Soviet did. Can't you accept the world the way it is?"

He held her away from him and looked at her young face. He felt himself drawn to her beauty.

"I accept it, believe me . . . I accept it. But the world you know, the world they have taught you about—it isn't the way things really are. Last night you saw the world as I know it, and it frightened you. Those were Soviet weapons they were firing at us . . . Soviet mortars . . . Soviet rockets. That is the world as I know it."

"And if you had to kill my brother—knowing he was my brother—would you?" she asked.

He answered without hesitation. "Yes. If he threatened my country, yes."

Anya moved away from him. She was frightened again. She was also sad and frustrated.

The moment was interrupted by the sound of an approaching helicopter. When Taft disembarked moments later, Gross went to greet him. Anya turned away and walked up the beach toward the infirmary. Perhaps Sasha needed her. She knew that Michael certainly didn't.

Leonid sat on the hospital cot watching Sasha eat lunch. The Israeli nurse had just left the room, and they were alone.

"Is there much pain?" He was concerned.

"No. They gave me a shot." She tasted the broiled fish. It was good.

"Do you want a taste?" she offered.

"No, thanks. I'm not hungry."

"The battle bothered you?" It was a friendly question, but Leonid was offended.

"What is that supposed to mean?" he snapped.

"Nothing, Leonid. It just scared the hell out of me. I was never near combat before, not a firefight anyway. Were you?"

"No." His tone softened. "It was frightening, wasn't it? It wasn't that I was scared . . . just overwhelmed a little. They were trying to kill us. I mean it was aimed at us specifically. Colonel Somoroff is sure of that."

The sun's rays filtered through the plain white curtains that covered the window of the stark, white room. The light bounced off the walls and brightened everything. It gave the room an antiseptic look, clean and sterile.

Sasha swallowed some food. She studied Chomsky. She thought it strange that two KGB agents, highly trained in the art of interrogation, could not get one another to speak the truth. The atmosphere of the room demanded truth.

"How did they know we were here?" she asked.

"The Israelis don't know. They feel that the prisoners they took really don't know either."

He reached into his pocket and took out a pack of American cigarettes.

"Where did you get those?" she asked. He offered one and she took it.

"Captain Gross gave them to me this morning. I like him."

"Yes," she said, "I like him, too. Did you see how he protected Anya last night? That was brave."

"Do you think I am a coward?" He was angry.

"Leonid, please . . . it has nothing to do with you. Being

in combat for the first time has to be frightening. I admit it,
why can't you?''

Chomsky got off the bed and walked to the window. He
watched Anya walking toward the infirmary from the beach.
''Anya's coming. Your American friend just arrived in that
helicopter. Gross is with him.''

Sasha Andreyev set aside her tray and lit the cigarette.
''Leonid, before she comes, tell me what is on your mind.
Please.''

He looked at her. The last thing he wanted to do was admit
his feelings about being afraid last night. Yet he felt he had to
talk to somebody.

''I was frightened last night. When I thought I was hit I
almost panicked. Then when I saw it was just pieces of fish I
felt stupid . . . like a coward.''

''You aren't a coward. You came and helped me when you
saw I was hurt. That's not a coward's way. Don't you see
that?''

''There's more. Later, when we were in the dining hall I
watched the Israelis, the commandos. They are without fear . . .
killers.''

''I disagree,'' she answered firmly. ''They have a purpose
and soil to defend. They have no choice but to fight bravely.''

''There is always a choice. I was in Kabul for two weeks. I
saw our soldiers there. I didn't see any combat, but the
Afghan tribesmen gave them a battle. One night I went out
and got drunk with a few officers from the GRU. They talked
about the resistance those shepherds put up against our elite
troops. It was fearful. They captured some and interrogated
them for days. They never broke.''

''What has that to do with these Israelis?''

''I looked into their eyes last night. There was a determination there that was like the officers in Afghanistan described.''

Sasha sat up in bed. She had missed something, and she
felt as though she had been seduced by the cordiality of the
Israelis.

''You mean,'' she began, ''that this is the enemy and we
are in his midst? I know about that. I've been in America for
two years.''

He moved close to the bed and glared at her. ''No. Not like
the Americans. We will never fight the Americans. But some-

day we may have to fight these people, and I don't think we could win—or if we did, we would pay a terrible price."

"But we *would* win." She was definite.

"Maybe. But remember Colonel Valarian and the story that Colonel Somoroff told about his visit to the GRU office. That is not stuff of this earth—it is supernatural."

"So you don't like the idea of coming here and asking these people to help us?"

"No. Can't you see it?" He was intense.

"See what, Leonid? Say it!"

He put his cigarette out and looked at Sasha. He began, "If Valarian is a supernatural being, or thing, or even the devil himself, then hasn't it occurred to you that his opposite might also exist? I am talking about God."

Sasha was shocked at the word. It had never occurred to her. It wasn't part of her vocabulary.

Leonid continued, "And what frightens me, my dear fellow communist, is that if this God exists, then surely it was He whom I saw in the faces of those soldiers. Perhaps they *are* chosen people . . . perhaps He walks with them. Think about that, Comrade!"

Anya Somoroff entered the room and was confronted by two stunned faces staring at her.

"Hi. You two look just like you just saw a ghost," she joked.

They were not in a joking mood.

Michael Gross and Andy Taft joined ben Kagan and Peter Somoroff at the guest house. They were just finishing their conversation with Rabbi Vogel and Rabbi Asher, who were about to leave for Zefat.

"I'll call you as soon as I have an answer," Asher said as he shook Arie's hand. Then he reached his hand to Peter Somoroff and grasped his firmly. Vogel did the same.

"Colonel, I hope my call is good news. I promise that I will try to convince them to see you, to hear your case. Until then, shalom."

"Shalom," answered Peter. "And thank you."

"How is Sasha?" Andy asked General Kagan after greetings were exchanged.

"She is fine. I expect she will be up and around later."

"Good," he said. "I have some news for you."

He handed Arie a copy of the DIA message without signatures. Ben Kagan read it carefully and passed it to Peter Somoroff.

"This should give the premier some more ammunition against Marshall Malenkov."

Peter read the message, then spoke. "It will not do much. This is PLO business, not Soviet. There will be a denial of involvement, the usual."

"Not if we can identify that frogman as a Soviet."

"What frogman?" asked Taft. "You didn't tell me anything about a frogman, Michael," he said to Gross.

Gross didn't answer, deferring to the general.

"We don't know who he is," said Peter Somoroff. "I suggested that the general give you the man's fingerprints and dental x-rays. You can send them to Washington and they can be passed to our embassy there. Perhaps he can be identified. If he is a Soviet, then the military computer will seek him out for us."

"You mean Valarian's record section?" Andy asked sarcastically.

"No, Mr. Taft," answered Peter. "This man is not in the Army. I am sure, if he is a Soviet, that he came from the Navy. Colonel Valarian won't see the request for several days."

"Fine," said Andy. "I want to see Sasha for a few minutes. Michael tells me that we are going back to Tel Aviv tonight."

"Colonel Somoroff and I will remain here overnight. The others will go back with you," answered Arie.

"Very good. If you have that material for me when we leave, I'll get it on the satellite tonight. We should have an answer in two days at the outside."

Arie sent Michael off to get the prints and x-rays. Andy went down to the infirmary to see Sasha. The remaining two men sat on the guest house porch, preferring to keep out of the sun. Peter watched Andy and Michael walk together.

"We have a good group here, General."

"Yes, excellent. Now let's hope that Rabbi Asher can convince those fanatics in Zefat how good we really are."

"Rabbi Vogel was there for some of it. They'll have to believe him." Peter sounded hopeful.

"Vogel has spent twelve years in your prisons. These men

may live secluded lives, but they are not fools. They will test him severely. I hope he has the strength."

"Does he really have to go with us now?" Peter asked. "One night interrupted by an attack isn't much of a reunion after twelve years."

Arie looked at the Soviet and smiled. "My dear Colonel Somoroff, without Rabbi Vogel there is no story. Asher alone could not convince them."

As ben Kagan fell silent, Peter watched Asher and Vogel get into a small truck and drive away toward Zefat.

~ 35 ~

The room was still dark although it was nearly eight AM. Major Rosteveli slept comfortably in Fannie Beshevsky's arms, his head resting on her matronly bosom. The phone startled him. It took a moment to orient himself in the darkness. Fannie stirred and hugged his face into her.

"That might be for me, Fannie."

She slid her body across his and reached for the persistent phone.

"Hello," she said sleepily. Then she was suddenly awake. It was Meyer Plotkin, one of the leaders of the Synagogue. She listened intently for a moment, then spoke. "I'll be there as soon as I can. Don't do anything."

She hung up. Rosteveli reached over and turned on the bedside lamp. "What is it, Fannie? What's wrong?"

Her face was white. Her breath was labored. He held her and tried to calm her.

"Tell me."

"That was Meyer Plotkin, the shamus—he takes care of the Synagogue every morning. He said that it has been desecrated. Rabbi Posner is gone. His apartment has been ravaged."

"What about the guards?" asked Rosteveli.

"They're dead. All of them *dead*!" she screamed in terror.

Serge Rosteveli was on his feet in a leap. "Get dressed. Fast."

He went to the phone and called Lubyanka. Captain Bonyon answered the private line.

"Bonyon? Take a squad of men and get over to the Synagogue. Take a medical team, too. Don't ask me any questions, just listen and do as I say. I want the place sealed off. No police. No GRU. No one except our people. I'll be there in twenty minutes.''

When he hung up he saw that Fannie had not moved from the bed.

"Fannie," he shouted, "get dressed. We have to find out what happened."

The woman shook herself back to reality and began to dress. "They took Rabbi Posner, didn't they," she said quietly.

"We can't be sure, darling. We have to see for ourselves."

When Rosteveli and Fannie arrived, Captain Bonyon had done as ordered. They found him in the sanctuary, standing amid overturned benches. The Torah scrolls were unwound, torn, and scattered around the room. The word *Yevrei*, Russian for Jew, was painted on the walls and over the ark. The captain had moved the dead KGB guards into the sanctuary and covered them with sheets from Rabbi Posner's apartment. Fanny was devastated. Rosteveli talked quietly to Bonyon.

"Is there any sign of the rabbi?" he asked the stunned captain.

"No, sir. We searched the entire building. We only found those bodies," he answered, pointing to the corpses placed neatly in a row against the front wall.

The major glanced at the bodies. He fought to contain his anger.

Fannie bent down near one of the Torah scrolls and began to roll it up onto its spindle.

"I want to show you something, Major," said Bonyon, walking toward the dead KGB men. Rosteveli followed.

When they reached the first body the captain bent over and removed the sheet covering the corpse. It was the detail corporal, hand-picked by the major. The man's throat had been cut and his tongue removed. He was naked, and on his stomach a Star of David was carved into his skin.

"Just like the Grochenko woman in Leningrad," remarked Bonyon.

"Are they all like this?" asked Rosteveli.

"Yes, sir. All six."

While he spoke Fannie took the scroll and walked to the ark to replace it. She held it in one arm while she opened the ark doors with her other hand.

"Six you say?" questioned the major. "There were seven men assigned to this detail."

Then Fannie screamed. The seventh man was stuffed into the ark. He too was naked and the star was carved on his abdomen. He also had the word *Yevrei* carved on his forehead.

Hatred welled up in Rosteveli as he held Fannie, trying to calm her hysterics.

"Captain," he called. "Get that man out of there and have someone take Mrs. Beshevsky to Lubyanka. I want her under our protection. Then get some more men down here to clean this place up. But keep it sealed."

He guided Fannie to the captain, then walked toward the front door.

"Major?" said Bonyon. "Where are you going?"

"To finish some old business. I'll see you later." He closed the door behind him, keeping the image of Isadore Kantrowitz sneaking through the same door, in his mind's eye.

Five candles flickered in the black chandelier above Valarian's desk. The old rabbi lay on the floor in front of him. His arms were bound tightly. He bled from a bad head wound. Valarian was pleased.

"Stand up, Jew," he commanded.

Posner didn't move. Even if he wanted to obey he did not have the strength to get up. The people who had roused him from his bed were brutal. He was sure ribs were broken, and he suspected his left ankle was also badly injured.

Valarian moved around in front of his desk and kicked the rabbi.

"Get up I said, you obscenity!"

"I can't," Posner answered weakly.

Valarian reached his foot out and hooked it beneath Posner's shoulder, then flipped him over on his back. The rabbi screamed with pain.

"Before I destroy you, you will tell me what your Jew-loving friends were doing in Palestine. They are dead now, so it doesn't matter."

"Dead?" Posner muttered. "Dead?"

"What were they doing there?" Valarian demanded.

"I don't know. I was only a go-between."

"Liar!" he bellowed.

Then one of the candles above him began to glow. A disciple was calling.

"Metsky," he shouted.

The major promptly opened the office door and entered the cold room. "Take this garbage downstairs and lock him up. I will deal with him later."

Metsky pulled Posner to his feet and dragged him out of the office. Valarian went to his shiny desk and lay down to receive his disciple's message. A few moments later, when Achmed Sharit reported the failure of the mission, he was glad he had kept the rabbi alive. Sharit then felt his master's wrath.

A cold chill gripped Viktor Servioff when he heard the pounding on his door. No one knew he was home. It was midday. The young boy who lay next to him was also startled.

"Who is it?" Servioff shouted.

"I'm afraid," said the boy. He got out of bed and began to search for his clothing.

"Stay here," commanded the KGB captain. "Who is it?"

The pounding continued. Servioff got out of bed and put on a robe. The pounding grew louder. He was afraid his neighbors would begin to complain. He moved quickly to the door and unlatched the bolt.

As soon as the door was free, Rosteveli burst into the room. The force of his entrance threw Servioff to the floor. Rosteveli was on top of him in a flash, smashing him in the face with his large fist. The big Georgian was incensed.

"You *filth*. I'll kill you, you miserable deviate."

The young boy, now dressed, tried to run past the major to the door, but Rosteveli caught him with one hand and threw him across the room, back toward the bedroom. The boy stayed where he fell, in a state of fright.

Rosteveli stood and pulled Servioff to his feet. The captain trembled in front of the large man.

"Major Rosteveli . . . what is it? Why are you doing this?" he whined.

Rosteveli reached down and grabbed him by the balls and twisted.

"I will only ask you once, so you better give me the truth, or I will rip them off."

The pain was extreme. Servioff's face contorted in agony.

"What . . . *what*?"

"Who told you to go to the Synagogue last night?"

"What . . . what synagogue . . . I don't—"

That was all he could say. Rosteveli squeezed and pulled at the same time, then threw the KGB captain against the wall on top of the boy.

The boy whimpered, but did not move.

Rosteveli took a knife from his pocket and opened it slowly.

"I am going to cut them out, one at a time. And you are going to eat them in front of your little lover here. Do you hear me?"

With all the pain, Viktor Servioff knew that the major meant to do what he said. He was panicked. His body began to shake uncontrollably. The boy slid out from under him.

"Stay where you are, sonny," the major commanded. "Stay with your playmate. I'll deal with you later."

Then Rosteveli had an idea. He grabbed the boy and held him by the hair.

"How would you like to be castrated, little man?"

"Please . . . please . . ." the boy whimpered. "I didn't do anything . . . please . . ."

"Who sent you here?"

"No one," he answered innocently. "I come here often. By myself."

The major grabbed the boy's pants and pulled them down in one quick motion. He pointed the knife directly toward his hairless crotch.

"You are about to be a soprano for the rest of your life, my little liar. Is a lie worth that?"

"No . . . *please* no . . ." The boy looked at Servioff, lying helpless on the floor beneath him.

"Then tell me who sent you here. Now!"

"Major Metsky—he sent me. He always sends me."

Rosteveli remembered the short GRU major from the Synagogue. He shoved the boy aside and bent down over Servioff.

"So it was Metsky. Servioff, you're a dead man. Get dressed."

He kicked the captain into action, handcuffing him to the frightened boy before they left. An hour later Rosteveli sent a prearranged message to Sasha Andreyev via the embassy in Washington. *"Call home. Flame is burning."*

~ 36 ~

The road north to Zefat was scenic. Mount Tabor rose above off to their left. Since it was a clear day, the highest mountain in Israel, snow-capped Mount Atzmon, stood out majestically in front of them. The late afternoon sun cast long shadows along the highway.

They had left Kibbutz Ginnosar after the Chinook helicopter took off with the rest of the group. Sasha was able to travel, and though Chomsky took their parting uneasily, he accepted Somoroff's order without argument. Peter knew Chomsky had something on his mind, but there was no time for discussion. He also sensed a strain between Gross and his daughter. Perhaps it was just the raid last night. Everyone's nerves were on edge.

An hour later they entered Zefat and drove directly to the building that housed the ultrareligious sect that followed the teachings of the ancient Rabbi David ben Zimrah.

The house was in an old part of Zefat where the architecture was mixed with Spanish and Moorish influences. Peter felt as though he were traveling back in time, to a long-forgotten world. It made him uneasy.

It was an old house, very worn. There were no lights visible from the narrow street. Ben Kagan parked the jeep in an alley adjacent to the house and turned the motor off. Suddenly there was absolute silence. Arie and Peter sat for a moment listening to nothing. It was eerie. Far down the alley, a door opened and warm light poured out against the wall, now blue after sunset. The familiar figure of Rabbi Sholem Asher came toward them. He carried an oil lantern and walked slowly until he stopped in front of the jeep.

"How was the trip?" he asked.

Peter and Arie got out of the jeep and came around to greet him.

"Peaceful, Rabbi. And how are you?" Arie asked.

"All things considered, I'm fine."

"Did they give you a hard time?" asked ben Kagan.

"Not as hard as they will give you and our Soviet friend here. They were upset that I didn't come through the proper channels, but they seemed to accept my explanation and Vogel's tale. The attack last night did the trick, I think. Come on, let's go."

"Now?" asked Peter, surprised that it was happening so fast. He had expected to spend the night in Zefat and present his case tomorrow.

"Right now. They are waiting. Do you have everything you need, Colonel Somoroff?"

Peter carried his attaché case and the small leather bag he had so carefully protected throughout the journey. It was evidence that surely would convince the rabbis, or so he hoped.

The five men seemed to be part of the room, frozen in their places at the end of the table. The room itself was dimly lit. Only three oil lamps burned on the far wall behind the old men. The other walls were not visible. Peter surmised that the room was larger than it now appeared.

The introductions were formal and in Hebrew. Peter understood only a few Hebrew words, but he distinctly heard ben Kagan's name and his own spoken. The man on the far left spoke first. His English was precise.

"We will speak in English, Colonel Somoroff. If during this meeting we must defer to Hebrew, please understand that it will be for clarification, not for secrecy. Also, we would like you, and General ben Kagan, to understand that we are not impressed by the plea of your premier. You are here because Rabbi Asher has been convinced that your experience with the man you call Valarian contains a certain particle of truth."

"It is all true," Peter interrupted.

The old man in the center turned his gaze to Peter Somoroff. Never in all his years of confrontation with men of power had Peter seen such eyes. They were deep black pools that burned right through him, as though they were lasers.

"Colonel." The old man's baritone voice cut through the air like a sword. "I am Rabbi Levi Lemach ben Abraham. I want you to understand that it was you who requested our council. This is our temple. These are our ways. General ben Kagan will tell you that he has never been here. Very few have. Many believe this is a place to be feared, to be avoided. Perhaps they are correct in that assumption. In any case, we do not assume truth, we search for it and try, with humility, to understand its meaning. Now, please sit down and tell us your story. Be precise. Take your time."

As Peter sat down in the chair at the end opposite Rabbi Abraham, he studied the other men from the temple. The man who had spoken first was the youngest. His beard was dark and not as long as the others'. Rabbi Abraham had a snow-white beard and a marvelous mane of long white hair. He wore a black skullcap. The two men to his left also had white beards. Both looked frail. One was nearly bald. They wore black, shawl-like coverings over their heads. The fifth man had dark, almost black skin. His beard was a mixture of grey and black, yet his eyes were light blue. He wore a small miter on his head. Peter could not make out the rest of their clothing. General ben Kagan sat to Peter's left. Rabbi Asher sat on his right, between Somoroff and the old men.

Peter spoke after all were seated. "Where would you like me to begin, Rabbi?" He addressed his question to Rabbi ben Abraham.

"Start with this man Menoff and the file. That was the beginning for you, wasn't it?"

Peter prepared to begin, then realized that someone was missing. "May I ask where Rabbi Vogel is?"

"He will join us later, if we need him." The answer was final.

Peter began. It took two hours to tell the complete story. He was careful and precise, referring to his notes several times. The rabbis never moved. They never took their eyes from his face. They never interrupted Peter, nor did they show any sign of acknowledgment. Yet Peter was sure that each of them could repeat his tale verbatim. He had never witnessed such concentration. It was as though he were speaking into a human sponge that absorbed words and stored them neatly within a billion cells.

When Peter had completed the story he carefully checked

his notes to be sure he had covered everything. Satisfied, he looked at Rabbi Abraham.

"That is all?" questioned the old man.

"No, Rabbi, there is more, but before I go on I would like to know what you think about Valarian."

The man with the miter spoke rapidly in Hebrew to Rabbi Abraham. Rabbi Asher entered the conversation. Peter understood none of it, and ben Kagan saw his confusion. He leaned over to Peter and tried a simultaneous translation.

"That one wants to throw you out. He says you are rude . . . no, excuse me, godless and lost and stupid. Sorry, Colonel. Asher is speaking on your behalf. The old man wants to know what you have in the leather case. . . . The other one isn't convinced, but Rabbi Abraham is curious. . . . Asher has told them you have told us that there is more . . . so . . . okay."

Rabbi Asher turned to Peter Somoroff. He was not friendly.

"Colonel Somoroff, Rabbi Zahor thinks you are a fool not to obey Rabbi Abraham's instructions, and he is annoyed with you. I suggest—"

Before Asher could finish his statement, Peter stood and faced the dark-skinned rabbi with the miter.

"Rabbi, I am sorry that I offended you, and I apologize for my actions. I have lost my son, my only son, to this maniac. I have come to believe things that I would never, in my wildest dreams, have imagined could be true. I have seen, with my own eyes, the power of God, of God Almighty at work through my prayers . . . your prayers. I am a desperate man representing the leader of my country, who is more desperate than you can imagine. If I am anxious, please understand my impatience, but I must learn some things so that the rest of the story can make sense to me as well as to you. If that is being a fool, then please, I beg you, give a fool the benefit of the doubt."

Rabbi Zahor's expression did not change. Rabbi Abraham smiled. Then he raised his hands, palms out, toward Peter and spoke. "Please calm down, Colonel Somoroff. I will answer your question."

Rabbi Abraham stood and walked to the wall behind the table. He took one of the oil lamps and motioned to Peter to join him as he walked toward the wall on Peter's right. As the rabbi neared the wall, Peter came close to him. The man was taller than Peter. His black robes touched the floor. Peter looked at the wall where the lamp cast its light. He nearly lost his breath. There, in plain sight, was the acrostic he had found on the wall of Celia and Boris Menoff's apartment. Although the letters were ancient Hebrew he knew it was the acrostic. Beneath it were several Hebrew words. The rabbi saw the recognition and confusion in Peter's face. His long white fingers pointed to the acrostic and then to the Hebrew words.

"This is the same as you found in your friend's apartment. This is the name of a spirit, Beelzebub. He is a subprince." His hand moved to the next word, which was smaller than the name of Beelzebub. The lamp showed several words of the same size in a column below. The rabbi translated the names.

"Alcanor, Diralisen, Ergamen, Lamalon, Tachan, Tromes, Nominon . . ." He reached the bottom of the column and pointed to the next column.

"Amatia, Licanen, Gotifan, Igurim, Ikonok, Balfori, Iamia . . ."

That column was finished and he moved to another. In all there were forty-nine names under that of Beelzebub.

"These are the servants of the spirit subprince Beelzebub. They serve him. They are his slaves, in a manner of speaking, and he can impart great power to them, if he wishes."

The rabbi lifted the lamp so that it illuminated the wall above the acrostic. There Peter saw a name larger than the rest.

"Who is that?" he asked.

"That is Belial, one of the four high princes. The superior spirits. Beelzebub serves him. He is a very powerful spirit, and one of darkness."

"Is he the devil?" Peter was caught up in a current from which he could not escape, as though it were a magnet drawing him to the wall and to the power that he knew it held.

"The devil is a Christian belief. You might say, or could say, that this is the devil, as you know it. That is not as we know it. Come around the room with me and I will show you many devils."

He moved along the wall and Peter saw acrostic after acrostic, each with a Hebrew word above it, each with a single word below it, each with a list of names below that.

Some were joined by lines etched into the ancient stone. Others were written in a different script, and many different colors served as background to the names. Once in a while Rabbi Abraham would stop and translate a few of the names.

"Habhi, Enaia, Plirok, Molin . . . Astarot, a subprince . . . Ethan, Buk, Semlin . . . Amodeus, a subprince . . . Goleg, Pachei . . . Magot, a subprince . . ."

The old man came to a halt near a very large acrostic. He lifted the lamp so that the name above it was clear.

"This is an old friend of the Christian world—Shaytān—Satan. He is a prince. There are four dark princes—Lucifer, Leviathan, Belial, and our friend here, Satan."

"Then the devil is not just one spirit?" Peter was totally absorbed.

"Let's sit down and talk a little, Colonel Somoroff. Perhaps you would like some tea?"

They walked back to the table, and the rabbi replaced the oil lamp on the wall. He spoke to Rabbi Asher, and Sholem left the room.

Peter returned to his chair to find Arie ben Kagan looking like he had seen a ghost.

"That's something!" said Peter.

"It gives me the creeps. I don't care for this world of theirs."

"We have to believe it is the world as it really is, yours and mine," Rabbi Abraham said. "You just refuse to give it any attention. But no matter. We are here when we are needed. Now, Colonel Somoroff, let me answer your question about this Valarian. From what you and Rabbi Vogel have told us, he could be any one of these spirits. Perhaps even one of the subprinces. I believe he is one of the dark ones, one of those fallen from the grace of God, may His name be praised forever. Ah, here is the tea."

Sholem Asher entered the room with a heavy silver tea service. Peter was startled by the beauty of the pot and the delicate china cups.

"We are not totally uncivilized," joked Rabbi Zahor, in a gesture of forgiving Somoroff. Peter accepted the gesture with a nod. When the tea had been served they settled down again. Rabbi Abraham continued.

"So, Colonel, when we ask for all you know, we do so only because the possibilities are many. We knew that from

Rabbi Vogel. He was unable to narrow it down. He did not have enough information. Anything else you can tell us will help.''

Once again, everyone in the room concentrated on the KGB colonel. As he was about to speak, Rabbi Vogel entered the room and sat between ben Kagan and the two younger rabbis, directly across the table from Rabbi Asher. Peter acknowledged Vogel and began to speak.

''Before we came here, to Israel, I separated from our group for approximately two weeks. Something was bothering me about Menoff's file and the business of the missing Captain Barnowski. I told you I had gone to see his wife in Gorki and that Valarian had refused to remove the disgrace of calling him a deserter from the military records. I went back to Gorki and visited Barnowski's wife once again. This time I brought an enhanced photograph of Valarian. We do that by computer. She was sure it was a picture of her husband, even though Valarian is badly scarred from burns. But why, I thought, would Barnowski change his name and identity and, more important, desert this woman whom he loved so dearly? It puzzled me. Yet she insisted it was a picture of her husband. I could not shake her from that conviction.''

Peter sipped his tea and turned to ben Kagan. ''Now, General, I will share a KGB secret with you. We have been doing a great deal of work with ESP—extra sensory perception. We have identified certain people we call sensitives—mediums, if you like. Some of the work has been quite promising. In any case, I returned to Moscow and borrowed one of these subjects.''

He turned back to the five rabbis. Their expressions told him that they were extremely interested.

''Her name is Natasha Zelenko. She is a very accomplished medium. I took her to Volgograd, which was Stalingrad until we renamed it in 1961. There is a great memorial hall there called Mamayev. It is a huge monument with an eternal flame. The names of twenty million heroes of the Soviet Union who died for their country cover the walls. It is a stirring place, visited by millions of Soviets every year. It is a place of sadness, courage, and pride. Captain Barnowski's name is not there. I thought that Natasha might be able to tell me if his spirit was there. She could not, though she tried for five hours. It was a terribly wearing experience for her be-

cause she told me that many spirits filled the hall. We stayed
overnight in Volgograd. Having researched Barnowski, I know
he had disappeared in the battle for the city. The next morning we visited the battle area where his unit fought. It was on
Mamayev Hill. It is now a park. A few momentos of the war
still remain. There was a concrete bunker, overgrown and
decaying, in the middle of a field. Natasha Zelenko was
drawn to it like a magnet. I had to run to keep up with her.
When we got to the bunker she kept turning in a circle
saying, 'He is here. . . . Someone is here . . . was here . . .
but it is wrong.' She went to the bunker and began to rub the
worn concrete. Then she began to scratch at it, clawing like a
dog trying to dig up a bone. 'In here . . . it is in here . . .' ''
She was trembling but very excited, very agitated. I ran back
to the car and brought the tire iron. I used it to dig into the
old doorway of the bunker. It took nearly an hour, but we got
inside. Natasha shook violently once inside. When I tried to
calm her she pushed me away. There was horror on her face.
She suddenly screamed and ran out. I found her on the
ground, exhausted.''

Rabbi Abraham muttered a prayer to himself. Peter noticed
it.

'' 'He is in there,' she told me. 'But there are two of them.
Not really two of them, because they are the same. One is
German,' she said. 'An officer, but not just a German. He is
also a Turk. There are three, four, all mixed together.' It
didn't make any sense to her, but it was all she could tell me.
She said the German was the strongest, except that Barnowski
was nearby, too. She told me it was a very high-ranking
German officer. That was all she could tell me, and truthfully
I was afraid for her health. She was exhausted. I sent her
back to Moscow, and I stayed in Volgograd, using the KGB
computer there to find out what German units were in the area
during that battle. Then I got lucky. On the day that Barnowski
disappeared from his unit, a report was filed that the body of
a German colonel, an SS colonel, was found in the area. He
was identified as Waffen SS Colonel Wilhelm Hendricks, a
Nazi of very high stature and a man who was extremely close
to Hitler himself.''

Now ben Kagan reached over and touched Peter's arm,
interrupting him.

"Wilhelm Hendricks, you say? He is one of those still on the top of the Mossad list."

"Well, you may remove him, General. He is dead."

"Please continue," asked Rabbi Zahor, now extremely interested.

"I contacted our office in East Berlin, and while I flew there, they dug up the files on Colonel Hendricks."

Peter reached into his attaché case and took out a folder. He passed a large black and white photograph across the table to Rabbi Abraham. He held another in his hand.

"That is the enhanced photograph of Nickolai Valarian. This," he said as he passed the second photograph to the rabbi, "is an enhanced photograph of the infamous SS Colonel Hendricks."

The other rabbis leaned toward Rabbi Abraham and examined the pictures.

"It is the same man," said Rabbi Abraham slowly.

"The German is burned, just like Valarian," commented Rabbi Zahor.

"May I see those?" asked ben Kagan. The photos were passed to him, and he studied them carefully.

"Yes," he said, "I would say the resemblance is uncanny. But many people look alike."

Peter was not happy with ben Kagan's skepticism, but he continued with his story.

"Not only do the two men resemble each other, but their stories are strangely similar. Valarian was found badly wounded with burns near Volgograd. We don't know exactly where, but let us assume it was near the bunker. His records begin there. There is no record of the man before that time. Supposedly all his records were destroyed in the fires in Leningrad. Colonel Hendricks, also badly burned, was from Mainz, in West Germany, or so the records say. He received his burns in quite a different place. The SS records show that he was in combat in Turkey during World War One and was found wounded and burned near the city of Istanbul. The German officers ran the Turkish Army, but when the war in Europe went against them, they pulled all of their officers out of Turkey. Hendricks was one of those officers—but his records in Mainz were destroyed by a fire in the city hall. So, like Valarian, his life begins for us when he is returned from Turkey badly wounded and burned. His rise with Hitler is

documented, and his anti-Semitic activities are well known.
Coincidence, General ben Kagan?''

The Mossad chief shrugged. Peter smiled. He now reached
into his attaché case and withdrew still another photograph.
He passed it to Arie, who examined it and passed it on to
Rabbi Abraham. It too was an enhanced photo. The rabbi
who sat to the left of Rabbi Abraham took it and lifted it close
to his face. He peered into the picture, then looked down the
table at Somoroff and put the photo down. But he said
nothing.

"Who do you think that is?" Peter asked aloud.

"It is Valarian," said ben Kagan. He stood and placed the
new photo next to the picture of Valarian. "See, the face is
the same."

"No," said Rabbi Abraham, "I would say it is Hendricks.
Look at the eyes and the scar on the nostrils. It is the
German?" He looked to Peter for confirmation.

"It is neither!" said Peter firmly. He reached across the
table and placed the three pictures side by side facing Rabbi
Abraham.

"Gentlemen, no matter what you may think of the KGB,
and I make no excuses, some of us are just ordinary policemen. I have been called a boring, plodding detective many
times. But that training is extremely useful."

He reached into his attaché case and removed a small
notebook, opening it and checking some notes.

"When you have a difficult case, the first thing you look
for are consistencies. Facts that appear and reappear. They
are the best link to the truth. Here I have a Soviet named
Valarian who is burned and without any previous record." He
pointed to the photo of Valarian.

"Here I have Hendricks, who was killed near the place that
Valarian first appears . . . according to the record." He
pointed to the photo of Hendricks.

"And here," he said, pointing to the third photo, "we
have not Valarian, General . . . not Hendricks, Rabbi Abraham . . . but General Mustafa Ismet Bayar, adviser to Abdul-
Hamid the Second and Mehmed the Fifth, rulers of the Ottoman
Empire. He was a butcher, responsible for the brutal slaughter
of Serbians, Bulgarians, Russians, and along with them, as
many Jews as he could lay his hands on."

"How do you know this?" asked a stunned ben Kagan.

Before Peter could answer, the rabbi who had closely examined the photo spoke.

"Because, as Colonel Somoroff told us, he is a detective. I will venture a guess that this General Bayar was killed near the place where the burned young Hendricks was found."

"In the same building in Istanbul, Rabbi," answered Peter. Satisfaction filled his voice.

"And the picture?" asked Rabbi Abraham.

"Once you know what you are looking for, once a pattern emerges, the rest is easy. It took three days for our embassy in Turkey to supply it. While they searched, I began to track down the history of General Bayar. Do any of you want to guess what I found?"

The rabbi on Abraham's left spoke again. His name was Rabbi Malachi.

"Of course you found that he was also burned in war and that no previous record existed."

"Exactly. He supposedly came from the seaport of Izmir. But there I lost track of his history."

"Where was he found burned?" asked Rabbi Zahor.

"That is the problem. His family were sea captains. Ship owners of some kind. The records are very bad. He arrived in Izmir aboard a Syrian ship in or about 1863. The ship was called the *Tartus*. It was a merchant vessel, but I believe it was a slaver—a ship that carried slaves to America."

"America?" Rabbi Zahor whispered. "Can you trace it?"

"Do you think it is necessary, Rabbi Zahor?" Peter asked.

Rabbi Abraham spoke. "No, Colonel Somoroff. I do not believe it is necessary. In any case I am sure that you will find a similar circumstance regarding the birth of Mustafa Ismet Bayar, but I doubt if there will be any photographs. You have made your point, and you have made it well. Is there anything else you have to say?"

Peter reached over and picked up the leather bag he had carried. He carefully opened the drawstring and removed an object wrapped in burlap. He gently placed the burlap on the table and unfolded the cloth. From within the folds he removed two pieces of shiny mahogany. He placed them side by side in front of the rabbis. On each was a small mark, an impression in the wood, much like a seal in wax.

"I went to Mainz and tracked down Wilhelm Hendricks's house. It had survived the bombing of World War Two and is now owned by a very nice automobile salesman and his family. They have completely redecorated. Actually the house has been occupied by several different families since the war. Still, I am a detective, so I asked if I could have a look around. It took more than an hour, but I found one of these marks in the wood over the door that supposedly led to the colonel's bedroom. The people were kind enough to let me remove the section of wood. The other piece comes from the doorway of General Bayar's bedroom in Izmir. That house is also intact. It was luck.''

Rabbi Asher reached for one of the pieces of wood. He passed it to Vogel. The other rabbis examined the mark very carefully, muttering to each other in Hebrew as it went from hand to hand.

''Do you know what this is?'' asked Rabbi Levi Lemach ben Abraham.

''Yes. I have seen it before,'' answered Somoroff.

''Where?'' The old man leaned forward, and Peter sensed that he had come to a critical juncture in the meeting. He took the piece of wood from Rabbi Vogel, placing it in front of him and taking one last look at it before he answered. The mark was worn, but there was no mistaking its form—clearly the outline of a dragon, a Chinese dragon, impressed into the wood. It was the same dragon he had seen carved into the jade and silver ring that Valarian wore.

''Valarian wears this symbol on a ring.''

''Where does he wear this ring?'' the old rabbi asked.

''On his right hand, middle finger.''

''Ahhhh.'' Rabbi Abraham sighed. He leaned back in his chair, folded his hands in his lap, and closed his eyes. His head nodded slowly. The others watched him intensely. Peter felt his heart skip several beats. Then Rabbi Abraham opened his eyes and reached his hand across the table to Peter Somoroff.

''You are a brave man, Colonel Somoroff, and a most intelligent one, too. Come with me, please.''

The old man stood, took a lamp again from the wall, and led Peter through the door out into a hallway. The others all remained behind. Peter stayed close behind the rabbi, who led the way up a flight of stairs to the second floor of the temple. They then walked down another hallway and stopped in front of a large, heavy mahogany door. The old man reached under his cloak and removed an ancient key, which he used to unlock the door.

The room was dark. Rabbi Abraham moved carefully with the lamp in front of him after telling Peter to remain near the door. He lit three oil lamps in the front of the small room. Peter's eyes adjusted slowly to the new light, which was brighter than the lamp that the rabbi held.

"Come over to me," commanded Rabbi Abraham.

As he walked toward the bright lamps, his eyes caught sight of a glittering object below them. Nearing the rabbi, Peter saw a cluster of jewels, spread out on a table that was covered with fine white cloth. As he came closer he saw that the jewels were set into what appeared to be a breastplate made of hammered gold. He stopped next to the rabbi and beheld a large table on which were spread various robes, miters, jeweled clasps, gold chains, and ornaments. It was a spectacular sight. The robes were blue and purple, made with intricate craftsmanship. Other pieces were scarlet, and still others brilliant white and deep blue, edged with gold thread.

The rabbi looked at Peter. "No outsider has ever seen this before. It is our greatest treasure and, we believe, a gift from God, Holiness unto Him."

"What is it all?"

"Have you ever read the Bible, Colonel Somoroff?"

"Long ago. The New Testament, but I don't remember anything."

The rabbi led Peter to a wooden stand, upon which a large and very old Bible rested. Rabbi Abraham opened the book to Exodus Chapter 28. The words appeared to be hand-lettered in Hebrew; actually, as Peter learned later, they were Aramaic.

"Let me translate this for you. Hold the lamp for me, please."

The rabbi's finger moved across the words as he translated them into English. He spoke slowly, with a deep, rich voice.

"And take thou unto thee Aaron thy brother, and his sons with him, from among the children of Israel, that he may minister unto me in the priest's office, even Aaron Nadab and Abihu, Eleazer and Ithamar, Aaron's sons. And thou shalt make holy garments for Aaron thy brother for glory and for beauty."

Rabbi Abraham went on to read the incredibly detailed instructions for fashioning Aaron's garments and breastplate—meticulously laid out in that ancient holy book. Peter stood throughout it all, completely enthralled.

Finally, the rabbi closed the book slowly, then bent and

kissed the ancient cover. He straightened up and turned to
Peter Somoroff.

"That is the word of God, praised be His name forever and
ever, as He gave it unto Moses and the children of Israel. We
are those children. . . . We are Israel today, risen out of the
ashes once again."

He moved past Peter back toward the table that held the
marvelous breastplate and garments. Now Peter saw all of
those things that the Bible spoke of, and he was amazed that
he remembered each and every item. There was the miter
with the plate of pure gold, inscribed in Hebrew and set on
blue lace. The breastplate contained twelve gemstones, each
different, each meticulously inscribed with Hebrew writing.

"The copies are exact, Rabbi Abraham. Just like it said in
the Bible."

The tall old man looked down at Peter with a smile. His
hands touched his long white beard. He stroked it.

"But, Colonel Somoroff, you miss the point. These are not
copies. These are the originals."

His hand pointed toward the ceiling in a gesture of victory.

"But how?" asked Peter.

"By the grace of God, and a brilliant archaeologist named
Sholem Asher."

Peter felt understanding growing in him, but the rabbi was
not yet finished. He guided Peter to the far wall and held the
lamp up to it. There he saw row upon row of symbols, above
the numerical acrostic that Rabbi Vogel had drawn upon
Misha Karkov's head in Lubyanka. To the left of the symbols, in a box surrounded by a rainbow of brilliant colors,
was the Chinese dragon, an exact copy of those on the wood
he had removed from the Nazi's door frame and the Turkish
general's house. But this dragon was carved in a piece of
jade, just like Valarian's ring.

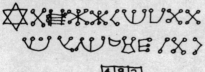

~ 37 ~

The great doors of the hall were closed and the Council of Ministers of the Supreme Soviet was officially in session. This was a special meeting called by the General Secretary of the Party Marshall Malenkov, and although Premier Alexeyevich objected privately to the other ministers, he was unable to overrule Malenkov's request.

Ivan Alexeyevich counted his support around the large square table. He knew he would lose the day. The corpulent general secretary wasted no time in getting down to business. It had all been planned the day before when he met with Nickolai Valarian at GRU headquarters. The marshall had adjusted to his master quickly. The rewards were most pleasurable. He reveled in his new-found power. But he also understood that the master could punish as intensely as he could reward.

"The business of this meeting," he began, "is simple, and I might add, long overdue. We all mourn the loss of our comrade, Boris Menoff, and the untimely death of his wife. He will always be remembered for his great contributions to our nation. But his ministry is unfilled, and we must get on with the business of guiding the Soviet Union's glorious destiny."

The premier observed his adversary with great interest. Something about him was different, changed. It was subtle, yet it was there. He wondered if the other ministers noticed it too. Malenkov seemed younger, stronger. His aging skin looked smoother and firmer. His eyes, lately milky with age, were now clear and intense. Malenkov stared at the premier

215

as he spoke, and Alexeyevich was forced to look away from his gaze.

"My recommendation is therefore that we now appoint a new Minister of the Interior. I wish to nominate Colonel Nickolai Valarian, Chief of Security and Records, GRU, and a hero of the Soviet Union. May I have your comments?"

The first to speak was General Josef Porikin, head of the KGB. He was Peter Somoroff's superior and an old friend of Premier Alexeyevich.

"Marshall Malenkov, with all respect, this post has always been the province of the KGB. I am familiar with Colonel Valarian, and although I respect his zeal and efficiency, I feel he is not the caliber of man to sit on this august council."

"Thank you," said Malenkov, immediately ignoring Porikin's remarks. "Does anyone else have a comment?"

Premier Alexeyevich waited for a moment, hoping that one of the other ministers would speak out. No one did. Malenkov had them in his pocket. The battle was lost before it began, but before giving up, the premier decided to go on the record against Valarian.

"I have a few words to say on this matter, Comrades," he began, "and I hope that you will weigh my words carefully. With all respect to my old and dear friend, Marshall Malenkov, I too must disagree with his choice for this most critical position. I stress critical, because we must face the fact that the world is changing rapidly and our adversaries grow bolder every day. This ministry in times past was totally involved with the internal affairs of our great country. What it did was not seen by the outside world. Today things are different. No matter how we try, the world watches us and knows what is happening inside our borders. Dissidents arise at every turn. The population demands more goods and services; they are aware of the living standards of other nations, especially in America and western Europe. We are watched and scrutinized. To appoint Valarian is to wave a bloody flag at our enemies and give them grist for their propaganda mills. I speak mostly of his brutal treatment of Soviet Jews. The American press has had a steady flow of information about him, and in my opinion his appointment would signal that we condone the oppression he advocates."

His words fell heavily upon the meeting. Their impact was solid and sensible to many of the rulers of the USSR.

Malenkov sat unmoved.

"Premier Alexeyevich, I respect your opinion. But I disagree for exactly the reasons you have just stated. I am tired of having the western nations, and especially America, dictate policy in this room. They are our enemy. Have we forgotten Premier Khrushchev's promise to bury them? Have we grown soft and afraid of our own beliefs?"

The big man slammed his fist down on the table, shaking it and spilling several water glasses nearby.

"I am fed up with this business. It is time that we assert ourselves again. No one objected when we dealt with the Czechs or the Hungarians or the Poles. There was no disaster when we extracted our price from the Americans in Vietnam. When we roared into Afghanistan the world squeaked back at us. What we do inside our own country is really of little consequence to the capitalists. They are too busy looking after their own interests."

"We have heard this argument many times in this room, Marshall Malenkov," answered Alexeyevich. "But you ignore the truth when you disregard our dependence on their technology, their wheat, their money. The world grows smaller. We cannot hide behind our borders when it is convenient."

Malenkov stood at the end of the table opposite the premier. The rotund man seemed taller than usual. His presence loomed over the entire assembly. He spoke slowly, with a menacing tone in his voice.

"We have never hidden, Comrade Alexeyevich. But our business is just that, our business. A man of Valarian's strength is just what we need to move away from this obscene dependence you speak about. I for one deny it. I refuse to have it direct our destiny. It is time that we assert ourselves to the full measure of our potential. I curse this policy of appeasement, and I curse those who would lie down and have us surrender our destiny."

He sat down facing the premier and folded his meaty arms across his chest in defiance.

Ten minutes later Nickolai Valarian became the Minister of the Interior of the Union of Soviet Socialist Republics—and moved one step closer to the chaos he had preordained. Malenkov called Valarian personally and, in the presence of the Council, congratulated and welcomed him. As Malenkov walked from the meeting room, he experienced his master's reward pulsing through his body. Ecstasy filled his senses.

Rabbi Posner was near death. The GRU major stood over him defiantly.

"There are many places left on your body to cause you more pain, Jew," Major Metsky said. "Many more places. I will continue, or you can die now in peace. The choice is yours."

His words sounded far away to Posner, as if in an echo chamber. He wanted no more pain. His will to resist was gone.

"What do you want?" he whispered.

"Where are they going in Israel? Who are they going to see?"

"Don't know . . . Vogel used . . . Kemiot . . . spoke of Zefat . . . Kemiot . . ."

"What is Kemiot?"

"To the old ones . . . Hassidim . . . from ben Zimrah . . . please . . . no more . . ."

Metsky felt Valarian call, and he left Posner bleeding on the floor of the damp cell. He slammed the door, putting the room into total darkness. The rabbi tried to drag himself to the cot but was unable to move. He felt a sensation growing in his chest. It became intense rapidly. Pains shot through his left arm and leg. His back arched.

"Oh . . . oh . . ." he gasped, feeling his heart beating wildly. "God forgive me," he muttered. "Shema Yisraeil: Adonai Eloheinu . . . Adonai . . ."

His heart stopped and he died.

After Metsky delivered Posner's words to Valarian, the colonel dismissed him. There was much to do. Marshall Malenkov had told him of General Porikin's objection to his nomination. Valarian was now Porikin's superior insofar as KGB operations within the Soviet Union were concerned. But before he dealt with the KGB chief, he had to know what Somoroff had accomplished in Israel. He contacted Achmed Sharit in Acre immediately. The old Arab was delighted at being able to serve his master so soon after the failure of the attack on Ginnosar.

"You will go to Zefat, to the place of the old Jews of

Zimrah. Tell me if Somoroff is there. Find out all you can. Kill him if you can."

Valarian had two disciples outside the Soviet Union. Achmed Sharit had been in the holy land for a very long time. A disciple was always kept there since the days of Rabbi Jesus and his confrontation with a prince of darkness. It was a troublesome place for Valarian. He needed eyes there at all times.

Sharit was uneasy when he heard that he must go to Zefat. He had been in the city before, and it caused him great discomfort. Something had existed in Zefat in the last few years that was most disturbing. He was weak and unsure of himself in Zefat. But his master commanded. There was no alternative but to obey.

"I will be there before dawn, Master. I know the place of the Zimrah."

"Contact me as soon as you know anything," said Valarian. He broke off the contact with a small reward for Sharit. Then he placed a call to General Porikin and requested that the KGB chief visit him that afternoon. When the general begged a delay due to illness in his family, Valarian insisted that the matter to be discussed was far more important than Porikin's domestic problems, causing the general to feel hatred for Valarian. It was exactly what the new minister wanted Porikin to feel. It would make their confrontation more agitated, and that meant the general would be more easily controlled by Valarian's will.

The KGB chief was in Valarian's office within an hour. It was his first visit to the newly appointed minister's sanctuary.

"You should speak to the building superintendent," Porikin suggested after greetings had been exchanged. "I'm sure they can supply more heat to this office."

"The temperature is exactly the way I want it, General," Valarian answered.

"To each his own, Commissar. Now what can I do for you?" There was sarcasm in his voice.

"A few small but nevertheless important matters concerning the operations of the KGB."

"I am sure that you understand, Colonel Valarian," the general replied quickly, "that the affairs of the KGB are totally under my jurisdiction. I report to the premier directly."

"Yes, of course, General. I am only concerned with the

operations as they apply internally to the Soviet Union. Those operations are under my jurisdiction, as I understand my duties.''

''What operations concern you?'' The general was curt.

Valarian smiled and leaned forward in his chair, placing his scarred hands palm down on the shiny desk.

''Please understand, General Porikin, that I am not a politician. I am a soldier accustomed to taking and giving orders and carrying out my duties as efficiently as possible. I understand that certain members of the Council of Ministers were . . . shall we say . . . opposed to my appointment to this post. That is understandable, and I bear no malice toward this opposition. I am informed that even our great premier had reservations about me.''

General Porikin was surprised at the reasonable tone of Valarian's voice, but he remained wary, knowing full well the sadistic reputation he enjoyed.

''That is to be expected, as you say. Now what operations of the KGB concern you?''

Valarian slid a folder containing a computer printout from the narrow center drawer of his desk. He opened the folder and pretended to read the printout for a moment. After several seconds had passed he looked up at General Porikin.

''I am aware that the KGB maintains a wing of Lubyanka under its total control. I wish that control to be transferred to my ministry today.''

''That wing is used strictly for international purposes, Colonel.''

''And if I could prove to you that what you say is not the case?''

''That is not possible.''

''Ah, General, but I have proof that it is not only possible, but that it is being used to subvert the policies of our government!''

His words were strong and threatening.

''I will look into the matter immediately. Is there anything else?''

''Yes, General Porikin. Are you familiar with the activities of . . .''—Valarian looked at the printout once again—''of a Colonel Somoroff?''

''I am. He is in charge of the Moscow Bureau of the KGB

and certain international assignments that I am not free to discuss."

"With Israel?"

Porikin was stunned.

"Israel? What the hell are you talking about?"

Valarian stood and leaned across the desk, pointing a finger at the powerful general.

"I have no interest in your activities outside the Soviet Union, General Porikin. Not yet anyway. But if I were you I would have a meeting with Premier Alexeyevich as soon as possible and pose the question to him."

Valarian sat down and put the file away. He reached for his communications console and buzzed his secretary.

"I expect to take control of the Lubyanka wing tomorrow morning. My men will be there at eight AM. If Colonel Somoroff's visit to Israel is international KGB business, then it is not my affair. I will inform the Council of Ministers of this adventure in any case, because I believe they have the right to know that someone in our government is carrying on relations with a sworn enemy of the Soviet Union. Good afternoon."

An hour later General Porikin left the premier's office in a state of shock. As much as he admired and supported Ivan Ivanovich Alexeyevich, he was certain that the man had lost his senses. He could not deny Valarian access to Lubyanka. The premier told him that he was unable to move against Valarian until Peter Somoroff returned from Israel. All that the general could do was to warn Major Rosteveli. The premier had begged him to lend the operations whatever support he could, but only with unofficial sanction. It was completely off the record. Porikin liked Somoroff. He had also been a good friend of Boris Menoff. He left the Kremlin and instructed his driver to go directly to Lubyanka. Major Rosteveli had a great deal of explaining to do in the next few hours.

As he left the Kremlin walls behind he did not notice the dark blue Skoda, driven by Valya Pernick, following him.

— 38 —

For centuries Zefat was predominately an Arab city. During the war of independence for the State of Israel, it was a bitter battleground. The Israelis prevailed after a long conflict.

It is in a beautiful part of Galilee. The spectacular light, a strong blue-white, has made it a mecca for artists and craftsmen of all types. But Zefat is also a city of mystical heritage. It is an ancient city, said to be one of the holiest places in Israel, and a center of learning for centuries. The modern code of Jewish law, Shulhan Aruk, was written in Zefat by Joseph Caro. In the sixteenth century it was the home of the Kabbalists, led by the famous Rabbi Hayyim ben Joseph Vital. Here art and mysticism blend against a background of tourists enjoying the climate and beauty of the city.

Achmed Sharit parked his old Chevy in the municipal lot near the entrance to the old part of Zefat. It was morning. He appeared to be an average tourist, wearing walking shorts and a straw hat with his hair tucked under, clean-shaven, with the ever-present 35 millimeter camera slung around his neck. He wore a blue denim shirt and matching blue jogging shoes. At first glance he was just another schoolteacher or businessman on holiday. For several minutes he lingered near the tourist information booth, examining brochures and clicking photographs of the nearby buildings. Then he sauntered slowly toward the narrow street and entered the old city.

Rabbi Abraham and Peter Somoroff had returned to the conference room and continued their discussion throughout the night. Questions had been answered, schedules discussed and revised, plans drawn and confirmed. Rabbi Abraham announced that he was convinced of the validity of Somoroff's story and Boris Menoff's suspicions. The rabbis then said a prayer for the departed Menoffs and, with Peter's permission, another for his son. Afterward, Peter asked the first question.

"Can you identify which of the spirits is Valarian?" he asked, gesturing to the columns of names on the walls.

"Not with certainty," answered Rabbi Abraham. "The ring is a clue that he may be one of the subprinces, and if that is the case we must be very careful because then we are dealing with a very powerful spirit. There are eight subprinces, and they serve the highest of the fallen angels."

"Fallen angels?" questioned Peter.

"Archangels. There are four of them—Lucifer, Leviathan, Satan, and Belial. The subprinces, two at a time, serve these dark and fallen archangels. Lucifer is served by Astarot and Oriens, Leviathan is served by Magot and Piamon, Satan by Asmodeus and Ariton, and Belial by Beelzebub and Amaimon." As he spoke, Rabbi Abraham pointed out each name to Peter where they were listed on the walls above and below the acrostics.

"Could it be that Valarian is one of the archangels?" Peter asked.

Rabbi Zahor drew in his breath and muttered a silent prayer. Rabbi Abraham's voice dropped an octave lower than normal, and it sounded cold.

"Pray with all your might that such a thing is not true. To confront one of those cursed spirits is to stand at the very brink of iniquity. It is to look into damnation itself and see the awesome power of God, may His name be blessed forever and ever."

All in the room muttered, "Amen."

"Then how will you know which of these is Valarian? There are hundreds on these walls." Peter was lost in a world he didn't comprehend.

Rabbi Abraham spoke patiently to the Soviet. "The mark on Misha Karkov's shoulder you spoke about, the red triangle with the backward C, is a clue. From Rabbi Vogel's description of his contact, although Vogel is not trained, I believe we can eliminate those who serve the archangel Lucifer. He is always associated with light and fire. I have heard nothing of flames or heat in your story. As a matter of fact you said that

Valarian's office was a very cold place. So I think we can count Lucifer's followers out of our contemplations. Leviathan's, too, do not fit into the mold of the man you have described. He is a creature of the sea and water, of flood and famine. That leaves the followers of Satan and Belial to consider."

"Does it matter which one?" Peter asked naively.

Rabbi Zahor smiled and answered. "It matters a great deal. These archangels have experienced God's wrath, blessed be His name forever, because each has defied the Lord's word and commandment. Each has been given a different punishment for falling from His grace. The powers granted to the fallen archangels, their subprinces, and their servants are only granted by God's grace, blessed is He."

"I don't understand," interrupted Peter. "How can God grant them power if he has cast them out? It doesn't make sense."

"Colonel," Rabbi Malachi's tone was tutorial, "no matter who has controlled this land, our temple has been in Zefat for more than five hundred years. In that time we have learned that man's assessment of what makes sense, and God's assessment, may He reign forever, are two different matters. The very name *Israel* means *God strives*. We do not question His ways, blessed is He, but yearn only to understand what He wishes to reveal and act upon what He guides us to. Can you understand that?"

Peter just spread his hands, acquiescing to the rabbi's words, which he had no background to deny. It was beyond his grasp.

"Let me explain it in a different way," said Rabbi Abraham patiently. "In this house, this temple, are records dating back more than four thousand years. We study them every day and ponder their meaning. It has been the work of our temple for centuries, always against the background of our devotion to God and to His law. Since creation, many have fallen from God's grace. Their souls have been cast to the fallen archangels, bound forever to do their bidding. But all—all that occurs in heaven and on earth—all is under the direction and plan of the Lord, blessed is He. The fact that He has placed evil and temptation before us is not a new thought or fact. The definition of what is evil has always been the province of man upon earth. We can only ponder right and wrong and remain pure and true to the laws that God has given. The doubters can ask, who says that God gave us these laws? Prove it to me. We cannot prove it in the modern sense. It requires an act of faith. Without that faith, any definition of good and evil is impossible. We, as Jews, have kept a faith we believe is true and acted upon it. We have never attempted to convert others to our beliefs. We have paid dearly in blood for our faith. Yet we prevail. We survive. That is witness enough for us. We pray continually that God, may His name be blessed forever, will someday reveal Himself to the world and pass His word to all. Until that time we can only remain constant in our devotion and steadfast in our belief. We do not ask the world to follow us, but from time to time, as you are a witness, some have come seeking our help."

Peter nodded, knowing that he was the only non-Jew in the room. How much had he missed, he wondered, in casting out thoughts of God and religion in return for the Soviet state?

"What will happen now?" Peter asked, accepting their statements.

"We will need some time to identify the spirit that is Valarian and to prepare Rabbi Asher for his journey to the Soviet Union. You can return to Tel Aviv and make your arrangements for the trip with our most able General ben Kagan and his organization."

It was to be Rabbi Sholem Asher who would confront Valarian and deal with the spirit that inhabited that body. Any one of the five older rabbis would have been able to perform this function, but because of the arduous journey and the physical stamina required in the process, a younger man would better serve the cause. Part of Asher's daily life was to keep himself prepared to perform the rites that were needed to confront the fallen spirits. This meant physical fitness, piety and prayer, and strict adherence to the commandments and Talmudic law. But Asher also held a special place in the temple founded by Rabbi David ben Zimrah four centuries ago because he had discovered some of its most cherished artifacts, the robes and breastplate and miter of Aaron.

Nowhere in the world does a more intricate and frustrating road map to the past exist than in Israel. More than a map, an entire book, the Holy Bible, is filled with places and events that actually existed and happened in this diminutive country. So much to explore in so small a space. Yet the surface has hardly been scratched. Over the centuries, destruction, looting, and foreign occupation have desecrated many of the places and turned biblical history to dust. The constant translation and retranslation of biblical text has obfuscated true meaning and design. Only with the discovery of the famous Dead Sea Scrolls were the students of the Bible able to begin to reconstruct the actual map of the ancient land. Rabbi Asher was one of those scholars, who centered his efforts in particular on the elusive travels of Aaron, brother of Moses and the acknowledged first priest of the nation of the Israelites after their escape from years of bondage in Egypt. It was Aaron and the sons of Aaron, of the tribe of Levi, who were the priests of the new nation. The priestly clothes, breastplate, and miter, as described in the Book of Exodus, were lost at the time of the destruction of Jerusalem by the Babylonian king, Nebuchadnezzar. They never surfaced after that. After the Six-Day War, Israeli troops occupied all of Jerusalem for the first time since the tiny state was born, and the Jews were in total control of their most holy place. Sholem Asher led one of the first archaeological teams into the city and personally supervised the careful restoration of the famous Western Wall, all that was left of the previously destroyed Temple of Solomon.

Six years after the occupation of the old city, Asher began a dig near the base of the wall. The exact spot was determined from records discovered in Crete and Tyre regarding the famous temple. These little-known military records were part of a naval log kept by the Greek admiral Theacus, whose job it was to keep Alexander the Great's Army supplied during the long Mideast campaign of conquest. The place of the dig had been a supply depot. Asher hoped to find remnants of Greek occupation. Some were found, but the most extraordinary find was a tunnel that wound under the old temple grounds and out toward the Moslem holy place known as the Dome of the Rock. Its existence was kept secret for six months while Asher and his crew of students carefully excavated as much of the tunnel as they could without causing a disastrous cave-in. Their digging came to an abrupt halt when they discovered they were directly below the famous Moslem shrine. In fact, had they continued, it was believed they would have caused the collapse of the mosque that shelters the Rock, from which it is said Muhammad ascended to heaven. Some also believe it is the sacrificial rock upon which the patriarch Abraham was to sacrifice his only son Isaac when the Lord tested his faith.

It was on the last day of their dig, when the tunnel was to be sealed, that Rabbi Sholem Asher discovered a chamber revealed by workmen installing support beams. The discovery was made in the late afternoon. Rabbi Asher was the only member of the archaeological team on the site at that time. When he realized what the chamber contained he emptied the tunnel of all the workers. Then he quickly sent word to three of his most trusted assistants, who were at the dig in twenty minutes. It took several hours to prepare the discovery for shipment, but Sholem knew what he had found was of great importance to the rabbis at Zefat. The entire chamber was emptied and crated by only four people, Asher and the students. They brought the crates out of the tunnel that night and drove directly to Zefat. Fortunately for Asher, Israel was engaged in the Yom Kippur War at the time, and though he drove the treasure out of Jerusalem under the watchful eyes of Israeli soldiers, it was never searched, nor was his trip to Zefat questioned. By giving the vestments to the rabbis, Sholem Asher had supplied a most powerful tool for their work. Rabbi Levi Lemach ben Abraham felt it was certainly God's design that one of their own, namely Rabbi Asher, had made the discovery. Now the priestly garb, so carefully designed as commanded by God, was in the hands of the people who knew its meaning and how to use it.

The five rabbis, Asher, Vogel, ben Kagan, and Peter completed their meeting and retired outside to an inner patio for breakfast. Peter and Arie would drive Rabbi Vogel back to Kibbutz Ginnosar where they would call Mossad headquarters and request a helicopter pickup. Peter was surprised at his appetite, thinking that the night's excitement would make it impossible to eat. He ate three eggs and toast and drank local fresh-squeezed orange juice and several cups of coffee. He sat with Rabbi Abraham, listening as the old man talked about the early origins of their belief and how the sect came into existence, about the ridicule and persecution they received, even from other Jews, and about a few triumphs over the dark spirits that they had enjoyed. Their greatest excitement had come with the discovery of Aaron's garments. Rabbi Abraham believed that they were sent to them at that special time for a definite purpose. He quietly informed Peter Somoroff that he believed this was the time, especially if the spirit was a subprince. The priestly garments of Aaron would drive Valarian from the Soviet Union. "But can they never be destroyed?" questioned Peter.

"When it comes to the will of God, blessed be He, we cannot use the word *never*. Our judgment, according to the ancient writings, is that God has put the archangels of darkness and their servant spirits in our midst for His own purposes. Only He may destroy them. Remember that at one time, so it is written, they were close to Him and were numbered among his most faithful servants. Their ways are their punishment. We can only be God's instruments on earth—" The old man was about to continue when something stopped him in midsentence. He shuddered. Rabbi Zahor stood at the far end of the patio, poised to move like a cat. Rabbi Malachi was also on his feet and alert. The youngest rabbi, David Hashomer, and the fifth one, Rabbi Solomon ben Levi, also stood, their faces turned in the direction of the street beyond the patio wall.

"What is it?" asked Peter of General ben Kagan.

"I don't know. They all felt something at the same time," he answered, then got to his feet and touched Rabbi Asher on the shoulder.

"What is it, Sholem?"

Asher raised his hand, gesturing to Arie to be silent. Only the sounds of a few songbirds and the faint noise of the distant city traffic echoed inside the patio walls. Rabbi Abraham motioned to Solomon ben Levi and David Hashomer. Both rabbis acknowledged his unspoken command and left the patio quickly. Rabbi Abraham gestured to Rabbi Zahor, and he too left, moving in the opposite direction through the kitchen toward the street. Then Rabbi Abraham whispered into Sholem Asher's ear, and he too quickly left the patio, with Rabbi Vogel close behind. The old man gestured for Peter and Arie to be seated. Rabbi Malachi remained standing. He positioned himself near the entrance to the patio and blocked the doorway with his body and flowing robes by stretching his arms outward. Then Rabbi Abraham sat down. "Let us finish our breakfast," he said in a voice louder than usual. "We have a great deal of work to do in the next few days."

Peter began to speak, but the rabbi put his finger to his lips, telling Peter to be silent. He seemed to be counting to himself. Arie looked at Peter and shrugged, not knowing what was happening. Suddenly Rabbi Abraham was on his feet, his hands outstretched, his face lifted toward the sky. As he spoke Arie translated for Peter. It was an old prayer that ben Kagan knew by heart, Isaiah 45:18.

"For thus saith the Lord that created the heavens; God himself that formed the earth and made it; he hath established it, he created it not in vain, he formed it to be inhabited: I *am* the Lord; and *there is* none else. . . . I *am* the Lord; and *there is* none else. . . . I *am* the Lord; and *there is* none else. . . ."

He kept repeating the last line of the prayer over and over, louder and louder.

Then Peter heard a yell of pain coming from the street beyond the patio. A man was running and screaming. There were sounds of a scuffle and more yelling. Then silence.

Rabbi Abraham relaxed and smiled, turning his head toward Peter and Arie.

"Today is a wonderful day, my friends. God has sent us a great gift. Let us have a look."

He led them past Rabbi Malachi, back to the meeting room. Ahead in the hallway, Peter saw the other rabbis firmly holding a man who looked to be a tourist. Rabbi Zahor and Rabbi Hashomer each held an arm, Rabbi ben Levi and Rabbi Vogel each held a leg, and strangest of all, Rabbi Asher gripped the man's mouth, his fingers spreading the jaws open. Then Peter saw that the man's tongue was lashing about Asher's hands. It was a long tongue, and each time it struck Sholem it left a trail of blood oozing from the rabbi's hands.

"What in God's name!" exclaimed ben Kagan as they followed the group into the meeting room. The struggling man was thrown on the table but still restrained. Rabbi Abraham went immediately to the man's neck and ripped his shirt away.

"Come over here, Colonel Somoroff. Look at this. God has truly sent us a precious gift, and we know how to deal with it, praised be His name!"

There on the man's shoulder was the red arrowhead and backward C, an exact duplicate of the mark Peter had seen on Misha Karkov in Lubyanka.

"*A disciple*," he exclaimed. "You have caught a disciple."

"Yes. Do you know him?"

Peter studied the man carefully. He wanted to be sure. "No," he said firmly. "I have never seen him before."

In the pause that followed, the man's tongue extended to an impossible length, reaching for the mark on his shoulder. Rabbi Abraham saw this and grabbed the tongue firmly in his hand. It glowed and burned. Peter smelled burning flesh, but the old man held on tightly.

"Malachi," he yelled. "Bring me the knife."

The fifth rabbi entered the room in a split second, his hand fumbling under his robe. He ran toward Rabbi Abraham and handed him a dagger. Peter noticed the now-familiar twelve stones in the handle—like those of Aaron's breastplate—as Rabbi Abraham gripped the knife and raised it above his head. His other hand still held the prisoner's red-hot tongue.

"Thou has forgiven the iniquity of the people; thou hast covered all their sins. Selah!"

He pulled the tongue upward, causing the man's head to leave the table. It was incredibly long, over two feet. With one swift motion Rabbi Abraham sliced through the fleshy tongue near to the man's mouth. Blood gushed red, then it became all colors of the rainbow, flowing onto the man's face and then onto the table. The fluid glowed and sizzled as it spread.

"That thy way may be known upon earth; thy health among nations." Everyone in the room said a loud "Amen."

"Amen," said Peter, too.

In the GRU headquarters building across from Petrovisky Park, Nickolai Valarian, newly appointed Minister of the Interior of the Soviet Union, watched in horror as one of the candles above him burned brighter than normal. The flame shot up in the air, almost touching the ceiling. Blood dripped slowly from his mouth onto the brilliant mahogany desk. Then it began to gush and spurt, splattering onto the surface in front of him. He could not control it. His mind and powers were totally absorbed in the excruciating pain that emanated from his mouth.

It stopped only when Rabbi Abraham in Zefat heated the knife blade and cauterized the prisoner's wound. He did not want the man to bleed to death. He had much use for a live disciple, and Valarian knew that until Achmed Sharit was dead, he would have no peace.

~ 39 ~

Tel Aviv is a modern city, a jewel set on the shore of the Mediterranean. Several high-rise buildings, steel and glass, soar skyward in the bright Middle-East sunlight. The Mossad, Israel's fabled intelligence agency, occupies the top three floors of one such building. It is the nerve center of one of the finest intelligence-gathering organizations in the world. Several times the American CIA and the British MI5 has been indebted to the Mossad for hard information they were unable to gather.

On the top floor of Mossad headquarters there are five well-furnished apartments, as well as executive offices and the high-tech communications center. It was here that Sasha Andreyev, Anya Somoroff, and Leonid Chomsky stayed while Somoroff was in Zefat. Sasha continued to receive medical treatment for her wound, which had become infected. She was confined to bed. Leonid spent a great deal of time with her during those two days while they waited for Somoroff's return. Anya was a different story. She was in love with Michael Gross, and he was in love with her.

It was a new experience. Anya had been an exceptional student in secondary school. She spent most of her free time at the Polytechnic Museum, situated quite near Lubyanka on the south side of Dzerzhinsky Square. After finishing secondary school with honors, and because her father was a high-ranking official, she was chosen to attend the famous Polytechnical Institute in Omsk. Her area of concentration was chemistry with a minor program in solid-fuel rocket engine design. All of her young life had been devoted to science and the precise discipline that accompanies such work. Love was a new sensation. She could not control her feelings as she might control a laboratory experiment. The result was a Ping-Pong effect where she constantly moved from deep emotion to total rejection of her feelings. It was beginning to wear her down.

Michael Gross, on the other hand, had been in love before. Tragically, his first love, and wife, had been killed when her truck, delivering vegetables from a kibbutz where they lived, ran over a land mine. She was critically wounded but lingered in the hospital for two weeks before dying. The experience left Michael bitter and angry. Shortly after her death he applied for active duty in the Army and was recruited by the Mossad one year after that. He spoke several languages, a natural talent that Mossad put to use immediately. They taught him several more, enabling him to work in such diverse places as Algeria, South Africa, the Soviet Union, and China. He was one of their top agents, but he also possessed good managerial skills. This talent led General ben Kagan to offer Gross the job of Assistant Manager of Operations. It meant less travel. After all the years of dangerous living and occasional killing, Michael jumped at the opportunity. The pain of his wife's death had faded, leaving fond memories and an occasional ache. A little-known fact about Michael Gross's exploits on behalf of the Mossad was that despite his youth and because of his fluency in Spanish, he became one of the front men in the famous snatch of Adolf Eichmann in Argentina.

Now he sat on Anya's bed, high above Tel Aviv, those exploits far from his thoughts. He watched the lovely young Soviet woman move from the window and sit in the armchair next to a small telephone table.

"Can't you relax for a moment?" he asked in a soft voice. "You keep moving around the room like an imprisoned animal. What is it?"

Anya was not ready to tell him how she felt. She didn't want to appear weak or dependent to the handsome Israeli. Yet something inside cried out for her to embrace him and tell him that she loved him. It was unbearable to the point of distraction. Reaching for an answer to explain her nervous state, she replied, "I'm just worried about my father."

"He will be here soon. I sent a helicopter up to Galilee for them. Relax, they are fine. They said it went very well."

She didn't respond but folded her hands in her lap and nodded. A moment later she was on her feet again, walking to the window. She watched the busy Tel Aviv traffic below but saw nothing. Then she felt Michael standing behind her. As he spoke she turned to look at him, not realizing he was very close. Their bodies touched. She could not pull back because she was against the window. He didn't give ground either.

"Anya," he whispered, "why do you avoid me?"

Stunned by his tone, she pushed past him and moved to the other side of the room.

"I'm not avoiding you. What makes you think I'm avoiding you?"

"You keep running around this room like a rabbit. Stop for a moment!"

Anya caught herself and made a conscious effort to calm down. She sat on the bed, folding her hands in her lap. "Michael, please sit down. You make me nervous."

"No," he answered, looming over her as he moved to her side.

"I don't want to sit down."

"Michael, please!" she commanded.

"Okay, okay, I'll sit." He started to sit next to her.

"Not here. Go sit in the chair," she said, pointing to the armchair.

"I sit on the bed, you sit in the chair . . . you sit on the bed, I sit in the chair. What are we playing here, musical chairs?" He laughed and sat in the chair.

"Okay. So now I am in the chair and you are on the bed. Are you comfortable?"

"You are making fun of me. I don't like it," she answered.

He leaned forward, his large hands outstretched. "What do you want, Anya? Can't you tell me?"

"What do you want?" she replied.

"To make love to you," he answered quickly and firmly.

She was shocked. She flushed with excitement. But she was not angry.

"Ha." It sounded hollow and false. "What a thing to say. It's so rude."

"What do you know about it? I say what I feel and you

laugh. Rude? You think it is rude to tell someone that I love her?"

"You didn't say that. You said that you wanted to make love to me."

"It's the same thing, little Russian."

"That's not the way I was taught!"

"So," he said, leaning back in the chair, "tell me what you were taught. I can always learn. Israelis are a very learning people."

"What can I tell you? Love is not just making love . . . it's caring and working together for a goal. It's respect and children. A home. Those things. Not just the bed."

"You do all this with a stranger?" he questioned.

"No, of course not. People have to get to know one another. Have common interests. Common beliefs."

"Ah," he said, pointing his large index finger upward. "Ah . . . now we are getting somewhere. It's because I said I would have to kill your brother, may he rest in peace, if it were necessary. You think we have little in common? That, my dear Anya, is bullshit. Let me tell you about what I tried to say on the beach the other day. I was talking about the business of survival. It's a business everyone in this country works very hard at—we have to, you know. Tell me, Anya, those rocket engines you design in Omsk—are any of them going to transport atomic bombs to Israel someday?"

"What are you talking about? What bombs?"

"The nuclear weapons that sit on top of your rockets. You do design engines, don't you?"

"How do you know? Who told you that?" She was surprised.

"This is Israel, little Anya, and you are sitting inside the headquarters of the Mossad. Central intelligence, you know about that. You should, your father is a big fan of ours."

"My father doesn't tell me his business."

"Well, his business is our business, and we have a very fat file in the computer downstairs that tells me all about him and his family . . . and what they do . . . and where they are. But it doesn't tell me what they think or how beautiful they are inside. You are beautiful inside, you know. And outside it isn't too bad either. So that's who told me, a printout from a computer."

"You think I'm beautiful inside?" she asked, her voice

softening. "Even when I build rockets that could bring death to your country?"

"That's something neither of us can do anything about. Why don't we both stop talking about death and think a little about life?" Michael pleaded.

Anya studied him, her large brown eyes examining his rough face inch by inch. What did she feel for this man? What was it about him that caused the lightness inside, the rush of adrenaline, the shaking? Are you my love, she wondered? Can I be in love with you? You are almost twice my age. As she thought and looked, he stood and came to the bed. He was beside her before she realized it, his hand outstretched to her.

"Anya," he was whispering again. "Anya. Stop being a scientist for a moment. Stop being a Soviet for a moment. Let me love you. Let us be human, nothing more."

Her hand touched his, and like a flower it was held in his large petal-like fingers as they closed about hers. She was lifted to her feet and engulfed in his embrace. His hands slid up and held her head in a gentle cradle. She relaxed into them, feeling their strength and warmth as they pulled her mouth toward his. It was a soft, caring kiss, followed by a longer, stronger kiss, which was followed by a passion that she had only read about in novels her grandmother kept secreted in the old breakfront in her room. Anya was Natasha in *War and Peace*, swept into her forbidden lover's arms by circumstances beyond their control. To hell with the world, she thought, this is a man, my man, and he is now and with me. And I will be with him.

Moments later they were in bed, lost within each other, exploring new-found sensations of love.

"I have never done this," she whispered, her words coming as she exhaled rapidly.

"And I have never done this with you either, Anya. But it will be good, I promise you."

"I love you, Michael."

"And I love you," he answered, holding and touching her gently, aware that this was her first experience and wanting it to be perfect.

Perhaps perfection was not reached, he thought later, but they certainly came close. But the helicopter landed on the roof above them after only an hour of lovemaking. It brought with it the shudder of reality and the awareness of difficult days ahead.

Three rooms away from where the lovers lay, Leonid Chomsky and Sasha Andreyev also heard the helicopter arrive. Leonid went to the door, but it was locked. He would have to use the phone to call the guard at the end of the hall. Even though they were guests of the Mossad, their movements were restricted. Whenever they wished to move around or go outside, an agent was assigned to accompany them. Leonid went to the phone. Sasha stopped him.

"It may not be Colonel Somoroff. Why don't you wait and see?"

"He was due about now. Gross said they were coming at about three. It's almost three," he said looking at his watch.

"They will come for us when they are ready. I'd like to have your company, if you don't mind."

Leonid didn't mind at all. He liked Sasha. She had been an excellent sounding board for him. They had discussed his feelings about the Israelis in great detail. Much of what she said made sense. He wanted more than ever to continue his training so that he could get assignments outside the Soviet Union. It was apparent to him that there was much to see in the rest of the world and much to learn. He envied her wisdom and experience.

The sound of the door opening interrupted his thoughts. Andy Taft entered the room.

"Good afternoon." Andy greeted both of them. "How's the patient?"

Sasha acknowledged him with a smile and a gallant wave of her hand. "Mending, Comrade Taft. It must be the chicken soup." It was obviously an American joke, which Chomsky didn't understand. He always felt alienated from Sasha when she and Andy talked about American things and customs. But the explanations never made much sense to him, so he had stopped asking and just accepted their private jokes.

"Good," said Andy, bending and kissing her hand. "You look beautiful."

"Why thank you, Mr. Taft. You're so very kind." She now spoke with the funny slow accent that Leonid understood was Southern American.

"My pleasure, darling, and may I say an honor?" Andy too affected the accent. Leonid grew impatient.

"Have you heard from Washington?" He interrupted their game. Andy turned to him and was all business.

"Yes. Good news . . . and bad news. Your people have identified the frogman. He is from a unit stationed in" —Andy referred to notes written in a small leather-bound pad he carried in his coat pocket—"Vladivostok. The naval base. Ninth Submarine Attack Group. He's a bit of a hero. The records show he led the underwater demolition teams that helped clear Haiphong Harbor for the North Vietnamese after we mined it, in the good old days."

Leonid wasn't smiling. Andy continued.

"His name is—was—Yuri Danoloff. He was a captain. As far as the Eastern Command knows he is on special assignment to the GRU. Fancy that. Oh yes, he spoke Arabic and Farsi." Andy closed the notebook, letting Leonid know that was all he had to tell.

"Colonel Somoroff and General ben Kagan have just arrived, so I think we will have a meeting soon. Have you seen Gross around?"

"No," said Sasha. "Andy," she continued, "were there any messages for me from the embassy?"

"Oh, thanks for reminding me. They said to tell you that there was an inquiry from Major Metsky of GRU regarding your whereabouts a month ago. They said they told him that you were, and continue to be, in Washington."

"So he knows about my involvement," she mused almost to herself. But she was not disturbed. "We better tell Colonel Somoroff about that," she told Andy.

"Fine," he said. Then addressing Leonid, he continued, "I'm going to catch up with ben Kagan and your boss now. Do you want to come along?"

Leonid looked at Sasha. She waved him off.

"Go ahead. I want to get some sleep. The more I rest, the sooner I'll be out of here and back in the thick of things."

Andy let Chomsky go through the door first, then closed it and casually locked the outside bolt. He caught Leonid looking at him, put his arm around the young KGB officer, and guided him down the hall, saying, "Orders are orders, my friend. When in Rome, one follows the Romans' wishes . . .

or something like that. Let's see what the big boys have been up to.''

He slid his arm from Leonid's shoulder and headed for ben Kagan's office. As they passed Anya's room the door opened and Michael Gross exited, nearly knocking them over.

''Hey, honk before you turn, Michael,'' Andy joked.

Gross closed the door quickly and by habit fastened the bolt. Leonid Chomsky studied the big Israeli's face, but it was noncommittal.

''Where are you headed?'' Gross asked.

''To see the boss,'' Leonid responded. ''Both our bosses. They're back.''

''Yes, I heard the chopper. Okay, let's go.''

The three men walked briskly toward ben Kagan's office. Leonid looked back at Anya's room just once.

— 40 —

Major Anton Metsky stared at the empty corridor. The guard station was deserted, and all the rooms were bare. Even the furniture was gone. The men he had sent to inspect the holding cells reported that they too were empty. The entire KGB unit assigned to this wing of Lubyanka had disappeared. *The master will be furious,* thought Metsky, *but it is not my fault this time.*

The night before, Valya Pernick reported that General Porikin had gone directly from the Kremlin to Lubyanka, but when Metsky tried to contact Valarian he was unable to reach him. He tried by phone, he tried the dacha, he even went to his own quarters and attempted contact through the mark on his shoulder. But when his tongue touched the backward C it bled profusely, causing him great pain. He then went to Valarian's office at GRU headquarters, but the master was not there. However Metsky did notice that one of the candles in the chandelier had turned upside down and was burning brightly. He knew that a disciple must be in trouble, and that that was what was distracting Valarian. Still Metsky would not make the decision to move against the KGB unless Valarian ordered it. So he waited until morning and followed the original instructions, but it was too late. Porikin must have warned Rosteveli and moved the section to a safe place during the night. He withdrew his men, leaving two behind just in case someone returned, but he knew it was a long shot. Once he was back in his staff car he telephoned Valarian and told him the bad news. The master was still distracted and ordered him back to headquarters.

After finishing with Metsky on the telephone, Valarian turned back to face Valya Pernick. The bleeding had stopped, but the pain was still with him. He spoke slowly.

"Our brother in Palestine is trapped. The Jews in Zefat have him, and there is little I can do for the time being. If I were there it would be a different story, but I cannot go at this time. You will have to go in my place."

"Yes, Master," she replied eagerly. "Whatever you command."

"These old Jews have some power over us. They cannot stop us, but they know many of our ways. They must be destroyed. I should have done it long ago."

"I will do it now," she said with conviction.

"Don't misjudge them. You must be very careful. Once long ago, their kind drove me out of that place. I have sworn to return and destroy them. Soon the time will be right, and this country, the Soviet Union, will be my instrument. I almost succeeded with the Germans. This time we will not fail. Then only those Jews in America will be left, and they will go quickly. When it is done, my brothers and I and all that follow us will inherit this earthly domain."

Valya beamed with joy at Valarian's words. This was the promise made to all disciples. This was the covenant of the fallen archangels.

"Before you leave the Soviet Union I will give you my seed. You will bear a child and give birth in Palestine. Nurture it. Name it Sifon, follower of Asmodeus and Ariton. He will be our instrument from the inside when we attack."

It was the highest achievement that a female disciple could attain—to bear a son for her master. Valya was filled with anticipation. Valarian stood, after first removing a packet of papers from his middle drawer.

"These will enable you to enter this accursed Israel. Now we will go to the dacha to conceive the child."

To Valarian it was a task to be done. To Valya it was the supreme act of her life. As they drove north on the Leningrad Road past the Frunze Central Airfield, Valya trembled with excitement. Valarian's thoughts were concentrated on the suffering of Achmed Sharit. He silently cursed Peter Somoroff. Driven by hatred, he swore to kill this KBG adversary whom he had so badly underestimated. Then he cursed God.

• • •

The effort expended during the night had exhausted everyone in the section. Major Rosteveli was proud of the group and had told them so before his own exhaustion forced him to sleep. General Porikin's reaction to the operation was very negative. Rosteveli had no choice but to call the premier to discuss Valarian's order for the GRU to take over the KGB Lubyanka wing. He had been careful to assure the premier that he was calling only because Peter Somoroff had left strict orders not to jeopardize the operation under any circumstances. The premier thanked him and then spoke to General Porikin for ten minutes. After that conversation Porikin ordered Rosteveli to be ready to move the entire operation in two hours. The highest-ranking KGB official had joined the group.

Like thieves in the night, they moved by truck and bus across Dzerzhinsky Square, past the Bolshoi and the Lenin State Library, across the Kamenny Bridge south to the old Donskoy Monastery. They settled in the basement of the old orthodox stronghold, which had become the Architectural Museum. The KGB kept the basement as a place for secret interrogation, and lately as a holding prison for political dissidents before their trials. The move was only temporary until safer accommodations could be secured outside of Moscow.

Rosteveli slept for three hours. He had asked General Porikin to advise the embassy in Washington of the move, so that they could pass the information to the DIA contact. He hoped that Colonel Somoroff would contact him soon.

Captain Bonyon had not yet slept. He supervised the guard roster and made sure that the prisoners—Dr. Brodsky, the two policemen from Pushkin, the morgue sergeant, and especially Captain Servioff—were under lock and key and secure. Fannie Beshevsky and Marina Grochenko became roommates. There just wasn't enough room otherwise. The two women liked each other and seemed happy with the arrangement. Fannie took it upon herself to nurse the young ballet dancer, who still required sedation from time to time. Marina was healing. The bone grafts and kneecap replacements were successful. She could never dance ballet again, but she would walk.

There was no trace of Rabbi Posner. Serge Rosteveli feared

the worst for the old man, but he kept his thoughts to himself, not wanting to upset Fannie. Bonyon reported to the major.

"We have the floor secured. I have plainclothes men in the museum."

"How many?"

"Six, Major. I also have men in cars outside the monastery walls. General Porikin is arranging for the museum to be closed this week. He is sending a squad of his men. They will pose as workmen doing repairs."

"Are you satisfied?" the major questioned. He had grown to admire the efficiency of the Army officer.

"Yes, sir. I think we can hold off detection for a while, but I will feel much better when we are out of the city."

"What about secure phones?"

"General Porikin suggested that we use the museum phones. There would be no reason for them to be tapped, and it would seem like business as usual. Anyone tapping the phones will have discovered us. By then secure phones won't matter."

Rosteveli agreed. There was little he could do now, except wait for Somoroff to contact them.

"Tell the men they are restricted to the grounds for now. There will be no contact with our headquarters until I sweat that bastard Servioff and find out who else in our group is working for Valarian and Metsky."

The rabbis had gone through almost half the rituals used to detect and identify particular spirit servants of the subprinces and archangels. Each archangel had two subprinces that served them. Each subprince had a number of spirits serving him, each with particular talents and powers, but all subservient to the dark princes. Having decided that Valarian was a follower of either Satan or Belial, the field was narrowed, but it still left over one hundred possible spirit servants to check. The process was well worth the effort, because once they could identify the servant, then they could identify the subprince and the archangel that controlled it. Knowing this, they would prepare Asher with the proper prayers and rituals.

Rabbi Levi Lemach ben Abraham worked to identify the spirit, assisted by Rabbi Zahor. In a room above them, Rabbis Malachi and Solomon ben Levi began to prepare Rabbi Sholem Asher for his confrontation with Valarian. Although Peter and Arie had returned Rabbi Vogel to Kibbutz Ginnosar, that had only been a guise. Within hours, as prearranged, Vogel was back in Zefat taking the holy vows of the sect and receiving the same instruction and training as Asher. It was a rule of the sect of David ben Zimrah that at least two men be so prepared at all times.

Rabbi Abraham sat at a small table in a Spartan room. He closed the book of spirits that follow the subprinces Beelzebub and Amaimon.

"That is the last of the servants of Belial," he said to Rabbi Zahor.

"Then it is Satan's servant we seek," answered the dark rabbi.

"It would seem so," said Rabbi Abraham. "Perhaps we have missed something here."

He watched the prisoner carefully. Sharit was awake. The bleeding had stopped. He hung upside down from a chain fastened to the stone ceiling.

"Turn him toward those that follow Asmodeus and Ariton," he commanded.

Rabbi Zahor unhitched a pully attached to the chain and slowly turned the disciple to the left, stopping when Sharit's head faced the wall bearing the acrostic and names that Rabbi Abraham had specified. Then the old man took the next book of spirits, the third on the table, and began the ritual. The title of the book read, *The Third Book of Sacred Magic Given by God unto Moses, Aaron, David, Solomon, Saints, Patriarchs, and Prophets, Which Teacheth Divine Wisdom.* He opened the book and began the prayers.

"We have faithfully observed that which hath been taught unto us, and have with a good will obeyed the commandments of God. Be certain that this veritable and loyal wisdom accorded to us by His grace shall render the perfidious Satan to be our slave together with his pestiferous generation, for they can not do otherwise. We command this sacred operation in His name, blessed be He, knowing this power is granted for fear of God, in no way used for evil. God the eternal hath wished herein to leave us our free will, but woe unto him who shall abuse His divine grace."

He motioned to Rabbi Zahor, who took a pointed silver instrument with the twelve jewels set in the handle from a purple case on the small table. The dark rabbi dipped the point into a bowl of water and prayed.

"Let the fear of God be ever before the eyes and heart of him who shall possess this divine wisdom and sacred magic."

He then dipped the point of the instrument in a silver bowl filled with oil. Again he prayed as he lifted the jeweled knife and pointed it at Sharit's back.

"To know all manner of things past and future, which be not however directly opposed to God and to His most holy will."

He moved quickly to the hanging prisoner and with the instrument drew an acrostic on his back in blood.

When the last letter had been drawn in the lower right-hand box, Sharit's body shuddered and jerked like a fish on a hook out of water. Rabbi Zahor stepped back. Rabbi Abraham nodded. Now they were getting somewhere. But still he was troubled.

The first thing that Leonid Chomsky noticed about Peter Somoroff was that he had aged. In just a few days his boss seemed ten years older. The colonel's dark hair had been greying, but now Leonid noticed new streaks of white along the temples. The most striking change was around Somoroff's eyes. There were lines and cracks, crow's-feet deep and long, radiating along his high cheekbones toward his ears.

They sat casually in ben Kagan's corner office. The afternoon sun poured brightly into the large room, making ben Kagan's body a filmy silhouette as he stood against the window.

Andy Taft sat on the sofa with Leonid Chomsky. Michael Gross took a chair near the communications console on his boss's desk. Peter Somoroff stood near the Mossad chief.

"Before we finalize our plans," began Peter, "have we any information from Washington?" He spoke directly to the

DIA agent. "Yes, sir," answered Andy, taking out his note-book and reading his notes aloud.

Peter had no reaction, except a quick glance to Chomsky.

"Second, Major Metsky has made inquiries in Washington about Sasha Andreyev. He was especially interested in her whereabouts during the time she was in the Soviet Union working with you. The embassy covered for her. They told Metsky that she was in Washington then and that she still is there."

"Good," said Peter. "Does Sasha know this?"

"Yes, sir," answered Leonid, trying to show his boss that he had been working while he was away. Andy understood the young Soviet's need and nodded in agreement.

"There was another message for you, Colonel, addressed to Sasha." Andy read from the notebook to be sure of his accuracy. "Flame is burning," said the American.

Peter was alert. He looked at Chomsky, but obviously the message was news to him also.

"Say that again," Somoroff commanded.

"Call home. Flame is burning. That was the entire message. What does it mean?"

"It means that Major Rosteveli has a serious problem. When did it come in?"

"This morning."

Peter turned to General ben Kagan. He was obviously agitated. "Is there any way we can get a telephone line patched into the Soviet Union from here?" His tone was an urgent command to the Israeli general.

"It is possible," answered Arie calmly, "but you will have to tell me what this is about. I will request a line on the American satellite, and you can be sure that they will record the conversation. Let's be sure the call is absolutely necessary."

"Rosteveli wouldn't call unless it was a crisis. I must speak to him as soon as possible."

"Do you have the number?" ben Kagan asked.

Peter gave him the secure number at the wing in Lubyanka. Ben Kagan instructed Gross to have the call placed and patched into his office. Gross left the meeting on the run. The call would have to be placed on a special phone hookup, and Michael was one of the few people who knew the code to connect with the American satellite.

A moment after Gross left, ben Kagan's phone rang. The general answered, then put the call on hold.

"It's for you, Andy. There's a messenger from your embassy downstairs. He has an urgent communiqué for you. You better go down and get it." Andy left quickly. Ben Kagan told the front-desk guard to hold the messenger there for Mr. Taft.

Five minutes later Gross canceled his first call and began to make the connection for Peter Somoroff to talk to Major Rosteveli. It was the first time that the CIA, DIA, KGB, and Mossad had knowingly shared a phone line. Usually they tried to listen in on one another's conversations. Arie ben Kagan was amused at the irony.

As Somoroff spoke rapidly in Russian to Major Rosteveli, the others in the room listened silently. Andy, who had returned to the office, was the only one who did not understand fluent Russian, so Chomsky translated Peter's side of the conversation for him. They were all able to get the gist of things. Gross was particularly upset when he surmised that Rabbi Posner was missing. Peter told Rosteveli that he would be back in the Soviet Union in no less than two days and that the KGB major should keep an extremely low profile. He ordered Rosteveli to leave the interrogation of Captain Servioff to him, and under no circumstances was he to harm the KGB traitor. Peter knew that Servioff was an important link to Valarian, and especially to Metsky. Homosexuality is a crime in the Soviet Union, and the punishment is severe. Peter could make a case against Metsky by breaking Servioff and put the GRU major in prison for a long time.

After the call was completed, Peter Somoroff briefed everyone on the recent events in the Soviet Union.

"I think we have to move quickly," he told ben Kagan.

Throughout the trip back to Tel Aviv, and during the meeting, ben Kagan had been quiet, letting the Soviet colonel give orders and direct the course of events. Now Arie's tone of voice changed. He became the chief of the Mossad again, totally in command.

"Colonel Somoroff, before you leap ahead to what you perceive as the plan of action, let me remind you that although we have cooperated thus far in aiding Premier Alexeyevich with this problem, we still have to clear our actions with my prime minister. Let us not forget that our countries are basically at war and that there are no official relations between us.''

The events of the past few days had distracted Peter Somoroff. He was so involved with the Al Fatah attack, the rabbis in Zefat and the progress they had apparently made, that he momentarily had forgotten where he was and under what circumstances he had been allowed into Israel.

"Forgive me, General ben Kagan," he began formally. "I have been swept up in the events. I am, of course, your guest, and you correctly remind me of the political implications of this visit. How shall we proceed?"

The Israeli intelligence chief was not without compassion for the Soviet problem. He'd vowed to pursue it to a conclusion. But he still had to extract whatever his government wished from the Soviet premier. It was, after all, the rationale behind allowing the KGB into Israel in the first place.

"I will request a meeting with the prime minister this evening. I hope to have an answer for you in the morning. Until then, please accept the hospitality of the Mossad. Unfortunately you will have to remain on these premises until further notice. Michael," he said as he prepared to telephone the prime minister, "please make Colonel Somoroff comfortable and see that the others have whatever they need. Then come back here."

Gross stood. The others sensed their dismissal and began to leave the office.

"Mr. Taft," General ben Kagan said, "can you remain here for a few moments?"

Andy sat down. Leonid and Peter left with Gross. After the door was closed the general turned his attention to the young DIA agent.

"Mr. Taft, let us assume that a satisfactory political arrangement can be reached with Premier Alexeyevich, or at least that he will be willing to discuss the matter with the prime minister. Therefore a meeting will have to be arranged. It is implied in the premier's letter."

"I drew the same inference, General."

"Good. I would like you to arrange a meeting place outside of Israel but close enough to both the Soviet Union and Israel so that the heads of state can get to the destination quickly and undetected."

"That means either Europe or North Africa." Andy was tracking ben Kagan accurately.

"Precisely. Any ideas?"

"We cooperate with the CIA. They control most of the safe houses in both places. I think we can arrange something in Morocco, Algeria, or France."

"My choice would be France, Mr. Taft." The general's response was quick.

"I'll get right on it. How do you want to handle the security?"

"You arrange that with your people. I am sure the KGB will want their own people on the site, too. We will match them with my people."

"How many can you bring?"

"That will depend on the Soviets. From what I can see, there are not too many KGB agents involved in the matter. Your group should be responsible for the major share of security."

"What about travel arrangements?"

"Let the Soviets take care of their own. I will get the prime minister into France. We have a trade mission up there now."

A few moments later Andy headed for the American Embassy. General ben Kagan called the prime minister and made an appointment to see him later that evening.

The dacha was dark. Valya Pernick lay on the black satin cover of Valarian's bed. She was completely nude and in a trance. The small table containing the disciples' candles had been moved to the foot of the bed. One of the candles burned dimly upside down. Sharit was still a prisoner. Valya's candle had been moved to the center of the pentangle. Its flame was long and straight, burning to a narrow taper ten inches high. Valarian entered the room, dressed in a long black robe. He wore a cardinal red miter with a backward C embroidered on the front. The shape of the arrowhead and miter were the same. As he crossed the room to the foot of the bed, the candlelight illuminated fine needlework on the robe, similar in quality to the work done on Aaron's robes and vestments. However the symbols woven into this robe were oriental in design. The dragon on his ring was duplicated on the back of the robe. He raised his hands over the candle representing Valya, and the flame grew higher and more intense. On the

bed, Valya arched her back. Her lips parted and her long
tongue licked wildly out in front of her. Rainbow-colored
spittle dripped from it. She moaned.

Valarian's hands moved down into the flame of her candle
and parted it so that it now formed a V. Simultaneously,
Valya's legs parted, exposing her vagina, swollen and drip-
ping with multicolored ooze. Her moaning grew louder and
more intense. Valarian moved from the parted flame and slid
onto the foot of the bed. He opened his robe to lie on top of
Valya, covering her completely. He entered her quickly,
without passion or emotion. Valya's tongue reached up toward him. He opened his mouth and allowed her tongue to
enter, sucking it so that her head was lifted from the black
satin bed. Her tongue turned bright red, then black. With one
hard thrust he deposited his seed in her, then disengaged. He
moved back to the table and closed the parted flame. Valya's
legs also closed. Valarian put her candle back outside the
pentangle in its proper place. It returned to normal size. Then
the master gazed at Sharit's upside-down candle and pondered
his next move.

Valya slept, but now she was two. Inside her womb,
already attached and being nurtured, was a tiny fetus. It
would grow rapidly, coming to term in a few short weeks. Its
power would be awesome enough to wreak havoc on the Jews
of Israel, and it would forever be part of Valarian and his
followers of iniquity.

Back at Zefat, Rabbi Abraham knew something was terribly wrong. The prisoner was not revealed. His identity remained a secret. He had gone through the list and ceremony
for all the servants of the final two subprinces, Asmodeus and
Ariton. There had been no reaction. Sharit had an erection for
a few moments, but that made no sense to the old rabbi.

"Who are you?" Rabbi Abraham muttered to himself.
Then in a blinding flash, the rabbi knew the answer.

"Quickly," he said to Rabbi Zahor. "We have been de-
ceived by our own stupidity. This is not just a servant.
Quickly. We can lose him if we make a mistake. Step away
and bring me the ram's horn."

Sharit lifted his head and stared at the rabbi. His eyes were
bright red and glowing with hatred. His mouth opened, and
although his tongue had been removed words still came forth.

"Yes, Jew. You have made a mistake. I am not a servant of princes—*I am a subprince!*"

The chain burst into thousands of pieces, and the naked prisoner flipped and landed on the floor upright. His mouth remained open, and the words, spoken as though from within a deep subterranean cavern, echoed out at Rabbi Abraham.

"I am Asmodeus, subprince of the archangels!" He spread his arms. "This is my domain. It was I who built your temple in Jerusalem, it was I who should be the rightful ruler of Israel. You vermin, descendant of Solomon who exiled me unto Egypt. I am returned to claim my birthright. The day is near."

Laughter echoed from the empty mouth. Rabbi Zahor entered the room carrying a large and ancient shofar.

"Do it now!" screamed Rabbi Abraham. *"For the sake of God!"*

Rabbi Zahor lifted the horn to his lips and sounded a blast that shook the room. But it was too late. The body of Achmed Sharit lay dead on the floor. The spirit of the evil subprince Asmodeus was gone.

Back at the dacha Valarian watched the upside-down candle flame die. The black wax melted into an indistinguishable lump at the corner of the pentangle.

"Be patient, Asmodeus, my son," he said. "You shall again reign over all Israel."

~ 41 ~

The lobby of the ultramodern Hôtel Méridien had taken the look of a World War I airplane hangar. Five vintage bi- and tri-wing planes had been placed on display in the lobby. The famous French Air Show was in progress at Le Bourget Airport to the north and Orly to the south. By invitation, an Israeli trade mission was present. The prime minister had arrived undetected and in disguise as a member of the mission. Captain Gross would handle transportation and security to the meeting place for the prime minister.

The words *Sopwith Camel* went through ben Kagan's head as he walked to the crowded registration desk. What a circus, he thought. He registered under the name of Richard Henderson and presented an American passport to the desk clerk, who would hold it for a few hours while it was checked with customs and the French Sûreté. Arie followed the bellboy to the elevators and then up to his suite.

When he was alone, Arie checked his watch and swept the room for bugs. There was no reason for the room to be bugged, but years of discipline made the act second nature to Mossad agents wherever they went. Satisfied, he turned on the TV and phoned a local number.

"Hi. Dick Henderson here," he said in an affected midwestern American accent. "I'm calling for Bill Green."

The voice at the other end said, "I believe Mr. Green is at lunch. May he return your call?"

"No, I'll phone tomorrow if it doesn't rain." Arie hung up. Three minutes later his phone rang.

252

"Dick," said the caller, "welcome to Paris. How was the trip?"

"Fine. Just fine. I have the samples. When do you want to meet?"

"I have meetings all afternoon. But dinner is good, okay?"

Mr. Green, otherwise known as Andy Taft, followed the prearranged conversation accurately.

"Dinner is fine, Bill."

"Good. I'll pick you up at eight. Okay?"

"Great." Arie hung up and lay back on the bed. He had time for a nap, knowing the night ahead would be long and arduous. Before he slept, the events of the past few days filtered through his mind like a high-speed newsreel. He still found it hard to believe that his prime minister and the premier of the Soviet Union were about to meet. He also sensed that the rabbis in Zefat had not told him everything.

He had met with the prime minister at 8:00 on the evening of his return from Zefat with Peter Somoroff. The Israeli leader requested that ben Kagan's superior, the diminutive clockmaker from Beersheba, also be present at the meeting. But it was Arie ben Kagan's show. He convinced both men that the Soviet premier's problem was within the scope of the Zefat sect, and although he couldn't assure success, he did feel that there was a basis for negotiation with the Soviet leader.

"How much do you feel we can extract from the Soviets?" the prime minister had asked.

"Who can say?" answered Arie. "I believe it depends finally on your judgment, if you decide to meet with Alexeyevich."

"I have no doubt that I will request such a meeting. I am only concerned to the extent that we have the ability to deliver a solution."

The wily chief of the Mossad spoke carefully. "Mr. Prime Minister, if I may share an opinion?"

"Certainly," said the Israeli leader, who, among few of his countrymen, knew the power this little old man controlled. "That is why I wanted you here."

"It seems to me that we have to go along with General ben Kagan's assessment of this situation. The rabbis in Zefat have agreed to allow Rabbi Asher to confront Valarian. They must therefore feel that he can be effective. That business is beyond my understanding, but if that is the tool we must use, then let us use it. The negotiations with the Soviet premier must be based on the attempt, not the success, of our Rabbi Asher. Let's not promise what we cannot deliver.''

"Then you recommend," said the prime minister, "if I understand you correctly, that we base our demands on our cooperation only. And if we succeed, then we will have even stronger cards to play later.''

The old man nodded his agreement.

"Done!" said the prime minister. "General ben Kagan, you will make all the necessary arrangements?"

The meeting was adjourned. Ben Kagan spent most of the night planning the logistics with Michael Gross. By morning they were ready to present the plan to Colonel Peter Somoroff and the Soviet agents.

Before the meeting, ben Kagan contacted Taft regarding the safe house in France. The DIA had assured Andy that a small chateau north of Paris would be perfect. Several agents had begun clearing the area. Others were en route from the United States to supplement the DIA's European section. The president of the United States had been briefed that night regarding the whole fantastic story, and he had ordered a special watch room set up in the Executive Office building basement to monitor the operation from the American point of view.

Peter Somoroff studied the plan silently as he sat reading in ben Kagan's office. Leonid, Sasha, and Andy also had copies. Gross had committed it to memory. Anya Somoroff did not attend the meeting. Peter felt that the less she knew, the better off she would be in case of capture. He looked up from the plan folder as he finished.

"Excellent, General," he began. "The only factor that we cannot know until I return to Moscow is whether Premier Alexeyevich is able to travel on such short notice. However, I can see him immediately upon my return and notify our embassy in Washington. The French Air Show will supply a good cover.''

Arie interrupted him. "I think we will have to establish direct communications. If all goes well and the big shots can work out an agreement, then we will have to move swiftly.

Andy,'' he said to the young American, ''you said that the president has established a situation room in Washington?''

''Yes, sir,'' answered Andy.

''I assume that involves a direct and secure satellite linkage?''

''Yes, General. That traffic is not on the NATO channels. We are using a sideband on the Tyros weather satellite system.''

''Excellent. Our weather people have access to those frequencies. If your people can link the KGB section of the Soviet Embassy in Washington to the situation room, we can establish direct contact with Moscow, Paris and Tel Aviv from here.''

Peter shook his head in amazement at the intellect displayed by ben Kagan and at his grasp of technical capabilities.

''No problem, General,'' answered Andy, ''as long as the president clears it.''

''Does he have to know?'' asked ben Kagan.

''That's not my decision. I'll suggest it, but remember I have a boss in Washington, and he is answerable to the president.''

''Fair enough,'' said the Israeli. ''Other than that, if there are no objections, I think that Project Flame should begin to move to Paris.'' He looked around the room. Leonid Chomsky spoke.

''What about Sasha? She is still unable to travel.''

Arie thought for a moment, then answered the young KGB lieutenant. ''Miss Andreyev's presence is not required in Paris. Once we decide our next move, she can be notified through Mossad headquarters. Perhaps it will be best if she returns to Washington. You did say that GRU Major Metsky was inquiring after her, didn't you? It would be good for him to find her there.''

Everyone agreed, including Sasha, who was still weak from her wound.

Michael Gross's security force would leave for Paris immediately and link with the DIA. Leonid and Anya would fly to Athens with Polish passports and then back to Paris. They would pose as newlyweds. Taft would leave immediately for Paris under one of his regular covers, that of Bill Green, American businessman stationed in Paris. The DIA maintained an office on Rue Washington. He would be accompanied by the firm's Middle-East representative, known to this group as Rabbi Sholem Asher. Arrangements would be made under a NATO diplomatic agreement for them to bring luggage through customs without inspection; therefore it would guarantee safe entry for the priceless vestments of Aaron that Asher would need if he were to go on to the Soviet Union. General ben Kagan would go to Paris only after he had received confirmation from Peter Somoroff on the Tyros link. Once confirmed, Gross and the prime minister would become part of the trade mission to the air show. Finally, Peter Somoroff would be on his way to Moscow, via Rome, in a few hours.

After everyone had left his office, ben Kagan ordered a helicopter. Twenty minutes later he lifted off the Mossad rooftop and instructed the pilot to radio a flight plan to Zefat. The one disturbing fact that he had told no one was that Rabbi Abraham had contacted him and urged that he come as quickly as possible to the old temple in Galilee. There was a new problem, and it was important.

He reached Zefat at midday. A jeep and driver were waiting for him at the small tactical air base outside the city of artists. The driver waited in the narrow alleyway alongside the temple, as Rabbi Solomon ben Levi met Arie at the side door and silently escorted him through the cool dark hallways to Rabbi Abraham's private study in a sparsely furnished cell in the basement of the temple.

The old man dismissed Rabbi ben Levi and immediately got down to business.

"Thank you for coming so quickly, General. We have a much larger problem, I fear, than what was originally anticipated. First let me ask you if the prime minister has agreed to meet with the Soviet premier."

Arie had originally planned to keep that information top secret until the final arrangements were completed, and then only those with a definite need to know were to receive the information. The rabbis in Zefat were not on his list of people to be informed. Rabbi Asher would be in Paris with all the tools necessary for his mission to Moscow. The Zefat rabbis could infer that the deal was struck, but they would not know with certainty until the deed was done.

"I will have to defer an answer to that question, Rabbi Abraham," began Arie, "until I know what the new problem is and how it affects our operation."

The old rabbi, although native to Israel, had not been a

recluse. In his younger years he had traveled throughout the world, serving those in need of the particular talents and knowledge possessed by the followers of Rabbi David ben Zimrah. In fact, these followers had been worldwide travelers since the sixteenth century, for theirs was work that never ceased. The archangels of darkness had many disciples and servants. Their travels and accomplishments were recorded and kept in the temple archives. Even a cursory reading would show that many cases involved extremely delicate political and diplomatic negotiations. Rabbi Abraham understood ben Kagan's hesitancy.

"I will not argue with you, General. The security of your work is as necessary as our own self-imposed secrecy. There are disturbing facts in this matter that I cannot really explain clearly. I just don't know for a fact that what I suspect is really true. Rabbi Asher knows what to look for, and when he is convinced that my suspicions are correct, he will inform you, and we will know what to do. But in order to be prepared, I must request that you obtain clearance for Rabbi Zahor and Rabbi Hashomer to enter the People's Republic of China."

The madness grows, thought ben Kagan. First the Soviet Union, now China.

"May I ask why, Rabbi?"

The old man saw how perplexed the Mossad general was. He knew he would have to reveal the awesome possibility of Valarian's true identity.

"The prisoner we took the other day is dead. His life was taken by the spirit that controlled him. I believe that spirit is Valarian. But we think that we were able to identify the spirit that inhabited the body of our prisoner. This means that his birth—and I am talking about the body we captured, not the spirit that inhabited it—was not of Jewish or Moslem sanction. Yet he was native to this land. The spirit that possessed him was most powerful. I believe it was that of a subprince, who, as I explained the other night, are among the most high in this order of evil. They are answerable only to the dark archangels themselves. We believe this man was possessed by Asmodeus, servant to Shaytān himself."

General ben Kagan chose his next question carefully. Somehow he sensed that the Soviet premier's problem had taken on new, ominous proportions.

"Are you saying that Valarian is Satan himself?"

"I am saying that this might, and I stress *might*, be the case." Rabbi Abraham's words were firm.

"What has China to do with all of this speculation?"

"That is a long and complex story. Colonel Somoroff brought us many clues. The prisoner added to our knowledge. You must understand—and this is most important—that where one of the four dark archangels are involved directly, and this is truly a rare occurrence, there is always subterfuge, deceit, guile . . . in other words, things may not be what they appear to be. But let us assume that Valarian is Shaytān himself. We must then assume that he has revealed his presence for a most evil reason."

Arie interrupted, a fear growing inside needing to be expressed. "Excuse me. Are you saying that he has planned all of this? That we are being led into a trap?"

"Not necessarily. But it is possible. With a fallen archangel anything is possible. Only God, blessed is He, knows the truth."

Ben Kagan's mind raced with a hundred new thoughts. Had Somoroff duped them? Was the prime minister in danger? Was the premier himself a follower of Valarian? Was it all a fabrication to embarrass Israel—or worse . . . ? The knot in his stomach grew tighter.

Again, Rabbi Abraham was able to read Arie's emotions.

"Be calm, General. There are positive facts that we cannot refute. The experiences of Colonel Somoroff and Rabbi Vogel, I am convinced, are true. Our own experience with our prisoner is not a figment of imagination. I was in the room. I confronted the spirit, and although we have never ourselves seen a subprince, we have in our possession many records of our forebears experiencing similar spirits. This knowledge protected us. The spirit Asmodeus was driven from here. He cannot, or he will not, inhabit just any body. His needs and services to the archangels of darkness are special. He must have a special body."

"What kind of body?" Arie asked, the intelligence officer in him gaining control of his emotions.

"One born of a disciple, a spirit servant. One conceived by the dark archangel himself."

"A child of Satan?"

"Exactly. We will not have to worry about Asmodeus for several weeks."

"You mean the child has been conceived for some time?"

"No," said the rabbi patiently. "It is, or was, conceived only when Shaytān knew that we could hold our prisoner indefinitely. It was then that he destroyed the body of this evil man and ordered Asmodeus out. We can assume another child grows in an unholy womb somewhere in the world."

"Can it be here?" Then Arie remembered the old man's request for entry into China. "In China?"

"No," Abraham answered quickly. "It will not be in China. It may very well be here. Learn from Peter Somoroff's tale of this man, this spirit that inhabits Valarian. We know his must be the body of the missing Captain Barnowski. And before that the Nazi Hendricks, and before that the Ottoman butcher Bayar. He appears where Jews are slaughtered in great numbers. Shaytān is peculiar that way. His brothers, Lucifer, Leviathan, and Belial, the other dark archangels, have other missions in this world. Shaytān pursues us because of our covenant with God, king of the universe. He attacks God through our persecution. Once in a while he will stir up evil and hatred for other causes. It is possible he was a slaver in America and fomented the evil of their Civil War and the persecution of the black man. But we are his target. From that he has never wavered since we drove him out of this land when the Rabbi Jesus refused his temptations."

It was the first time in his life that Arie ben Kagan had ever heard a rabbi refer to Jesus Christ as a rabbi, or in any way tie him to the Jewish faith. He was stunned.

"There is more for you to know," the old man continued.

"Although we seem a small sect, few in numbers, we reach throughout the world and are in constant contact with followers and believers in all lands. This is one of our great strengths, and one of our deepest secrets. I trust you will keep it thus?"

"Of course," answered Arie. "What about China? Why there?"

"Our contacts in China have always believed that this one, Shaytān, originated in their land. Recent facts have been discovered to support this belief. I cannot go into details. We do not have the time. But if Valarian is the archangel Shaytān, then we must be prepared to trap him, capture him, and remove him to a specified location deep inside China. Rabbi Zahor and Rabbi Hashomer must be allowed to prepare the way as a contingency. I cannot stress the importance of this matter too strongly. For you, it must be an act of faith.''

Ben Kagan knew there was no point in argument. He had been warned of possible deception, and he would be on his guard from this moment on, watching Somoroff and the Soviets with new eyes. He would instruct Michael Gross to dispatch a secret force, unbeknownst to the DIA and KGB, to Paris for further security.

"When do you want the rabbis in China?" he asked, implying acceptance of the rabbi's story.

"Immediately. Whatever their route, they must get to the city of Sian as quickly as possible. Once there they will know where to go and whom to contact. I can say no more.''

Ben Kagan sensed the meeting was over. He had one more question. "Rabbi, let me be frank. If we assume that Valarian is Satan himself, can you guarantee control over him?"

"Ours is not a business of guarantees," the old man answered. "We are only instruments of God, blessed is He. He will guide us and He will make us strong . . . if that is His will. One thing I can say that I do believe—Valarian has no idea that we have the ancient vestments of Aaron. They are our strength. He has miscalculated, and God has allowed us what appears to be a moment of possible triumph. We must take it. We cannot question its wisdom. To have the covenant is to be prepared to act!''

The tall glass window in his room glowed with the night lights of Paris. Arie was not sure whether he had slept or only daydreamed through the three hours that had passed since he had spoken to Andy Taft. It was nearly 7:00 PM. He would take a shower, have a drink at the crowded bar in the lobby, and meet the young DIA agent outside the hotel under the gleaming chrome and glass canopy that extended in front of the hydraulic and electric sliding doors of the Hôtel Méridien.

As he prepared for the night ahead, Rabbi David Hashomer, his skin darkened with makeup, and Rabbi Zahor, a man of Yemenite birth who needed no makeup, joined a group of Egyptian engineers boarding the special Boeing 747 for the long trip to China. It had required a personal scrambler call from the Israeli prime minister to the Egyptian president to arrange the cover and the trip. Incongruous nations were joining forces, and that made General ben Kagan feel a little better. Still, he would keep Rabbi Abraham's warning about deceit in the forefront of his mind.

━ 42 ━

Arie greeted Andy with a hug and perhaps too much backslapping.

"Hey," said Arie as the young American exited the car and met him on the curb under the canopy. "It's good to see you, you old son of a bitch. You look great!"

Andy accepted the Israeli's embrace and guided him quickly to the car, a black Citröen, slightly scruffy and dull. After they pulled out of the driveway Taft spoke.

"Everything is in place. Premier Alexeyevich has arrived with Colonel Somoroff. The air show was a godsend. We couldn't have fabricated a better cover."

Arie reflected momentarily on Andy's use of *godsend*, remembering Rabbi Abraham's final words in Zefat. The young man continued, excitement obvious in his voice.

"The prime minister is in the Israeli Embassy. Your security people will move him in an hour. Nothing suspicious there, since you always offer protection for your nationals when they travel. Our people have the chateau totally secured for a radius of two miles. We will eat dinner at a small restaurant in Saint-Germain near the Île de la Cité."

"Is that the one that looks out onto Notre-Dame?" Arie asked.

"Yes, sir. The best food in Paris."

"I've eaten there. Good choice."

Andy turned off the Champs-Élysées onto Rue de Rivoli. Arie could see the illuminated spires of Notre-Dame ahead, pointing as a beacon in the clear Paris night.

"We shall have to decide on a topic of discussion during

262

dinner,'' the general said. ''Do you know anything about farming, Andy?''

''Yes. I was raised on a farm in southern Illinois.''

''What did you grow?''

''Soybeans and corn. We kept dairy cattle, too.''

''Good,'' said the Israeli general. ''Then it will be animal husbandry.'' Arie relaxed, enjoying the sights of the City of Lights.

''Do you think we will have a deal with the Soviets—I mean Israel, that is?''

''Cattle, my friend,'' answered ben Kagan, ''the topic is cattle from now on. When the time comes to change the subject, I will tell you.''

Andy felt as though his hand had been slapped. ''It's your show, General,'' he responded as he turned the Citroën onto the bridge leading across the Île de la Cité to St.-Germain.

Anya Somoroff combed her long black hair nervously. The room was charming, but very small. She and Leonid kept tripping over each other, carefully avoiding embarrassment, especially when it was time for bed. The young KGB lieutenant had slept on a chair near the garret-type window that afforded them a wonderful view of the famous rooftops of Paris. They were supposed to be honeymooners, so separate rooms were out of the question. Still Anya felt that Michael Gross had purposely arranged for the small hotel near the Pont Royal to embarrass Leonid Chomsky after the argument the men had had regarding Anya and Michael's relationship in Tel Aviv.

It really was none of Leonid's business. In the end Anya had been the peacemaker, but she knew Leonid still held the Israeli captain in contempt. The trouble began when Gross relayed the results of the interrogation of the Arab officer, captured the night of the attack on Kibbutz Ginnosar, to the Soviets in Tel Aviv. Her father took the information calmly. He told General ben Kagan he would look into the matter when he returned to Moscow that night. But Leonid took exception to the report. She recalled his words clearly.

''How do you know those attackers were controlled by Soviet advisers, as you call them?'' Leonid had demanded.

Gross had been calm and deliberate, sensing the young Soviet's animosity.

"The Arab officer admitted that to Major Horowitz during the interrogation."

"Was the man tortured?" Leonid demanded.

"Our procedures are none of your business, Lieutenant," Michael answered.

"If he was tortured, he would say anything. I don't believe it."

Before Gross could answer, Peter Somoroff intervened. "Leonid. Enough of this. I will confirm the matter tomorrow in Moscow. Drop it." Peter was sure that his assistant was wrong. Still he had to calm the atmosphere. But it didn't work. Chomsky was agitated. He moved swiftly across the room and confronted his superior.

"You will excuse me, Colonel Somoroff, but I cannot take the word of this man as fact. You should know better, sir. He has spent his time making advances to Anya in your absence."

The words tumbled out of Chomsky's mouth, shocking everyone in the room. Gross jumped to his feet in a rage. He began to cross the room toward Leonid with clenched fists.

"You bastard," he roared. "You have no right—"

Ben Kagan yelled, *"Michael,"* stopping the big Mossad agent in his tracks. "Michael! Sit down!"

Gross obeyed automatically, but his anger did not subside.

"I apologize, Colonel Somoroff," the general said. His thoughts leaped back to Rabbi Abraham's words regarding subterfuge and deceit spread by Satan. Could this distraction be part of Valarian's plan?

Peter Somoroff spoke calmly to no one in particular in the room. "I apologize for Lieutenant Chomsky's outburst. We are all highly strung over this business. Let's remain calm."

Anya then spoke, feeling that the air must be cleared of this side-issue. "Michael and I are in love, Father. It is not the dirty thing that Leonid infers. Perhaps it is unfortunate, but it happened. Perhaps Leonid was thinking about Marina Grochenko . . . perhaps he misses her too much . . . I forgive you, Leonid."

She stood and extended her hand to Chomsky. He took it, but averted his eyes. Michael crossed the room and extended his hand to the young Soviet officer. They shook hands, and a sense of calm returned to the room.

Leonid now came out of the bathroom. Anya turned to him, swirling her dress in a pirouette.

"How do I look?"

"Beautiful," he replied, and meant it. "We should be going soon. I made a reservation in the small café across the street. The car is parked there, too."

They crossed the narrow street to the Café D'Or. Leonid checked his car before they went into the restaurant. He took no notice of the black Peugeot parked three cars away, nor did he see the man behind the wheel duck down when Chomsky momentarily looked up the street. It was a man whose face he knew intimately from Moscow—Major Anton Metsky, disciple of Nickolai Valarian.

Three days ago the master had summoned him to his office. Metsky sensed that Valarian's plans were coming to a head, that the day of reckoning and triumph promised to all disciples was at hand. There was much to do. Anton had arranged the final details of Valya Pernick's immigration to Israel. The necessary papers and false records had to be prepared quickly. In addition, an intensive search for Rosteveli and the rest of the missing occupants of the now-deserted KGB Lubyanka wing was to be instigated. Valarian authorized his disciple to make use of whatever GRU forces he required to get the job done. Finally, the new Minister of the Interior instructed Major Metsky to keep a watch on all flights emanating from Israel. Agents were to patrol every European and American airport that serviced flights from Tel Aviv. All passengers were to be photographed and identified by the GRU, but Metsky was to look for Somoroff, his daughter, Chomsky, Sasha Andreyev, and Rabbi Vogel in particular. Somehow Valarian knew they were about to leave Israel. And he was right.

Metsky also noticed that one of the candles above Valarian's desk was extinguished. He thought to inquire but knew better. The disciples were kept apart to do their separate acts. Only when absolutely necessary were they brought together. This was understood, and in the years that Metsky had served Valarian, only the recently departed Misha Karkov and Valya Pernick were known to him as disciples. Misha's candle had been replaced with another's, but its identity remained a mystery to the GRU major. The new candle glowed evenly. The one that had been upside down was now dark. His interest was not missed by Valarian, but no explanation was given.

Within twenty-four hours he reported back to his master. The results of the surveillance were excellent.

"Colonel Somoroff was identified in Rome. He is on his way back to Moscow on Aeroflot flight one-seventy-one," he began, referring to his notes when necessary. Valarian listened carefully but made no comment.

"We nailed Chomsky and Somoroff's daughter in Athens. They had fake Israeli passports upon entry, but then left using their Polish documents, on a BOAC flight to Paris. I had them followed. They are registered as man and wife at the Hôtel Pont Royal." He looked up from his notes. "That is all we have at the moment. Valya Pernick is on her way to Israel through the placement agency in Vienna. She is traveling as a Jewess immigrating from here. I have over one hundred men searching for the KGB unit, but there is nothing to report yet."

"I want you to go to Paris, Anton," Valarian began. "I want you to grab Somoroff's daughter and find out what she knows. If you have to kill Chomsky, do it. I will deal with Colonel Somoroff. Contact me when you have completed your mission." He dismissed Metsky. Within ten hours the major was in East Berlin, passing through the Brandenburg Gate into the west. Six hours later he arrived in Paris.

Now he watched the young Soviet couple dining in the restaurant. His plan was working perfectly. The next move, he thought, was to get into the back seat of Chomsky's car and wait for his prey. It was his last thought. The big Israeli put three nine-millimeter bullets through Metsky's brain in two seconds. Gross opened the door of the Peugeot, shoved the dead Soviet into the passenger seat, and speedily drove away down the narrow street.

Back in Moscow it was nearly midnight. Nickolai Valarian had telephoned Premier Alexeyevich three times, but the Soviet leader had not yet returned the calls. He was about to dial Marshall Malenkov so that the general secretary could demand a meeting on his behalf with the premier and Peter Somoroff. As he reached for the push-buttons on his console he felt the pain of the Israeli bullets in his own head. He knew Metsky was dead. The candle representing the major flickered above the shiny mahogany desk. Rising quickly,

Valarian stood on the desk and removed the dying candle. He placed it in front of him, gently caressing it with his scarred hands. His tongue slid out and encircled the flickering flame. He held the flame on the tip of his tongue, slowly drawing it back into his mouth. Then he swallowed the fire.

"Stay in the body," he commanded. "We still have use for it."

Then he telephoned the marshall, his newest disciple, and instructed the Soviet leader to arrange the meeting. An hour later he learned that Premier Alexeyevich was nowhere to be found. He had disappeared from the face of the earth. Peter Somoroff was also gone. For the first time since the defeat of the Nazis became apparent, Valarian felt the hand of God upon him and he was deeply concerned.

At that moment, the Illutian aircraft was receiving final landing instructions from the Orly control tower. On board, the Soviet mission to the French Air Show fastened their seat belts in preparation for landing. At the rear of the giant Soviet airliner, hidden from view by drawn curtains and protected by two KGB agents, Peter Somoroff and Premier Ivan Ivanovich Alexeyevich also prepared to land. But they would not be attending the air show. Project Flame was firmly ensconced in Paris, eagerly awaiting their presence.

Michael Gross passed the DIA checkpoint, was recognized, and was passed through. The guards at the KGB checkpoint questioned him about the dead body in the front seat for five minutes. Each group knew the members of the others by sight. They had worked in concert for the past three days, checking and double-checking security arrangements. Still the Soviets went by the book. They had to be certain that Gross's passenger was truly dead. Satisfied, they passed Gross on toward the chateau. The final approach checkpoint was Is-raeli. By plan, only the cars containing the prime minister of Israel and the Soviet premier would be allowed to drive to the chateau. All others would walk from the final checkpoint, a distance of one hundred meters. Michael instructed his men to park the Peugeot behind their checkpoint in a small clearing and lock the doors. Satisfied, he walked slowly toward the house smoking an aromatic French cigarette. He was sur-prised to see a limousine parked near the side entrance to the building. As he approached, two DIA guards signaled him to halt. Both men had leashed Doberman pinschers. Both carried Uzi machine guns.

By design, known only to the DIA, Premier Alexeyevich and Peter Somoroff had arrived an hour early. In the final analysis, no one really trusted the other, yet. Peter and Ivan Ivanovich sat alone in the large central dining room of the classic chateau. A large stone fireplace dominated the room. Alexeyevich stood near the fire, the mantel rising a good three feet above his head. He sipped a brandy and studied Peter Somoroff as the KGB colonel prepared the long dining table for the meeting. It was handmade of heavy oak, with ornate carving on the curved legs. Eight massive chairs, containing the same carving motif, were placed four across from four. Peter opened his large attaché case and distributed thick files onto the table in front of each chair.

Outside the door to the dining room, two DIA agents sat silently, their hands folded on top of their loaded machine gun pistols. Within the house four more DIA men, plus two KGB and two Mossad, patrolled. Each group had an attack dog. Outside, on the inner perimeter, more DIA men were stationed. The second perimeter and checkpoints were manned by Mossad, the next perimeter checkpoint by KGB. The final checkpoint and outside perimeter were completely in the control of the DIA European section. Listening devices and infrared-sensitive TV cameras scanned all approaches to the chateau. The American president had ordered a wing of Cobra gunships held secretly ready at the nearby NATO base in St.-Denis. As an extra precaution the DIA had two jet helicopters behind the chateau just in case the heads of state needed to make a hasty departure. Things were secure.

Three kilometers to the north, a special Israeli strike team, including Commando Sergeant Sarah Steiner and Corporal Ahron ben Levi, hero of the Ginnosar attack, plus two hand-picked commandos, made a final check of their equipment and routes to the chateau. General ben Kagan had ordered their undetected presence as an extra precaution after his meeting with Rabbi Abraham. The general was not totally convinced of the sincerity of the Soviet premier. But the group would only move on a radio signal from ben Kagan, who had the transmitter installed in his lighter. If he sensed a trap, he would ask Gross for a cigarette and key the radio.

As Michael was about to enter the chateau he saw the headlights of Chomsky's car stopping at the final checkpoint. He looked at his watch. They were on time. But he had to find out why the premier and Somoroff had arrived early, since he knew the limo was not his prime minister's.

Peter finished placing the files on the table and poured himself a brandy. He joined the premier near the fireplace.

"To Boris Menoff," he said, raising his glass toward Alexeyevich.

"And Celia." Both men drank deeply.

"Is that all of it?" the premier asked.

"Everything is committed to paper. The original is in the safe in Tel Aviv."

"Incredible." Ivan Ivanovich studied his old friend. He saw the new lines of age in his face and the white hairs. "Who would believe such a story?"

"I do," Peter answered flatly, staring into the fire, thinking of his son, his family, his country, and the story he had related to Premier Alexeyevich, Major Rosteveli and General Porikin in Moscow earlier.

His flight from Rome had been uneventful, but he was sure he was being followed when he arrived in Moscow. As previously arranged he drove directly to the Kremlin and met with Premier Alexeyevich. Arrangements had been made for the flight to Paris by General Porikin. After relating the events in Germany, Turkey, and Israel, Peter inquired about the Soviet frogman, Captain Yuri Danoloff, and the advisers supposedly working with the special Al Fatah unit in Lebanon. General Porikin, through Premier Alexeyevich's office, had given the problem to General Kubyshev in Chita. The man had been young Peter Somoroff's commander and took his murder very hard. When Porikin told him that this information was tied to the murder, the Far-East commander tore through his headquarters and wrung necks until he had the answers. What he found upset him terribly. Colonel Nickolai Valarian, through the records section of the GRU and with the blessing of Marshall Malenkov, had siphoned off top officers, specialists in terrorism and guerrilla warfare, and by cutting special assignment orders lifted them to his command, eventually placing them in the Middle East, totally under his orders and his assistant, Major Anton Metsky. The Soviet Union, like any huge bureaucracy, is layered and smothered by tons of paperwork and computer tape. A man can disappear for months, and as long as the records appear to be in order, no one questions the absence.

"Valarian has built a private army right under our noses," General Kubyshev had told General Porikin. When advised of the situation, Premier Alexeyevich ordered General Kubyshev to return the men to the Soviet Union immediately. If Marshall Malenkov questioned the order, he was to be referred to the premier.

Rosteveli had related his capture of Captain Servioff with emotion and anger. When he finished, Peter had a few questions.

"Did you strip him?"

"I didn't have to. The swine was naked when I found him with his little boy. He had no marks on him like that dog Karkov."

"Is there any sign of Rabbi Posner?"

"No, sir. It was Servioff who took our people out, so we must assume that Metsky and Valarian have him. But I doubt that he is alive."

"He was a brave man." Peter spoke more to the premier than to the others. "He loved this country even though we treated him so poorly."

Porikin was uncomfortable with the tone of Peter's voice.

"Colonel Somoroff, I know that you have had an arduous journey, a fantastic journey. But these Jews—Israelis—they are still enemies of the Soviet Union. I hope you have not grown soft."

Peter Ilyavich Somoroff measured his superior carefully. Had he completely missed the point of the entire adventure? Peter restrained his emotion and spoke calculatingly to General Porikin.

"I realize that no one in this room has been where I have been. You have only my word to judge. I believe the evidence is overwhelming. These enemies—Israelis, Soviet Jews—enemies you call them, have contributed more than we can to the solution of this problem, assuming there is a solution. I am not a political man, just a policeman. I know little of the affairs of state. Two months ago, in this office, Premier Alexeyevich handed me a pitifully small file that belonged to

Boris Menoff. Boris gave his life for that file. My son gave his life, too. A beautiful young dancer lies crippled; the entire reputation of the KGB is threatened. Enemies you call them? A man, a rabbi whom we kept incarcerated in Tostuya for twelve years, whose family was told he was dead, came out of the northern wasteland and risked his life for the Soviet Union. Enemies? You did not know the old man Posner. Major Rosteveli can tell you what a patriot he is . . . was. I saw the bodies of many dead Israeli soldiers who defended me—me, a Soviet. Do you want me to go on? Let me just say that these things we are fighting, this Valarian, now a minister of the Soviet, a member of the executive council of the Presidium, has no place among us. He is evil, and we must be rid of him or I fear we are all doomed. Our enemy is here, and his one wish is to destroy us . . . to destroy the Soviet Union. I am not soft, General Porikin, I am deeply afraid.''

An hour later Peter Somoroff and the premier left through a secret tunnel under Red Square that led to the basement of the Cathedral of St. Basil. They were followed by Major Rosteveli and General Porikin, both of whom felt much wiser having spent the last few hours with Peter Somoroff.

Michael Gross double-checked the inside guards and then went to the small bedroom on the second floor where Rabbi Asher waited with the vestments of Aaron. Michael knocked, and Sholem's voice called out in Hebrew.

"Who calls?"

"A son of Aaron, of the tribe of Levi," answered Michael.

Rabbi Asher unlocked the door and admitted the Mossad agent.

"Everything okay?" Michael asked, glancing around the beautifully furnished room.

"I feel like Louis Quatorze. Is everything going all right?"

"Fine, Sholem. I'll come and get you when we are ready."

The light from the crystal chandelier glittered off the solid gold and jeweled breastplate that lay on the pale blue bedspread. Sholem had laid out the vestments in preparation for the meeting in case the prime minister and premier wanted to view them.

"It's the real thing?" asked Michael, still unable to believe that the treasure of his people actually existed.

"In this city of couturiers we have a garment by the

ultimate designer. God Himself, may He reign forever, ordered these. They are as real as you and I.''

"Well, take good care of them, my friend," Michael said as he prepared to leave.

"With my life," said Sholem Asher. "With my life."

Michael met Anya and Leonid in the foyer at the bottom of the ornate staircase. He kissed Anya, then checked his watch. Right on schedule. They walked together to the doors of the dining room. The DIA guards stood and checked their IDs. Anya Somoroff had met the premier many times. As a young girl she remembered many visits to his beautiful home in Odessa. He was always kind to her, a gentle man. Leonid had not been told of the early arrival of the premier. He was not prepared to meet Ivan Ivanovich Alexeyevich and was shocked to see him standing in the room when he entered. Michael Gross also felt a tingle of extreme excitement when he viewed the premier. Peter rushed across the room and embraced Anya.

"Ah," he exclaimed, "safe and sound. How are you? How was your trip?"

"Fine . . . wonderful. Leonid took good care of me. How are you?"

Peter realized that Leonid and Michael were standing very stiff near the door. He shook their hands and guided them toward Premier Alexeyevich, who had started to cross the room. Before he could introduce them, the premier took over.

"Anyanochkya, how beautiful you are." He was effusive and sincere, moving to extend his hand to Leonid Chomsky. "And you are Lieutenant Chomsky. Your country owes you a great debt."

"An honor to meet you, Premier Alexeyevich." Leonid could hardly get the words out of his throat. The premier then turned to Michael Gross. Before he could speak, Michael introduced himself in fluent Russian.

"I am Captain Michael Gross of the Mossad. It is an honor to meet you, Premier Ivan Ivanovich Alexeyevich. I am at your service."

Alexeyevich was taken aback. He quickly gathered his thoughts. "Shalom aleichem, Captain Gross," he said. "The Soviet Union owes you a great deal also. It is my honor."

• • •

Back in Paris, ben Kagan and Taft enjoyed a superb dinner and excellent wine. They had escargot with a light Chablis, boeuf bourguignon with fresh vegetables and puffy little potatoes that melted in their mouths, and drank a full-bodied house Burgundy. Dessert was a cheesecake that made ben Kagan moan with delight. He left the table only once and politely, in perfect French, asked the proprietress, a handsome woman from Brittany, to use the phone for a local call. At these prices, thought Arie, I should be able to call Australia. He phoned the Israeli Embassy and with a prearranged code instructed the prime minister's guards to begin the journey to the chateau.

A half hour later, Andy Taft and he passed the last checkpoint. They parked in the clearing next to a small black Peugeot. Ben Kagan questioned the guards about the car, and they told him that Michael Gross brought it. Arie doubled back to the car and peered in at the corpse. Having memorized Somoroff's file, he immediately recognized the man as Major Anton Metsky of the Soviet GRU. How in God's name did Gross grab him? thought ben Kagan as he walked toward the chateau with Taft. Both men presented their IDs to the outside DIA patrols. Arie noticed both limousines parked at the side entrance. He heard the slow whip of the helicopter blades turning behind the chateau. Their motors were running in anticipation of trouble.

"Where is the dish?" he asked Andy as they neared the door.

"On the other side of the house," he answered. "We have checked and double-checked the linkup. When everyone is in, we will make the final connection to the meeting room. Then you will have immediate contact with General Porikin through the Soviet Embassy in Washington, your headquarters in Tel Aviv, and the president's situation room, if you wish." He was proud of the American efficiency exhibited throughout the past few days.

"Excellent," said ben Kagan. "Anytime you want to come to work for us, let me know. There's only one problem."

Always serious, Andy questioned, "What's that?"

"You don't look Jewish." Ben Kagan laughed to himself. "Now let's get this show on the road."

Both men presented their IDs to the guards at the dining room door and entered the room.

At the same time, Anton Metsky's eyes popped open, but he did not move.

~ **43** ~

The amenities were completed without delay. The atmosphere
was tense. Everyone was anxious to begin. General ben
Kagan and Andy Taft found the others already seated at the
long oak table. The two heads of state sat opposite one
another. Peter Somoroff sat to the left of the premier; Arie's
seat was to the right of his prime minister. Leonid Chomsky
sat on the premier's right, Michael Gross opposite him. The
Soviets had one extra person, Anya Somoroff, who sat next
to her father. General ben Kagan shook the premier's hand
firmly and bowed slightly. He introduced Andy Taft, who
shook hands with the Soviets. The American then took the
seat at the head of the table.

"We have one more thing to do, if you will wait just a
moment," said Andy. He reached under the table and pressed
a button. A moment later two DIA men quietly entered the
room carrying telephone equipment. They placed one instrument in front of the premier, another in front of the Israeli
prime minister, and a third next to Taft. The two men gave
each head of state operating instructions in their native language. Finally they connected a speaker system and placed it
in the center of the table. They left as silently as they had
entered. Within fifteen seconds Taft's phone buzzed. A voice
from the communications truck parked outside announced that
the system was operative.

"We can begin," Taft said.

The Soviet premier spoke first.

"If I may," he began, "I would like to suggest that
Colonel Somoroff conduct this meeting. He is most familiar

with all of the details." He looked at the Israeli prime minister for approval.

"I have no objection to that suggestion," said the prime minister. "But," he continued, "these people all around us, Premier Alexeyevich, have done their work. We have all read the file. We have all heard first-hand accounts. I believe we are all convinced that the beast Valarian must be removed." He spoke slowly in halting English. The premier nodded his agreement.

"Up to this point," he continued, "there has been unprecedented cooperation between our countries. The old wounds have been set aside. In effect, the slate can be wiped clean, if we wish."

A troubled expression crossed the premier's face. Where was the Israeli leading him?

The prime minister went on. "From the last report of"—he stopped to check a name in his file folder—"General Porikin regarding the private army that Valarian and Marshall Malenkov have gathered into our part of the world, and by the appointment of Colonel Valarian to your executive council, I would say that we don't have much time left to fight these forces."

The premier felt uneasy. "Mr. Prime Minister." Alexeyevich spoke in English. "There is no doubt of the appreciation we have for your efforts and those of your countrymen in this matter. But I am premier of my country. I am in charge of its affairs, not Marshall Malenkov or Colonel Valarian."

The prime minister raised his hand, interrupting Ivan Ivanovich. "Please. I did not mean to infer that you have no control over events in your government. I am a little clumsy in English. Forgive me. I am trying to say that it seems to me the only real business we have to conduct in this clandestine meeting is that you and I reach an agreement regarding the future."

Alexeyevich suddenly admired the Israeli prime minister. He liked the direct approach. To him, and obviously to the Israeli, most diplomacy and protocol were nineteenth-century bullshit. He leaned across the table and looked directly into the prime minister's eyes.

"Good. Would you rather do this privately?"

The prime minister smiled. He too liked directness when there was business to be done.

"I personally like to have a witness or two, if you don't mind. It keeps me honest. Besides, they have all worked so hard and faced such danger that it would be unfair to exclude them from the final hondling."

"I am not familiar with that word," remarked the premier.

"Bargaining, dealing—it's a Yiddish expression."

"Oh," Alexeyevich said. "Then fine. What do you want in exchange for your help?"

"If you will excuse me, Premier Alexeyevich," he said slowly, gathering his thoughts for what he perceived to be the key remark that would set the tone of their negotiations. "I do not think that it is my place to suggest actions to you. What we came to do, we will do . . . but the things that we now discuss are things that you must undo. That is what interests me."

Touché, thought Peter Somoroff to himself. He silently hoped that the premier would respond positively. This was one area they had not discussed. Peter was not a politician, and he certainly was not a maker of policy.

"Very well," began the premier. "This is what I propose we do after Valarian is gone." He then began a litany of actions that the Soviet Union would take. It included free immigration, opening of synagogues, a decree allowing Jews access to all aspects of Soviet life, a review of all Jews held in prison and release of those who were arrested for political or religious reasons, recognition of the State of Israel, a trade agreement including sale of petroleum products and import of Israeli goods, and an effort to intervene in the peacemaking process with those Arab nations with which the Soviet Union had some influence.

As the premier droned on, naming concession after concession to the utter amazement of all in the room, the body of Anton Metsky stirred inside the small Peugeot. He unlocked the door farthest from the nearby Israeli checkpoint, slowly opened it, and slid out onto the ground. With catlike movements he rushed into the woods and circled behind the chateau.

At the dacha, Valarian lay on his bed. His eyes were closed, his tongue extended, multicolored, with a flame at the tip touching a mass of black wax he held in his hands. The wax melted and ran down his arms, enveloping them like long gloves, skin-tight and glistening. When his hands and arms were covered with the wax, he rose from the bed and moved around the room with the same catlike motions as the body of Metsky in faraway France.

Following the orders of his master, Marshall Malenkov began to notify the members of the executive council of the Presidium of the Supreme Soviet that he was calling a special meeting the next afternoon. He informed each minister and member of the council that he had proof Premier Alexeyevich was a traitor to the Union of Soviet Socialist Republics and that he intended to expose him publicly.

The Egyptian airliner landed in Karachi, Pakistan, for refueling. A Buddist monk boarded the plane and spoke briefly with Rabbi Zahor and Rabbi David Hashomer. The monk would make the final connections and arrangements for the rabbis to get from Chungking to Sian, their final destination.

Premier Alexeyevich completed his proposal. He sat back, waiting for a reaction from the Israeli prime minister. The answer came surprisingly fast.

"I am delighted with your attitude and humbled by your generosity. Thank you. I, however, have a different view of things."

Tension gripped the room. General ben Kagan, recalling the advice of the chief of the Mossad, stayed relaxed. He knew what was coming, but he strained, listening to exactly how the prime minister would express the Israeli attitude.

The body of Anton Metsky knelt in the woods behind the helicopters. The pilots and crews were aboard, ready to take off at a moment's notice. The DIA patrol and attack dog moved past the helicopters. They began a sweep of the area around the communications truck, its large microwave dish pointed skyward. He heard a low hum emanating from the truck. If he moved swiftly he could pass between the helicopters unnoticed. He crouched, ready to run.

Valarian knelt in the same position in his bedroom, his eyes still closed, his black wax gloves glistening, his tongue extended with the flame at the tip. Suddenly he stood and began running in place.

The body of Anton Metsky began running between the helicopters toward the chateau. He aimed at the wooden cellar door that was recessed below the main building line. Three stone steps led down to the door.

The breastplate of Aaron began to tremble on the bed. At prayer, Rabbi Asher did not notice the glittering, jeweled movement.

The prime minister's voice was friendly, almost pleading. "Here we sit, representing armies, weapons, past animosity. Let's be honest, a state of war has existed between our countries. To do all these things you say, I believe, would be unexplainable and impossible for the rest of the world to understand. We are not here discussing matters of reality as the world knows it, or even as we know it. It is not natural, it is supernatural. I do not know, honestly, what these rabbis from Zefat can do. They themselves admit we are dealing with things unknown. Things we do not understand. So, my fellow human being, I cannot, and they cannot, guarantee any success in this endeavor. And if we do succeed, it will be some time before we know what we have actually accomplished. Let me propose a different course of action." He paused again, carefully choosing his words in the foreign tongue.

"Let us, the rabbi, do what he can against Valarian. Then, no matter what happens, let us vow to ease the tensions between our countries. We can start in small ways. Slowly—or putting it another way, as fast as circumstances and the world will allow. Just as long as we understand that our goals of peace and harmony are common. If you wish to allow immigration, fine. If you can apply persuasion to those who would destroy us, then I will swear not to attack or instigate action against them. Later we can recognize one another, trade, grow together. We can make a start and leave a legacy for those who follow us as leaders. Because this much I know, and you will too when the time comes—if we . . . Rabbi Asher, that is, is able to drive this evil one away, then it is clear that there is a force of good in this world. And He is helping, and He will fulfill the promise: 'Blessed are the peacemakers, for they shall be called the children of God.' ''

Ivan Ivanovich repeated the expression in Russian. He reached across the table and shook the prime minister's hand just as a loud crash sounded below them.

Valarian leaped through the air, his wax-coated arms extended. Anton Metsky leaped through the air, his hands extended the same way, and smashed through the cellar door, splintering it as he passed through into the chateau basement. The sound brought two teams of DIA men running toward the shattered door. They released their dogs and both animals disappeared into the dark cellar. A moment later the two dogs' bodies flew back through the door and fell to the ground twitching. They were decapitated.

The breastplate rose from the bed, suspended in midair. Rabbi Asher ran to it. As he grasped the ouches at the shoulder, it took on a life of its own and moved to his chest, fitting snugly. Down below he heard a beast in the foyer.

Michael Gross moved to the door of the dining room. Arie ben Kagan shoved his prime minister under the table. At the same time Peter Somoroff performed a similar service for his premier. Chomsky drew his pistol and followed Gross. Peter motioned for Andy to get on the phone and find out what had happened.

"Stay away from the door!" ben Kagan yelled at Michael. "Let them handle it outside." He fingered the cigarette lighter radio transmitter in his pocket, undecided whether to call in the strike team. Their orders were to kill everyone except the Israelis. He had no doubt they could accomplish their mission.

Valarian stood in the middle of his candlelit bedroom. He moved his head around as though he were looking or smelling for something. His eyes were closed. His tongue began to drip the rainbow fluid onto the floor.

Asher placed the miter on his head. Driven by a force beyond his control, he left the room and headed down the stairs toward the foyer.

The DIA guards at the dining room door were on their feet, machine guns aimed toward the foyer.

Metsky broke through the door from the basement into the foyer with a roar. Behind him the Americans fired machine gun bullets into his body. They had no effect. He turned and roared again back toward the gunfire. Then he spit a rainbow of fluid, splattering the guards. They screamed in agony, unable to avoid the searing liquid. It ate into their clothing and weapons like acid. Metsky turned and started toward the dining room.

Rabbi Asher saw the man below and knew who he was. The rabbi leaped over the curved banister and flew onto Metsky's back. As the jewels on the breastplate touched the dead Soviet major, his flesh seared and smoked. He screamed like a wounded bull elephant, shattering the large crystal chandelier hanging above the foyer. It splintered and fell onto the black and white marble floor.

Valarian was slammed to the floor of his bedroom. His eyes popped open in shock. Blisters appeared on his skin at the same points where the jewels touched Metsky's body.

Inside the dining room, Gross could no longer contain himself. Chomsky too looked pleadingly at Colonel Somoroff. Both men wanted action.

"Be careful, Michael," said ben Kagan.

"Go with him, Leonid," Somoroff ordered.

Both men rushed to the door. Taft was talking to the truck and, by walkie-talkie, to the perimeter guards and helicopter crews. No one knew what had happened. Michael and Leonid rushed past the guards at the door.

"Stay here," Michael ordered. He ran to the foyer entrance and saw the incredible sight. Splinters of crystal lay all over the floor. The sickly smell of burning flesh drifted up through the open basement door. On the floor in front of him was Rabbi Asher, dressed in the vestments of Aaron, struggling on top of a man whose face was hidden. The man had his tongue wrapped around Sholem's throat, and it pulsed with brilliant colors. It was choking the life from the brave rabbi. Asher's hands were pushing down on the other man, trying to free himself from the unbelievably long tongue, but his strength was almost gone. The man underneath Asher was screaming in pain. Michael could not see where the pain was coming from.

Leonid rushed past Michael and tried to help Asher. The moment he touched the man on the floor his hands burned.

He leaped back, screaming in pain, his pistol dropping to the floor. Michael now rushed up and put his pistol to the man's head, startled to see it was the man he had killed earlier that evening. The bullet holes were clearly there, yet the man was alive. He fired into the head six times, but it had no effect on Asher's attacker. Suddenly Sholem Asher's body collapsed onto Metsky. The miter fell onto the Soviet's face, its gold medallion landing on his forehead. He went stiff, then shook violently and was still. The long tongue turned red, then black, and withdrew into the open mouth. Michael pulled Asher's body off the man he had seen die twice, for he had no doubt that Major Metsky was once more dead. But so was Sholem Asher.

Valarian lay on the floor of his bedroom exhausted. His eyes had rolled up into his head; the scars on his face and body smoldered in twelve places. Though his lips did not move, words were still clear.

"And still I curse you . . ."

⇒ 44 ⇒

"He was coming for us," said Premier Alexeyevich. "The rabbi saved our lives."

Peter Somoroff was angry. A medivac team from the helicopter tended to Leonid Chomsky's burns in a corner of the dining room. The premier sat at the table next to the prime minister. Both men drank large brandies. All had removed their jackets. Michael Gross carefully folded Aaron's vestments. Anya stood by him, wanting to help but afraid to touch the sacred clothing. Arie ben Kagan ran his fingers over the twelve jewels embedded in the gold breastplate. His thoughts drifted back thousands of years. The only one with a cool head was Andy Taft. He patiently waited on the phone while the international connections were patched in and the necessary people were brought to their ends of the line.

"Why the hell didn't you tell us you had killed Metsky?" Somoroff finally asked. He directed the question to ben Kagan.

The Mossad general came back to reality. He removed his hand from the breastplate.

"Because I found out just as I arrived. At first I thought Gross had told you. Then the meeting started, and the excitement of the discussion made me forget. It is my fault. Don't blame Michael. It is unfortunate history. I am frightened. This is a powerful thing . . . I just don't know."

Peter knew there was no point in discussing what might have been. Even if he knew Metsky was dead, what would he have done? What would it have meant? He remembered Misha Karkov dying a few moments after Rabbi Vogel used him. He knew that Misha had been killed from the outside, ot by Vogel. Would he have taken steps to watch the body of Metsky? He didn't know. Taft interrupted his thoughts.

"Everyone's on the line. If it's okay I'll put it on the speaker. That way we can all listen and talk."

The premier and the prime minister became attentive. Peter and Arie moved to the table and sat, side by side, opposite their countrymen. Both leaders gestured for ben Kagan to speak. They knew the first order of business was in Israel.

"Dov? This is General ben Kagan in France."

A clear voice, sounding as though it were in the next room, answered promptly.

"General ben Kagan, Dov Aharoni here. Miss Andreyev is with me."

"Good. Who is in Moscow?"

"General Porikin here. Major Rosteveli is with me." He spoke in Russian. Michael Gross translated simultaneously. "Are you all right, Premier Alexeyevich?"

"Yes," answered the Soviet leader. "I am fine."

"Hold on a moment, General Porikin. Who is on the line in Washington?"

There was a pause. Then the familiar voice of the American president came from the speaker on the table.

"This is President Simonson. My greetings to Premier Alexeyevich and Prime Minister Mintz." The American, as always, was formal and proper. "We are at your service here in America."

The premier and prime minister thanked him. Arie continued. "Dov? Leave Miss Andreyev on the line. I want you to dispatch a helicopter to Zefat from the base at Migdal immediately. Get word to Rabbi Levi Lemach ben Abraham that he is urgently needed in Tel Aviv. Tell him we have serious trouble and we must speak to him. Tell him that Rabbi Asher is dead. Do it now."

"Yes, sir." The man was gone from the line.

"I am here," said Sasha. "What happened?"

"We are not exactly sure what happened. There was an attack. The man was killed, but so was Rabbi Asher, may he rest in peace. He gave his life for us."

"Oh . . ." Sasha was moved to tears. Everyone could hear her sob for a moment.

"May I speak?" asked General Porikin.

"Go ahead," said ben Kagan.

"Premier Alexeyevich, may I speak freely?" The KGB general was not used to having so many people listen to his phone calls, especially an American president and an Israeli prime minister.

"Go ahead," said Alexeyevich. He was annoyed at the man's hesitancy.

"Marshall Malenkov has called a special meeting of the executive council for tomorrow afternoon. He called me just an hour ago. He said that you were a traitor and that he was going to expose you."

Peter Somoroff's heart sank. Valarian was winning. They were unable to stop him now. Rabbi Asher was dead, and with him their only hope of immediate victory.

"Does he know I am here?" asked Ivan Ivanovich.

"I don't think so, Premier, but he knows you have dropped out of sight. He suspects you are out of the country. I am sure that is why he called this meeting."

"Then I will confront him. I will be back in Moscow tomorrow morning." Alexeyevich was firm.

"Is there anything we can do?" asked the American president.

Arie ben Kagan spoke again. "Excuse me, Mr. President. We need some time to decipher exactly what has happened here. The man who attacked was a dead man. Somehow he came to life."

"What? Did I hear you right?" The president was confused.

"Yes, sir. The copy of the Menoff file and Colonel Somoroff's report that you received are true. . . . As fantastic as it sounds, believe us, it is all true. We are dealing with supernatural forces. We need some time to speak to our experts in Israel. About an hour. In the meantime, is it possible for you to lodge a protest to the world press stating that the head rabbi of Moscow, Rabbi Posner, has been arrested and incarcerated without cause by the new Minister of the Interior of the Soviet Union? It must be a very strong protest, if it is agreed to by Premier Alexeyevich." Ben Kagan looked at the premier for support.

"I totally agree, Mr. President," said the premier. "It is a good tactic. General Porikin, I want you to see that *Pravda* and *Izvestiya* release the same story as soon as the complaint is lodged. See that it gets onto the morning news on television without comment. Nationwide. Is that clear?"

"Yes, sir," answered a shocked Porikin.

Peter Somoroff spoke next. "Major Rosteveli, how is the security of our unit?"

"We are still in the same place, Colonel Somoroff. I do not believe we have been detected. The GRU are all over the city, but our cover is still good."

"How many men do you have there?"

"Twenty-five, sir."

"Is there any news of Rabbi Posner?"

"No, sir. May I ask who attacked you, Colonel?"

Being aware of security, even though the Tyros system sidebands were rarely used, Somoroff chose his words carefully.

"It was the one who brought little boys to your friend."

"Is he dead?"

"We believe now he is."

"Good," said Rosteveli. There was satisfaction in his voice.

"We will keep these lines open until Rabbi Abraham can join us."

Andy Taft looked at his watch and stood. "We have sequenced an irregular change of frequencies on the system. If for a moment you think you are cut off, just wait. The connection should come back in ten seconds after the line appears to go dead."

As they waited for Rabbi Abraham to arrive in Tel Aviv, the Egyptian 747 crossed the Burmese border and entered Chinese air space on a vector toward Chungking. At a distance almost equal from Chungking but to the northeast, the sleek new Lear Commander, recently delivered by the CIA to Chinese intelligence, lifted off the runway at Sian carrying General Tsung Ming Lee, commander of worldwide Chinese intelligence services, and Dr. Tsu Heng, supervisor of the archaeological dig near the ancient city of Sian. It too maneuvered to a vector heading that would bring it to Chungking. They would arrive an hour before the Egyptian plane landed.

In his dacha, Nickolai Valarian literally licked his wounds. The seared flesh began to heal. He then contacted his newest disciple, Marshall Malenkov. The portly general secretary felt the pleasure of reward after he informed his master that the meeting of the executive council was confirmed. By tomorrow night Malenkov would be the sole ruler of the Soviet Union. Valarian was pleased. He alone knew who would really rule the Soviet Union and, through its military power, wreak havoc on the world.

~ 45 ~

It was nearly midnight when Rabbi Abraham joined the satellite hookup. He had been wakened by Major Horowitz's assistant banging on the old temple door. The helicopter ride through the dark skies was frightening, but by the time they arrived in Tel Aviv atop Mossad headquarters, he was enjoying the sensation of flight. Rabbi Malachi had gone down to Kibbutz Ginnosar to bring Rabbi Vogel back to the temple. Rabbi Solomon ben Levi prepared for Vogel's return and silently prayed for the soul of Rabbi Sholem Asher.

During the hour and a half that it took to bring Rabbi Abraham down to Tel Aviv, exhaustion began to wear heavily on the people at the chateau. Premier Alexeyevich and Prime Minister Mintz had settled in armchairs near the fireplace and discussed world affairs. Both men sincerely liked one another. Michael and Anya sat quietly holding hands. The medics had given Leonid Chomsky a sedative to ease the pain of his burns. He slept. Peter and Arie sat at the long table discussing the options now that Rabbi Asher was dead. Valarian had the upper hand, of that there was no doubt. They speculated on the possibility that he also had control of Marshall Malenkov, though they did not broach the subject to the premier. Somoroff was outmanned in Moscow, given that Valarian now controlled the GRU and perhaps all of the KGB people left in Peter's office. One bright spot was General Porikin, but Peter didn't think that the general actually believed Valarian possessed supernatural powers.

Taft's phone buzzed, alerting everyone in the room.

"Go ahead," he said. "Okay, patch it." He hung up and

told everyone that the rabbi was coming on the line. The
speaker on the table squealed with static.

"General ben Kagan? This is Dov Aharoni. I have Rabbi
Abraham for you."

The old rabbi's voice was calm and clear. He spoke in
Hebrew. Michael translated for the Soviets.

"General ben Kagan . . . is Sholem dead? Is it true?"

"Yes," said Arie. "He was killed by a man whom we
thought was already dead."

"Was the man marked with the red triangle and the backward C?"

"Yes, Rabbi. But he was killed earlier this evening. Somehow he came back to life. He was dead, I tell you. How is
that possible?" Arie was excited. His cold, logical mind had
been pushed too far with the night's events, and he wanted an
answer he could understand. Rabbi Abraham sensed his distress.

"Calm down, General. I believe I know what happened.
Every detail is important. Think carefully. A great deal depends on what might seem to you insignificant."

Ben Kagan told the rabbi as much as he knew and allowed
Gross and Leonid, who was now awake, to tell what they saw
and did. They called in the two DIA door guards to confirm
every detail of what occurred in the foyer. When they finished, ben Kagan also related the events that had recently
transpired in the Soviet Union. "We have little time," said
Rabbi Abraham. His voice was strong, filled with decision.

"What has happened, Rabbi?" asked the prime minister.
"What can we do?"

"This must be a message from God, blessed is He. I now
know who Valarian is . . . what he is, and how we must deal
with him." Everyone moved closer to the speaker, hanging
on every word the old man spoke. "Valarian is the evil one
himself, this fallen archangel, *Shaytān!* Only the archangels
can raise disciples from the dead."

A chill swept through everyone around the table. The
American president said, "Good Lord!" General Porikin's
translator literally shouted the name *Satan* to the KGB chief.
No one spoke for a moment. Peter took control of the situation, gesturing for Michael to translate for him.

"Rabbi, this is Colonel Somoroff. Can we stop Valarian?"

"Yes, Peter, it is possible." It was the first time the rabbi
had used Somoroff's first name. It gave him strength.

"Valarian must act forcefully now," the rabbi continued. "He must suspect we have a powerful tool to use against him. But he is vain and arrogant, so he will doubt what his intelligence tells him. It is our only chance. He will refuse to accept that we have found Aaron's holy robes and breastplate."

"What do we do?" Peter asked, his confidence growing.

"It will take extraordinary actions by those with you and by those who are listening. It will require an act of faith, and above all, finally, a belief in God Almighty. Without that we are all lost."

Somoroff spoke for everyone in the room. "We are with you, Rabbi Abraham. Just tell us what to do."

The rabbi began to rattle off a list of things that had to be accomplished within the next twelve hours. Michael continued to translate aloud. Anya committed it all to paper.

They were all to return to Moscow as quickly as possible. General Porikin was to try to keep their arrival secret. The general suggested a military base in Dubna. He would have helicopters waiting to transport them directly to the Kremlin.

They must assume that Marshall Malenkov was under Valarian's control. The premier was to contact the general secretary and request a meeting in Alexeyevich's office before the executive council meeting. He would demand that Valarian be there, too. The rabbi suggested that the premier use Peter Somoroff as bait. Peter agreed.

There was no need for the prime minister to journey to Moscow. He would return to Tel Aviv. The prime minister adamantly declined.

The most difficult part of the plan was that the four rabbis, Abraham, Malachi, ben Levi, and Vogel, plus Sasha Andreyev, had to get to Moscow immediately. That meant an Israeli plane had to fly into Soviet airspace. In an unprecedented move, President Simonson, his military adviser in the operation room, and General Porikin, with a patch line directly to General Kubyshev in Chita, devised an extraordinary flight plan. An Israeli tactical bomber, capable of landing on an aircraft carrier, would transport the people from Israel to the American Sixth Fleet flagship currently cruising in the Mediterranean off Cyprus. They would transfer to an American missile-launching jet helicopter, which would take them to a Soviet aircraft carrier now stationed off the Turkish coast. From there a Soviet scout plane would bring them to the base at Dubna. If all went well, the plane from Paris would arrive a half hour before the Israeli contingent.

They would need ten people in the premier's office besides the premier and Peter Somoroff. Ben Kagan explained that this was a minyan, a minimum congregation. There had to be at least ten present when prayers were said.

Rabbi Abraham preferred that the ten be Jews. Peter suggested that to bring strangers into the situation now might jeopardize everything, especially if someone new panicked. The rabbi reluctantly agreed. The ten would be Rabbi Vogel, Rabbi Abraham, Rabbi Solomon ben Levi, Rabbi Malachi, Prime Minister Mintz, Michael Gross, General ben Kagan, Fannie Beshevsky, Major Rosteveli, and Andy Taft. Anya Somoroff protested at being left out, but Rabbi Abraham assured her that she was needed to help Rabbi Vogel. Sasha Andreyev, because of her wound, was unable to be present. She would return to Moscow to recuperate.

Instructions were given as to how the vestments of Aaron were to be packed and handled. Rabbi Abraham would also be bringing several large cases from Israel.

As the details were finalized at the chateau, the helicopter crews were told to stand by for a flight to Le Bourget Airport. The premier telephoned his embassy in Paris and instructed them to prepare the Illutian aircraft immediately for the return to Moscow. When they were in Soviet air space, the flight plan would deviate to the base at Dubna.

Everyone, except Arie ben Kagan and the Israeli prime minister, was surprised when Rabbi Abraham asked about transportation to China. The Mossad general had kept that part of the operation secret. It took several minutes for the rabbi to explain what was needed and why. Premier Alexeyevich and Peter Somoroff were annoyed with ben Kagan. Would they ever learn to completely trust one another? Ben Kagan apologized. Dov Aharoni was in contact with the Egyptians. He told everyone that the plane was now on its final approach to Chungking and that the Egyptians would handle clearance for the Soviet plane, if and when it made the trip to Sian.

Premier Alexeyevich told General Porikin to replace all the security forces near his office with hand-picked men. He was to go to the executive council meeting as though nothing was wrong and await Premier Alexeyevich's call. Because of his burns, Leonid Chomsky's assignment was to take command of the group hiding in the Architectural Museum. The sedative and the thought of seeing Marina Grochenko made him happy, but his disappointment at not being in on the kill was obvious.

When everything was completed, Rabbi Abraham said a prayer that the day ahead would bring success.

The Illutian 600 lifted majestically off the runway at Le Bourget. The Israeli bomber carrying its unlikely passengers skimmed across the dark Mediterranean as the first rays of blue and purple far to the east announced the new day. In each aircraft, Rabbi Abraham's prayer echoed through the minds and souls of those who would soon do deadly combat with Satan.

"Send out Your light and Your truth; let them lead us, let them bring us to Your holy mountain, to Your dwelling place.

"When evil darkens our world, give us light.

"When despair numbs our souls, give us hope.

"When we stumble and fall, lift us up.

"When doubts assail us, give us faith.

"When nothing seems sure, give us trust.

"When ideals fade, give us vision.

"When we lose our way, be our guide!

"That we may find serenity in Your presence, and purpose in doing Your will. Amen."

~ 46 ~

Small groups of students, soldiers, tourists, and Muscovites dotted the enormous expanse of Red Square at midday. Faint signs of spring were evident, adding a bounce to the children's gait. The sun was bright, causing mounds of snow, gathered from many shovels all winter, to send trickles of water onto the pavement. The air smelled of spring, that special freshness promising eternal renewal.

None of the sights and smells were of interest to Nickolai Valarian as his car approached the Kremlin. He drew some comfort from viewing the Cathedral of St. Basil with its extraordinary mosquelike towers and colorful domes. The once-zealous church, begun by the infamous Ivan the Terrible, was now an antireligious museum. Soon, he thought, all of the churches will serve the same purpose.

Marshall Malenkov sat at his desk and reread the dismal computer projection for wheat production in the next decade. The Minister of Agriculture, a former Ukrainian farmer himself, relied heavily on computer science for his forecasting. Malenkov understood little of computers, other than their ability to launch and guide missiles and keep track of the enemies of the Soviet Union. He made a mental note to dismiss the minister at the first opportunity. Then he could blame future failures on the ineptitude of the man. The Canadians would sell wheat and grain to the Soviets. Once in control of the government, Malenkov could outbid the Chinese masses and raise the market price beyond their means. Fight capitalism with capitalism, he thought as he closed the report and set it aside. Today there were much more important matters at hand. He looked at his desk clock, stood, buttoned his grey suit jacket, and began his journey to Premier Alexeyevich's office in the Kremlin Great Palace. He decided to walk. He liked spring, and it was in the air today. A good sign. As he left the Council of Ministers' building his eyes fell upon the old Kremlin Arsenal across the way. The czar defended the Kremlin from the Revolutionary Army from that arsenal. But today, thought General Secretary Marshall Malenkov, today there is no defense great enough to stop him. Today he would triumph.

New faces patrolled the halls outside the premier's suite of offices. They made the assistants and secretaries nervous. All telephone calls were routed to the message secretary. All appointments had been canceled. Those older government workers who had been around during the old purges felt a similar atmosphere pervade. They silently went about their work, trusting their bureaucratic obscurity would protect them.

Three miles to the southwest, Leonid Chomsky hugged Marina Grochenko for what seemed the thousandth time. He could not get enough of her. How good she smelled and felt. His hands were bandaged, so he did his touching with his face. The months spent on this case and the strain of Marina's injury had taken their toll on the young man. He was tired as he lay next to her, knowing in a few moments he would have to be ready and alert.

"I will have to go soon," he said, his face buried in her smooth neck.

"I know. I'm frightened. Do you think we can beat him?"

He didn't want to answer. He had always had doubts about the old rabbi and the other Jews. Everything he had ever learned in the Soviet Union told him that religion was nonsense and that Valarian would win. On the other hand, he held a deep respect for Peter Somoroff, and there was no doubt in Peter's mind that this was the only way to destroy Valarian. Leonid slid his face down between Marina's small breasts and breathed deeply. Her robe opened. As he began to pull away, knowing it was time to leave, he saw the fresh pink scar on her abdomen. His love would always carry the Star of David on her body. He stared at it, wondering and finally hoping that Peter Somoroff was right.

"I'm proud of it," Marina said, her voice barely a whisper.

Chomsky stood, then bent and kissed her softly on the lips, lingering for a minute, rubbing his lips along hers. He then kissed both her eyes, turned, and silently left the room. She watched him until the door closed, then put her hands on the scar and prayed.

In the next room Sasha also prayed.

The Soviet aircraft carrier scout plane had been a half hour late, due to bad weather over the Balkans. It had to sweep wide to the east and fly over the Black Sea to avoid menacing spring thunderstorms. The American president had arranged clearance for it to pass over Greek and Turkish air space, then on to Dubna.

They all arrived by helicopter at the Kremlin just before ten in the morning. Now, as noon approached, everything that could be done was done. The plan had been rehearsed, everyone knew his role. The unknown factor—what could Valarian do . . . and what would he do—remained on everyone's mind. But strangely, Rabbi Abraham's inner strength and belief affected even the most cynical among them, General Porikin. He had left the premier's office at eleven-thirty, after first making a call to Marshall Malenkov assuring him that, as head of the KGB, he had an extreme interest in hearing about the premier's treason. He had told the general secretary that if the allegations were true, he would like the honor of arresting Ivan Ivanovich Alexeyevich himself. What he didn't tell Malenkov was that three buses loaded with KGB security forces were parked behind Lenin Mausoleum, ostensibly to handle the crowds expected on a fine spring day but under secret orders to surround the Great Palace after Nickolai Valarian's car entered the Kremlin.

Premier Alexeyevich and Peter Somoroff sat nervously near the ornate samovar, sipping tea. The first call, from Captain Bonyon, came at twelve-fifteen. He was dressed in his Army uniform, olive-colored with red officer trim, mingling with the crowds in Red Square. He walked slowly to his command car and notified the premier and the KGB commander at the buses that Valarian had entered the Kremlin. The second call came moments later, announcing that Marshall Malenkov had left his office and was walking to the Palace.

"I will sit at the desk," said the premier, repeating what they had rehearsed. "You stay near the fireplace. Marshall Malenkov must be near you when we strike."

The premier moved to the center of the room and stood on a beautiful Persian rug, looking down at a cluster of pale flowers woven centuries ago.

"And this is where Valarian must be when the time comes."

Peter nodded his agreement, knowing it would all happen very fast. Everything must be exactly right.

The others divided into teams. Rabbi ben Levi and Andy Taft would be on the south side; Rabbi Malachi and Prime Minister Mintz would take the north; Michael Gross and General ben Kagan had the most difficult assignment, the west side; Fannie Beshevsky and Major Sergei Rosteveli had the east. Valarian would not go toward the east, Rabbi Abraham suspected. The old man would be at the door, behind Valarian. The south team waited with Rabbi Abraham in the small anteroom outside the main door leading to the premier's inner office. The north team hid behind the heavy drapes that framed the window behind Alexeyevich's desk. The east team waited in the premier's bathroom. The west team, which would work along the fireplace wall, was secreted in the roomy coat closet. Fannie Beshevsky held Rosteveli's hand tightly. He gripped the Torah in his other hand, resting it upon his shoulder. Gross held the Torah for his team. The ancient parchment seemed small and frail against the big man's body, but he held it tenderly, with respect. The rabbis each held the Torahs for their teams. Rabbi ben Levi instructed Taft. When the time came, Rabbi ben Levi would give him the sacred scroll spindle, and ben Levi would move. Prime Minister Mintz also requested that Rabbi Malachi move for their team. He did not know if he would have the energy to make the run. His age was a factor. The sleepless night had drained his strength.

Anya Somoroff silently watched Rabbi Vogel. The robes, chains, and vestments were beautiful. Even the famous Oruzheinaya Palata in the west wing of the Palace, which held many of the great Czarist treasures, had nothing to compare with the workmanship and beauty of Aaron's garments. Since he had begun to dress, Rabbi Isadore Vogel had spoken only prayers. It was as though Anya were not in the room, although she passed each part of the garment to him when he pointed to that which he needed next. They had gone over the ceremony briefly. Anya wondered why one of the other rabbis didn't help him dress. Rabbi Abraham explained that in the final moments before the confrontation, Rabbi Vogel would self-induce a trancelike state. When he entered the premier's office he would have to move swiftly or Valarian would escape. A distraction would help. Anya would precede him through the door and serve that purpose. She would run across the room, keeping Valarian's attention away from the door. That would give Rabbi Vogel the extra moment he needed because Valarian would feel him before he saw him, and they hoped that in the time it would take Valarian to realize what was happening, Rabbi Vogel could be in position to begin the ceremony.

He was nearly dressed. He looked magnificent, beyond priestly—he seemed ephemeral, on another plane of existence. She wondered at the strength of this humble man who had spent so much time in the frozen wasteland of Siberia. After freedom, how could he risk his life when he had just been reunited with a family who thought he was dead? Yet none of that was apparent in his face. He was a man with a mission. The breastplate with its twelve jewels set in hammered gold was in place and attached to the gold chains at his shoulders. All that remained in the premier's private file room was the miter. She held it, surprised at the weight. The gold medallion gave the miter the appearance of being heavy, yet it was light. The touch of the fine blue linen on her hands calmed her. Rabbi Vogel whispered prayers in Hebrew as he touched each stone on the breastplate separately. Then he motioned for her to pass the miter, and as he placed it on his head, he uttered the final prayer. Anya heard the premier's heavy office door open and felt the thunderous steps of Marshall Malenkov as he entered the room.

She moved to the file room door and put her hand on the knob, straining for her signal to enter the room. Rabbi Vogel stood silently behind her. The team members tensed, awaiting their cue. In the anteroom outside the front door, Rabbi Levi Lemach ben Abraham felt Marshall Malenkov pass and knew he was Satan's disciple. Then the old man shuddered and whispered a prayer toward Jerusalem heard only by God. Nickolai Valarian, the dark archangel himself, was approaching. The old man felt his awesome power pulsing through the

Kremlin Palace walls. A lifetime of preparation had preceded this moment. Many lifetimes.

Malenkov closed the door behind him. There they were, he thought, brazen traitors, trapped by their own stupidity. He saw that Valarian had not arrived, but feeling victory in his grasp, he immediately attacked both men in the office.

"You are finished, Ivan Alexeyevich. You and this sneaking, Jew-loving traitor will never have a chance to sell out this country again. I will destroy you both today!"

He stood in the middle of the room, pointing a meaty finger at the premier. Alexeyevich sat calmly at his desk, though his heart was beating rapidly and his folded hands trembled.

"Please have a seat," he said to the agitated general secretary. "Your accomplice is late. Perhaps he has lost his courage?"

The overweight Marshall walked toward Peter Somoroff, who gestured for him to sit near the fireplace.

"Would you like some tea?" he asked quietly.

"No, Jew-lover. You are a disgrace to the Soviet Union." He folded his hands, deciding now to remain silent until Valarian arrived.

Out in the long corridor, Nickolai Valarian approached the premier's office cautiously. Something felt very wrong. His eyes darted among the paintings that hung along the marble hallway. They all depicted the glory of the Soviet Union and the Revolution. But he knew that before those days, religious works of art decorated this part of the Palace. He always felt uneasy inside the Kremlin walls. It had once been a place of religious fervor. Many spirits once occupied this space. God's name had constantly been evoked here. That is why I am uneasy, he thought. Many of the religious objects still remained in the building. After today he would have them removed. That thought enabled him to put aside his doubt and open the premier's door. As he entered the room, Malenkov rose to greet him, but it was Peter Somoroff who approached from his place near the fireplace.

"Colonel Valarian," Peter said in a friendly manner, "please come in. We have been waiting for you."

Peter placed himself between Malenkov and Valarian. It was the premier's turn to speak.

"Come in, Minister Valarian. I have waited a long time to meet you."

Alexeyevich did not get up. He gestured for Valarian to come to him. Valarian sensed an old, disturbing presence in the room. Peter's movement distracted him. The premier's gesture distracted him. But this discomfort. What was it? He moved toward the premier's desk. Malenkov could not restrain himself, but his outburst, too, distracted the evil archangel.

"I have told these Jew-loving pigs that their time is over. The executive council is waiting. We have their full support."

Nearby, Anya listened for her cue. The premier looked down at the rug. Valarian was almost in the right spot.

"Minister Valarian, or should I say Commissar Valarian, I am not a man who runs from a fight, especially if that fight is just. We can, I believe, discuss our differences like reasonable men."

"Weakling," Malenkov said with a sneer. "Nothing can save you now!"

Somoroff observed that Valarian was almost on the prearranged spot. The fact did not escape the premier either.

Rabbi Vogel's eyes stared ahead, in a trance. It was as though he could see through the door into the room. He knew exactly where Valarian stood. He began the ceremony with the first prayer uttered silently to himself.

"May the grace of the Lord, and the defense and the protection of His holy angels, never depart from me; nor from all those who by Your means and by the will of God shall receive this operation! So be it!"

The premier stood. He breathed deeply and spoke the Hebrew words. "God is upon you, brother of Lucifer, Leviathan, and Belial!"

Valarian was stunned.

Anya rushed into the room screaming. She ran past the front of the premier's desk to the samovar table.

"Murderer!" she screamed. "Murderer of my brother! Kill him—*kill him!*" She pointed a finger at Valarian. He started to lift his hand to silence her when he felt Rabbi Vogel enter the room. He swooned from the power of Aaron's vestments. The joints of the body he inhabited grew weak. Rabbi Abraham entered the room behind him and stood as a guard at the door.

"What is this?" demanded Malenkov. Peter Somoroff had moved next to him and blocked his view of Vogel. He tried to get past Somoroff, but the KGB colonel shoved the large man down into an armchair.

Vogel's voice filled the room with a strength that it had never before contained. He moved deliberately to his position in front of Premier Alexeyevich's desk in full sight of Valarian. The yellow color of the gold breastplate reflected a light onto the fallen archangel. It enveloped him in a gold mist.

"Then I will remember my covenant with Jacob," Vogel began, "and also my covenant with Isaac, and also my covenant with Abraham will I remember; and I will remember the land."

"Aaron!" Valarian gasped.

Behind Valarian, Rabbi Abraham said, "Amen."

Satan heard him and turned around to face the old rabbi. Vogel spoke again.

"A land which the Lord thy God careth for: the eyes of the Lord thy God are always upon it, from the beginning of the year even unto the end of the year."

Valarian was spun around involuntarily toward Vogel.

The four teams revealed themselves and took their positions in the four corners of the room. Malenkov shuddered at the sight of the Torahs, but he didn't know why. He tried to rise from the chair, but he couldn't. Vogel spoke again.

"Blessed is the Lord our God, Ruler of the universe, Rock of all creation, Righteous One of all generations, the faithful God whose word is deed, whose every command is just and true."

"Amen," said Rabbi Abraham again, causing Valarian to spin around once more and face the old man at the door.

"Hear, O Israel; the Lord is our God, the Lord is One."

Valarian spun back to Vogel. Rabbi Abraham spoke. "Our God is One; Our Lord is great; holy is His name."

Valarian spun back to the door again. His tongue slid out of his mouth, glowing with rainbow colors.

Vogel's voice doubled in volume, shaking the room. "Blessed is the Lord our God, Ruler of the universe, who has chosen us from all peoples by giving us his Torah. Blessed is the Lord, Giver of the Torah."

Valarian spun back again and fell to his knees. His tongue

dripped colored fluid onto the Persian rug, but it was not
absorbed.

From each corner of the room the teams began their part of
the ritual. Andy held the holy scroll, and Rabbi ben Levi
unwound it along the south wall of the office. At the same
time, Prime Minister Mintz held his Torah, and Rabbi Malachi
unwound it along the north wall. Likewise Fannie Beshevsky
held hers, and Serge Rosteveli unwound it along the east
wall; and, finally, Michael Gross held his Torah, and Arie
ben Kagan unwound it along the west side of the office.
Together they formed a box around Valarian with Vogel
inside and the rest of the people in the room outside.

Valarian screamed a primeval wail. Parts of his body began
to break. An arm cracked, a leg split in half, fingers dropped
from his hands.

Rabbi Vogel touched the first stone in the breastplate, the
sardius. "This is the tribe of Reuben. Upon it Thou hast
granted fertility unto our people that we may be numbered
and serve You." With the sound of an electrical arc, a bolt of
light shot from the stone and struck Valarian.

He touched the next stone, a topaz, as those holding the
Torahs moved a step closer to Valarian, tightening the box of
sacred scrolls around him.

"This is the tribe of Simeon. Upon it Thou hast granted
love for Thy people Israel and for all the world." Again the
square tightened and a colored bolt of light shot out. Valarian
writhed on the floor now, pieces of flesh falling from his
face.

The next stone was an emerald.

"This is the tribe of Levi. Upon it Thou hast granted
wisdom and an open heart that we may forever serve You."
The box tightened. Green light flashed, and Valarian's rain
bow fluid turned green.

The next stone was a carbuncle, much like the topaz only
clear red.

"This is the tribe of Judah. Upon it Thou hast given u
great strength that we may endure all manner of persecution
yet rise again to put our hands on the necks of our enemies."

Valarian stood, his fingerless hands raised in defiance
even as pieces of his flesh fell from them. A voice from
within him emitted sounds in an ancient and long-forgotten
tongue. The box tightened a little more. Fannie Beshevsky

esitated at the sounds Valarian made. Those who held the
orahs formed the corners of the box. They were outside and
ould not see Satan. Rabbi ben Levi, the youngest of the ben
imrah rabbis, was next to Fannie. He urged her on with a
omforting word, ''Courage!''

Inside the ever-tightening square, Rabbi Vogel touched the
ext stone, a sapphire, purple-blue in color.

''This is the tribe of Issachar. Upon it Thou hast given
omfort and healing. Yet it shall be health to Thy navel, and
narrow to Thy bones.'' Valarian's spine broke and he crum-
led to the floor, paralyzed as a bolt of purple-blue light
truck him.

The next stone was a ligure. Vogel touched it, his strength
rowing as he watched Valarian fall to the floor.

''This is the tribe of Zebulun. Upon it Thou hast granted
efreshing sleep and goodwill. As Leah bore Zebulun saying,
Now my husband will sleep with me.' ''

Valarian's eyes closed. The scroll square tightened even
nore. Half the distance had been covered. There remained six
tones.

Vogel touched the jacinth.

''This is the tribe of Dan. Upon it Thou hast overturned the
raven image forever.'' The light from the stone enveloped
atan's head, and Valarian's body was flipped to lie face-
own in the pool of his own fluid.

The next stone was an agate.

''This is the tribe of Naphtalí. Upon it Thou hast planted
s firmly on Thy earth, to do Thy bidding and stand secure in
hy way.''

Face down, Satan cried out for his brother Lucifer.

Vogel touched the next stone, a sea-green beryl.

''This is the tribe of Asher. Upon it Thou hast enriched the
arth and promised nourishment; as for Asher, his bread shall
e fat.''

The parchment box was almost upon Valarian, the ancient
Hebrew writing facing him.

The next stone touched was the multicolored jasper. Rabbi
Vogel now stood over Valarian, the Torah on the north side
lmost upon his back.

''This is the tribe of Benjamin. Upon it Thou hast bridled
he tongue of evil and restrained the blood of temptation.''

A multicolored light emanated from the stone, causing the

long tongue of Satan to turn red, then black. It slid into his mouth. His entire body turned red, then black, then white, and it appeared to be that of another man. Artillery Captain Barnowski, inhabited by Satan so many years ago in Stalingrad, had returned.

Rabbi Vogel put his hand upon the next stone. It was a large onyx.

"This is the tribe of Joseph. Upon it Thou hast gathered Thy people and given Thy word that we might spread it even unto the world with success." The light from the stone spread out and touched the Torahs.

There was only one stone remaining to be touched. The Torahs surrounded Satan, and each of the people holding them leaned over the body on the floor. They also enveloped Rabbi Vogel, who now stood straddling Satan.

He bent under the parchments and touched the last stone. It was a large and brilliantly cut amethyst. His voice had finality about it and possessed great determination.

"And this is the tribe of Gad. Upon it Thou hast granted great courage and put Gad in the forefront against our enemies."

He knelt beside the now-rigid body and put his hand upon the face of the man who had been known as Nickolai Valarian, Wilhelm Hendricks, Mustafa Ismet Bayar, and countless other doers of evil throughout the course of history. Had this man been with Cortés? Had he stood next to Nero and Ramses? Was it he who whispered in the ear of Attila and rode with Genghis Khan?

Rabbi Abraham directed those who held the Torahs to place them over the body on the floor. Rabbi Vogel stood and stepped back. The ceremony was not yet complete. After the Torahs were placed, everyone moved against the walls, as they had been instructed to do. The ancient parchments rippled with a life of their own. Peter Somoroff, totally awed by what he had witnessed so far, looked over at Marshall Malenkov. The man was dead, his face twisted with unspeakable agony, strangled by his own tongue, which was wrapped around his fat neck.

Vogel stood over the undulating parchments.

"Thou hast forgiven the iniquity of Thy people; Thou hast covered all their sins. Selah."

One of the Torahs began to roll itself up onto its spindle. Rabbi Malachi and Rabbi Solomon ben Levi left the room.

"That Thy way may be known upon the earth; Thy saving health among all nations."

"Amen," said Rabbi Abraham.

A second Torah began to wind onto its spindle.

"The Lord shall command the blessing upon thee in thy storehouses and in all that thy settest thine hand unto; and He shall bless thee in the land which the Lord thy God giveth thee."

The third Torah began to wind.

The two rabbis returned to the room carrying ancient silver and jeweled covers for the Torahs.

"Thou shalt no more be termed forsaken; neither shall thy land anymore be termed desolate; but thou shall be called Hephzibah, and thy land Beulah, for the Lord delighteth in thee, and thy land shall be married."

"Amen," said Rabbi Abraham as the last scroll began to wind onto its spindle.

Within a moment the four Torahs were wound, covering the body on the floor from head to toe. The fluid was gone from the rug, the pieces of flesh, fingers, and bones were nowhere to be seen. Rabbi Vogel removed the miter from his head and knelt, placing it on the head of the body underneath the first Torah. He stood and spread his hands out, turning slowly and blessing all in the room.

"The Lord bless thee and keep thee."

Everyone bowed their heads.

"The Lord make His face to shine upon thee, and be gracious unto thee."

Peter, Anya, Ivan Ivanovich, Sergei Rosteveli, and Andy Taft knelt, keeping their heads bowed.

"The Lord lift up His countenance upon thee, and grant unto thee, unto this nation, unto Israel, unto the world, everlasting peace. Amen."

Everyone in the room said, "Amen."

The Torahs snapped shut, their spindles locking tight, totally rewound and ready for the silver cases.

Rabbi Abraham knelt and took the miter from the head of the body and placed it back upon Vogel's head.

"You have earned this, Rabbi, son of Aaron of the tribe of Levi. You are blessed forever."

The other rabbis took the Torahs and carefully placed them in their silver cases.

"And now we have a long journey ahead of us," said Rabbi Abraham. "We cannot rest until Shaytān is returned to his earthly tomb."

Rabbi Vogel would return to Zefat with Aaron's vestments but not the breastplate. That would be bound as a cover over the four Torahs that now contained Satan's spirit. Michael Gross would accompany him. The premier had to deal with the executive council. He would then return and work out a formal agreement with Prime Minister Mintz. Peter, Arie and Andy would accompany Rabbis Abraham, ben Levi, and Malachi to Sian, China. The others would remain in Moscow and take a long-deserved rest. Anya asked to go to Israel with Michael, but Peter told her to wait until he returned. Her mother and grandmother needed her now. Before they left for the airbase in Dubna, Peter made one important phone call to Gorki. Katarina Barnowski answered the phone on the second ring.

"Mrs. Barnowski, this is Colonel Somoroff. I want to tell you that your husband's body has come home. He is a hero of the Soviet Union, and his name will have a prominent place in the Hall of Heroes at Mamayev."

As the helicopter carrying the travelers to China lifted off the Kremlin landing pad, Peter Somoroff breathed deeply. The spring air was sweeter than it had ever been before. He watched Moscow pass underneath the swift helicopter as it headed north to the waiting Illutian aircraft. In his left hand he fingered the jade dragon ring that Rabbi Abraham had given him to hold during the long journey to China. Somehow it seemed less menacing now that he held it in his hand.

~ 47 ~

The tomb appeared to be no more than a large dirt mound rising above the yellow clay plain. It stood against the majestic backdrop of Tsung Nan Shan, a part of the Tsinling Shan Mountains, its snow-capped peaks forming an impenetrable barrier to the north. On the plain below, busy farmers tended their crops, working with ancient tools, stooped in their labor.

Peter and Arie stood at the entrance to the huge, canopied dig. It stretched out underneath a plastic roof for more than four hundred yards. Most of the statues still remained covered by the native yellow clay. Tsu Heng demanded extreme care in unearthing each and every figure. He was among the few men who knew their real purpose.

Sian is in central China, in Shensi Province. Its history dates back to the dawn of Chinese civilization. For centuries it was believed that the earth-covered tomb was that of the first emperor of the Chou dynasty, buried nearly four thousand years ago. Heng had been very patient in explaining the history of the area to the visitors from Moscow. Fortunately the Chinese venerated ancient ways and ancestors, so that the tomb lay untouched and unopened all these years. The discovery of the buried figures, found one mile south of the tomb, and two other groups of figures, discovered to the east and west, brought the wise Taoist scholar to Sian in time.

Peter and Arie walked back into the prefabricated building along the dirt road that ran down the middle of the dig. To both sides, terra-cotta figures, life-size and fantastically lifelike, stood partially unearthed. Groups of workers carefully removed clay from several figures. Each statue was different.

305

All were warriors in full battle dress. Each face and uniform was unique unto itself. Many were mounted on horses, their spears and lances set firmly in ornate saddles. There were exactly six thousand figures in this dig. The digs to the east and west contained a thousand more. As the two intelligence officers walked toward the center of the dig, General Tsung Ming Lee and Andy Taft joined them.

"I still can't grasp the enormity of this place," said Peter.

"Impossible to believe, even though I see it with my own eyes," remarked Andy.

The Chinese general walked with them silently. He had been here before. The first time was when the initial discovery had been made by a farmer using a new tractor-driven plow. The blade of the steel plow had struck one of the figures. The peasant thought he had hit a rock and stopped to remove it, only to find that the rock was the sculptured head of an ancient warrior. As more heads were discovered, Dr. Heng was called in to take charge of the area. That was ten years ago. While the dig progressed, he had secretly ordered a special team of Taoists, Buddhists, and Confucianists to excavate the entrance of the emperor's tomb under his supervision. As soon as he saw the seal on the bronze door he knew the meaning of the terra-cotta figures and the purpose of the tomb.

History records that Sian was the first place in China where missionaries of the Buddhist, Jewish, Muslim, and later Christian faiths formed a common community. When the archaeological discoveries were made, Dr. Heng confirmed the reason why the ancient religious practitioners had gathered in this place.

As the four intelligence officers walked through the dig, Dr. Heng, two Taoist monks, a Buddhist monk, a Muslim mullah, Rabbis Abraham, ben Levi, and Malachi, and a Nestorian priest—who followed the doctrine that Christ had two distinct and independent natures, divine and human—were about to enter the tomb.

The Illutian jet had landed at the Sian airport at dawn after a seven-hour journey from the Soviet Union. It took most of the morning to remove the seals from the huge bronze door that bore the dragon mark similar to that on the ring worn by Valarian. The men spoke few words as they labored to gain entrance to the tomb. The four Torahs with the breastplate still serving as a cover were guarded by the Taoist monks. They burned incense and prayed over the trapped spirit of Satan while the others worked.

When the door was opened, a gust of stale, foul air rushed by the diggers. The Torahs shook violently.

"We must hurry!" commanded Dr. Heng. He turned on a large flashlight and entered the tomb first. The others followed close behind. The chamber floor was covered with human and animal skeletons and skulls. In the center of the small, square room stood a throne of solid gold, grotesquely beautiful, with carvings of all manner of creatures resembling gargoyles, winged serpents, and dragons. The walls contained the same acrostics found in the temple at Zefat, and along with them, the lists of archangels of darkness, the subprinces, and the servant spirits. All of the writing was Chinese, but in ancient, almost forgotten characters. On the ceiling above the throne, the name of God was written in Hebrew—Yahweh.

"Bring the Torahs," said Rabbi Abraham, and the monks obeyed his command. He told them to place the scrolls on the throne. When that was done, he led the others in prayer. He and the other rabbis spoke in Hebrew, Dr. Tsu Heng and the Taoists in Chinese, the mullah in Farsi, the Buddhist in Japanese, the Nestorian priest in Latin. Although there were different tongues, the prayer was the same and understood by all.

"He that dwelleth in the secret place of the most High shall abide under the shadow of the Almighty.

"I will say of the Lord, He is my refuge and my fortress: my God; in Him will I trust.

"Surely He shall deliver thee from the snare of the fowler, and from the noisome pestilence.

"He shall cover thee with His feathers, and under His wings shalt thou trust: His truth shall be thy shield and buckler. Thou shalt not be afraid for the terror by night; nor for the arrow that flieth by day.

"Nor for the pestilence that walketh in darkness; nor for the destruction that wasteth at noonday.

"A thousand shall fall at thy side, and ten thousand at thy right hand; but it shall not come nigh thee.

"Only with thine eyes shalt thou behold and see the reward of the wicked.

"Because thou hast made the Lord, which is my refuge, even the most High, thy habitation.

"There shall be no evil befall thee, neither shall any plague come nigh thy dwelling.

"For He shall give His angels charge over thee, to keep thee in all thy ways.

"They shall bear thee up in their hands, lest thou dash thy foot against a stone.

"Thou shalt tread upon the lion and the adder; the young lion and the dragon shalt thou trample under thy feet.

"Because He hath set His love upon me, therefore will I deliver Him, I will set Him on high, because He hath known my name. He shall call upon me, and I will answer Him; I will be with Him in trouble; I will deliver Him, and honor Him. With long life will I satisfy Him, and show Him my salvation."

All present raised their hands toward the name of God above the throne. They all then left the tomb. Rabbi Abraham and Dr. Heng remained. The others gripped the heavy tomb door, ready to slam it shut. Rabbi Abraham walked to the throne, while Dr. Heng held the lamp upright behind him.

"Must you take the breastplate?" asked the Chinese scholar.

Rabbi Abraham reached out and put his hands on the heavy gold and jeweled piece.

"If we are to continue our work, then we will have need of its power. His three brothers, Belial, Leviathan, and Lucifer, remain free in the world. The day will come when we discover their earthly tombs, as you have discovered Shaytān's. When they are all put to rest, then the work will be done."

He gripped the breastplate and pulled it from the silver-encased Torahs. Holding it tightly he ran toward the tomb door, following Dr. Heng and the lamp. Behind him he heard a primeval roar, but he did not look back. Once outside, the others slammed the door shut and replaced the seals and locks. The ground shook under them, and the sound of Satan, trapped inside, reverberated through the heavy door.

"Cover the door with dirt," commanded the doctor. It was done.

Later the entire group stood in the middle of the dig, saying their goodbyes and promising to remain in constant contact. The world had changed because of their actions and faith.

"And he will always remain in the tomb?" asked Peter

Somoroff as he returned the dragon ring to Rabbi Abraham. The rabbi studied the jade and silver ring for a moment, then gave it to Dr. Heng. The Chinese archaeologist bowed to the rabbi, then turned to Peter to answer his question.

"He will remain as long as we keep our vigil."

"And as long as the world wishes him to remain entombed," added the old rabbi. "Remember that once he and his dark brothers were all entombed. It was man who released them and gave them entrance to human souls. Therefore man can do it again."

"Not while I am alive," promised Peter.

Suddenly there was a disturbance near the front door of the large prefabricated building. Peasant workers were running from one of the statues they had just unearthed, yelling in fear.

To the disbelief of everyone, the terra-cotta statue had come alive. It was a fierce horseman, his ancient leather helmet strapped squarely on his head, his hands gripping the reins, his spear raised in the throwing position, galloping out of the yellow clay, up onto the road, and out toward the front door. The group ran toward the door with Peter Somoroff leading the way.

Out on the plain a goatherd moved toward the tomb, urging his small flock along. From a distance he seemed an ordinary peasant, going about his daily work. The statue horseman come to life galloped toward the man. Suddenly the man began to run toward the tomb. But he ran on four legs. The bottom half of his body was that of a goat. The horseman drew back his spear and let it fly through the air toward the satyr. It hit its mark directly at the base of the spine where the man-half joined the goat's body. It crumpled on the plain. At the same time the horseman froze in motion and crumbled to dust.

When the group reached the dead goat-man they immediately observed the mark on his back—a red arrowhead containing a backward C.

"The subprince . . . the disciple Ariton," said Rabbi Abraham sadly. "It begins."

"It has never ended," added Dr. Tsu Heng.

◆◆ EPILOGUE ◆◆

It was a joyful spring for those who had worked so hard to defeat Satan. The tensions in the world had relaxed a bit. An unexplainable desire to cooperate had arisen in international politics. Disarmament meetings were in progress. The Soviet Union and China had withdrawn massive armies from their common border. The Americans were once again shipping wheat to the Soviet Union. The most surprising development was the establishment of a Soviet Consulate in Jerusalem and Israeli consulates in Moscow, Minsk, and Kiev. This followed the recognition of the State of Israel by the Soviet Union.

Peter and Nadja Somoroff had recently returned from Israel, where they attended their daughter's wedding to Michael Gross. The trip was especially thrilling for Grandma. To her surprise, there was even a growing attendance at her church in Moscow.

Leonid Chomsky, now a captain, married Marina Grochenko in a small Orthodox church in Leningrad.

Andy Taft and a recuperated Sasha Andreyev remained friends in Washington.

Rabbi Vogel had rejoined his family at Kibbutz Ginnosar but made frequent trips to Zefat. There was still much work to be done by the followers of Rabbi David ben Zimrah. Communications from Sian revealed that eight more statues had come to life to protect the tomb, destroying intruders. Satan continued to call his servants to free him.

The tomb of the fallen archangel Leviathan lay undiscovered in the frozen wastelands of the northernmost tip of Norway on one of the barren islands of Nordkapp.

The tomb of the fallen archangel Belial was hidden under the Great Salt Lake in Utah, in the United States. Its existence, spoken of in the ancient tales of the southwestern American Indians and their ancestors, the Incan and Mayan civilizations, also remained undiscovered.

The tomb of the third fallen archangel of darkness, Lucifer, was known only to the nomadic aborigines of the vast Australian outback. They avoided the place, a dusty, dirt-covered mound in the middle of nowhere. They never spoke of its existence.

These three spirits, the brothers of Satan, still roamed the earth. Even if they could be captured, without knowledge of the whereabouts of their tombs they could never be contained.

The biblical story of the Israelites' entrance into the land of Canaan centers around the city of Jericho. It is said that Joshua sounded the ram's horn, the shofar, and the walls of the city crumbled. Excavations begun in the twentieth century by German archaeologists revealed parts of the ancient walled city. A few miles away, at Khirbat Qumran, the famous Dead Sea Scrolls were discovered. Further excavations throughout the twentieth century offered proof that this part of Israel was a crossroads for many civilizations, covering a period of almost thirteen thousand years before the birth of Christ.

On a late summer afternoon, construction workers near Jericho noticed the figure of what appeared to be a woman, dressed in black, climbing the steep hills above them. They yelled to her, but she paid no attention to their warning.

It took Valya Pernick, now known as Luba Linsky, a Soviet immigrant, an hour to find the right cave. This was the place where her master had confronted the Rabbi Jesus, offering him dominion over the kingdom of Israel in return for his worship. It had often been Shaytān's dwelling place in the days before Christianity took hold in the world.

She climbed through the narrow opening and rested against the cool cave wall. The child came quickly, feet first and marked with the red arrowhead and backward C. She held the bloody infant, licking it with her long tongue as it suckled at her full breast. She felt totally fulfilled.

"Here he is, Master!" she said proudly. "Here is your son!"

The spirit of Asmodeus entered the cave eager to claim his new earthly body. The child wrenched itself from her arms and rolled onto the cave floor between her legs. Asmodeus became the child. As the afterbirth came out from between Valya's legs, the child reached for it and sat eating the bloody mass.

The tomb in Sian shook slightly. A Chinese peasant working in a nearby field turned and walked toward the ancient mound. At the eastern dig, the statue of an archer slowly turned his head, drew an arrow, and placed it in his bow. He stood and aimed toward the peasant as he approached the tomb door.